Augustus Toplady

The Works of Augustus M. Toplady

Vol. VI

Augustus Toplady

The Works of Augustus M. Toplady
Vol. VI

ISBN/EAN: 9783337120580

Printed in Europe, USA, Canada, Australia, Japan

Cover: Foto ©Raphael Reischuk / pixelio.de

More available books at **www.hansebooks.com**

THE

W O R K S

OF

AUGUSTUS T. OPLADY, *A.B.*

Late Vicar of Broad Hembury, Devon.

IN SIX VOLUMES.

VOL. VI.

L O N D O N:

PRINTED for the PROPRIETORS,

AND SOLD BY

W. Row, Great Marlborough-street; J. Parsons, Pater-noster-row; J. Deighton, Holborn; Herbertt, Pall-mall; J. Mathews, Strand; Wilson and Co. York; Phorson, Berwick; Brown, Bristol; Penny, Exeter; Cooke, Oxford; Nicholson, Cambridge; and J. Barker, Russell-court, Drury-lane.

1794.

why

SKETCH of CONTENTS.

VOL. VI.

CHAPTER VII.

APPENDIX.

XXXIII.

THE

SCHEME

OF

CHRISTIAN AND PHILOSOPHICAL

NECESSITY

ASSERTED.

In Oppofition to Mr. JOHN WESLEY's Tract   that Subject.

"Adeò ſtat et permanet invicta ſententia, omnia neceſſitate fieri. Nec eſt hîc ulla obſcuritas, aut ambiguitas. In Eſaiâ dicit [Deus], conſilium meum ſtabit, et voluntas mea fiet. Quis enim puer non intelligit.quid veliat hæc vocabula, conſilium, voluntas, fiet, ſtabit?" Luther, de Servo Arbitrio, ſect. 19.

"Quæ nobis videtur contingentia, ſecretum Dei impulſum fuiſſe. agnoſcet fides." Calvin, Inſtitut. l. 1. c. 16.

"Quid igitur, inquies, nullane eſt in rebus, ut iſtorum vocabulo utar, contingentia? Nihil caſus? Nihil fortuna?—Omnia neceſſariò evenire Scripturæ docent." Melancthon, Loc. Com. P. 10. Edit. Argentor. 1523.

"There is not a fly, but has had infinite wiſdom concerned, not only in its ſtructure, but in its deſtination." Dr. Young's Cent. not fab. Letter II.

PREFACE.

YESTERDAY's poft brought me a packet from London, including, among other papers, a fmall tract, recently publifhed by Mr. John Wefley, entitled, " Thoughts upon Neceffity." I had no fooner perufed thofe " Thoughts," than I refolved to bring them to the teft: arid am now fetting about it.

During fome years paft, I have, for the moft part, ftood patiently on the defenfive, againft this gentleman. It is high time, that I take my turn to invade ; and carry the arms of truth into the enemy's own territory.

Mr. Wefley's tract, above-mentioned, was fent to me, by a well-known, and very deferving, London clergyman. So much of whofe letter, as relates to the faid tract, fhall, for the amufement of my readers, be fubmitted to their view.

" I went, laft night, to the * Foundery ; expecting to hear Pope John : but was difappointed. After hearing a Welfhman, for an hour and twenty minutes, on Pfalm lxxxiv. 11, preach up all the herefies of the place ; a man, who fat in the pulpit, told him to ' give over ;' for he feemed to bid fair for another half hour, at leaft. But he came to a conclufion, as defired. Then this man, who feemed a local preacher, ftood up, with a pamphlet in his hand, and addreffed the auditory in the following manner:

" I am defired, to publifh a pamphlet upon Neceffity and Free-will : the beft extant, that I know of,

---

* Mr. Wefley's principal meeting-houfe in London.

in the * Englifh tongue ; by Mr. John Wefley, price three-pence. . I had purpofed to have faid a good deal upon it : but the time is elapfed. But, in this three-penny pamphlet, you have all the difputes that have been bandied about fo lately. And you will get your minds more eftablifhed, by this three-penny pamphlet, than by reading all the books that have been written for and againft. It is to be had, at both doors, as you go out.

" I beg leave" (adds my reverend friend), "to tranfmit you this here faid fame three-penny wonder."

'Upon the whole, this muft have been a droll fort of mountebank fcene. Attended, however, with one moft melancholy and deplorable circumftance, arifing from the unreafonable and unfeafonable pro-lixity of the long-winded holderforth : which cruelly, injudicioufly, and defpitefully, prevented poor Zany from puffing off, with the amplitude he fully intend-ed, the multiplex virtues of the doctor's three-penny free-will powder.

Never do that by delegation, fays an old proverb, which you can as well do in *propriâ perfonâ*. Had Doctor John himfelf got upon the ftage, and fung,

"Come, buy my fine powders, come buy dem of me;
" Hare be de beft powders dat ever you fee :"

Who knows, but the three-penny dofes might have gone off, " at both doors," as rapidly as peas from a pop-gun ?

My bufinefs, for a few fpare hours; fhall be, to amufe myfelf, by analyfing this redoubtable powder. The chemical refolution of fo ineftimable a fpecific into its component parts (a fpecific, _

" The like whereto was never feen,
" Nor will again, while grafs is green,")

---

* Query. Does the faid lay preacher, whoever he may be, know aught of any other tongue ?

may,

may, moreover, be of very great and fignal ufe. It were pity, that the *materia medica*, of which it is made up, fhould remain a fecret. Efpecially, as the good doctor defigned it for general benefit. To make which benefit as univerfal as I can, I do hereby give notice, unto all philofophers, divines, and others, who have poifoned their intrails, by unwarily taking too deep a draught of Neceffity : that they may, at any time, by help of the following decompofition, have it in their power to mix up, for their own immediate recovery, a competent *quantum* of the famous Moorfields powder: whofe chief ingredients are,

An equal portion of grofs Heathenifm, Pelagianifm, Mahometifm, Popery, Manichæifm, Ranterifm, and Antinomianifm ; culled, dried, and pulverized, *fecundum artem :* and, above all, mingled. with as much palpable Atheifm as you can poffibly fcrape together from every quarter.

Hæ tibi erunt artes. Follow the above prefcription, to your life's end, and you will find it a moft pleafant, fpeedy, and infallible antidote againft every fpecies and effect of the baneful neceffitarian nightfhade. It is the *felix malum,*

> ———— *Quo non prefentius ullum*
> *(Pocula fi quando fævæ infecere novercæ,*
> *Mifcueruntque herbas, et non innoxia verba)*
> *Auxilium venet, ac membris agit atra Venena *.*

But though Mr. John Wefley is the vender, and the oftenfible proprietor, of this efficacious threepenny medicine ; the original difcovery of the noftrum is by no means his own. He appears to have pilferred the fubftance, both of his *arcana medendi,* and of his cavils againft the true philofophy of colours, from the refuted lucubrations with which a certain North-Britifh profeffor hath edified and en-

---

* Georgic. l. 2. 127.

B 3   riched

riched the literary public. Let the ſimple, however, be on their guard, leſt Mr. Weſley's ſpiritual
medicines have as pernicious influence on their
minds, as the quack remedy, which he * recommends for the gout; had on the life of Dr. T——d,
the late worthy dean of N——ch.

By way of direct Introduction to the following
ſheets, allow me to premiſe an extract from the
commentary of a very great man on thoſe celebrated
lines of Juvenal:

" *Nullum numen habes ſi ſit pudentia ; ſed te nos facimus,*
fortuna, deam, cœloque locamus.

'*Dicit autem hoc poëta, ob fortunam : quæ non ſolum*
nullum numen eſt, ſed nuſquam et nihil eſt. Nam cùm
ſciamus omnia in mundo, maxima et minima, providentiâ
Dei gubernari ; quid reſtat de fortunâ, niſi vanum et inane
nomen ? ——— *Unde, rectè dicitur, tolle ignorantiam è*

---

* In Mr. Weſley's book of Receipts, entitled " Primitive Phyſic,"
he adviſes perſons, who have the gout in their feet or hands, to apply raw lean beef ſteaks to the part affected, freſh and freſh every
twelve hours. Somebody recommended this dangerous repellant, to
Dr. T. in the year 1764, or early in 1765. He tried the experiment. The gout was, in conſequence, driven up to his ſtomach and
head. And he died, a few days after, at Bath: where I happened
to ſpend a conſiderable part of thoſe years; and where, at the very
time of the Dean's death, I became acquainted with the particulars
of that cataſtrophe.
I am far from meaning to inſinuate, becauſe I do not know, that
the perſon, who perſuaded Dr. T. to this fatal recourſe, derived
the recipe immediately from Mr. Weſley's medical compilation. All
I aver, is, that the recipe itſelf is to be found there. Which de-
monſtrates the unſkilful temerity, wherewith the compiler ſets himſelf up as a phyſician of the body. Should his quack pamphlet come
to another edition, it is to be hoped that the beef ſteak remedy will,
after ſo authentic and ſo melancholy a *probatum eſt*, be expunged
from the liſt of ſpecifics for the gout. It is, I acknowledge, an effectual cure. Cut off a man's head, and he will no more be annoyed
by the tooth-ach. Alas, for the *ingenium velox*, and for the *audacia*
perdita, with which a raſh empiric, like Juvenal's *Græculus eſuriens*,
lays claim to univerſal ſcience !

Grammaticus, Rhetor, Geometres, Pictor, Aleptes,
Augur, Schœnobates, Medicus, Magus! Omnia novit !

perſonis,

perſonis, fortunam de rebus ſuſtuleris. Quia enim homines rerum omnium cauſas non perſpicimus, ut eſt mortalium cæcitas; fortunam neſcio quam vagam, irritam, inſtabilem, nobis fingimus. Quòd ſi cauſas rerum latentes & abditas nobis inſpicere daretur; non modò nullam eſſe talem fortunam videremus, verùm etiam omnium minima, ſingulari Dei providentiâ, regi. Et ſic fortuna nihil aliud eſt, quàm Dei providentia, ſed nobis non perſpecta. Et rectè divinus ille Seneca: fortuna, fatum, natura, omnia ejuſdem Dei nomina, varie ſua poteſtate utentis *."

i. e. " The poet, in this place, levels his arrows at fortune or chance : which is not only no goddeſs, but a mere nothing, and has no exiſtence any where. For ſince it is certain, that all things in the world, both little and great, are conducted by the providence of God ; what is chance, but an empty unmeaning name ? Hence it has been rightly obſerved, Take away man's ignorance, and chance vaniſhes in a moment. The true reaſon, why any of us are for ſetting up chance and fortune, is, our not being always able 'to diſcern and to trace the genuine cauſes of events : in conſequence of which, we blindly and abſurdly feign to ourſelves a ſuppoſed random, unreal, unſteady cauſe, called luck, or contingency. Whereas, were we endued with ſufficient penetration to look into the hidden ſources of things, we ſhould not only ſee that there is no ſuch power, as contingency or fortune ; but ſo far from it, that even the ſmalleſt and moſt trivial incidents are guided and governed by God's own expreſs and ſpecial providence. If, therefore, the word, chance, have any determinate ſignification at all, it can mean neither more nor leſs than the unſeen management of God. In which ſenſe, the admirable Seneca makes uſe of the term : Fortune (ſays that philoſopher) and Fate, and Nature, are but ſo many dif-

---

* Lubini Comment. in Juvenal, Sat. 10. P. 454. Edit. Hanoviæ, 1619.

ſerent

ferent names of the one true God, confidered as exerting his power in various ways and manners."—
But, with Seneca's good leave, as the words *fortune,*
chance, contingency, &c. have gradually opened a door
to the grofleft Atheifm ; and as they require much
fubtilty and prolixity of explanation, in order to
their being underftood in any other than an atheiftical fenfe ; it is more than expedient, that the words
themfelves fhould be totally and finally cafhiered
and thrown afide.

I have only to add, that if, in the fucceeding
Effay, any reader fhould imagine I exprefs my
meaning with too much plainnefs; it may fuffice, to
obferve, that there is no end, to the capricious refinements of affected and exceffive delicacy.

Quod verum, atque decens, curo, & rogo, & omnis in
hoc fum.

Language, like animal bodies, may be phyficed,
until it has no ftrength left. We may whet it's
edge, as the fool fharpened his knife, and as fome
are now for reforming the Church, until we have
whetted the whole blade away.

Broad. Hembury, January 22, 1775.

C H A P. I.

Neceffity defined: and its Confiftency, with voluntary Freedom, proved.

A L I Q U I S in omnibus, nullus in fingulis. The man, who concerns himself in every thing, bids fair not to make a figure in any thing.

Mr. John Wefley is, precifely, this *aliquis in omnibus.* For, is there a fingle fubject, in which he has not endeavoured to fhine?—He is alfo, as precifely, a *nullus in fingulis.* For, has he fhone in any one fubject which he ever attempted to handle?

Upon what principle can thefe two circumftances be accounted for? Only upon that very principle, at which he fo dolefully fhakes his head: viz. the principle of neceffity. The poor gentleman is neceffarily, an univerfal meddler: and, as neceffarily, an univerfal mifcarryer. Can he avoid being either the one or the other? No. "Why, then, do you animadvert upon him?"

1. Becaufe I myfelf am as neceffary an agent as he:—2. Becaufe I love to "fhoot folly as it flies:" —3. Becaufe, as, on one hand, it is neceffary that there fhould be herefies among * men; it is no lefs neceffary, on the other, that thofe herefies fhould be diffected and expofed. Mr. Wefley imagines, that, upon my own principles, I can be no more than "a clock." And, if fo, how can I help ftriking? He himfelf has, feveral times, fmarted, for coming too near the pendulum.

Mr. Wefley's incompetence to argument is never more glaringly confpicuous, than when he paddles in metaphyfics. And yet I fuppofe, that the man who has modeftly termed himfelf, and in print too, "The greateft minifter in the world;" does, with

* 1 Cor. xi. 19.

equal

equal certainty, consider himself as the ablest meta-physician in the world. But his examinations are far too hasty and superficial, to enter into the real merits of subjects so extremely abstruse, and whose concatenations are (though invincibly strong, yet) so exquisitely nice and delicate. One result of his thus exercising himself in matters which are too high for him, is, that, in many cases, he decides peremptorily, without having discerned so much as the true state of the question; and then sets himself to speak evil of things which, it is very plain, he does not understand. Or, (to borrow the language of Mr. Locke), he " knows a little, presumes a great deal, and so jumps to conclusions."

I appeal, at present, to his " Thoughts upon Necessity." Thoughts, which, though crude and dark as chaos, are announced, according to custom, with more than oracular positiveness : as though his own *glandula pinealis* was the single focus, wherein all the rays of divine and human wisdom are concentred.

His thoughts open thus.

1. " Is man a free-agent, or is he not ?"—Without all manner of doubt, he is; in a vast number and variety of cases. Nor did I ever, in conversation, or in reading, meet with a person, or an author, who denied it.

But let us, by defining as we go, ascertain what free-agency is. All needless refinements apart, free-agency, in plain English, is neither more nor less, than voluntary agency. Whatever the soul does, with the full bent of preference and desire ; in that, the soul acts freely. For, *ubi consensus, ibi voluntas, &, ubi voluntas, ibi libertas.*

I own myself very fond of definitions. I therefore premise, what the Necessity is, whose cause I have undertaken to plead.

It is exactly and . diametrically opposite, to that which Cicero delivers concerning *fortuna*, or chance, luck, hap, accidentality, and contingency; invented by

the

the poets of second antiquity, and during many ages, revered as a Deity, by both Greeks and Romans. " *Quid est aliud sors, quid fortuna, quid casus, quid eventus ; nisi quum sic aliquid cecidit, sic evenit, ut vel non cadere atque evenire vel aliter cadere atque evenire, potuerit *?*" i. e. Chance, fortune, accident, and uncertain event, are then said to take place, when a thing so comes to pass, as that it either might not have come to pass at all ; or might have come to pass, otherwise than it does.

On the contrary, I would define necessity to be that, by which, whatever comes to pass cannot but come to pass (all circumstances taken into the account); and can come to pass in no other way or manner, than it does. Which coincides with Aristotle's definition of necessity (though, by the way, he was a freewiller himself): Το μη ενδεχομενον ΑΛΛΩΣ ιχειν, αναγκαιον φαμεν †: We call that necessary, which cannot be otherwise than it is.

Hence the Greeks termed necessity, Αναγκη: because ανασσει, it reigns, without exception, over all the works of God ; and because αναγχει, it retains and comprizes all things within the limits of its own dominion. The Romans called it *necesse & necessitas ;* *quasi ne cassitas,* because it cannot fail, or be made void : *& quasi ne quassitas,* because it cannot be moved, or shaken, by all the power of men ‡.

I ac-

---

* Cic. De Divinat. L. 2.

† Apud Frommenium, Lib. 2. cap. 9.

‡ The immediate parent, or causa proxima, of necessity, is fate ; called, by the Greeks, ειμαρμενη : because it invincibly distributes to every man his lot. They termed it also πεπρωμενη, because it bounds, limits, marks out, adjusts, determines, and precisely ascertains, to each individual of the human race, his assigned portion both of active and passive life. Fate was likewise sometimes metonymically stiled μοιρα, or the lot, i. e. the res ipsissimas, or very actions and felicities and sufferings, themselves, which fall to every man's share.

The Latins called fate, fatum : either from fiat, i. e. from God's saying, Let such and such a thing come to pass : or simply, à fando; from God's pronouncing the existence, the continuance, the circumstances, the times, and whatever else relates to men and things.

If

I acquiesce in the old distinction of necessity (a distinction adopted by Luther *, and by most of, not to say by all, the found reformed divines), into a necessity of compulsion, and a necessity of infallible certainty.—The necessity of compulsion is predicated of inanimate bodies ; as we say of the earth (for instance) that it circuits the sun, by compulsory necessity : and, in some cases, of reasonable beings themselves ; viz. when they are forced to do or suffer any thing, contrary to their will and choice.—The necessity of infallible certainty, is of a very different kind ; and only renders the event inevitably future, without any compulsory force on the will of the agent. Thus, it was infallibly certain, that Judas would betray Christ: he was, therefore, a necessary, though a voluntary, actor, in that tremendous business.

2. " Are a man's actions free, or necessary ?"— They may be, at one and the same time, free and necessary too. When Mr. Wesley is very hungry, or very tired, he is, necessarily, and yet freely, disposed to food, or rest. He can no more help being so disposed, than a falling stone can help tending to the earth. But here lies the grand difference. The stone is a simple being, consisting of matter only : and consequently, can have no will either to rise or fall.—Mr. Wesley is a compounded being, made up of matter and spirit. Consequently, his spirit, soul,

If we distinguish accurately, this seems to have been the order, in which the most judicious of the antients considered the whole matter. First, God :—then, his will :—then, fate ; or the solemn ratification of his will, by passing and establishing it into an unchangeable decree :—then creation :—then, necessity ; i. e. such an indissoluble concatenation of secondary causes and effects, as has a native tendency to secure the certainty of all events, sicut unda impellitur undâ :—then, Providence ; i. e. the omnipresent, omnivigilant, all-directing superintendency of divine wisdom and power, carrying the whole preconcerted scheme into actual execution, by the subservient mediation of second causes, which were created for that end

* Vide Luther. De Servo Arbitrio, Sect. 43.—Edit. Noremb. 1526.

or will, (for I can conceive no real difference between the will, and the foul itfelf) is concerned in
fitting down to dinner, or in courting repofe, when
neceffity impels to either.   And I will venture to
affirm, what he himfelf cannot deny, that, neceffarily
biaffed as he is to thofe mediums of recruit; he has
recourfe to them as freely (i. e. as voluntarily, and
with as much appetite, choice, defire, and relifh),
as if neceffity was quite out of the cafe : nay, and
with abundantly greater freedom and choice, than if
he was not fo neceffitated and impelled.

It would be eafy, to inftance this obvious truth,
in a thoufand particulars ; and in particulars of infinitely greater moment, than relate to common life.
Let me juft, *en paffant*, illuftrate the point,, from
the moft grand important topic which the whole
compafs of reafoning affords.

It was neceffary (i. e. abfolutely and intrinfically
inevitable), 1. That the Meffiah fhould be invariably * holy in all his ways, and righteous in all his
works :——2. That he fhould die for the fins of
men.   •

Yet Chrift, though, 1. neceffarily good (fo neceffarily, that it was impoffible for him to be otherwife); was freely and voluntarily good : elfe, he
could not have declared, with truth, my meat and
drink [i. e. my choice, my appetite, my defire] is,
to do the will of him that fent me, and to finifh his
work ·†—2. Though he ‡ could not avoid being put
to

---

* I never knew more than one Arminian, who was fo tremend-
oufly confiftent, as to maintain, explicitly and in words, that it was
poffible for Chrift himfelf to have fallen from grace by fin, and to
have perifhed everlaftingly.   I muft, however, do this gentleman the
juftice to add, that he has, for fome years paft, been of a better
judgment.——But the fhocking principle itfelf is neceffarily involved
in, and invincibly follow. upon, the Arminian fcheme of contingency ; whether the afferters of that fcheme openly avow the confequence, or no.

† John iv. 34.

‡ To deny the neceffity of Chrift's fufferings, i. e. to confider
them as unpredeftinated, and as things which might, or might not,
have

to death, as a facrifice for fin; yet he died voluntarily, and therefore freely. Elfe, he would not have affirmed, that he was even ftraightened, until it was accomplifhed *: i. e. he wifhed, and longed, for the confummation of his obedience unto death.

Need I add any thing more, to prove that freedom and neceffity are not only compatible, but may even co-alefce into abfolute unifons, with each other ?

But, "how do they thus coalefce ?"—By the wife appointment of God, who is great in counfel, and mighty in working †. A Chriftian will be fatisfied with this anfwer. And philofophy itfelf cannot rife to an higher.

C H A P. II.

The Neceffity of Human Volitions proved, from the Nature of the Connection fubfifting between Soul and Body.

MR. Wefley afks, 3. "Is man felf-determined, in acting; or is he determined by fome other being?"—I fcruple not, to declare, as my ftedfaft judgment, that no man ever was, or ever will, or ever can be, ftrictly and philofophically fpeaking, felf-determined to any one action, be that action what it may.

Let us examine this point. It is neither unimportant, nor unentertaining.

have happened; is to annihilate, at one ftroke, the whole dignity and importance of the Chriftian religion. Scripture is, therefore, extremely careful to inculcate, again, and again, in the ftrongeft and moft explicit terms which language can fupply, that the whole of Chrift's humiliation, even his death itfelf, was infallibly and inevitably decreed. See, among many other paffages, thofe which occur in the 4th chapter of this Effay.

   * Luke xii. 50.   † Jer. xxxii. 19.

There

There is * no medium between matter and fpirit. Thefe two divide the whole univerfe between them. Even in man's prefent complex ftate, though body and foul conftitute one compofitum; yet are the two component principles not only diftinct, but effentially different, from each other. Their connection, though aftonifhingly intimate, occafions no mixture nor confufion of this with that.

Notwithftanding which, the nature (or, if you pleafe, the law) of their junction is fuch, that they reciprocally act upon each other. A man breaks a limb: or is wounded in a duel. The body, and the body alone, receives the injury: but the injury is no fooner received, than it operates upon the foul. For it is the foul only, which feels pleafure or pain, through the medium of the bodily organs. Matter can no more feel, or perceive; than it can read, or pray. To fuppofe otherwife, were to fuppofe that a violin can hear, and a telefcope fee.

If, therefore, the foul is the feeling principle, or fole feat of perception; it follows, as clear as day, that the foul is no lefs dependent on the body, for a very confiderable portion of its [i. e. of the foul's own] phyfical happinefs or mifery; than the body is dependent on the foul, for its [i. e. for the body's] inftrumental fubferviency to the will. Confequently, the foul is (not felf-determined, but) neceffarily determined, to take as much care of the body as it [the foul] in its prefent views deems requifite: becaufe the foul is confcious of its dependence on that machine, as the inlet and channel of pleafing or of difagreeable fenfations. So that, in this very extenfive inftance, man's volitions are fwayed, this way or that, to the right hand or to the left; by confiderations, drawn from the circumftance of that neceffary

---

* I am obliged, here, to take thefe two particulars for granted: as the adhibition of the abundant proofs, by which they are fupported and evinced, would lead me too far from the object immediately in view.

dependence

dependence on the body, which the foul cannot poffibly raife itfelf fuperior to, while the mutual connection fubfifts.

An idea is that image, form, or conception of any
thing, which the foul is impreffed with from without *. How come we by thefe ideas? I believe
them to be, all, originally, let in, through the bodily
fenfes only. I cannot confider reflection as, properly, the fource of any new ideas : but rather as a
fort of mental chemiftry, by which the underftanding contemplatively analyfes and fublimates, into
abftract and refined knowledge, fome of thofe ideas
which refult either from experience, or from information ; and which were primarily admitted through
the avenues of fenfe. Without the fenfe of hearing,
we could have had no juft idea of found: nor of
odours, without the fenfe of fmelling : any more
than the foot can tafte, or the hand can hear.

The fenfes themfelves, which are thus the only
doors, by which ideas, i. e. the rudiments of all †
knowledge, find their way to the foul ; are, literally
and in the fulleft import of the word, corporeal.
Hence, the foul cannot fee, if the eyes are deftroyed :
nor feel, if the nervous functions are fufpended : nor

---

* Are not the powers of fancy an exception to that doctrine which
maintains, that all ideas originally accede, ab extra, to the mind?
—Not in the leaft. Though I may form (for inftance) an uncertain, or at beft an incomplete, idea of a perfon I never faw ; yet
that idea is either drawn from defcription, or, if purely imaginary,
is a combination of conceptions, every one of which came at firft
into the mind through the fenfes, and which it affociates on principles of real or fuppofed fimilitude.

† The reader will obferve, that I am, here, fpeaking of no other
than of natural and artificial knowledge. Spiritual knowledge, divinely impreffed on the foul in its regeneration by the Holy Ghoft,
comes not, hitherto, within the compafs of the prefent difquifition.
Though to me, it feems extremely probable, that this moft adorable
agent often condefcends to make the fenfes themfelves (and efpecially the fenfe of feeling ; to which fingle fenfe, by the way, all the
other four may, fub diverfo modo, be reduced) the inlets of his bleffed
influence. There is a fpirit in man : and the infpiration of the Almighty giveth them underftanding. Job xxxii. 8.

hear,

hear, if the organs of that fenfe are totally impaired. What learn we from this? That the foul, or mind, is primarily and immediately indebted to the body, for all the ideas, (and confequently, for all the knowledge) with which it is furnifhed. By thefe ideas, when compared, combined, or feparated, the foul, on every occafion, neceffarily regulates its conduct : and is afterwards as dependent on the body for carrying its conceptions into outward act, as it was for its fimple reception of them at firft.

Thus, the foul is, in a very extenfive degree, paffive as matter itfelf.

Whether the fibres of the brain do no more than fimply vibrate ; or whether they be alfo the canals of a vital fluid agitated and fet in circulation, by the percuffions which it receives from the fenfes ; the argument comes to juft the fame point. The fenfes are neceffarily impreffed by every object from without ; and as neceffarily commove the fibres of the brain : from which nervous commotion, ideas are neceffarily communicated to, or, excited in, the foul ; and, by the judgment which the foul neceffarily frames of thofe ideas, the will is neceffarily inclined to approve or difapprove, to act or not to act. If fo, where is the boafted power of felf-determination?

Having taken a momentary furvey of the foul's dependance on the body ; and of the vaft command which the body has over the foul (fo great, that a difeafe may quickly degrade a philofopher into an idiot ; and even an alteration of * weather diffufe a
temporary

* Lord Chefterfield's remark is not ill founded. " I am convinced, that a light fupper, a good night's fleep, and a fine morning, have, fometimes, made an hero, of the fame man, who, by an indigeftion, a reftlefs night, and a rainy morning, would have been a coward." Letter 117.—Again : "Thofe who fee and obferve kings, heroes, and ftatefmen, difcover that they have head-achs, indigeftions, humours, and paffions, juft like other people : every one of which, in their turns, determine their wills, in defiance of their reafon." Letter 173.—Human excellence, truly, has much to be proud

temporary stupor through all the powers of the
mind) ; let us next enquire, on what the body itself
depends,

of! and man is a sovereign, self-determining animal! an animal,
whom too rarified or too viscous a texture, too rapid or too languid
a circulation, of blood ; an imperfect secretion of spirits, from the
blood, through the cortical strainers of the brain ; or an irregular
distribution of the spiritous fluid, from the secreting fibres, to the
nervous canals which diffuse themselves through the body :—these,
and a thousand other involuntary causes, can, at any time, in less
than a moment, if God please, suspend every one of our sensations ;
stagnate us into stupidity ; agitate us into a fever ; or deprive us of
life itself !

Yet, let it be observed, that thought and reason are, at all times
and amidst all circumstances whatever, essentially inseparable from
the soul : whether it dwell in a well-organized and duly-tempered
body, or in a body whose construction is ever so unfavourable, and
whose mechanic balance is ever so broken and impaired.   But in the
latter case (especially in swoons, epilepsies, &c.) the soul cannot unfold and exercise its faculties, as when the material machine is in
right order.   Thus, we cannot say, with metaphysical propriety,
that a person in a fainting-fit, or that even the most absolute idiot on
earth, is an irrational being : but only, that he has not the service of
his reason.   Nor can we say, of a madman, that he has lost his understanding : but only, that the proper use, or direction, of it, is
perverted.

It is true, indeed, that, as idiotcy seems to be rather a quid defi-
ciens, than a το positivum ; and may therefore be immediately occasioned by the bad mechanism (i. e. by a vitiated arrangement and
motion) of the corporeal particles, whether fluid or solid :—So, on
the other hand, madness seems to have more in it of the το positivum ;
and, consequently, to be the effect of an higher and more absolute
cause.   What can that cause be? I am strongly and clearly of opinion, with Mr. Baxter (not Baxter the puritan, but Baxter the great
modern philosopher), that all madness whatever proceeds from the
powerful and continued agency of some separate spirit, or spirits,
obtruding phantastic visions on the soul of the insane person.   If the
majority of dreams are but the madness of sleep, what is madness,
properly so called, but a waking dream ? For, as that most accomplished metaphysician very justly reasons, " The soul, in itself, is an
uncompounded, simple substance, and hath no parts, and therefore
properly no constitution : neither is it liable to any change, or alteration, in its own nature.   The inert matter of the body could never
affect it thus [i. e. could never so affect the soul, as to occasion mad-
ness].   That could only limit the faculties of the soul, farther and
farther, or deaden its activity : but not animate it after such a terrible manner.   Hence there is no other way for its being affected in
this manner, but the cause I have already assigned.——There is, indeed, a great difference, and variety, in the phenomena of reason
disturbed.

depends, for the sources of those innumerable ideas, which it is the vehicle of transmitting to the intellect:

disturbed. But, universally, the disease could not be lodged in the soul itself: nor could the matter of the body affect it any other way, than by deadening (i. e. by impeding] its activity; which, I think, is never the case in these appearances. In short, the disorder of matter might make a man a stupid idiot; subject him to sleep, apoplexy, or any thing approaching to its own nature: but could never be the cause of rage, distraction, phrensy, unless it were employed as an instrument by some other cause: that is, it cannot of itself be the cause of these disorders of reason. If the inertia of matter infers any thing, it infers thus much." Baxter's Enquiry into the Nature of the human Soul, vol. ii. p. 141, 142.—I no more doubt, that mad persons, at this very day, are dæmoniacs, or influenced and agitated by incorporeal and invisible beings; than I can doubt, that some people were so possessed, at the time of our Lord's abode on earth. Such an assertion will, probably, sound romantically strange, to a prejudiced, and to a superficial, ear. But (let the fact itself really stand how it may), I think I can venture to pronounce, that the philosophy of the opinion, as stated and argued by Mr. Baxter, is irrefragable —Examine first, and then judge.

Unembodied spirits, both friendly and hostile (ευδαιμονες, & κακοδαιμονες], holy and unholy, have more to do with us, in a way both of good and evil, than the generality of us seem to imagine. But they themselves are, all, no more than parts of that great chain, which depends on the first cause, or uncreated link: and can only act as ministers of his will.

Luther relates several uncommon things, concerning his own converse with some of the spiritual world: which, however fanciful they may, primâ facie, appear; are by no means philosophically inadmissible. For so saying, I am sure to incur a smile of contempt, from pertlings and materialists: the former of whom sneer, when they cannot reason; and wisely consider a grin, and a syllogism, as two names for the same thing. When it can be solidly proved, that the gums are the seat of intellect; I will then allow, that a laugher shews his understanding and his wit every time he shews his teeth. Was ridicule the legitimate test of truth, there could be no such thing as truth in the world; and, consequently, there would be nothing for ridicule to be the test of: as every truth may be, and in its turn actually has been, ridiculed, by some insipid witling or other. So that, to borrow a lively remark from Mr. Hervey, "The whim, of making ridicule the test of truth, seems as suitable to the fitness of things, as to place harlequin in the seat of lord chief justice." Moreover, ridicule itself, viewed as ridiculously usurping the office of a philosophical touch-stone, has been ridiculed, with much poignancy, and strength of sense, by the ingenious pen of the late Dr. Brown, in his Essay on Satire:

"Come,

lect: and, without which tranfmiffion, the intellect, implunged in a mafs of clay, could have had no more idea of outward things, than an oyfter has of a tinder-box. An unactive confcioufnefs of mere torpid exiftence would have been the whole amount of its riches, during its inclofure in a prifon without door, window, or crevice.

The human body is neceffarily encompaffed by a multitude of other bodies. Which other furrounding bodies (animal, vegetable, &c.), fo far as we come within their perceivable fphere, neceffarily imprefs our nerves with fenfations correfpondent to the objects themfelves. Thefe fenfations are neceffarily (and, for the moft part, inftantaneoufly) propagated to the foul : which can no more help receiving them, and being affected by them, than a tree can refift a ftroke of lightening.

Now, (1.) if all the ideas in the foul derive their exiftence from fenfation; and, (2,) if the foul depend, abfolutely, on the body, for all thofe fenfations; and, (3.) if the body be both primarily and continually dependent, on other extrinfic beings, for the very fenfations which it [the body] communicates to the foul ;—the confequence feems, to me, undeniable : that neither the immanent nor the tranfient acts of man (i. e. neither his mental, nor his outward operations) are felf-determined ; but,

"" Come, let us join awhile this titt'ring crew,
And own, the idiot guide for once is true :
Deride our weak forefathers' mufty rule,
Who therefore fmiled, becaufe they faw a fool.
Sublimer logic now adorns our ifle :
We therefore fee a fool, becaufe we fmile ?
 Truth in her gloomy cave why fondly feek ?
Lo, gay fhe fits in laughter's dimple cheek :
Contemns each furly academic foe,
And courts the fpruce free-thinker and the beau.
 No more fhall reafon boaft her pow'r divine :
Her bafe eternal fhook by folly's mine.
Truth's facred fort th' exploded laugh fhall win;
And coxcombs vanquifh Berkley by a grin!"

on the contrary, determined by the views with which an infinity of surrounding objects necessarily, and almost incessantly, impress his intellect.

And on what do those surrounding objects themselves, which are mostly material (i. e. on what does matter, in all its forms, positions, and relations), depend? Certainly, not on itself. It could neither be its own creator, nor can it be its own conserver. In my idea, every particle of matter would immediately revert into non-existence, if not retained in being, from moment to moment, by the will of him who upholds all things by the word of his power*, and through whom all things consist †.

Much less, does matter depend on the human mind. Man can neither create, nor ‡ exterminate, a single atom. There are cases, wherein he can alter the modes of matter: so as to form (for instance) certain vegetable fibres into linen, linen into paper, and paper into books. He can also throw that linen, or paper, or books, into a fire; and thereby dissolve the present connection of their particles, and annihilate their modal relations. But, notwithstanding he has all this in his power (though, by the way, he will never do either one or the other, except his will be necessarily determined by some effectual motive); still the seeming destruction amounts to no more than a variation. Not an individual particle of the burnt matter is exterminated: nor even its es-

---

* Heb. i. 3.
† Col. i. 17.
‡ To all her other antiphilosophical absurdities, Arminianism adds the supposed defectibility of saving grace: by giving as her opinion, that the holy principle in a renewed soul is not only a corruptible and perishable seed, but that it, frequently, and actually, does suffer a total extinction and a final annihilation. Or, as Mr. Wesley and his fraternity vulgarly express it, " He who is, to-day, a child of God, may be, to-morrow, a child of the devil." As if the principle of grace were less privileged than a particle of matter! and as if man, who cannot annihilate a single atom, were able to annihilate the most illustrious effect of the Holy Spirit's operation! Credat Judæus, &c.

sential

fential relation, to the univerfe, fuperfeded. There
would be, precifely, the fame quantity of folid fubftance, which there now is, without the lofs of a cor-
pufcular unit, were all the men, and things, upon
the face of the earth, and the very globe itfelf, reduced to afhes. Confequently, matter is abfolutely
and folely dependent on God himfelf.

Thus have we, briefly, traced the winding current
to its fource. The fcul, or intellect, depends on its
ideas, for the determinations of its volitions : elfe, it
would will, as a blind man walks, at a venture and
in the dark.—Thofe ideas are the daughters of fenfation; and can deduce their pedigree from no other
quarter. The embodied foul could have had no
idea of fo much as a tree, or a blade of grafs, if our
diftance from thofe bodies had been fuch, as to have
precluded their refpective forms from occurring to the
eye.—The fenfes, therefore, are the channels of all
our natural perceptions. Which fenfes are entirely
corporeal : as is the brain alfo, that grand centre, to
which all their impreffions are forwarded, and from
whence they immediately act upon the immaterial
principle.—Thefe corporeal fenfes receive their impreffions from the prefence, or impulfe, of exterior
beings (for all our fenfations are but modes of motion).—And every one of thofe exterior beings is dependent, for exiftence, and for operation, on God
Moft High.

Such is the progreffion of one argument (and it is
but one among many), for the great doctrine of
philofophical neceffity : a chain, concerning which
(and, efpecially, concerning the determination to
action, by motives arifing from ideas) Mr. Wefley
modeftly affirms, that " It has not one good link
belonging to it." Serioufly, I pity the fize of his
underftanding. And I pity it, becaufe I verily believe it to be a fault which he cannot help : any more
than a dwarf can help not being fix feet high. Lame
indeed are all his commentations :

                              " But

" But better he'd give us, if better he had."

I shall close this chapter, with submitting a few plain and reasonable queries to the reader.

1. How is that supposition, which ascribes a self-determining will to a created spirit, less absurd, than that supposition, which ascribes self-existence to matter?

2. In what respect, or respects, is the Arminian supposition of a fortuitous train of events, less atheistical, than the epicurean supposition of a fortuitous concourse of atoms?

3. If man be a self-determining agent, will it not necessarily follow, there are as many first causes (i. e. in other words, as many gods), as there are men in the world?

4. Is not independence essentially pre-requisite to self-determination?

5. But is it true in fact, and would it be found philosophy to admit, that man is an independent being?

6. Moreover, is the supposition, of human independence and self-determination, sound theology? At least, does it comport with the scriptural account of man? For a specimen of which account, only cast your eye on the passage or two that follow.—The way of man is not in himself: it is not in man that walketh to direct his own steps *.—Without me [i. e. without Christ], ye can do nothing †.—In him [i. e. in God] we live, and are moved (κινεμεθα), and have our existence ‡.—It is he who worketh all in all §.—It is God, who worketh in you both to will and to do ‖.—Of him, and to him, and through him, are all things ¶.

---

* Jer. x. 23.   † John xv. 5.   ‡ Acts xvii. 28.
§ 1 Cor. xii. 6.   ‖ Phil. ii. 13.   ¶ Rom. xi. 36.

7. May

7. May we not, on the whole, soberly affirm, that the scheme of necessity is philosophy in her right mind? And that the scheme of contingency is philosophy run mad?

CHAP. III.

Several Objections, to the Scheme of Necessity, answered.

IT seems most agreeable to the radical simplicity, which God has observed in his works, to suppose, that, in themselves, all human souls are equal. I can easily believe, that the soul of an oyster-woman has, naturally, the (unexpanded) powers of Grotius, or of Sir Isaac Newton: and that what conduces to raise the philosopher, the poet, the politician, or the linguist, so much above the ignorant and stupid of mankind, is not only the circumstance of intellectual cultivation, but (still more than that) his having the happiness to occupy a better house, i. e. a body more commodiously organized, than they.

The soul of a monthly reviewer, if imprisoned within the same mud walls which are tenanted by the soul of Mr. John Wesley, would, similarly circumstanced, reason and act (I verily think) exactly like the bishop of Moorfields. And I know some very sensible people, who even go so far, as to suppose, that, was an human spirit shut up in the skull of a cat, puss would, notwithstanding, move prone on all four, purr when stroked, spit when pinched, and birds and mice be her darling objects of pursuit.

Now, though I can, by no means, for my own part, carry matters to so extreme a length as this;

yet,

yet, I repeat my opinion, that much, very much, depends on corporeal organization. Whence the ufual remark, that a man is (I would rather fay, appears to be) fenfible and ingenious, according to his dimenfion and folid content of brain. That is, as I apprehend, the foul is more capable of exerting its powers, when lodged in a capacious and well-conftructed vehicle. I dare believe, that the brain of Dr. Thomas Nowell is, to that of Mr. John Wefley, as two to one, at the very leaft. And yet, all this is the refult of abfolute neceffity. For, what is brain, but matter peculiarly modified? And who is the modifier? Not man, but God.

I juft now hinted the conjecture of fome, that an human fpirit, incarcerated in the brain of a cat, would, probably, both think and behave, as that animal now does. But how would the foul * of a cat acquit itfelf, if inclofed in the brain of a man? We cannot refolve this queftion, with certainty, any more than the other. We may, however, even on this occafion, addrefs every one of our human brethren in thofe words of that great philofophic neceffitarian, St. Paul; and afk, who maketh thee to differ from the loweft of the brute creation? Thy Maker's freewill, not thine. And what pre-

---

* Let not the reader ftart, at that expreffion, ' The foul of a cat.' For though the word, fo applied, may feem ftrange to thofe who have not weighed both fides of the queftion (it would have feemed very ftrange to me, about fifteen years ago); yet, on giving the caufe an impartial hearing, the fcale of evidence will, in my judgment, ftrongly decide for an immaterial principle in brutes.

I mean not, here, to difcufs the argument. But let me hint, that one principal hinge, on which the enquiry turns, is: Do thofe inferior beings reafon, or do they not? If they do (be it in ever fo fmall a degree), they muft confift of fomething more than body: i. e. they muft be compounded of matter and fpirit.—If they do not reafon at all (and we may as well doubt whether they can feel at all); we may fet them down for mere material machines.—He, however, who ferioufly thinks, that even birds, or infects, are watches; may, with equal eafe, while his hand is in, advance a few fteps higher, and fuppofe, that men are clocks, i. e. larger watches of the three.

eminence haft thou, which thou didft not receive
from him ? Not the leaft, nor the fhadow of any.——
Now, if thou didft [not acquire, but] receive it, as
a diftinguifhing gift of his free and fovereign pleafure,
why carrieft thou thyfelf proudly (καυχασαι), as though
thou hadft not received it* ?

    " He, who through vaft immenfity can pierce ;
    " See worlds on worlds compofe one univerfe ;
    " Can tell how fyftem beyond fyftem runs ;
    " What other planets circle other funs ;
    " What vary'd being peoples ev'ry ftar :
    " May tell, why Heav'n has made us as we are."

What the poet could not tell, the Bible does.——
" Why are we made as we are ?" Even fo, Father :
for fo it feemed good in thy fight. Which is anfwer
enough to fatisfy me.

I take the truth of the matter to be this . All the
intellectual diftinctions, which obtain throughout the
whole fcale of animated exiftence, from the brighteft
angel down to man, and which give advantage to
one man above another ; which intellectual diftinctions defcend, likewife, in juft gradations, from
man, to the minuteft animalcule ; are diftributed,
to each individual, in number, in meafure, and in
weight †, by the fovereign will and the unerring
hand of God the only wife. The ufes, to which
thofe intellectual powers fhall fubferve ; the term of
their duration ; and, in fhort, every circumftance
relative both to them and their poffeffors ; I confider
as falling under the regulation of God's determining
and permiffive decree before time, and of his ever-
prefent and ever-acting providence in time.

According to this fcheme of things (a fcheme,
which, when fairly weighed, will be found the moft
chearful to men, and the moft worthy of God, which

---

    * 1 Cor. iv. 7.   † Wifd. xi. 20.

was ever proposed to the human mind), that melancholy, that absurd, that atheistical fiction, whose name is Chance, has nothing to do with God or with his works. On the contrary, the golden chain of necessity, providence, or fate (it is no matter which you term it), is let down, from the throne of the supreme, through all the ranks of animated and of unanimated creation : guiding and governing every individual spirit, and every individual atom, by such means, and in such a manner, as best comport with the dignity, the efficacy, the wisdom, and the love, of him who holds the chain, and who has implicated every link.

Thus, he doth according to his will, in the armies of heaven, and among the inhabitants of the earth ; and none can stay his hand, or say unto him, What doest thou * ? Hence it is, that the very † hairs of our heads are all numbered in his book ; and not one of them can fall from its pore, without the leave of Heaven. He is the guardian of sparrows ; and will not let what we account the meanest insect expire, until the point of time, divinely destined, is come. He not only tells the number of the ‡ stars, and calls them each by name ; but notices and directs the very particles of § dust, which float in the atmosphere. The ‖ sun shines not, but at his command : nor can a ** wind blow, but by authority from him. May we not say, of necessity, what the Psalmist says, of the central luminary, round which our globe is wheeled ; that there is nothing hid from the heat thereof ?

And yet, there are those, who think, that necessity makes no part of the Christian system !

Mr. Wesley is, or pretends to be, of this number. Let us give a concise hearing to the difficulties, which, in his estimation, clog the scheme of evan-

---

* Dan. iv. 35. † Matth. x. 29, 30. ‡ Psalm cxlvii. 4.
§ Isaiah xl. 12. ‖ Job ix. 7. ** Psalm cxxxv. 7.

gelical

gelical and philofophical fate : though they are fuch
as have been refuted again and again.

1. " There can be no moral good, or evil; no
virtue, and no vice."

So thought * Ariftotle; and his difciples, the
Peripatetics. Hence, they defined moral virtue to
be an elective habit, flowing originally from free-
will, and rendered eafy by repeated acts.

It is no wonder, that proud heathens fhould thus
err; feeing they know not the Scriptures, nor the
power of God. But Mr. Wefley fhould remember,
that he has read, and profeffes to believe, a book
which tells him, that a man can receive nothing,
except it be given him from heaven +; that we cannot even think a good thought ‡, unlefs God breathe
it into our hearts ; and that it is the Father of our
Lord Jefus Chrift, who muft work in us that which
is well-pleafing in his fight §.

Nor fhould his lordfhip of Moorfields forget, that
he has folemnly fubfcribed (to omit all prefent mention of articles and homilies) a certain liturgy : in
which liturgy, among a thoufand other paffages
equally excellent, God himfelf is addreffed, as the
fole being, from whom all holy defires, all good
counfels [or fincerely devout intentions], and all
juft works, do proceed. The fupreme is, likewife,
in the fame " Calviniftical and Antinomian Prayer-
book," declared to be the almighty and everlafting
God, who maketh us both to will and to do thofe
things that be good, and acceptable to his divine

---

* And yet Ariftotle, though a vehement, was not (any more than
his difciple of the Foundery) a confiftent, freewill man. Hence,
Ariftotle, being once afked, " Who can keep a fecret?" made this
odd anfwer: He that can hold red-hot coals in his mouth.—Surely,
Freewill muft be very feeble, and Neceffity irrefiftibly potent, upon
this principle! Not to afk: If Freewill cannot, on a proper occafion,
fhut the mouth of the man that has it; how can it bring him virtue,
and fave his foul?

† John iii. 27.   ‡ 2 Cor. iii. 5.   § Hebr. xiii. 21.

majefty.

majefty. And, in abfolute harmony with this neceffitating principle, the faid book befeeches the bleffed
Father and governor of men, that by his holy infpiration, we may think thofe things that are good ;
and that we may, by his merciful guidance, faith-
fully perform the fame. If this is being, what Mr.
Wefley terms, " a fine piece of clock-work;" I
heartily wifh and pray, that I may, every hour of
my life, be fo wound up.

But ftill, fays the objector, " moral good, or
evil," cannot * confift with neceffity. I, on the
contrary, fay, that it both can, and does. Mr.
Wefley does not confider the tremendous confequences, which unavoidably flow from his pofition.
For, if neceffary virtue be neither moral, nor praife-
worthy ; it will follow, that God himfelf (who, without all doubt, is neceffarily and unchangeably good)
is an immoral being, and not praife-worthy for his
goodnefs ! On the fame horrible Arminian principle,
it would alfo follow, that Chrift's moft perfect obedience (which was neceffary : for he could not but
obey perfectly) had no morality in it, was totally
void of merit, and entitled him to neither praife,
nor reward ! The axiom, therefore, which dares to
affirm, that " neceffity and moral agency are irre-
concilable things ;" lays, at once, the axe to the
root both of natural and revealed religion, and ought
to be hiffed back again by all mankind to the hell
from whence it came.

* " The hacknied objection to the doctrine of neceffity, from its
being [pretendedly] inconfiftent with the idea of virtue and vice,
as implying praife and blame, may be fully retorted upon its op-
ponents. For, as to their boafted felf-determining power (were the
thing poffible in itfelf, and did not imply an abfurdity), by which
they pretend to have a power of acting independently of every thing
that comes under the defcription of motive ; I fcruple not to fay,
that it is as foreign to every idea of virtue or vice, praife or blame,
as the groffeft kind of mechanifm that the moft blundering writer in
defence of liberty ever afcribed to the advocates for moral neceffity."
Dr. Prieftley's Exam. of Beattie, &c. p. 178.

The

The crucifiers of the Son of God perpetrated the moſt immoral act, that ever was, or ever will be, committed.   And yet, I am expreſsly aſſured, by the written teſtimony of the Holy Ghoſt, entered on a record which will continue to the end of time, that Herod, and Pontius Pilate, and the people of the Jews, were gathered together againſt Jeſus, for to do whatſoever God's hand and God's counſel had fore-determined to be done *.   So that, upon Chriſtian principles at leaſt, neceſſity and moral evil (by the ſame rule, alſo, neceſſity and moral good) may walk ✝ hand in hand together.   If Mr. Weſley prefers Ariſtotle and the other gentlemen of the Lycæum, to the inſpired writers ; and chuſes the peripatetic ſcheme of freewill, rather than the Bible ſcheme of neceſſity ; he muſt, for me, go on to hug an idol that cannot ſave.

The whole cavil amounts to preciſely this. If God is the alone author and worker of all good ; virtue ceaſes to be virtue : and, if God is the free permitter of evil, vice ceaſes to be vice.   Can any thing be, at once, more impious, and more irrational, than the letter and the ſpirit of theſe two propoſitions ?

In one word : thoſe modes of actions, called virtue and vice, do not ceaſe to be moral, i. e. to affect our manners, as creatures of God, and as members of ſociety ; be thoſe modes occaſioned by what they may.   Acts of devotion, candour, juſtice, and beneficence, together with their oppoſites, are, to all intents and purpoſes, as morally good or evil, if they flow from one ſource, as from another : though no works can be evangelically good and pleaſing to God, which do not ſpring from his own grace in the heart. But this latter circumſtance is entirely of ſpiritual

---

* Acts ii. 23. and iv. 28.   ✝ I have largely canvaſſed this point, in a former tract, entitled, " More Work for Mr. John Weſley."

conſideration.

confideration. It has nothing to do, off or on, with the mere * morality of actions. Good is morally, i. e. religioufly excellent, or focially beneficial ; and evil is morally, i. e. religioufly bad or focially injurious ; whether men be felf-determining agents, or not. Light is light, and darknefs is darknefs ; flow they from the right-hand, or from the left.

2. We are told, that, on the hypothefis of neceffity, man is " neither rewardable, nor punifhable ; neither praife, nor blame-worthy."

No objection can be more unphilofophical than this, becaufe it quite lofes fight of the very point in debate ; viz. of neceffity itfelf : by which, certain caufes inevitably produce certain effects, and certain antecedents are inevitably concatenated with certain confequences. It is fufficient, therefore, to anfwer : that the will of God has eftablifhed a natural connection between virtue and + happinefs, vice and mifery. This divine eftablifhed connection is fo indiffoluble, that, even in the prefent ftate of things, happinefs never fails to enter at the fame door with virtue ; nor does mifery ever fail to tread upon the heels of vice.

Some fenfualifts, however, profefs otherwife : and affirm, that their own deviations from the moral path are neither attended, nor followed, by any pungent briar, or grieving thorn. Their draughts are all balmy and nectarious, without a drop of wormwood or of gall, to allay the fweetnefs, or to embitter the remembrance.

Thofe gentlemen muft, however, excufe me from taking their word for this. I do not believe one fyllable of it to be true. Both Scripture, and the nature of the cafe, and the obfervations I have

* Morality, is, I think, ufually, and very juftly, defined to be, that relation, or proportion, which actions bear, to a given rule.— Confequently, neither neceffity, nor non-neceffity, has any thing to do with the morality of action.

+ I hear fpeak of intellectual happinefs or mifery.

made,

made, unite to render me quite pofitive, that the way of tranfgreffors is hard* : that even in the midft of laughter, they have a tinge of forrow in their hearts ; as well as that the end of their mirth is hea-vinefs†. They may, for a time, like the Lacedæ-monian Boy, conceal the wolf that is eating out their very intrails ; and fet the glofs of an outward Sardo-nian fmile, on the inward pangs they endure : but the great law of neceffity, from which neither the virtuous nor the licentious are exempt, affures me, that this pretended eafe is mere diffimulation and grimace.

One of the moft fenfible men I ever knew, but whofe life, as well as creed, had been rather eccen-tric, returned me the following anfwer, not many months before his death, when I afked him, " whe-ther his former irregularities were not both accom-panied, at the time, and fucceeded, afterwards, by fome fenfe of mental pain ?" Yes, faid he : but I have fcarce ever owned it, until now. We [mean-ing, we infidels, and men of fafhionable morals] do not tell you all that paffes in our hearts.

The fact, then, plainly is, that rectitude of man-ners faves people from much uneafinefs of mind ; and, that the perpetration of moral evil involves in it a Trojan horfe, whofe hidden force puts their comforts to the fword. I have feen inftances of this, in very high, as well as in more humble, life : not-withftanding all the labour and art, which have been obtended, to vail it from the eye of man. They who plough iniquity, and fow wickednefs, reap the fame‡ : the crop is always, more or lefs, fimilar to the feed. The wicked man travelleth with pain, all his days ; and a dreadful found is in his ears§ ; let him fay what he will to the contrary. So that we

---

* Prov. xiii. 15. † Prov. xiv. 13.
‡ Job iv. 8. § Job xv. 20, 21.

may almoſt aſſert, with * Seneca, "*prima & maxima peccantium pœna eſt, peccaſſe :*" i. e. the very commiſſion of ſin is its own primary and capital puniſhment.

God himſelf has joined the chain together : no wonder, therefore, that its links cannot be put aſunder. Hence, I conclude, that, let what ſeeming conſequences ſoever flow from the poſition of neceſſity, God would have not tied moral and natural evil together, into one knot, if moral evil were not juſtly puniſhable. And, while facts, indiſputable facts, ſay, aye ; facts I will ſtill believe, though ten thouſand imaginary inferences were to ſay, no.

I muſt likewiſe add, that, if we ſhut out the doctrine of neceſſity, which aſſerts the inſeparable connection of moral evil with intellectual (and, often, with external) infelicity ; men will want one of the moſt rational ✝ motives, which can poſſibly induce
them

---

* Epiſt. Lib. 16. Ep. 2.—When St. Paul ſpeaks (Eph. iv. 19.) of ſome who were απηλγηκοτες, which we render, paſt feeling (though it may better be rendered, quite ſunk in indolence and idleneſs; totally enervated, and diſſipated ; enemies to all honeſt, manly, and laborious employ :) there is no neceſſity for ſuppoſing even the Engliſh phraſe to import, that thoſe wretched people were void of inward horror and tormenting anguiſh ; but that they were quite void of outward decency, and had no feelings of delicacy : for there is a ſort of refinement (though bad is the beſt), which even vice itſelf is capable of.

When the ſame apoſtle ſpeaks, elſewhere (1 Tim. iv. 2.) of the κεκαυτηριασμενων, or perſons whoſe conſciences have been ſeared as with an hot iron ; the word (not to canvaſs, here, the ſeveral critical ſenſes which it will admit of) may be fairly conſidered, as importing neither more nor leſs than this, that they carry a fearful brand, or mark of condemnation, in their own minds; though they may endeavour to toſs off matters, outwardly, with an air of ſeeming unconcern.

✝ Should any be ſo pitiably undiſcerning, as to aſk, "What can neceſſity have to do with rational motives?"—I anſwer : that there are numberleſs caſes, wherein certain motives appear ſo very rational to the mind, as to be abſolutely cogent, and incline the will effectually. For, the finally predominant motive conſtantly and infallibly determines the will : and the will, thus neceſſarily determined, as conſtantly and infallibly (all extrinſic impediments removed)

them to an hatred of vice. And ſo great is the de-
pravation of human nature, that, were it not for the
thing neceſſity, virtue neither would nor could have
any ſort of exiſtence in the world.

As for that mixture (or, rather, interſperſion) of
good and evil, which obtains throughout our ſublunary planet; this, likewiſe, I acknowledge to be the
conſequence of actual and reigning neceſſity. But
this, in a philoſophic eye, reflects no more blame on
neceſſity itſelf, than the two contrary powers of
attraction and repulſion can reflect diſhonour on the
wiſdom of him, who, for good reaſons, endued matter with thoſe oppoſite properties.

Couſin german to the ſecond, is Mr. Weſley's

3d. Objection: namely, that, if univerſal neceſſity
determine all the thoughts and actions of man,
" there can be no judgment to come;" i. e. God
cannot, in the laſt day, judge and ſentence mankind
according to their works. I have *, elſewhere, amply
refuted this empty cavil. But, as it is now haſhed
and ſerved up again in a different diſh, I will give it
another examination, before we diſmiſs it from the
table.

The objector forgets one main circumſtance, of
no ſmall importance to the argument: viz. that
the judgment day, itſelf, and the whole proceſs
of the grand tranſaction, together with every
thing that relates to it, directly or indirectly;
are, upon the Chriſtian ſcheme, no leſs neceſſary and inevitable, than any intermediate event
can be. An oak is not more the daughter of an

moved) determines the actions of the willer. *Non eſt intelligentis*
cauſæ, ſine fine ſibi propoſito, agere.

If motives did not ſo operate on the mind; and if the mind, ſo
operated upon, did not give the law to the will; and if the will, ſo
biaſſed and conciliated, did not (*poſitis omnibus ponendis*) neceſſarily influence the conduct; actions and volitions would be uncauſed
effects: than which ideas it is impoſſible for any thing to be more
abſurd and ſelf-contradictory.

* More Work for Mr. John Weſley, p. 82—85.

acorn;

acorn ; than abſolute neceſſity will be the mother of that univerſal audit, wherewith ſhe is already pregnant.

But, obſerve. The ſcriptural is not a blind neceſſity, or a neceſſity reſulting (as ſome of the groſſer Stoics believed) either from the planetary poſitions, or from the " ſtubbornneſs of matter." I no where contend for theſe kinds of neceſſity : which, even admitting them to have their reſpective degrees of phyſical influence, in ſubordination to providence ; ſtill can never, by any Chriſtian (nor, I ſhould think, by any man of refined underſtanding), be conſidered as exerciſing the leaſt dominion over God himſelf, by inferring any ſort of cauſality on his interior purpoſes, or extrinſic operations.

On the contrary, neceſſity, in general ; with all its extenſive ſeries of adamantine links, in particular ; is in reality, what the poets feigned of Minerva, the iſſue of divine wiſdom : deriving its whole exiſtence, from the free-will of God ; and its whole effectuoſity, from his never-ceaſing providence.

Thus I affirm the day of judgment to be neceſſary : to-wit, becauſe God has abſolutely * appointed it. For his counſel ſhall ſtand, and he will do all his pleaſure †. It is alſo neceſſary, that there ſhould be conſcious beings, on whom to paſs ſentence ; and that there ſhould be both good and evil actions, on which the ſentence of the judge ſhould turn. We muſt, I think, admit this ; or, at one ſtroke, deny the certain futurition of a judgement-day. And, for my own part, I would much rather believe and maintain ſo important an article of revealed religion, though upon the principle of neceſſity ; than I would virtually deny it, as an Arminian, by imagining, either the great day itſelf, or the deciſions of the day, to be things of unfixed

* Acts xvii. 31.   † Iſaiah xlvi. 10.

chance,

chance, lying at fixes and fevens, and which confequently, may or may not take effect at all.

It is the doctrine of uncertain felf-determination,
which, by reprefenting events to lie at hap-hazard,
ftamps abfurdity on the fure expectation of a judgment to come. It is the doctrine of abfolute neceffity, alone, which, by refufing to hang any one
circumftance on a peradventure, affixes the feal of
infallible futurity to the day itfelf, to the bufinefs of
the day, and to all the antecedents, concomitants,
and confequences, of the whole.

That fide-face of Arminian free-will, which we
have hitherto furveyed, carries no more than a
fquinting afpect on the day of ultimate retribution;
by only leaving the day, and its retributions, at the
uncertain mercy of a may-be. Look at the other
profile (i. e. view the blind fide) of the Arminian
goddefs; and you will immediately perceive, that,
according to her fcheme of metaphyfics, it is utterly
impoffible there fhould be any day of judgment at
all. For,

He alone can be called "a felf-determining
agent," who is quite independent on any other agent
or agency whatever. If I may depend, for my being, for my ideas, and for my operations, on another; my being, and ideas, and operations, are and
muft be influenced and affected by that dependence.
Confequently, I am neither felf-exiftent *, nor felf-

---

* See p. 173. of a performance already quoted, namely, Dr.
Prieftley's mafterly "Examination of Dr. Reid's Inquiry into the
Human Mind, Dr. Beattie's Effay on Truth, and Dr. Ofwald's
Appeal to Common Senfe."—I cannot help obferving, what, by
this time, almoft every perfon knôws, and every impartial judge
muft acknowledge; viz the energy and fuccefs, with which Dr.
Prieftley has battered the free-will lanthorns (the Inquiry, the Appeal, and the Effay), in which the three northern lights had refpec-
tively ftuck themfelves and hung themfelves out to public view. It
lay, peculiarly, in Dr. Prieftley's department, to examine the
theory of thofe new lights and colours. And he has done it to
purpofe. Though, I am apt to think, that the luminous triumvirate,
like Æfop's one eyed ftag, received the mortal fhot from a quarter
whence they leaft expected it.

determined.

determined.—But, if I am an independent animal, I
am alſo, neceſſarily, * ſelf-exiſtent: and I not only
may be, but abſolutely muſt be (view what ſide of
the argument we will, neceſſity ſtares us in the face!)
I abſolutely muſt be a ſelf-determinant. Thus, ſelf-
exiſtence and independence neceſſarily enter into the
baſis of ſelf-determination, i. e. of Arminian or
Methodiſtical free-will.

Let us, for a moment, imagine ourſelves to be
what Mr. Weſley ſuppoſes us.

Lord of myſelf, is eſſentially connected with, ac-
·countable to none. Farewell, then, to the very
poſſibility of a judgment-day. Shall an independent
being, who can have no ſuperior, hold up his hand,
as a felon, at the bar?—Shall a potent ſelf-exiſter
deign to be puniſhed, for the evanid crimes of an
hour?—Shall a ſovereign ſelf-determiner ſubmit to
receive ſentence from the lips of another? Impoſſible. Paul was a knave, for aſſerting it. And Felix
was a fool, for trembling at the empty ſound.

What a truly Chriſtian tenet, therefore, is that of
free-will! How patly it ſquares with the Bible! And
with how good a grace does orthodox Mr. John
introduce his

4th Objection, that "the Scriptures cannot be
of divine original," if the doctrine of neceſſity be
true.

I, *è contra*, ſcruple not to declare, that no man
can conſiſtently acknowledge the "divine authority
of the Scriptures," without believing their contents:
i. e. without being an abſolute neceſſitarian. I will
. even add, that all the intentional defenders of
Chriſtianity in the world, who encounter Deiſm, or

* An independent creature is a contradiction in terms. To aſk,
" Whether the Deity might not endue created beings with philoſophical independence?" is to aſk, whether one God might not make
millions of others. I anſwer, No. And yet I do not, by ſo ſaying, " limit the Holy One of Iſrael." His power is ſtill infinite.
For, as ſome have well expreſſed it, an eſſential contradiction is no
object of power.

Atheiſm

Atheiſm itſelf, on any but neceſſitarian principles; ſuch defenders ever will, and inevitably muſt, have the worſt end of the ſtaff: for the Bible will ſtand on no ground but its own; nor can the cavillings of its doctrinal gainſayers (flimſy as their cavillings are) be hewn effectually in pieces, by any weapons but thoſe which the Bible itſelf ſupplies. Among others, it ſupplies us with the invincible two-edged ſword of predeſtination and neceſſity (which two edges, by the way, terminate, ſword-like, in one common * point): a weapon, peculiarly formed and tempered to penetrate the beſt mail of our modern unbeliev-ing Philiſtines; moſt of whom have ſenſe enough to laugh (and laugh they may in perfect ſafety) at

   " The pointleſs arrow and the broken bow;"

equipped with which, Arminianiſm comes limping into the field of battle.

---

* People do not ſee all things at once. The riſing of truth, up-on the mind, is commonly gradual; like the riſing of the ſun, on the world. Hence, ſome philoſophers, who are rooted neceſſitarians, either do not yet perceive, or forbear to acknowledge, the coïn-cidence of Scripture-predeſtination with phyſical and metaphyſical neceſſity.

But, all in good time. The more theſe doctrines are examined, and compared together, the more clearly and ſtrongly will they be found to ſuppoſe and ſupport each other. The Arminians are aware of this: and pelt both predeſtination and neceſſity, with equal rage, and with the ſelf-ſame cavils.

Nor without reaſon. For what is predeſtination, but neceſſitas imperata; or, the free and everlaſting determination of God, that ſuch and ſuch a train of cauſes and effects ſhould infalliby take place in time?—And what is philoſophical neceſſity, but predeſti-natio elicita; or, God's determination drawn out into act, by ſuccef-five accompliſhment, according to the plan pre-conceived in the divine mind?—Neceſſity (i. e. fate, or providence, to whoſe ceaſe-leſs agency all the laws and modes and the very being of matter and ſpirit inceſſantly ſubſerve) this neceſſity is, as a valuable perſon phraſes it, " a ſtrait line," however crooked it may ſometimes appear to us; " a ſtrait line, drawn from the point of God's decree." And as predeſtination is the point itſelf, from which the ſtrait line is drawn; ſo it is alſo the point, into which the line, progreſſively, but infallibly, reverts.

The

The *caput vivum*, of a dexterous infidel, is abfolutely invulnerable by the *caput mortuum* of free-will
nonfenfe, though the afinine jaw-bone were wielded
by the arm of a Samfon.

C H A P. IV.

Specimen of Scripture-Atteftations to the Doctrine of
Neceffity.

REFERENCES have already been made, in
the courfe of the prefent effay, to feveral Scripture paffages, wherein neceffity is invincibly and de-
cifively afferted. I will add a few others: and then
leave the reader to judge, whether neceffitarians, or
chance-mongers, give moft credit to the " divine
original of the Scriptures."

I withheld thee from finning againft me. Gen.
xx. 6.

It was not you that fent me hither, but God.
Gen. l. 5, 7, 8.

I will harden his heart, that he fhall not let the
people go. Exod. iv. 21.

It was of the Lord, to harden their hearts, that
they fhould come againft Ifrael to battle; that he
might deftroy them utterly. Jofh. xi. 20.

The ftars in their courfes fought againft Sifera.
Judg. v. 20.

The Lord maketh poor, and maketh rich; he
bringeth low, and lifteth up. 1 Sam. ii. 7.

They hearkened not to the voice of their Father;
becaufe the Lord would flay them. 1 Sam. ii. 25.

Thus faith the Lord: Behold, I will raife up evil
againft thee, out of thy own houfe; and I will take
thy wives, before thine eyes, and give them to thy
neighbour, and he fhall lie with thy wives in the fight

of

of this fun.—What was the confequence?—So they
fpread Abfalom a tent upon the top of the houfe;
and Abfalom went in unto his father's concubines,
in the fight of all Ifrael. 2 Sam. xii. 11. with
2 Sam. xvi. 22.

The Lord hath faid unto him [to Shimei], curfe
David. 2 Sam. xvi. 10.

And he [i. e. the evil fpirit] faid, I will go forth,
and I will be a lying fpirit in the mouth of all his
[Ahab's] propheis. And he [God] faid, Thou
fhalt perfuade him, and prevail alfo: go forth, and
do fo.—Now, therefore, the Lord hath put a lying
fpirit in the mouth of all thefe, &c. 1 Kings
xxii. 22, 23.

Both riches and honour come of thee, and thou
reigneft over all. 1 Chron. xxix. 12.

Then rofe up the chief of the Fathers of Judah
and Benjamin, &c; whofe fpirit God had raifed to
go up, to build the houfe of the Lord. Ezra i. 5.

The Lord gave, and the Lord hath taken away.
Job i. 21.

Man is born unto trouble, as the fparks fly upward (Job v. 7.). And, I am apt to think, fparks
afcend by neceffity!

He difappointeth the devices of the crafty, fo that
their hands cannot perform their enterprize. (Job v.
12.) Be men ever fo fhrewd, their utmoft dexterity
will not avail, unlefs the Great Superintending Creator ftamp it with efficiency.

Behold he taketh away. Who can hinder him?
Who will fay unto him [i. e. who has a right to
fay unto God], what doft thou? Job ix. 12.——
For he is not a man, as I am, that I fhould anfwer
him, and that we fhould come together in judgment. Ver. 32.

Vain man would be wife [and the puny prifoner
of a clod would be an independent, felf-determining
freewiller!] though man be born as a wild afs's
colt. Job xi. 12. What a thunderbolt to human
pride!

pride! To the το αυτεξυσιον. To αυτοδεσποτεια. To the τα εφ' ημιν. To αυτοκρατορια. To *liberum arbitrium.* To *ipſeitas.* To the Arminian herb called, ſelf-heal. To independency, ſelf-authority, ſelf-determination, ſelf-ſalvation, innate ideas, and other pompous no-things, with which man's ignorance and conceit ſeek to plat a wreath for the enrichment of his brows. Vain man, born as a wild aſs's * colt!

" How

---

* And we ſhould remain, to our dying day, nearly on a level with the animal to which we are compared, were it not for the care of thoſe about us, and did we not neceſſarily become parts of a ſo-ciety antecedently formed to our hands. In what a ſtate would the preſent generation be, had they not dropt (if I may uſe the expreſ-ſion) into an houſe ready built! i. e. if we had been cut off from all means of profiting by the wiſdom, the experience, the diſcoveries, the inventions, and the regulations, of thoſe who lived before us.— It is a circumſtance of unſpeakable convenience, to be the children of Time's old age.

Our mental powers, like a chicken in the ſhell, or a plant in its ſemen, are no more than virtual and dormant, until elicited by cul-tivation, and ripened by experience, attention, and reflection. Civil ſociety, dreſs, articulate language, with all other uſeful and orna-mental poliſhings which reſult from domeſtic and political connec-tion, are, in themſelves, things purely artificial and adventitious. If ſo, will it not follow, that (ever ſince the fall) man is, naturally, a wild animal? Some very able reaſoners have gone ſo far, as peremp-torily to pronounce him ſuch. The late Dr. Young, in his " Cen-taur not fabulous," appears to have thought, that the greater part of the human ſpecies profit ſo little by their acceſſory opportunities of improvement, as to go off the ſtage, ſemi ſavages, at laſt; not-withſtanding the inexhauſtible and omnipotent deluge of freewill, which that ingenious writer imagined every man to bring into the world with him. Strange, that ſo immenſe a reſervoir, inherent in the ſoul, ſhould yet leave the ſoul ſo dry!

With regard to the natural wildneſs of man, ſuppoſed and aſſerted by ſome philoſophers; thus much, I think, muſt be fairly admitted; that the hypotheſis derives much ſubſidiary force, from various per-tinent and well authenticated facts. For, if any credit be due to human teſtimony, there have been inſtances of expoſed infants, who were nurſed by foreſt animals; and, when grown up, went prone on all-four, with a ſwiftneſs greatly ſuperior to that of the nimbleſt running-footman: but totally unable (and no wonder) to form the leaſt articulate ſound. It is added, that, like any other wild crea-ture, they would fly from the human ſight (i. e. from the ſight of their own ſpecies refined), with a roar of fear and hatred, into the thickeſt receſſes of the woods.

Civilization,

" How keenly," ſays a fine writer, " is this compariſon pointed !—Like the aſs's : an animal, remarkable for its ſtupidity, even to a proverb.　Like
the aſs's colt : which muſt be ſtill more egregiouſly
ſtupid than the dam.　Like the wild aſs's colt :
which is not only blockiſh, but ſtubborn and in-
tractable ; neither poſſeſſes valuable qualities by nature, nor will eaſily receive them by diſcipline.　The
image, in the original, is yet more ſtrongly touched.
The comparative particle like, is not in the Hebrew.　Born a wild aſs's colt.　Or, as we ſhould
ſay in Engliſh, a mere wild, &c." (Hervey's Theron
and Aſpaſio, Dial. 13.)

He [i. e. God] is in one mind, and who can turn
him ? and what his ſoul deſireth, even that he doth.
He performeth the thing that is appointed for me.
And many ſuch things are with him.　Job xxiii.
13, 14.　Query : Who is ſelf-determiner ? Man or
God ? Surely, God.　Nor is he only the ſelf-determiner, but the all-determiner likewiſe ; throughout
the whole univerſe both of ſpirits and of matter.

For he looketh to the ends of the earth, and ſeeth
under the whole heaven : to make a weight for the

Civilization, though a very poor ſuccedaneum for that divine
image, originally impreſſed on our immortal part, and loſt by Adam's
tranſgreſſion, is, however, of very great ſecular importance.　Nay,
its importance is, with regard to millions of us, more than ſecular :
for it is often a providential means of qualifying us to receive and
underſtand that bleſſed goſpel, which, when made the vehicle of
divine power to the heart, iſſues in our recovery of God's image, and
in the ſalvation of the ſoul.

After all, let the inſtruments of our refinement, and of our knowledge (whether in things temporal, or in things ſacred), be who or
what they may ; and let us profit ever ſo deeply by our intercourſe
with the living, by converſe with the recorded wiſdom of the dead,
by the perceptions we receive from external objects, and by reflecting
on the ideas of which thoſe perceptions are the ſource ; ſtill, no advantages are any thing more to us, than divine Providence makes
them to be.　Let him, therefore, that glories, glory in the Lord.—
For, it is God, who teacheth us more than the beaſts of the earth,
and maketh us wiſer than the fowls of heaven. 1 Cor. i. 31.
Job xxxv. 11.

winds; and he weigheth the waters by meaſure. He made a decree for the rain, and a way for the lightening of the thunder. Job xxviii. 25, 26.

When he giveth quietneſs, who then can make trouble? and, when he hideth his face, who then can behold him? whether it be done againſt a nation, or againſt a man only. Job xxxiv. 29. Abſolute neceſſity ſtill.

By the breath of God, froſt is given; and the breadth of the waters is ſtraitened. Alſo, by watering, he wearieth the thick cloud: he ſcattereth his bright cloud. He cauſeth it to come; whether for correction, or for his land, or for mercy. Job xxxviii. 10—13. We ſee, from this, as well as from a preceding and from two or three ſubſequent quotations, that the air cannot be compreſſed into a current of wind; nor rain find its way to the earth; nor exhalations kindle into thunder and lightening; nor a river overflow its banks; nor ſuſpended vapours condenſe into ſnow or hail; nor water freeze, or, when frozen, thaw; without the expreſs appointment of God's will, and the hand of his particular providence. Second cauſes are but effects of his decree: and can operate no farther, than he, from whom they derive their whole activity, condeſcends to make uſe of them as mediums of his own agency.

The kingdom is the Lord's; and he is the governor among the nations. Pſalm xxii. 28.

O Lord, thou preſerveſt man and beaſt. Pſalm xxxvi. 6.

Except the Lord build the houſe, they labour in vain that build it. Except the Lord keep the city, the watchman waketh but in vain. Pſalm cxxvii. 1.

Whatſoever the Lord pleaſeth, that did he; in heaven, and in earth, in the ſeas, and in all deep places. He cauſeth the vapours to aſcend from the ends of the earth: he maketh lightenings, for the rain;

rain ; he bringeth the wind out of his treasuries. Psalm cxxxv. 6, 7.

He covereth the heaven with clouds, he prepareth rain for the earth, he maketh grass to grow upon the mountains. He giveth to the beast his food ; and to the young ravens, which cry. He maketh peace in thy borders, and filleth thee with the finest wheat. He giveth snow, like wool ; he scattereth the hoar frost, like ashes. He casteth forth his ice, like morsels ; who can stand before his cold? he sendeth out his word, and melteth them ; he causeth his wind to blow, and the waters flow. Psalm cxlvii. 8, 9, 14—18. What so variable and uncertain, humanly speaking, as the weather ? And yet, we see, all its modes and changes are adjusted and determined, from moment to moment, by divine impression: i. e. by a necessity, resulting from the will and providence of the supreme First Cause. Fire, and hail ; snow, and vapour; stormy wind, fulfilling his word ! Psalm cxlviii. 8.

Neither is material nature alone thus * " bound fast in fate." All other things, the " human will" itself not excepted, are no less tightly bound, i. e. effectually influenced and determined. For,

The preparations of the heart, in man ; and the answer of the tongue ; are from the Lord. Prov. xvi. 1. That is, men can neither think, nor speak; they can neither resolve, nor act, independently of providence.

The Lord hath made all things, for himself ; for the manifestation of his own glory, and for the accomplishment of his own designs : even the wicked, for the day of evil. Prov. xvi. 4. If so, he has endued none of his creatures with a self-determining power, which might issue in counteracting and defeating the purposes of his infinite wisdom.

---

* See Pope's Universal Prayer.

A man's

A man's heart deviſeth his way : but the Lord directeth his ſteps. Prov. xvi. 9. Yea, there are many deviſes in a man's heart : neverthelefs, the counſel of the Lord, that ſhall ſtand. Prov. xix. 21.

The lot is caſt into the lap : but the whole diſpoſing thereof is of the Lord. Prov. xvi. 33.

Even the king's heart is in the hand of the Lord, as the rivers of water : and he turneth it, whitherſoever he will. Prov. xxi. 1. Odd ſort of ſelf-determination, this !

Enémies and evil-minded men, are under the abſolute controul of God ; nor can their enmity, or their wickedneſs, do a jot more hurt, than he gives leave. O Aſſyrian, the rod of my anger. Iſai. x. 5. Thou art my battle-axe and weapons of war : for with thee will I break in pieces the nations, and with thee will I deſtroy kingdoms. Jer. li. 20. Very extraordinary declarations theſe, if men are ſelf-determining agents ! a ſelf-determining rod, for inſtance : a ſelf-determining battle-axe ; a ſelf-determining hammer ! Arminianiſm does that, which God, by the prophet, ſatirizes in the following lively terms : Shall the axe boaſt itſelf againſt him that heweth therewith ? or ſhall a ſaw magnify itſelf againſt him that ſhaketh it ? As if the rod ſhould ſhake itſelf againſt them that lifted it up ! or, as if a ſtaff ſhould lift up itſelf as though it were no wood ! Iſai. x. 15.—What ! is that noble freewiller, man, comparable to an axe, to a ſaw, to a rod, and to a ſtick ; not one of which can operate, or ſo much as move, but in proportion as it is acted upon ? This is worſe than being likened to Mr. Weſley's clockwork ! But who can help it ?

The prophet goes on, elſewhere. The Lord of hoſts hath ſworn [i. e. hath ſolemnly and immutably decreed], ſaying, Surely, as I have thought, ſo ſhall it come to paſs : and as I have purpoſed, ſo ſhall it ſtand. This is the purpoſe, which is purpoſed upon the whole earth ; and this is the hand
that

that is ſtretched out upon all nations. For the
Lord of hoſts hath purpoſed, and who ſhall diſannul
it ? And his hand is ſtretched out, and who ſhall
turn it back ? Iſai. xv. 24, 26, 27. Grand and
concluſive queſtions ! Queſtions, however, which
lordly Arminianiſm can ſolve in a moment. Who
ſhall diſannul God's purpoſe ? Why, human freewill
to be ſure. Who ſhall turn back God's hand ? Human ſelf-determination can do it, with as much eaſe
as our breath can repel the down of a feather !

I form the light, and create darkneſs : I make
peace, and create evil. I the Lord do all theſe
things. Iſai. xlv. 7.

Who is he that ſaith, and it cometh to paſs ;
when the Lord commandeth it not ? Lam. iii. 37.
The higheſt angel cannot.

Wiſdom and might are God's. He changeth the
times and the ſeaſons. He removeth kings, and
ſetteth up kings. He giveth wiſdom to the wiſe,
and knowledge to them that know underſtanding.
Dan. ii. 20, 21.

Locuſts, and other ravaging inſects, cannot afflict
a land, without a commiſſion under the great ſeal of
Providence. The locuſt, the canker-worm, the ca-
terpillar, and the palmer-worm ; my great army,
which I ſent among you. Joel ii. 25.

Shall there be evil in a city [viz. any calamitous
accident, as it is commonly called], and the Lord
hath not done it ? Amos iii. 6.—Impoſſible.

I cauſed it to rain upon one city, and cauſed it
not to rain upon another city.—I have ſmitten you
with blaſting, and mildew.—I have ſent among you
the peſtilence.—Your young men have I ſlain with
the ſword. Amos iv. 7—10.

They [Paul and Timothy] were forbidden of the
Holy Ghoſt to preach the word in Aſia.——They
eſſayed to go into Bithynia : but the ſpirit ſuffered
them not. Acts xvi. 6, 7. Had ſelf-determination
any thing to do here ?

A certain

A certain woman, named Lydia, heard us: whoſe heart the Lord opened, ſo that ſhe attended to the things that were ſpoken by Paul. Ibid. v. 14.

As many, as were ordained unto eternal life, believed. Acts xiii. 48.

I am carnal, ſold under ſin. For that which I do, ὃ γινώσκω, I am far from approving: for what I would, that do I not; but what I hate, that do I.—— To will is preſent with me: but how to perform that which is good, I find not. For the good that I would, I do not: but the evil which I would not, that I do.——When I would do good, evil is preſent with me. I delight in the law of God, after the inner man: but I ſee another law in my members, warring againſt the law of my mind, and bringing me into captivity to the law of ſin which is in my members. O wretched man that I am! Who ſhall deliver me from the body of this death? I thank God, through Jeſus Chriſt our Lord. So then, with the mind, I myſelf ſerve the law of God: but, with my fleſh, the law of ſin. Rom. vii. 14—25. According to the account which St. Paul here gives of himſelf, he no more dreamed of his being a ſelf-determiner, than of his having attained to ſinleſs perfection. No wonder that ſome flaming Arminians have a peculiar ſpite againſt this apoſtle!

In whom [i. e. in Chriſt] we alſo have obtained an inheritance: being predeſtinated, according to the purpoſe of him who worketh all things according to the counſel of his own will, Eph. i. 11.

Speaking of affliction and perſecution, the apoſtle comforted himſelf and his fellow-ſufferers, by reſolving all into neceſſity: that no man ſhould be moved by theſe afflictions; for ye yourſelves know, that we are appointed thereto. 1 Theſſ. iii. 3.

What idea St. James entertained, concerning free-will and ſelf-determination, fully appears from the following admonition: Ye know not [much leſs can ye be the diſpoſers of] what ſhall be on the

morrow.

morrow. For what is your life? it is even a vapour that appeareth for a little time, and then vanisheth away. Ye ought to say, if the Lord will, we shall live, and do this, or that. James iv. 14, 15.——— Why did St. James reason in this manner? Because he was endued with grace and sense to be a necessitarian.

So was St. Peter. Hence he tells the regenerated elect, to whom he wrote, Ye also, as lively stones, are built up, a spiritual house. 1 Pet. ii. 5. This is giving free-will a stab under the fifth rib. For, can stones hew themselves, and build themselves into a regular house? no more, in this apostle's judgment, can men form themselves into temples of the Holy Ghost. It is the effect of necessitating grace.

The prophecy came not, in old time, by the will of man: but holy men of God spake as they were moved by the Holy Ghost. 2 Pet. i. 21.——Necessity again.

There shall come, in the last days, scoffers, walking after their own lusts. 2 Pet. iii. 3.—But the apostle could not have been sure of this, without taking necessity into the account: or, as himself expresses it, unless they who stumble at the word, were appointed to disobedience. 1 Pet. ii. 8.

There are certain men crept in unawares, who were before, of old, ordained to this condemnation. Jude 4. If so, were not the sin and condemnation of those men necessary and inevitable?

CHAP. V.

Proofs that Christ Himself was an absolute Necessitarian.

LEST any, who may not, hitherto, have considered the subject, with the same attention that I have done, should be startled at the title of

this

this chapter; I ſhall adduce the larger evidence, in order to make good what the title imports. The reader will not, however, expect a ſynopſis of the whole evidence, by which this great truth is authenticated : for, were I to attempt that, I muſt tranſcribe well-nigh all the 89 chapters of the four evangeliſts.

It ſhould ſeem that our bleſſed Lord began his public miniſtrations with his ſermon on the Mount, recorded Matt. v. vi. and vii. In that diſcourſe, are the following paſſages.

One jot, or one tittle, ſhall in no wiſe paſs from the law, until all be fulfilled.

Thou canſt not make one hair white or black.

Your Father, who is in heaven, maketh his ſun to riſe on the evil and the good, and ſendeth rain on the juſt and on the unjuſt. Surely, man can neither promote, nor hinder, the riſing of the ſun and the falling of the rain !

Thine is the kingdom, and the power, and the glory, for ever.—How can a free-willer ſay the Lord's Prayer?

Which of you, by taking thought, can add one cubit unto his ſtature ? The word ἡλικια ſignifies both ſtature, and age. As we have no ſingle term, in Engliſh, which compriſes both thoſe ideas together; the paſſage ſhould be rendered periphraſtically : which of you, by being anxious, can either make addition to his ſtature, or prolong the duration of his life?

Be not tormentingly diſtreſſed, concerning futurity : for futurity ſhall take care of its own things. Sufficient unto the day is the evil thereof : i. e. commit yourſelves, in a believing and placid uſe of reaſonable means, to the will and providence of him, who has already lain out the whole plan of events in his own immutable purpoſe. The appointed meaſure of ſuppoſed evil is infallibly connected with its day, which no corrodings of imaginary anticipation can either ſtave off, or diminiſh.

" Reaſonable means! are not all means, hereby, ſhut out of the caſe?" No. Not in any reſpect whatever. For we know not what means God will bleſs, until we have tried as many as we can. But, when all tried, the reſult ſtill reſts with him.

I ſhall only quote one other paſſage, from the ſermon on the Mount.—The rain [of affliction] deſcended, and the floods [of temptation] came, and the winds [of perſecution] blew, and beat upon that houſe [the houſe of an elect, redeemed, converted ſoul]: but it fell not ; for it was founded upon a rock. That is, in plain Engliſh, it could not fall. It ſtood, neceſſarily: or, as the ſenſe is yet more forcibly expreſſed in St. Luke, when the flood aroſe, the ſtream beat vehemently upon that houſe, and could not ſhake it. Luke vi. 48.

In other parts of the goſpels, we find Chriſt reaſoning and acting on the higheſt principles of neceſſity.

I will ; be thou clean: ſaid he, to the poor leper. What was the conſequence ? And immediately his leproſy was cleanſed. Matt. viii. 3. The effect neceſſarily followed. The leper could not but be healed.

And, indeed, what were all the miracles wrought by Jeſus, but effects of his irreſiſtible and neceſſitating power ? Let the Chriſtian reader examine and weigh each of thoſe miracles, with this remark in his eye; and he will ſoon become a convert to the doctrine of neceſſity. Was it poſſible for thoſe miracles not to have taken effect ? i. e. was it poſſible for Chriſt's miracles not to have been miracles ? Was it chance, which armed his word with ability to heal and to deſtroy ? If ſo, farewell to all Chriſtianity at once. I can perceive no ſhadow of medium between neceſſity and rank infidelity.

Neither

Neither can I make any thing of the prophecies of Chriſt, unleſs thoſe prophecies be conſidered as infallible: i. e. as inferring a certain, or neceſſary, accompliſhment, in every part. For, if a ſingle predicted circumſtance can poſſibly happen, other-wiſe than it is foretold; the entire argument, for the truth of divine revelation, drawn from the topic of prophecy, moulders into duſt.

Nor is the Arminian ſelf-determining hypotheſis more compatible with (what is the eſſential baſis of prophecy) the fore-knowledge of God. If, for ex-ample, it ſo lay at the free-will of Chriſt's betrayer and murderers, that they might, or might not, have betrayed and crucified him; and if it ſo lay at the free-will of the Romans, as that they might, or might not, have deſtroyed Jeruſalem; it will follow, that thoſe events were philoſophically contingent : i. e. there was no certainty of their taking place, till after they actually had taken place. The ſelf-determining will of Judas might poſſibly have de-termined itſelf another way. So might the ſelf-de-termining will of every perſon concerned in the cru-cifixion of Chriſt. And ſo might the ſelf-determin-ing wills of thoſe Romans, who beſieged and razed Jeruſalem. Conſequently (on that principle,) divine fore-knowledge could not, with certainty, know any thing of the matter. For that which is not certainly future, is not certainly fore-knowable. It may be emptily conſidered, as poſſible : or (at the very utmoſt) be uncertainly gueſſed at, as not im-probable. But knowledge muſt be left out of the queſtion : for knowledge will ſtand on none but *

certain

---

* There are four links, which all the art of man can never ſepa-rate; and which proceed in the following order: Decree—Fore-knowledge—Prophecy—Neceſſity. Let us take a ſhort Scripture view of thoſe ſacred links, and of their connection with each other.

I am God, and there is none elſe; I am God, and there is none like me: declaring the end, from the beginning; and, from antient times, the things that are not yet done: ſaying, my counſel ſhall ſtand, and

E 3

I will

certain ground. God does not fore-know, but after-
know (i. e. he is never ſure of a thing's coming to
paſs, .

I will do all my pleaſure.——Yea, I have ſpoken: I will alſo bring
it to paſs. I have purpoſed: I will alſo do it. Iſaiah xlvi. 9, 10,
11. I admit, that this ſublime paſſage had immediate reference to
the certainty of Babylon's capture by Cyrus. But not to that only.
" The things which are not yet done," as well as that in particular,
are all known to Jehovah; and many of them explicitly predicted
likewiſe. And on what is God's abſolute and all-compriſing knowl-
ledge grounded? On the " counſel," or decree; and on the "pleaſure," or ſovereign and almighty determination; of his will.——By the
ſame rule, that God had predeſtinated, and did foreknow, the
exploits of Cyrus; he muſt have predeſtinated, and foreknown, the
exploits of every other man. Since, if any one being, or any one
fact, incident, or circumſtance, be unknown to God; every being,
fact, incident, and circumſtance, may be equally unknown by him.
But, putting matters upon the beſt footing on which Arminianiſm
can put them; the divine knowledge can neither be eternal,
nor infinite, nor infallible, if aught is exempted from it, or if
aught can happen otherwiſe than as it is foreknown.
  How great a ſtreſs God lays, on this his attribute of complete
and unmiſtaking preſcience; and how he claims the honour of it,
as one of thoſe eſſential and incommunicable perfections, by which
he ſtands diſtinguiſhed from falſe gods; may be ſeen, among other
places, in Iſaiah xli. 21, 22, 23. and xlii. 8, 9. and xliii. 9, 12.
and xlv. 21.——Well, therefore, might St. James declare, in the ſynod
of apoſtles and elders held at Jeruſalem, known unto God are all
his works, απ' αιωνος, from eternity. Acts xv. 18.
  The late excellent Mr. William Cooper, of Bolton, in New England, (I ſay, the late; becauſe I ſuppoſe that good man to be, ere
this time, gathered into the aſſembly of ſaints made perfect) obſerves, in the ſecond of his Four Diſcourſes on Predeſtination unto
Life, that it was the Scripture doctrine of God's omniſcience,
which proſelyted our famous Dr. South to Calviniſm. " I have
it," ſays Mr. Cooper, " from very good authority" [appealing in
the margin, to Dr, Calamy's Continuation, vol. i. p. 146.], "that,
ſome time after the Reſtoration, Dr. South being in company, at
Oxford, with ſeveral perſons of note, and among the reſt with Mr.
Thomas Gilbert, who was afterwards one of the ejected miniſters;
they fell into a converſation, about the Arminian points.——On
Mr. Gilbert's aſſerting, that the predeſtination of the Calviniſts did
neceſſarily follow upon the preſcience of the Arminians; the doctor
preſently engaged, that, if he [Gilbert] could make that out, he
[i. e. Dr. South] would never be an Arminian, ſo long as he lived.
Mr. Gilbert immediately undertook it: and made good his aſſertion,
to the ſatisfaction of thoſe preſent. And the doctor himſelf was, ſo
convinced, as to continue, to the laſt, a very zealous aſſerter of the
reformed

paſs, until it does or has come to paſs), if it be in the power of his creatures to determine themſelves to a contrary point of the compaſs.

"Oh, but God fore-knows to what particular point of the compaſs they certainly will determine themſelves." Pray, leave out the word, certainly; and likewiſe the word, will: for they ſtab poor ſelf-determination to the heart. If you retain theſe words and their ideas, you give up the very eſſence of your cauſe. For, what certainly will be, is no longer uncertain. And what is not uncertain is neceſſary, or will ſurely come to paſs, and cannot but do ſo: elſe, the certainty evaporates into nothing.

When Chriſt ſent his diſciples for an aſs's colt, which, he foreknew and foretold, they would find exactly at ſuch a place; he added, that the owner of the animal, on their ſaying, the Lord wants it, would immediately permit them to lead it away. They went to the village, and made up to the very ſpot; where every thing fell out preciſely, as their heavenly Maſter had predicted. Let me aſk: Was the man's conſent to part with his colt neceſſary; or was it uncertain? All circumſtances conſidered, had he power to refuſe, and might he actually have refuſed to let go his property? If (which was certainly the caſe) he could not poſſibly withhold his aſſent, Chriſt's fore-knowledge was real; and the man him-ſelf, what the ingenious Mr. Weſley would term, "a fine piece of clock-work;" but what I ſhould term, a neceſſary free-agent. If, on the other hand, he might have denied complying with the diſciples' requeſt, and could have diſmiſſed them without ſuc-ceſs; it will neceſſarily follow, that our Lord ſhot his arrow at a venture, ſent his meſſengers on a blind errand, and that his own fore-knowledge was not fore-knowledge, but random conjecture and ſur-

reformed [i. e. of the Calviniſtic] doctrine, againſt its various op-poſers."

miſe.

miſe. " Oh, but our Lord foreknew that the man
certainly would do as requeſted." Then the man
could not help doing it His volition was inevitable.
It could not have been infallibly known, that he
certainly would comply ; if that compliance was
antecedently uncertain, and if it could ſo have hap-·
pened that he might not have complied.

Thus does Scripture-prophecy (not one only, but
every individual prophecy in God's book) demon-
ſtrate, 1. The abſolute fore-knowledge of the three
divine perſons : and, 2. The unalterable neceſſity,
or indefeatable futurition, of things foreknown.

Either God is ignorant of future events, and his
underſtanding, like that of men, receives gradual
improvement from time and experience and obſervation (a ſuppoſition blacker, if poſſible, than atheiſm
itſelf !) or, the whole train of incidents, even to the
riſe and fall of a mote in the air, ever was, now is,
ever will be, and ever muſt be, exactly that, and no
other, which he * certainly knew it would be. Fore-
knowledge,

---

* Properly ſpeaking, it cannot be affirmed of God, that he either
did know, or that he will know ; but, ſimply, that he knows. For,
in Deum non cadunt prius & poſterius: there is no paſt, nor future,
to him. All is preſent, and unſucceſſive. The diſtribution of things,
into thoſe that have been, thoſe that are, and thoſe that ſhall be ; is,
indeed, ſuited to the flux condition, and to the limited faculties, of
beings like ourſelves, whoſe eſtimates of duration are taken from the
periodical journies of an opaque grain, round a lucid ſpeck termed
the ſun : but can have no place in him, of whom it is declared, that
a thouſand years are, with the Lord, as one day ; and one day, as
a thouſand years. And even this declaration, magnificent as it is,
falls infinitely ſhort of the mark.

When, therefore, I ſpeak of foreknowledge, as an attribute
eſſential to Deity ; I ſpeak, as St. Paul ſays, after the manner of
men. The ſimple term, knowledge, would be more intrinſically
proper ; but then it would not ſo readily aid the conceptions of ordinary perſons. Though, for my own part, I would, always, rather
call the divine knowledge, omniſcience, than give it any other
name.

Let me juſt hint, that, if all things, without exception, and without ſucceſſion, are eternally preſent, as an indiviſible point, to the
uncreated view ; neceſſity comes in, with a full tide. For that,
which

knowledge, undarkened by the least shadow of ignorance, and superior to all possibility of mistake, is a link, which draws invincible necessity after it, whether the Scripture doctrine of predestination be taken into the account or no.

Take a few more evidences of our Lord's necessitarianism.

When they deliver you up [to be tried as religious criminals at the Jewish and Heathen tribunals], take no thought how or what you shall speak. For it shall be given you, in that same hour, what you shall speak. For it is not ye that speak, but the spirit of your Father, who speaketh in you. Matt. x. 19, 20.

Are not two sparrows sold for a farthing? and one of them shall not fall on the ground, without your Father. But the very hairs of your head are all numbered. Matt. x. 29, 30.

O Father, thou hast hid these things from the wise and prudent, and hast revealed them unto babes. Matt. xi. 25.

It is given unto you, to know the mysteries of the kingdom of heaven; but to them it is not given. Matt. xiii. 11.

Without a parable spake he not unto them: that it might be fulfilled, which was spoken by the prophet. Matt. xiii. 34, 35.

---

which is always a philosophical now, can be no other, nor otherwise, than it is.—Not to add: that the Deity, whose view of all things is thus unchangeably fixed, and perpetual, and intransitory; must have within himself a constant and irremediable source of standing uneasiness, if any thing can happen in contrariety to his will, and so as to cross or defeat the wisdom and goodness of his designs. He must certainly interest himself, and very deeply too, in the accomplishment of a will which is all-holy, and all-right, and all-wise. Consequently, could such a will (and his will is precisely such) be frustrated, though but in one single instance; that frustration would necessarily be a calamity on God himself, and inflict essential and never-ending pain on the divine mind. Another (I think, irrefragable) proof, that nothing is left to contingency.

Flesh

Fleſh and blood have not revealed unto thee, but my Father who is in heaven. Matt. xvi. 17.

Upon this rock will I build my Church, and the gates of hell ſhall not prevail againſt it. Ver. 18.

The Son of man muſt go to Jeruſalem, and ſuffer many things, and be killed, and riſe again the third day. Ver. 21.

It muſt needs be [Αναϐκη ιϛι, there is a neceſſity] that offences come. Matt. xviii. 7.—Or, as St. Luke has it, it is impoſſible [ανενδικτον, it is not expectable] but that offences will come: Luke xvii. 1. Our Lord not only aſſerted the thing, which we mean by neceſſity; but even made uſe of the word itſelf. And ſo we find him doing, in three or four other parts of the goſpels. Nor is the ſenſe, in which he uſed the term, left ambiguous; as appears from comparing the two above paſſages together. Neceſſity is that, by which, things cannot, without the utmoſt folly and abſurdity, be expected to come to paſs any otherwiſe than juſt as they do. But Arminianiſm pays very ſlender regard to Chriſt's authority.

Go thou to the ſea, and caſt an hook, and take the fiſh that firſt cometh up: and when thou haſt opened his mouth, thou ſhalt find a piece of money. Matt. xvii. 27.

All men cannot receive this ſaying, ſave they to whom it is given. He that can receive it, let him receive it. Matt. xix. 11, 12.

To ſit on my right-hand and on my left, is not mine to give, except unto them for whom it is prepared of my Father. Matt. xx. 23.

Let no fruit grow on thee henceforward, forever. And, preſently, the fig-tree withered away. Matt. xxi. 19.

Whoſoever ſhall fall on this ſtone, ſhall be broken: but on whomſoever it ſhall fall, it will grind him to powder. Matt. xxi. 44.

Many

Many are called, but few are chofen. Matt.
xxii. 14.

Fill you up the meafure of your fathers. How *
can you efcape the damnation of hell? Matt.
xxiii. 32, 33.

I fend unto you prophets, and wife men, and
fcribes: and fome of them ye fhall kill and crucify,
and fome of them fhall ye fcourge in your fyna-
gogues; and perfecute them from city to city; that
upon you may come all the righteous bloodfhed
upon the earth. Matt. xxiii. 34, 35.—— Say not,
" Where is the juftice of this?" Juftice belongs to
another argument. We are not now treating of
juftice, but of neceffity. Keep to the point.

Two men fhall be in the field: one fhall be
taken, and the other left. Two women fhall be
grinding at the mill: one fhall be taken, and the
other left. Matt. xxiv. 40, 41.

---

* Monfieur Le Clerc (who would have thought it?) has a paffage,
fo full to the fenfe of this obfervable text, that one would almoft
imagine he defigned it for the very purpofe. " Pofito, hominem
peccato deditum effe; nec per totam vitam id habere, quod neceffariò poftulatur ad habitum peccati exuendum; inde colligimus, ne-
ceffitate confequentiæ, hominem in peccato manfurum, nec ullâ
ratione vitaturum pænas peccatori debitas impænitenti." Ontolog.
cap. 13.

I really wonder, at the above writer's expreffing himfelf thus.
But I do not wonder, to hear the excellent Luther remark as follows.
" Nonne clarè fequitur, dum Deus opere fuo in nobis non adeft,
omnia effe mala quæ facimus, et nos neceffariò operari quæ nihil ad
falutem valent? Si enim non nos, fed folus Deus operatur falutem
in nobis; nihil, ante opus ejus, operamur falutare, velimus nolimus."
(De Servo Arbitr. Sect. 43.) i. e. It is clearly evident, that, until
God is prefent in us by his own gracious influence, whatever we do
is evil: and we neceffarily do thofe things only, which have no
tendency to falvation. For if it is God alone who worketh falvation
in us, and not we in ourfelves; we can do nothing falutary, will we or
nill we, until he himfelf actually doth fo work in us. Well faid,
honeft Martin. To God's bleffing upon the bold and faithful affertion of fuch noble truths as this, we owe our reformation from
Popery. And nothing will finally preferve us from being carried
captive into the Popifh Egypt again, but the revival and prevalency
of the fame noble truths which at firft led us forth from that houfe
of bondage.

This

This night, before the cock crow, thou shalt deny me thrice. Matt. xxvi. 34. Might Peter not have denied him? and might Christ have proved mistaken?

If it be possible, let this cup pass from me. Matt. xxvi. 39.—But it was not possible.

Thinkest thou that I cannot now pray to my Father, &c. but how then shall the Scriptures be fulfilled, that thus it must be? Ver. 53, 54.

All this was done, that the Scriptures of the prophets might be fulfilled. Ver. 56.

And they crucified him, and parted his garments, casting lots; that it might be fulfilled which was spoken, &c. Matt. xxvii. 35. Nothing but mere necessity, from beginning to end!

My appeals to the other three evangelists shall be extremely concise.

He goeth up into a mountain, and calleth unto him whom he would, and they * came unto him. Mark iii. 13.

---

* It is precisely the same, in the spiritual conversion of the soul to God. None can come, until effectually called: and they, who are called effectually, cannot but come. For, as the profound and judicious Mr. Charnock unanswerably argues, "If there be a counsel [i. e. a display of godlike wisdom and design] in framing the lowest creature, and in the minutest passages of providence; there must needs be an higher wisdom in the government of creatures to a supernatural end, and in framing the soul to be a monument of his glory." Charnock on the Attributes. p. 373.—I have met with many treatises on the divine perfections; but with none, which any way equals that of Mr. Charnock. Perspicuity, and depth; metaphysical sublimity, and evangelical simplicity; immense learning, and plain, but irrefragable, reasoning; conspire to render that performance one of the most inestimable productions, that ever did honour to the sanctified judgement and genius of an human being. If I thought myself at all adequate to the task, I would endeavour to circulate the outlines of so rich a treasure into more hands, by reducing the substance of it within the compass of an octavo volume. Was such a design properly executed, a more important service could hardly be rendered to the cause of religion, virtue, and knowledge. Many people are frightened at a folio of more than 800 pages, who might have both leisure and inclination to avail themselves of a well-digested compendium.

If any man have ears to hear, let him hear. Mark vii. 16.

With men, it is impoſſible: but not with God. Ib. x. 27.

Except the Lord had ſhortened thoſe days, no fleſh ſhould be ſaved. But, for the elects' ſake, whom he hath choſen, he hath ſhortened the days. ——Falſe prophets ſhould ſeduce, if it were poſſible, even the elect. Mark xiii. 20, 22.

One of you, that eateth with me, ſhall betray me. Ib. xiv. 18.

All ye ſhall be offended, becauſe of me this night. Ver. 27.

The hour is come: the Son of man is betrayed, &c. Ver. 41.

But the Scriptures muſt be fulfilled. Ver. 49.

Many widows were in Iſrael, but to none of them was Elias ſent, ſave unto Sarepta, a city of Sidon, to a woman that was a widow. And many lepers were in Iſrael, in the time of Eliſeus the prophet: but none of them was cleanſed, ſave Naaman the the Syrian. Luke iv. 26, 27.

I muſt preach the kingdom of God to other cities alſo: for therefore am I ſent. Ver. 43.

Not one of them [i. e. not a ſingle * ſparrow] is forgotten before God. Ib. xii. 6.

All things that are written by the prophets, concerning the Son of man, ſhall be accompliſhed. For he ſhall be delivered to the Gentiles, and ſhall be mocked, &c. Luke xviii. 31.

There ſhall not an hair of your head periſh. Ib. xxi. 18.—i. e. before the appointed time.

Truly, the Son of man goeth [to crucifixion and death] as it was determined: but woe unto that man, by whom he is betrayed. Ib. xxii. 22.—

---

* " Oh blindneſs to the future, wiſely giv'n,
 " That each may fill the circle mark'd by heav'n!
 " Who ſees, with equal eye, as God of all,
 " An hero periſh, or a ſparrow fall." Popе.

What

What a different view did Christ entertain of predestination and necessity, from that which the Arminians profess to have! The Son of God connects
two ideas, which those gentlemen are for setting at
an infinite distance: namely, the determining decree of his Father, by which moral evil is effectually
permitted; and the penal woe, justly due to the
persons, who, in consequence of that effectual permission, are, necessarily, evil agents. I shall just
touch again upon this particular, when we come to
John xix. 11.

This, that is written, must yet be accomplished in
me, and he was reckoned among the transgressors:
for the things concerning me have an end [i. e. they
shall every one come to pass]. Luke xxii. 37.

This is your hour, and the power of darkness.
Ver. 53.

Ought not Christ to have suffered these things?
Ib. xxiv. 26.—i. e. Was there not a necessity for
those very sufferings, and were they not inevitable?
Certainty itself is not more certain.   The entire chain of his humiliation proceeded just
as it should, without one circumstance deficient,
or one redundant.   It all fell out, precisely,
as it ought: and ought to have fallen out,
precisely, as it did.   Why? Because God had decreed it, and because man's salvation (which was no
less decreed) required it.   It was predestinated,
that Christ should be delivered up to death, even to
the death of the cross, and there make his soul an
offering for sin.   But he could not have been betrayed, without a betrayer: nor crucified, without
crucifiers.   The means, therefore, no less than the
end, were necessarily included (as they always are)
within the circle of divine pre-appointment.

But I go on.

That, which is born of the flesh, is flesh: and that,
which is born of the spirit, is spirit.   John iii. 6.—
What is this but saying? Man, in his natural state,

is neceſſarily corrupt : man, in a regenerate ſtate, is neceſſarily biaſſed to God.

If thou kneweſt the gift of God, and who it is that ſaith to thee, give me to drink; thou wouldſt have aſked of him. Ib. iv. 11.—But ſhe did not know him, and therefore could not ſo pray to him. Our Lord, however, knew her to be one of his elect, and that the time of her converſion was very near. And, that ſhe might be converted preciſely at the very time appointed, he muſt needs go through the territory of Samaria. John iv. 4.

The hour is coming, and now is, when the dead [elect ſouls, but hitherto unregenerated, and of courſe dead to God] ſhall hear the [converting] voice of the Son of God; and, hearing, they ſhall live. · Ib. v. 25.—All true converſion is wrought by invincible power. The dead neceſſarily continue ſo, until they are neceſſarily raiſed to life. A dead ſoul, no more than a dead body, can neither quicken itſelf, nor hinder God from doing it. Whoever goes to Chriſt and heaven, goes thither by gracious neceſſity : a neceſſity ſo powerful, that it even makes him willing to go.

All that the Father giveth me, ſhall come to me. Chap. vi. 37.—They come neceſſarily : i. e. they cannot but believe with the faith which is of the operation of God.

This is the Father's will, who ſent me, that, of all which he hath given me, I ſhould loſe nothing; but ſhould raiſe it up again at the laſt day. Ver. 39.—God's will is neceſſity itſelf.

No man can come to me, except the Father, who hath ſent me, draw him.——It is written in the prophets, and they [i. e. my people] ſhall be all taught of God. Every man, therefore, that hath heard and hath learned [i. e. who has been drawn] of the Father cometh unto me, John vi. 44, 45.— Neceſſity, on both ſides ! until drawn, none can come : and, when drawn, none can ſtay away.

Therefore

Therefore ſaid I unto you, that no man can come unto me, except it be given to him of my Father. Ver. 65.

They ſought to take him; but no man laid hands on him, becauſe his hour was not yet come. Chap. vii. 30.—Until then, their hands were tied and bound with the inviſible, but adamantine, chain of neceſſity. And yet, I ſuppoſe, becauſe they did not ſee nor feel the chain, they looked upon themſelves as ſelf-determining free-agents!

Whoſoever committeth ſin, is the ſervant [δᾶλ◌, the ſlave] of ſin. Chap. viii. 34.—But according to the Arminian view of things, it is ſuch a ſlavery as was never heard of before: the ſlave is at perfect liberty all the while! I cannot believe this. On the contrary, I believe what follows:

If the Son ſhall make you free, ye ſhall be free indeed. Ver. 36.—Obſerve, until Chriſt make us free from the guilt and dominion of ſin, we are, neceſſarily, in thraldom to both. If he deliver us, we are, neceſſarily, emancipated from each.

Why do ye not underſtand my ſpeech? even becauſe ye cannot hear my word. John viii. 43.——A plain, pertinent, deciſive reaſon.

He that is of God, heareth God's words: ye therefore hear them not, becauſe ye are not of God. Ver. 47.—Either not choſen; or, at leaſt, not yet drawn and taught; of him.

I muſt work the works of him that ſent me, while it is day. Chap. ix. 4. Chriſt was under a neceſſity of doing ſo. He could not do any other.

Jeſus ſaid, for judgment I am come into this world: that they, who ſee not, might ſee; and that they, who ſee, may be made blind. Ver. 39.—Can any thing be more ſtrongly expreſſed than this?

A ſtranger will they not follow, but will flee from him: for they know not the voice of ſtrangers. Chap. x. 5.—i. e. The converted elect diſapprove of

falſe

falſe teachers, as neceſſarily as ſheep run away from a ſtrange man they are afraid of.

Other ſheep I have, which are not of this fold: them alſo I muſt bring, and they ſhall hear my voice. Ver. 16.—I muſt: and they ſhall. What is this but double neceſſity?

Ye believe not, becauſe ye are not of my ſheep, as I ſaid unto you. Ver. 26.—Conſequently, faith hangs, not upon man's ſelf-determination, but on God's own ſelf-determined election.

I give unto my ſheep eternal life, and they ſhall never periſh. John x. 28.—i. e. Their ſalvation is neceſſary, and cannot be hindered.

Lazarus, come forth! Chap. xi. 43.—Was it in Lazarus's power, not to awake and riſe up?

Though he had done ſo many miracles before them, yet they believed not on him; that the ſaying of Eſaias the prophet might be fulfilled, which he ſpake: Lord, who hath believed our report? and to whom hath the arm of the Lord been revealed? Therefore they could not believe, becauſe Eſaias ſaid again, he hath blinded their eyes, and hardened their heart; that they ſhould not ſee with their eyes, nor underſtand with their heart, and be converted, and I ſhould heal them. Chap. xi. 37—40. If an Arminian can extract free-will and ſelf-determination from theſe flowers, he poſſeſſes a very different alembic, from any which I am maſter of.

One of you ſhall betray me:—he it is, to whom I ſhall give a ſop when I have dipped it. And, when he had dipped the ſop, he gave it to Judas Iſcariot, the ſon of Simon. And, after the ſop, Satan entered into him. Then ſaid Jeſus unto him, That thou doſt, do quickly. Chap. xiii. 21, 26, 27.—Awful proceſs!

I will pray the Father, and he ſhall give you another comforter,—whom the world cannot receive, becauſe it ſeeth him not, neither knoweth him. John xiv. 16, 17.

Becauſe

Becaufe I live, ye fhall live alfo. Ver. 19.—
Chrift lives and reigns in glory, neceffarily : and fo
muft his people.

Ye have not chofen me, but I have chofen you,
and ordained you ; that ye fhould go and bring forth
fruit, and that your fruit fhould remain.   Chap.
xv. 16.

They have both feen and hated both me and my
Father : but this cometh to pafs, that the word
might be fulfilled which is written in their law ; they
hated me without a caufe.   Ver. 24, 25.

Father, the hour is come.   Chap. xvii. 1.—The
predeftined feafon of my crucifixion and death.

None of them [none of my apoftles] is loft, but
the Son of Perdition, that the Scripture might be
fulfilled.   Ver. 12.

The cup which my Father hath given me, fhall
I not drink it ? Chap. xviii. 11.—A cup, all whofe
ingredients were mixed in the Father's decree, and
adminiftered by Providence, though wicked men
were the inftruments of accomplifhing God's counfel.   *Qui vult finem, vult etiam media ad finem.*

Pilate faid unto them, Take ye him, and judge
him according to your law.   The Jews therefore
faid unto him, It is not lawful for us to put any man
to death.   That the faying of Jefus might be fulfilled, which he fpake, fignifying, by what death he
fhould die.   John xviii. 31, 32.—God had decreed,
and Chrift himfelf had foretold, that he fhould die
by crucifixion.   But had the Jews accepted of
Pilate's overture, Chrift could not have been crucified, for that was no Jewifh punifhment : he muft
have been ftoned.   To fulfil both decree and prophecy, they were divinely over-ruled, to let the
Romans be his executioners : in confequence of
which, he was affixed to the crofs.——Neceffitation
throughout !

Pontius Pilate was a free-will man.   He did not
believe neceffity.   He was a fturdy (not felf-deter-
miner,

miner, for no man can be really and truly that ; but
a) self-determinationist : i. e. he thought himself a
self-determining agent. Hence his speech to Christ:
Speakest thou not unto me? Knowest thou not, that I
have power to crucify thee, and have power to release
thee? To which the Lamb of God replied, Thou
couldst have no power at all against me, except it
were given thee from above : therefore, he, that delivered me unto thee, hath the greater sin. John
xix. 10.—Here, I presume, Mr. Wesley will step
in with his favourite universal demonstration, "Not
so."—" If the power both of the betrayer and of
the crucifier was given them, and from above too,
i. e. from God himself ; Judas and Pilate could have
no sin at all in acting as they did, so far from having
the greater sin by that means." The methodist
must excuse me, if I believe the testimony of Christ,
in preference to any cavil that can originate in
Moorfields.

Again. I assert, that the Roman soldiers had it
not in their power to break the Messiah's legs. For
that Scripture was necessarily to be fulfilled, which
had said, A bone of him shall not be broken. Chap.
xix. 33, 36.

On the other hand, I assert, that the soldier, who
penetrated the Messiah's side, did it necessarily.
Because, another Scripture had said, They shall look
on him whom they pierced; ver 37. So sure is that
axiom, *nihil est in effectu, quod non fuit in causâ.*

It was my intention, to have produced, at much
greater length than I have done in the close of the
foregoing chapter, the suffrages of the apostles, also,
on behalf of this doctrine ; who offer their evidence,
from every part of the inspired epistles. But, at
present, I waive this advantage : and, for brevity's
sake, refer the reader, indiscriminately, to any portion whatever of those writings, which he may first
open, or on which he may first cast his eye. Dip
where you will, your own reason (abstracted from

all conſideration of grace) muſt inſtantly perceive, that the illuminated penmen were as radicated neceſſitarians, as their divine Maſter.

And now, what can a fair and capable examinant think of the Arminian ſelf-determination doctrine? A doctrine which would impiouſly graft ſuch a monſter as contingency, on the religion of Jeſus Chriſt —a religion, which, from its Alpha to its Omega, preſents us with one grand, unbroken, and indiſſoluble, ſyſtem of neceſſity!

Is it any wonder, that men, who conſider the incarnation, miracles, prophecies, perſeverance, ſufferings, death, and ſalvation, of the Meſſiah himſelf, as things of chance; ſhould likewiſe maintain all other events to be equally fortuitous?

Hence, the alertneſs and rapidity, with which many of our modern Arminians (more conſiſtent, but at the ſame time more atheiſtical, than the generality of their predeceſſors), not content with trampling on God's decrees, are now verging toward a flat denial even of God's abſolute and unlimited knowledge.   Juſtly ſenſible, that their whole fairy ſcheme of chance, uncertainty, and contingency, is quite untenable, on the poſition of infallible preſcience; they make no ſcruple to rob (if they were able) the Deity himſelf of a perfection eſſential to his very being, rather than not ſtick the feather of free-will in the cap of man!

C H A P. VI.

An Argument for Neceſſity, deduced from the Balance of Human Life and Death.

WAS it not for that univerſal neceſſitation, which reſults from the effective and permiſſive will of God; all things would be, in a moment, unhinged,

unhinged, disjointed, and reverſed. Endleſs confuſion, wild irregularity, and the moſt horrible diſ-
order (to which the *materia prima*, or chaos, was harmony itſelf), would prevail throughout the natural
and the moral world.

The property of attraction, by which the earth,
and every other maſs of matter, cohere reſpectively
into one body, and become capable of the moſt
rapid motion, without diſſipation of their conſtitu-
ent particles; is one happy effect of phyſical neceſſity.
Analogous to which, but of incomparably greater
importance, is that *ineluctabilis ordo rerum*, or unalterable contexture of antecedents and conſequents,
wiſely pre-eſtabliſhed in the uncreated mind: through
the concealed energy of whoſe unerring appointment, every finite intelligent being both is and does,
preciſely, neither more nor leſs, than the ſaid unerring wiſdom of the Creator deſigned, or reſolved to
permit. And this is what I ſhould chuſe to call
moral neceſſity.

Suppoſing that calculation to be juſt, which eſtimates the adult inhabitants of our own globe at about
one hundred and fifty millions; or let their real
amount be what it may; who can poſſibly conceive
the boundleſs diſtractions and deſolations, which
muſt every where enſue, were ſo great a number of
fallen beings (like ramping horſes turned looſe into
a field) endued with a liberty of ſelf-determination,
and left at large to the exerciſe of it! For we muſt
take the exerciſe, and the outward operations con-
ſequent upon it, into the account: elſe mere ſelf-
determination would anſwer no other end, than that
of tantalizing and tormenting its reſpective poſſeſſ-
ors.——It is well for us, that, notwithſtanding our
wild and licentious arrogations of ſovereignty, the
ſame Almighty Parent, who, without aſking our
conſent, whirls our planet and our perſons round the
ſun, does, with equal certainty, and with as little
ceremony, roll us, and the inhabitants of all the

worlds

worlds he has created, on the central axis of his own
decree.

We have been gravely told, that this repreſenta-
tion of things is heatheniſm. You ſhould rather call
it, Bibleiſm. For, that fate, or neceſſity, which
the antient vulgar thought proper to worſhip as a
goddeſs, was, in their idea, the daughter of a blind,
fickle princeſs, called, Fortune or Chance: who was,
herſelf, the fabled daughter of a no leſs fickle old gentleman, named Oceanus. To which blind lady, and
her unſteady father, the ſcheme of Chriſtian neceſſity is
not in the leaſt related, either by conſanguinity, or
alliance.

I muſt, however, acquit the wiſer of the heathens,
from the abſurdity of looking upon chance, or fortune, as a reality. Senſible men knew better, and
laughed at the unphiloſophical chimera. Nor is the
antiquity, of the word itſelf, extremely high. It is
acknowledged, on all hands, that Τυχη (from whence
the Romans took their *fortuna*) was a term, invented long after the times of Heſiod and of Homer (in
whoſe writings it no where occurs); and was ſpawned by the atheiſtical imagination of ſubſequent
poets: from whom (I think) Ancus Martius adopted
it, and by building a temple to its honour, introduced
it, as a deity, among the Romans.

It ill becomes the Arminians to talk of heatheniſm.
Let them draw a ſolid line, if they can, between
fortune, and contingency. Let them ſhew us, how
the reſult of ſelf-determination differs from chance.
Let them reconcile their imaginary αυτεξουσιον, with the
neceſſary dependency of created beings, and with the
never-ceaſing agency of an * univerſally particular
providence.

* Mr. Pope aſks:

When the looſe mountain trembles from on high,
Shall gravitation ceaſe, 'cauſe you go by?

I anſwer, Yes. Either gravitation ſhall ceaſe, while I go by,
or I ſhall, in ſome way or other, be ſecured from ſuffering by its
effect

providence. When they have wrought thefe, and a few other fimilar impoffibilities, I will then abfolve their fcheme from heathenifm. I will even acquit it of atheifm.

Birth and death are the æra and the period, whofe interval conftitutes the thread of man's vifible exiftence on earth. Let us examine, whether thofe important extremes be, or be not, unalterably fixed by the neceffitating providence of God. If it appear, that they are ; we may the more eafily believe, that all the intercurrent events are under the controul and direction of the fame infallible hand.

I have heard it affirmed, that Defcartes, the French philofopher, was fo confiftent a free-willer, as to have believed, that death itfelf is abfolutely fubject to human felf-determination : that he confequently imagined, he had it in his power to protract his own age to any extent he pleafed, or to cut it precifely as fhort as he himfelf chofe : and would, very liberally, call any of his departed friends, who died with reluctance, fools ; for confenting to a change they did not wifh to experience. The antient Romans, notwithftanding the adulterations, with which the doctrine of free-will (and its natural attendant, fcepticifm) debafed and corrupted their theology, were yet, in general, fo decent, as to acknowledge, that death lay at the difpofal of a Deity, lefs capricious than fortune, and more powerful than any created will. Hence, their occafional reciprocation of *mors* and *fatum*. To intimate, that men cannot die, until God pronounces their doom : and that when he *fatus eft*, or iffues the word of fummons, the earthly vehicle can detain its gueft no longer.——

effect ; unlefs the will of God, to which all fecond caufes are abfolutely fubordinate, commiffion the " loofe mountain" to do me an injury. I am of the great Mr. Charnock's mind, that " There is underftanding, in every motion : and an eye, in the very wheel that goes over us and crufhes us." (Charnock on the Attributes, p. 419.)

Poor

Poor Deſcartes, with all his dreams of freewill, found
himſelf obliged to die, at the age of fifty-four !

I take the *ratio formalis*, or preciſe nature, of
death, to be neither more nor leſs than the effect of
ſeparation. The ſeparation of ſpirit from matter is
the immediate cauſe, and ſeems to exhauſt the idea,
of animal death. Now, only the ſame power, which
at firſt joined, can afterwards ſever, the two principles. Let the permitted means of diſſolving the
union be what they may, the diſſolution itſelf is an
act of God.

Whoever conſiders the relative alterations, the
domeſtic revolutions, the circulation of property,
and a multitude of other negative and poſitive conſequences, which, either directly or remotely, follow
on the deceaſe of the meaneſt human individual,
muſt ſoon perceive, that, was not the ſceptre of
death ſwayed by the determinations of Infinite Wiſdom, ſuch partial inconveniences muſt enſue, as
would, in their complicated amount, materially
affect, if not entirely reverſe, the whole ſyſtem of
ſublunary events. Some people (for inſtance) would
live too long. Others would die too ſoon. Some
would leave their aſſigned work, unfiniſhed : from
whence the Deity would be diſappointed of his views,
and ſurpriſed with a chaſm in his adminiſtration of
government. Others would ſurvive to do more than
their allotted buſineſs. From whence, the divine
plan would be diſconcerted ; the well-compacted
web become looſe, broken, and entangled ; and the
adminiſtration of Providence degenerate into a jumble of confuſion, perplexity, and abſolute anarchy.
In one word : God could not ſay, to any one of his
creatures, what he really does ſay to all and each of
them ; hitherto ſhalt thou come, and no farther.

Our entrance into life is determined and adjuſted,
by the ſame diſpoſing hand, which fixes and regulates our departure. Neceſſity brings us into the
world : and neceſſity carries us out of it. What man

upon

upon earth could help his being born at the very time and place he was? or could hinder himfelf from being the fon of fuch and fuch parents? or alter a thoufand concurring circumftances, by which his fubfequent ftate, and his very caft of mind, were effectually and necelfarily ftamped? How abfurd, then, muft it be, to imagine that the line, though fpun at firft by the hand of neceffity, is afterwards conducted, and at laft cut off, by the no-fingers of contingency! For it is impoffible to conceive any thing fo abfolutely contingent and uncertain, as the operations, and the exit, of a felf-determining actor. Efpecially, if we fuppofe him (and the Arminian fcheme does fo fuppofe him) to live in a world, where all about him is as precarious as himfelf; and where the great fheet of events, inftead of being let down by the four corners from heaven, is only a fortuitous complication of flimfy threads, much of which is ftill liable to unravelment, and the whole of which might never have been woven at all.

Might Charles the Firft have been the fon of Cromwell's parents? And might Cromwell have been born legal heir to the Englifh crown? Was it poffible for fir Robert Walpole to have been prime minifter to queen Elizabeth; and fir Francis Walfingham to have been fecretary of ftate to king George the fecond? Yet, all thefe impoffibilities, and millions of others, might have happened, upon the Arminian fcheme of chance. A fcheme, which, if admitted, turns every thing upfide down, and knocks every thing out of joint:

Diruit, ædificat, mutat quadrata rotundis.

Why was friar Bacon, and not fir Ifaac Newton, born in the thirteenth century? Why were not the living ornaments, of the prefent generation, born an hundred, or five hundred, years back? or referved to ages as remotely future? Arminianifm may tell me, that " All this is cafual: and that it was a chance, not only when and where the prefent race

F 4 of

of men might be born, and what departments they
ſhould fill ; how they ſhould act, and how and when
they ſhall die ; but whether they ſhould ſo much as
exiſt at firſt." I, on the contrary, diſcern ſuch in-
conteſtable traces of wiſdom, propriety, and deſign,
in the diſtribution of particular men through ſucceſſive periods of time, and in the whole connection of
event with event ; that, for my own part, I neceſſarily conclude, ſo regular a chain could not poſſibly
be hammered in the Cyclopæan den of contingency;
but that every depending link is fitted and fixed into each other, by the Supreme Intelligence himſelf ;
the diſpoſals of whoſe providence, like the covenant
of his grace, are ordered in all things, and ſure *.

As lightly as ſome people think of the Bible, that
book is the fountain of true metaphyſics. A book,
no leſs weighty, with the treaſures of philoſophic
wiſdom, than bright, with the healing beams of
evangelical conſolation. To this bleſſed oracle, I
now refer the queſtion ; whether human birth and
death be not the effects of divine neceſſitation ?

I ſhall not be very prolix. Two or three plain
and pertinent teſtimonies will anſwer the ſame purpoſe, as two or three hundred. Let us begin with
the article of birth.

Rachel ſaid unto Jacob, give me children, or
elſe I die. And Jacob's anger was kindled againſt
Rachel : and he ſaid, am I in God's ſtead ? Gen.
xxx. 1, 2.

Joſeph ſaid unto his father, they are my ſons,
whom God hath given me in this place. Gen.
xlviii. 9.

Thy hands have made me, and faſhioned me together, round about. Job x. 8.

* 2 Sam. xxiii, 5.—Thoſe of us, who go to Church, profeſs
ourſelves to be "tied and bound with the chain of our ſins." Why,
then, ſhould we deem ourſelves too grand to be tied and bound,
with the good, though not always perceivable, chain of providential neceſſity ?

Thou

Thou art he that took me out of the womb.
Pfal. xxii. 9.

Who holdeth [better rendered, who putteth] our
foul in life, and fuffereth not our feet to be moved.
Pfal. lxvi. 9.—i. e. God gave us life at firft, and
keeps us alive, until it is his pleafure to untie the
knot that binds us to the body.

Lo, children are an heritage of the Lord. Pfalm
cxxvii. 3.—Or, as the liturgy tranflation reads, Lo,
children and the fruit of the womb are an heritage
and gift that cometh of the Lord.

And the cafe fpeaks for itfelf. The birth of every
fingle infant is productive of no lefs than everlafting
confequences. Every infant (even fuppofing him to
die fuch) is an immortal being. But, fuppofing he
lives to bear an active part in life, fociety is very
materially concerned in his behaviour. Each adult
individual makes important movements, in the grand
circular fcale of events. The alteration of a fingle
birth, or of a fingle death, from the firft period of time
until now, would have occafioned fuch a difference,
that neither the vifible, nor the invifible world,
would have been as it is : i. e. fomething would have
been wrong, either in defect, or in redundancy.
None of us can tell, what may hang on the nativity
of the meaneft infant that is born of woman. But
the Creator knows ; for he is acquainted with his own
decrees, and orders matters accordingly.

Thou haft covered me [i. e. cloathed my foul
with a material body] in my mother's womb : in thy
book [of decree and providence] all my members
were written. Pfalm cxxxix. 13, 16.

To every thing there is a feafon, and a time to
every purpofe under the heaven ; [i. e. God has fixed an exact point of time, for the accomplifhment
of all his decrees : among which fixed and exact
points of time, are] a time to be born, and a time
to die. Ecclef. iii. 1, 2.

Who

Who * formeth the ſpirit of man within him. Zech. xii. 1.

'God, who ſeparated me from my mother's womb. Gal. i. 15.

Does it not appear, even from theſe few paſſages, that the doctrine of fortuitous nativity is as falſe and ridiculous, as that of equivocal generation ?

And the doctrine of fortuitous death is like unto it. Witneſs the following evidence.

The time drew near that Iſrael muſt die. Gen. xlvii. 29. Obſerve, 1. A time for Jacob's death was prefixed of God; and it is therefore called, the time; meaning, that preciſe time, and no other. 2. The time drew near; and the holy man was like a racer in view of the goal, or like a mariner in ſight of the haven where he would be. 3. He muſt die: which expreſſion does not denote any unwillingneſs in Jacob; but the certainty of his departure, when the deſtined moment ſhould arrive.

Can any incident be more ſeemingly fortuitous, than what we commonly call homicide, or one man's undeſignedly killing of another? And yet this, when it comes to paſs, is according to the ſecret will of God: who is poſitively affirmed to deliver the ſlain party into the hand of the ſlayer. Exod. xxi. 31.

---

* This text, and many other of ſimilar import, ſeem to intimate, that the body is firſt made; and that the ſoul, commanded into exiſtence for the purpoſe, is united to the body thus previouſly provided for its reception. The direct ſource, however, of the ſoul, is an enquiry attended with great metaphyſical difficulties; whether we ſuppoſe it to be of God's immediate creation, or to originate from parental tranſmiſſion. Much may be ſaid for each hypotheſis: and ſeveral weighty objections lie againſt both. It becomes us, to confeſs, that Scripture has not clearly decided the point; and, of courſe, that we know very little of the matter. In talibus queſtionibus, as Witſius ſays on another myſterious occaſion, magis mihi placet hæſitantis ingenii modeſtia, quàm inconſiderata determinandi pervicacia (Diſſert. de Michæele). This only we are ſure of, that God himſelf, and not chance, is (either mediately. or immediately, according to the good pleaſure of his own will) the formator, and the governor, of every ſpirit, and of every body, in the univerſe.

He

He [i. e. God] is thy life, and the length of thy days. Deut. xxx. 20. The author of that, and the meafurer of thefe.

The Lord killeth, and maketh alive : he bringeth down to the grave, and bringeth up. 1 Sam. ii. 6. Which exactly comports with what God fays of himfelf: I, even I, am he; and there is no God with me. I kill, and I make alive : I wound, and I heal; neither is there any that can deliver out of my hand. ▪ Deut. xxxii. 39.

Is there not an appointed time to man upon earth ? Are not his days alfo like the days of an hireling ? Job vii. 1. The ftipulated hours, of an hireling's labour, are afcertained beforehand : they confift of fo many, and no more.

Thou haft granted me life and favour; and thy vifitation hath preferved my fpirit. Job x. 12.

In whofe hand is the foul of every living thing, and the breath of all mankind. Job xii. 10.

Man's days are determined ; the number of his months is with thee : thou haft appointed his bounds, which he cannot pafs. All the days of my appointed time will I wait, until my change come. Job xiv. 5, 14.

Thou prevaileft for ever againft him [i. e. man cannot poffibly extend his own life a fingle moment beyond thy decree] : thou changeft his countenance [by death], and fendeft him away. Job xiv. 20.— Sendeft his body to the grave, and his foul to another world.

Lord, make me to know my end, and the meafure of my days; what it is. Pfalm xxxix. 4. But, unlefs God had fixed David's end, and had determined the meafure of his days; the Pfalmift would here have afked a queftion, to which God himfelf could only have anfwered, " O fon of Jeffe, 1 know no more of the matter, than you do. You have ftarted a problem, which I am unable to refolve : for there is no meafuring in the cafe."

Thou

Thou turneſt man to deſtruction. Pſalm xc. 3.

There is no man that hath power over the ſpirit, to retain the ſpirit [i. e. to retain the ſoul in the body, beyond the term divinely prefixed]; neither hath he power in the day of death. Eccleſ. viii. 8.

Behold, I will add unto thy days fifteen years. Iſaiah xxxviii. 5. Hezekiah thought, that his leaſe was juſt expiring, and that his ſoul muſt, almoſt immediately, turn out of its earthly cottage. No, ſays God; you have fifteen years to be added to thoſe of your days which are elapſed: and the ſaid future years are of my adding, no leſs than were the years that are paſt. "Oh, but God ſaid to Hezekiah, I have heard thy prayer, and have ſeen thy tears." True. And what does this prove? Not that God's decree is a * weathercock, ſhifting, and changing, and veering about, juſt as the breath of man's free-will happens to blow: but, that the Scriptural axiom is right, which ſays, Lord, thou haſt heard the deſire of the afflicted: thou prepareſt their heart [to pray for ſuch things as thou haſt decreed to give], and thine ear hearkeneth thereto. I muſt farther obſerve: that, if there be any meaning in words, Hezekiah could not die, until the remaining fifteen years had run out; and could not but die, when they were.

Which of you, by taking thought, can add one cubit, πρ@· ἡλικιαν αὐῖ8, to his term of life? Matth. vi. 27. Let us hear the reflections of that learned, pious, and truly reſpectable Arminian, Dr. Ham-

---

* "Prayer moves God, and overcomes him, not by cauſing any change in the divine will: for God is immutable; and what good he does in time for his people, he purpoſed before any time was.— But prayer is ſaid to overcome him, becauſe he then gives, what, from eternity, he purpoſed to give, upon their praying to him. For, when God decreed what he would do for his ſaints, he alſo purpoſed that they ſhall pray for the ſame; Ezek. xxxvi. 37.—Prayer's midwifry ſhall be uſed, to deliver the mercies which God purpoſeth and promiſeth. God's purpoſe to give, doth not diſcharge us from our duty to aſk." Gurnall's Chriſtian Armour, vol. iv. p. 17.

mond, on this text. After obſerving, that ἡλικια
ſometimes denotes " the quantity, or ſtature, of the
body ;" he adds : " So alſo doth it ordinarily ſignify,
age (and ſo doth אויף, which the Syriac here
uſes) ; and may poſſibly do ſo, here : 1. Becauſe the
dehortation, which this [queſtion of Chriſt's] is
brought to enforce, was particularly that concerning
ſolicitude for the life : and to that, this will be very
proper, of our not being able to add, by all our ſolicitude, the leaſt proportion to our age, and to enlarge the period of life πηχυν ἱνα, one cubit, i. e. one
ſmalleſt meaſure or proportion, beyond what God
hath ſet us. 2. It will be obſervable, that one cubit
being here ſet down as a very ſmall meaſure, would
yet be a very great proportion, being applied to the
ſtature of the body. Nay, ſuch as are come to their
full growth (as the far greateſt part of Chriſt's auditors were) could not thus hope to add one thou-
ſandth part of a cubit to their ſtature. On the
other ſide, a cubit will ſeem but a ſmall part, to the
many years of a long life. And he that is of the
fulleſt growth, may yet hope to enlarge the period
of his life ; and to that, generally, men's ſolicitude
is applied ; by diet, phyſic, &c. to acquire long
life, not to increaſe their ſtature. 3. The word πηχυς,
cubit, is ordinarily a meaſure of longitude of any
ſpace : and, particularly, of a race ; to which man's
life is compared. Job ix. 25. 2 Tim. iv. 7."

This truth may be farther argued, from another
paſſage, cited alſo in a preceding chapter, viz.
Matt. x. 29, 30. For, if not a ſparrow can die,
without God's expreſs commiſſion ; much leſs can a
man. And, if the very hairs of our heads are numbered, much more our days.

God giveth, unto all, life, and breath, and all
things : and hath made of one blood all nations of
men, for to dwell on all the face of the earth ; and
hath determined the times, before appointed, and
the bounds of their habitation.——For in him we
live,

live, and are moved, and have our being. Acts
xvii. 25, 26, 28.—Obſerve : 1. God is the giver of
animal life, as well as every thing elſe.—2. He has
multiplied us all, from one ſtock : viz. Adam.—3.
The times, i. e. the proper ſeaſons, of our birth and
death, and of all that we ſhall do or ſuffer between
the ſtarting-poſt and the goal, are determined, or
marked out with certainty and exactneſs, by him himſelf.—4. This determination, or adjuſtment, of our
times, is not a modern act of God, ariſing *è re nata*,
or from any preſent emergency of circumſtances and
ſituation of affairs : but a determination, inconceiv-
ably ancient. The times were fore-appointed, even
from everlaſting : for no new determination can
take place in God, without a change, i. e. without
the deſtruction, of his eſſence. *Quævis mutatio mors
eſt.*—5. The very places, which people inhabit, are
here poſitively averred to be determined and fore-appointed of God. And it is very right it ſhould be
ſo. Elſe, ſome places might be over-ſtocked with
inhabitants, and others totally deſerted : which would
neceſſarily draw after it the moſt pernicious conſequences; as ſtagnation of agriculture, famine, peſtilence, and general ruin to the human ſpecies.
Whereas, by virtue of God's having fore-appointed
and determined the bounds of our habitations, we
are properly ſifted over the face of the earth, ſo as
to anſwer all the ſocial and higher purpoſes of providential wiſdom.—6. If Deity has condeſcended to
determine, in what particular places our bodies ſhall
dwell; why ſhould it appear ſtrange, that he ſhould
alſo determine how long our ſouls ſhall dwell in their
bodies? Adverbs of time are no leſs important, than
adverbs of place. Nor, indeed, could omnipotence
itſelf determine the *ibi*, without likewiſe determining
the *quando*, and the *diu*.—Eſpecially, when we conſider, 7. That in him we, every moment, live, and
are moved, and do exiſt.

Moreover, if Chriſt's own teſtimony will have any
weight with ſelf-determinationiſts, the following text,
excluſively,

excluſively of all others, will ſet the point above diſ-
pute: where our Lord roundly affirms, that he himſelf keeps the keys of hell and of death.   Rev. i. 18.
Which declaration holds true, in every ſenſe the
words are capable of. He openeth, and no man can
ſhut : and ſhutteth, and no man can open.   Rev.
iii. 7.

Nor is Divine Providence the diſtributor **of** death
to man alone.   The very beaſts themſelves, which
are, by many, ſuppoſed to periſh utterly, are immortal, until God cut their thread.   Thou hideſt
thy face : [they are troubled. Thou takeſt away
their breath: they die; and return to their duſt.
Pſalm civ. 29.—It ſhould be remembered, that this
is more directly ſpoken, concerning thoſe ſmall and
great beaſts, and creeping things innumerable, which
inhabit the ſea.   So that fiſhes themſelves, from a
whale to a periwinkle, have the Creator himſelf for
the diſpoſer of their lives, and the determiner of
their deaths!

From the evidence alledged, conciſe and ſuperfi-
cial as my allegations have been, we may fairly (and,
I think, unanſwerably) conclude : that contingency
has nothing to do with births, or burials ; and, conſequently, that chance never yet added, nor ever
will add *, " a ſingle unit to the bills of mortality."

If, therefore, the initial point, from whence we
ſtart ; and the ultimate goal, which terminates our
race ; be thus divinely and unchangeably fixed: is
it reaſonable to ſuppoſe, that chance, or any free-
will but the free-will of Deity alone, may fabricate
the intermediate links of a chain, whoſe two extremes are held immovably faſt in the hands of God
himſelf?—Impoſſible.

---

* For this phraſe, a ſingle unit to the bill of mortality, ſee **Lord**
Cheſterfield's Letters : Lett. 336.

CHAP.

CHAP. VII.

*The ſuppoſed Gloomineſs of Neceſſity, conſidered.—The
Origin of Neceſſity.—Conciſe View of Manichæiſm.—The
Nature of Evil enquired into.—Curious Converſation-
Pieces of three Modern Philoſophiſers.—Several Aſſemblies of Divines vindicated.—Arminians themſelves
ultimately forced to make Neceſſity their Refuge.—Concluſion of the preſent Eſſay.*

1. GREAT declamatory pains have been taken,
to ſet the ſyſtem of neceſſity in a very
" gloomy" point of view: and to miſrepreſent it,
as made up of nothing but clouds, and ſhades, and
thick darkneſs. The ſame has been ſaid of religion
at large, and of virtue itſelf. But are virtue and religion therefore deformed and black, becauſe their
beauty and luſtre do not ſtrike a libertine eye? No
more is the ſcheme of neceſſity tinged with real
gloom, on account of a proud or prejudiced free-
willer's being pleaſed to aſſert it.

" I have ſometimes beheld," ſays an elegant
writer, " a ſhip of war, ſeveral leagues off at ſea. It
ſeemed to me to be a dim, cloudy ſomething, hover-
ing on the ſkirts of the horizon : contemptibly mean,
and not worthy of a moment's regard.—But, as the
floating citadel approached, the maſts aroſe. The
ſails ſwelled out. Its ſtately form, and curious properties, ſtruck the ſight. It was no longer a ſhape-
leſs maſs, or a blot in the proſpect: but the maſter-
piece of human contrivance, and the nobleſt ſpecta-
cle in the world of art." Hervey's Theron and
Aſpaſio, Dialogue 5.

Arminianiſm, if you pleaſe, is a region of darkneſs: but neceſſity, a land of * light. For I ſhould
be

---

* The pretended gloomineſs of neceſſity is urged, with moſt appearance (and it is but appearance) of plauſibility, againſt that branch
of Scripture-metaphyſics, which relates to the decree of reprobation.

Let

be glad to be informed, wherein conſiſts the chearfulneſs of believing, that the greater part, if not the
whole of ſublunary events, even thoſe of endleſs
concern not excepted, are delivered over to the
management of an imaginary goddeſs, called chance;
the mere creature of poetic fiction, and the moſt
unmeaning ſound that was ever admitted into
language?

Let me, for a moment, weigh the pretended horror of this principle; a principle, which occurs ſo poſitively and repeatedly, again
and again, in almoſt every page of the Bible; that the exiſtence of
God does not admit of more ſtrong and explicit proof, from the inſpired volume, than does the awful reality of non-election. What I
here mean to obſerve on this ſubject, I ſhall give, in the words of
part of a letter, which I lately ſent to a very eminent Anti-Calvi-
nian philoſopher, Dr. Prieſtley. "Why are Calvin's doctrines repreſented as gloomy? Is it gloomy, to believe, that the far greater
part of the human race are made for endleſs happineſs? There can,
I think, be no reaſonable doubt entertained, concerning the ſalvation
of very young perſons. If (as ſome, who have yet ſed themſelves in
this kind of ſpeculation, affirm,) about one half of mankind die in
infancy;—And if, as indubitable obſervation proves, a very conſiderable number of the remaining half die in early childhood;—And
if, as there is the ſtrongeſt reaſon to think, many millions of thoſe,
who live to maturer years, in every ſucceſſive generation, have their
names in the Book of Life: then, what a very ſmall portion, comparatively, of the human ſpecies, falls under the decree \f preterition and non-redemption!
  "This view of things, I am perſuaded, will, to an eye ſo philoſophic as your's, at leaſt open a very chearful viſta through the
'gloom;' if not entirely turn the imaginary darkneſs into ſun-
ſhine. For, with reſpect to the few reprobate, we may, and we
ought to, reſign the diſpoſal of them, implicitly, to the will of that
only king who can do no wrong: inſtead of ſummoning the Almighty to take his trial at the tribunal of our ſpeculations, and of
ſetting up ourſelves as judges of Deity."
  I might have added, that the purpoſe of God according to election is not reſtrained to men, either of any particular country, or
age of time, or religious denomination. Undoubtedly, there are
elect Jews, elect Mahometans, and elect Pagans. In a word, count-
leſs millions of perſons, whom Chriſt hath redeemed unto God, by
his blood, out of every kindred, and tongue, and people, and nation. Rev. v. 9.
  Only take a fair and diſpaſſionate ſurvey of the matter, as it is;
and the Arminian myſteries will be found a vox, et prætereà nihil.
For, who can count the duſt of Jacob, or the number of the fourth
part of God's elect Iſrael?

" Oh, but we deny chance, and maintain free-will.". Be fo good as to fhew me, how you can maintain felf-determining free-will, without fetting up the blind daughter of Oceanus upon her pedeftal. If the will of man be free, with a liberty *ad utrum-libet*; and if his actions be the offspring of his will; fuch of his actions, which are not yet wrought, muft be both radically and eventually uncertain: as depending, for their futurition, on an uncertain caufe, viz. on the uncertain volitions of an agent, who may, or may not, incline himfelf to the performance of thofe actions. It is therefore a chance, whether they fhall ever be performed, or no. For chance, and uncertainty, are only two words for the fame idea. So that every affertor of felf-determination is, in fact, whether he mean it or no, a worfhipper of the heathen lady, named, Fortune; and an ideal depo-fer of Providence from its throne.

Could Providence be really dethroned, with as much eafe as its influence is denied, dreadful indeed would be the ftate of things. For my part, I think, that all the chearfulnefs lies on the fide of neceffity. And for this plain reafon: becaufe, that Infinite Wifdom, which made, or permitted, us to be what we are, and to be circumftanced as we are, knows better, what to do with us, than we could poffibly know how to difpofe of our own felves.

It is my happinefs, to be convinced, that my times are in God's hand. Pfalm xxxi. 15. and that his kingdom ruleth over all. Pfalm ciii. 19. If any others can extract comfort from confidering them-felves as veffels failing over a dangerous ocean, with-out pilot, without chart, without infurance, and without convoy to a coaft unknown; much good may their comfort do them. I defire none of it.

Gloomy as the doctrine of Chriftian neceffity is ignorantly affirmed to be; it is the only principle, upon which any perfon can truly and confiftently, adopt that animating apophthegm, fo perpetually in

the

the mouth of St. Chryſoſtom, Bleſſed be God, for every thing that comes to 'paſs!——Whereas, the genuine language of an afflicted free-willer is, Alas! alas! what an unlucky accident was this! The very exclamation, which might be expected to iſſue from the lips of a melancholy, deſponding atheiſt.

If unreſerved reſignation, to the wiſe and fatherly diſpoſals of God; if contentedneſs and complacency, within our ſeveral ſpheres and ſtations; if thankfulneſs, for the bleſſings we enjoy; if the exerciſe of candour, lenity, and compaſſion, toward our miſtaken, our offending, and our afflicted fellow-creatures; if humility, and a deep ſenſe of our abſolute dependence on the arm of omnipotent love, for preſervation or deliverance from evil, and for the continuance, or increaſe of good; if the pleaſing conviction that nothing can hurt us, except God's own hand firſt ſign the licence; if a juſt confidence, that he will never ſign any ſuch licence, but to anſwer the beſt and wiſeſt ends; if an unſhaken perſuaſion, that whatever he does is, and muſt be abſolutely, and directly, right; and that whatever he permits to be done, is, and muſt be, relatively, conducively, and finally, right:—If theſe lovely virtues, and felicitating views (virtues and views which no neceſſitarian can, conſiſtently, be without), have any thing gloomy in them; it will follow, that the ſun is made up of darkneſs, and that beauty itſelf is a complication of deformity and horror.

When Mr. Pope penned the following verſes (in which the philoſophic inferences from the doctrine of neceſſity are ſummed up with equal truth and elegance), I cannot bring myſelf to ſuppoſe, that the poet was in a chearleſs, melancholy frame of mind. So far from being able to obſerve the remoteſt veſtige of gloom; I ſee nothing in them, but the luſtre of unmingled light, and the triumph of exulting joy.

" Submit.

" Submit.—In this or any other ſphere,
Secure to be as bleſt as thou canſt bear.
Safe in the hand of one diſpoſing pow'r,
Or in the natal or the mortal hour.
    All nature is but art, unknown to thee ;
All chance, direction which thou canſt not ſee.
All * diſcord, harmony not underſtood ;
All partial evil, univerſal good.
And, ſpite of pride, in erring reaſon's ſpite,
One truth is clear : whatever is, is right."

If, together with the philoſophic, we view neceſſity through the evangelic, medium ; nothing will
be wanting to render the ſurvey complete. Chriſtian
neceſſitarians, having ſung with Mr. Pope ; can alſo
ſing, as follows, in thoſe chearful lines of the late
excellent Mr. Hart :

" This God is the God we adore ;
    Our faithful, unchangeable friend :
Whoſe love is as great as his pow'r,
    And knows neither meaſure, nor end.

'Tis Jeſus, the firſt and the laſt,
    Whoſe ſpirit ſhall guide us ſafe home !
We'll praiſe him, for all that is paſt ;
    And truſt him, for all that's to come."

And ſo much for the pretended gloomineſs of neceſſity. Or, in other words, for the Æthiopic complection of that diſmal, melancholy doctrine, which
moſt dolefully aſſerts, that all things, without ex-
cepting the worſt, work together for the glory of
God, and for good to them that love him. Rom.
viii. 28. " Dri-plorable news indeed," as an old
lady once expreſſed it.

    2. To ſhew his ſkill in hiſtory and genealogy,
Mr. Weſley traces the origin of neceſſity. And
thus he makes out the pedigree.

* All diſcord, i. e. all the ſeemingly irregular and contrarient
diſpenſations of Divine Providence.

" That

" That man is not ſelf-determined; that the principle of action is lodged not in himſelf, but in ſome other being; has been an exceeding antient opinion : yea, near as old as the foundation of the world. It ſeems, none that admit of revelation can have any doubt of this. For it was unqueſtionably the ſentiment of Adam, ſoon after he had eaten of the forbidden fruit. He imputes what he had done, not to himſelf, but another : the woman whom thou gaveſt me. It was alſo the ſentiment of Eve : the Serpent, he beguiled me, and I did eat. It is true, I did eat, but the cauſe of my eating, the ſpring of my action, was in another."

Waiving all notice of the grammatical and the logical inaccuracies, which adorn this paragraph; I ſhall, with its author's leave, carry the antiquity of neceſſity ſomewhat higher up.

God himſelf is a neceſſary being. He exiſted, and could not but exiſt, without beginning. He exiſts, and cannot but exiſt, without end. Neceſſity, therefore, is co eval with, and inſeparable from, Deity; i. e. it is, truly and properly, eternal : as all his other attributes are. I would term neceſſity, in this view of it, *neceſſitas prima*.

With regard to Adam, he was ſufficiently inſtructed in the doctrine of neceſſity, during the ſtate of innocence. He could not but know, that he exiſted neceſſarily, and that every circumſtance of his ſituation was neceſſarily determined by a ſuperior hand.

For example. When he was well awoke from that deep ſleep, into which he had been neceſſarily caſt, without his own conſent firſt had and obtained; was not that ſingle incident (eſpecially when he adverted to the important effect of it) more than enough to impreſs a reflecting mind with the idea of neceſſity? The very miſſing of his rib, which he had involuntarily loſt on the occaſion, muſt have made him a neceſſitarian, ſuppoſing him to have

G 3 been,

been, what I make no doubt he was, a man of common underſtanding.

Eve, likewiſe, could not but know, that ſhe was
neceſſarily made, neceſſarily placed in Eden, and
neceſſarily conſigned to Adam.

I conclude, therefore, that the firſt man and his
wife were neceſſitarians, antecedently to their fall.
And if they, afterwards, endeavoured to account for
their fall, upon the principle of neceſſity; I muſt
declare, that, for my own part, I ſee neither the
impiety of the attempt, nor the lameneſs of the
reaſoning.

"Oh, but this makes God the author of their
falling." By no means in the world. It is the Arminian hypotheſis, which repreſents Deity as either
unſeaſonably abſent from the place, or as looking
unconcernedly on, while his feeble creature Eve was
chopping unequal logic with a mightier and more
artful being than herſelf. It is the free-will ſcheme,
which lays original ſin at the divine door: by ſuppoſing, that God ſtood neuter throughout the whole
affair; though he knew (if Arminianiſm will allow
him to have foreknown) that no leſs, than the ruin
of all mankind, would be the conſequence of that
neutrality.

When we ſay, that the fall of man came neceſſarily to paſs; it is only ſaying, that Satan is neither
too ſtrong, nor too wiſe, for God: and that Satan
would not have proved too ſtrong, or too wiſe, for
Eve herſelf, had it been the will of God *poſuiſſe obi-
cem*, i. e. to have hindered Satan from ſucceeding.
Now, if it was not the divine will to bar the enemy
from ſucceeding; and if it was really foreknown,
that, without ſuch bar, the enemy would ſucceed;
and if God could, without injuſtice, actually forbear,
at the very critical time, to put an effectual bar in
the way, though he certainly had power to do it:
the inference is invincible, that Adam and Eve fell
neceſſarily.

Nor

Nor is God's decree to permit the fall, liable to any one cavil, which will not hold, with equal or with ftronger force, againſt the actual permiſſion it- felf. " But why did God decree to permit the fall, and permit the fall according to his decree ?" For reaſons, the whole of which he has not thought pro- per to communicate. He giveth not account, to any, of his matters. Job xxxiii. 13. And this is too good an anſwer to ſo daring a queſtion.

Let me give our Freewillers a very momentous hint, viz. That the entrance of original ſin was one of thoſe eſſential links, on which the Meſſiah's incar- nation and crucifixion were ſuſpended. So that, if Adam's fall was not neceſſary (i. e. if it was a pre- carious, or contingent, event) ; it would follow, that the whole Chriſtian religion, from firſt to laſt, is a piece of mere chance-medley: and, conſequently, cannot be of divine inſtitution. Arminians would do well, to conſider, whither their principles lead them.

3. The true neceſſity is, *toto cælo*, remote and different from Manichæiſm: as indifputably appears, on comparing the two fyſtems together. Not to ob- ferve, that St. Auſtin (who, in his earlier part of life, had been * entangled in the Manichæan net)
was

---

* " The Manichæan fcheme," fays Mr. Wefley, " was formerly efpouſed by men of renown : St. Auguſtin in particular." But I will do St. Auſtin that juſtice which this gentleman withholds, by adding, that God converted him from Manichæiſm, while yet a young man ; and feveral years, before he was fo much as baptized into the Chriſ- tian Church.—The Methodiſt gces on : " Manichæiſm is now fo utterly out of date, that it would be loſt labour to confute it." Here- in, he is, to expreſs it as tenderly as I can, utterly miſtaken in his reckoning. I ſhall clearly prove, a page or two hence, that he him- felf is, in one refpect, as much ; and, in another refpect, abundantly more, a Manichæ, than either Scythian, Budda, or Manes.

Mr. Wefley, by a very fingular mixture of Manichæiſm, Pela- gianiſm, Popery, Socinianiſm, Ranteriſm, and Atheiſm, has, I be- lieve, now got to his ultimatum. Probably, he would go ſtill far- ther, if he could. But, I really think, he has no farther to go.——

Happy

was ultimately confirmed in his reſolution to renounce thoſe hereſies, by reading the epiſtles of that illuſtrious neceſſitarian St. Paul.

Manes, from whom Manichæiſm is (though very inaccurately) denominated; was by birth a Perſian, and flouriſhed toward the cloſe of the third century. His original name was * Cubric; which he afterwards dropped, for that of Manes.

One Scythian, an Arabian merchant, who had made himſelf maſter of the oriental philoſophy and theology, committed the ſubſtance of his collections to writing: and bequeathed his books, which were four in number, to a proſelyte of his, named Budda-Terebinthus. This Budda, ſettling afterwards in Perſia, reſided in the houſe of a widow, who had bought Manes for a ſlave. On Budda's deceaſe, the books of Scythian fell into Manes's hands; from whence he drew the generality of thoſe tenets which paſs under his name, and moulded them into a ſyſtem. In this odd manner, did Manes come to diſtinguiſh himſelf as an Hæreſiarch.

Happy ſettlement, after forty years infinity of ſhiftings and flittings hither and thither!

> " Thus weathercocks, which, for a while,
> " Have turn'd about with ev'ry blaſt;
> " Grown old, and deſtitute of oil,
> " Ruſt to a point, and fix at laſt!"

* " Mutato nomine, deinde Manis, vel Manetis, nomen adoptavit; Perſicum aliis, quod ὁμιλητὴν dicat, diſceptatorem, agoniſtam: aliis Chaldaïcum מאני, Græcè μανης, ex מאני, quod, Babyloniorum linguâ, ſignificat, vas, organum; quòd ſe σκεῦ۞ ἐκλεκλον dicerat, quo Deus, ad doctrinæ divinæ propagationem, uti vellet. Hinc videtur factum, ut falſæ doctrinæ auctorem talmudiſtæ vocarint מאני; quod Elias Levita à מאן Hæretico derivat. Et reverà priùs nomen Cubricus denotaſſe videtur כבב רי, vas vanum, contemnendum, fragile. Dein diſcipuli, ob invidiam Græcæ vocis, quâ Μανης deſignabat τον μαινονla τας φρενας, inſanentem, vel furentem; literâ dupiicatâ, & compoſitâ voce, quaſi eſſet μαννα χεων, manna fundens, fecere Manichæum."

Spanhemii Hiſt. Chriſtian. Sæc. 3.—Operum Tom. I. Col. 751, 752.

The

The amount of his ſyſtem was this :

" There are two co-equal, co-eternal, and independent Gods, or infinite principles, viz. God, properly ſo called ; *alias* light : and matter ; *alias* darkneſs.

" The firſt, is the author of all good : the ſecond, of all evil.

" The light God inſpired the penman of the New Teſtament ; the dark God inſpired the writers of the Old Teſtament. Conſequently, the Old Teſtament is worth nothing.

" Theſe Gods are real ſubſtance ; the one, a good ſubſtance ; the other, a bad.

" In the work of creation, the good being wrought part, and the bad being wrought part.

" The good being is the maker of human ſouls.

" The good being united himſelf to the elements of air and fire ; the bad being took poſſeſſion of earth and water.

" The evil God made the world, and the human body, and ſin, and magiſtracy.

" There is a Trinity ; but it conſiſts of Scythian, Budda, and Manes. Scythian's ſeat is in the ſun ; Budda's in the moon ; and Manes's in the air.

" The ſun in the firmament is Chriſt.

" Chriſt did not aſſume a real, but only a ſeeming body.

" The elect are thoſe, in whom the evil principle is quite done away.

" Matrimony does but unite us more cloſely to the evil God.

" Water-baptiſm is worth little.

" The ſouls of my auditors" [i. e. of thoſe who conſtantly attended his aſſemblies, and imbibed his doctrines] " are thereby changed into elect ſouls ; and ſo return, quite purified, to the good being.

" The ſouls of other people tranſmigrate, at death, into beaſts, and trees, and all kinds of vegetables.

" Inward

" Inward concupiſcence is a perſon. It is never healed, but it may be totally ſeparated from men. In the day of judgment, each concupiſcence ſhall be ſhut up in a globe, and there live in perpetual impriſonment.

" The good God, and the bad God, wage implacable and never ceaſing war againſt each other; and perpetually clog and diſconcert one another's ſchemes and operations.

" Hence, men are impelled, by forcible conſtraint, to good, or to evil; according as they come under the power of the good Deity, or the bad one."

Such is a ſketch of what I have been able to collect with certainty, of the abſurd and execrable tenets of Manes : which form a medley of Pythagoriſm, Gnoſticiſm, and almoſt every other iſm, both Pagan and Heretical, which that and preceding ages could ſupply. It is probable, that Budda improved upon Scythian, and that Manes improved upon both. Though, in reality, neither of the three, nor all the three together, were authors of the monſtrous opinions which conſtituted the jumble. The opinions were taken from a variety of other ſources; and the pilfering triumvirate, contrary to the practice of thieves in general, ſeemed reſolved to ſteal the worſt of every thing they could lay their hands on.

I believe, it is abſolutely impoſſible to trace, quite up to its ſource, the antiquity of that hypotheſis, which abſurdly affirms the exiſtence of two eternal, contrary, independent principles. The other oriental nations ſeem to have adopted it from Egypt. But whence the Egyptians had it, and when they firſt entertained it, we know not : at leaſt, I could never find out.

What led ſo many wiſe people, and for ſo great a ſeries of ages, into ſuch a wretched miſtake, were, chiefly, I ſuppoſe, theſe two conſiderations: (1.) That

That evil, both moral and phyſical, are poſitive things, and ſo muſt have a poſitive cauſe. (2.) That a being perfectly good, could not, from the very nature of his eſſence, be the cauſe of ſuch bad things.

But (1.) Evil, whether phyſical or moral, does not, upon a narrow inſpection, appear to have ſo much of poſitivity in it, as it is probable thoſe ancients ſuppoſed.

A man breaks his leg : i. e. the continuity, or coheſion of parts, natural to that limb, ceaſes to be integral. This is followed by the evil of pain. And what is pain? the abſence, or privation, of ſenſible eaſe antecedently enjoyed. A man's houſe is burnt down. The conſequence is, a loſs, or privation, of property. He does not poſſeſs as much as he poſſeſſed before. Thus (not to multiply needleſs inſtances), ſickneſs is a privation of health : and is, from thence, very properly termed, diſeaſe. Poverty is a deficiency of wealth and conveniences. Death itſelf, a ceſſation of animal life.

God forbid, that I ſhould even wiſh to extenuate the malignity of ſin. The omnipreſent Reader of hearts and hearer of thoughts knows, that, next after his own awful diſpleaſure, I dread and deprecate ſin, in all its forms, as the greateſt of poſſible calamities. Let us, however, with cautious and timid hand, put moral evil itſelf into the philoſophic ſcale.

When I was a boy, and began to read Watts's Logic, I well remember the ſurpriſe it gave me, to find, that ſo good a man ſhould venture to treat of ſin, in the 6th Section (pt.1. chap. 2.), under the title Of Not-Being. And I confeſs, I partly wonder at it ſtill. But let the doctor ſpeak for himſelf. " The ſinfulneſs of any human action is ſaid to be a privation : for ſin is that want of conformity to the law of God, which ought to be found in every action of man.——I think," adds the doctor, and in troth **I**

think

think ſo too, " we muſt not reduce ſuch poſitive beings as piety, and virtue, and truth, to the rank of non-entities, which have nothing real in them. Though ſin, or rather the ſinfulneſs of an action, may be properly called a Not-Being: for it is a want of piety and virtue. This is a moſt uſual, and perhaps the moſt juſt, way of repreſenting theſe matters."

Very happily, we have a fine definition of ſin, given us by a Logician who could not err. Παϛ ο ποιων την αμαρλιαν, και την ανομιαν ποιει· και 'η AMAPTIA εϛιν 'η ANOMIA. 1 John iii. 4. Every man, who committeth ſin, doth alſo commit illegality: for ſin is illegality.— Whence I conclude, in the firſt place: that ſin, ſtrictly conſidered, has more of negation in it, than of poſitivity; elſe, it could not have been properly defineable by a merely negative term. For, illegality imports no more, than a non-commenſuration to the law, as a rule, or meaſure of length and breadth.—But, Secondly, I infer, that, unleſs ſin had ſomething of poſitivity in it, the illegality of it could not be ſaid to be commiſſable: "Every man, who committeth illegality." And yet, after all, I do not clearly diſcern, how that can be, without the aſſiſtance of Dr. Watts's diſtinction (a diſtinction which is, I believe, admitted by moſt, if not all, metaphyſical writers) between actions themſelves, and the ſinfulneſs of them.

Critics explain פשע, one of the Hebrew words for ſin, by the Greek word αθεσια; which imports unſettledneſs, and, in particular, a not ſtanding to articles before agreed upon. חטא, the moſt uſual word for ſin, properly ſignifies, a not walking in the right road, and a not hitting the propoſed mark. עוה is obliquity, or crookedneſs: i. e. want of ſtraitneſs.

The Greek αμαρλια, moſt certainly, conveys a negative idea: and ſignifies, like the ſecond Hebrew word abovementioned, a falling ſhort of the mark.

The

The Latin *peccatum* (which ſome are for deriving from שׁגג) is alſo explained by *delictum*, i. e. a failure in duty. *Iniquitas, culpa, noxa, injuſtitia, impietas, ſcelus, vitium,* and a multitude of others; are, in ſtrictneſs, terms of negation.

But (2.), in what light ſoever we conſider thoſe modes of being and action, called natural and moral evil; whether we view them as poſitive qualities, or as negative, or as mixed; ſtill the queſtion returns, whether the great Firſt Cauſe, who is infinitely and merely good, can be, either efficiently, or deficiently, the author of them?

In my opinion, the ſingle word permiſſion ſolves the whole difficulty, as far as it can be ſolved in the preſent beclouded ſtate of human reaſon. Certainly, God is not bound to preclude evil from among his works. It is equally certain, that he can permit it, not only to obtain, but even to reign. And it is as certain, that he actually does ſo permit it. Why? Not for want of knowledge, to perceive it. Nor for want of power, to hinder it. Nor for want of wiſdom, to counteract it. Nor for want of goodneſs, to order all for the beſt. But becauſe it was and is his unſearchable * will (and the will of God

is

---

* And a ſtep, or an inch, beyond this, we cannot go. That God willed to permit evil, cannot be doubted, but at the expence, either of his wiſdom, or of his power. The reaſons why he willed it, are, perhaps, among thoſe arcana, which angels themſelves have not yet been allowed to ſee into.

I think, I may venture to aſſert, that the Scriptures throw hardly any degree of light upon the divine motive, or motives, to this permiſſion. And it appears inconteſtably plain, from the writings, and from ſuch authentic memorials, as remain, of the moſt ſagacious philoſophers of preceding ages, and of every civilized clime, the Chineſe themſelves included; that all their various hypotheſis (ſome of which were extremely ſubtil and ingenious) by which they ſtrained both judgment and imagination, to account for the primary exiſtence and introduction of moral and phyſical ataxy; terminated, univerſally, in the point from whence they ſet out, viz. We cannot tell.

Whoever deſires to ſee, at one view, as much as needs to be known, concerning the ſpeculations of the greateſt ſages among the ancients, is rectitude itſelf), to allow the entrance and the continuance of that ſeeming foil to the lovelineſs of his works.

Arminianiſm

on this inextricable ſubject; will enjoy a moſt refined amuſement (but attended, I think, with no feaſible ſolution of the difficulty immediately in point), by peruſing the ſecond part of that conciſe, elegant, judicious, and faithful ſketch of antique philoſophy, entitled, A Diſcourſe upon the Theology and Mythology of the Ancients. Written by the Chevalier Ramſay; an author, who, though, in my opinion, extremely fanciful and erroneous on ſome metaphyſical queſtions; yet deſerves to be loved and admired, as one of the moſt ingenious, polite, candid, and entertaining reaſoners, that ever added the enchantments of beauty to the dignity of virtue and to the riches of learning.

But ſtill, our utmoſt inveſtigations leave us, preciſely, where they began. We know ſcarce any of the views, which induced uncreated goodneſs to ordain (for, where infinity of knowledge and power and of wiſdom unite in the permitter, I ſee no very great difference between permitting and ordaining) the introgreſſion, or, more properly, the intromiſſion, of evil. For my own part, I can, with unrepining chearfulneſs, give God credit (and that to all eternity, ſhould it be his pleaſure to require me) for doing every thing well.

> " I know but this, that he is good,
> " And that myſelf am blind."

Can any body bring the matter to a more ſatisfactory iſſue? Si non, hoc utere mecum.

It might have been happy for that fine, but too excurſive Theoriſt, Dr. Conyers Middleton, if he had not, with more raſhneſs than good ſpeed, endeavoured to overleap that boundary, which God himſelf has fixed, to the preſent extent of human knowledge. Were we even to grant the doctor his favourite hypotheſis, viz. that the whole Moſaic account of the fall is merely allegorical; the origin of evil would ſtill remain as dark, and as deep at the bottom of the well, as ever. For to what does this boaſted allegory amount? Dr. Middleton ſhall give it us, in his own words (Works, Quarto. Vol. II. P. 149). " By Adam, we are to underſtand reaſon, or the mind of man. By Eve, the fleſh, or outward ſenſes. By the Serpent, luſt, or pleaſure. In which allegory, we ſee clearly explained the true cauſes of man's fall and degeneracy: that, as ſoon as his mind, through the weakneſs and treachery of his ſenſes, became captivated and ſeduced by the allurements of luſt and pleaſure, he was driven by God out of Paradiſe, i. e. loſt and forfeited the happineſs and proſperity, which he had enjoyed in his innocence."

With all the respect due to ſo very ſuperior a pen, I would offer an obſervation or two on this paſſage.——1. If Adam, and Eve, and

the

Arminianiſm (which repreſents moral and natural evil as entering and as reigning in defiance and contrariety to the will and with and endeavours of the Divine Being) co-incides ſo patly with the Manichæan dream of two almighty conflicting principles, who reign in ſpite of each other, and catch as catch can ; that I really wonder at the reverſed modeſty of thoſe free-willers, who are for ſhifting off

the Serpent, and the Trees of Knowledge and of Life, and the very Paradiſe where they grew, were all allegorical (i. e. fabulous and unreal) ; might not an atheiſt ſuppoſe, with equal reaſon, that the adorable Creator, whom this ſame hiſtory terms God, is as allegorical a being as the reſt ?——2. If the fall itſelf, as related in Scripture, be no more than a piece of moral fiction : what ſecurity have we, that the ſcriptural account of redemption, is not equally fictitious ? Indeed, where is the neceſſity, or ſo much as the propriety, and reaſonableneſs, of imagining, that an allegorical ruin requires more than an allegorical reſtoration?——3. Among a multitude of other objections, which clog the wheel of this unſatisfactory ſcheme, the following is one; that the difficulty of accounting for the riſe of evil, ſtills ſubſiſts in all its primitive and impenetrable obſcurity. For, (1.) How came the "allurements of luſt and pleaſure," to exiſt at all? eſpecially, in a ſtate of abſolute innocency ?—(2.) How came man's "outward ſenſes" to be ſo very eaſy of acceſs, as to fly open, like the doors of an enchanted caſtle, at almoſt the firſt appearance of this ſaid gigantic lady, called " Allurement?"—(3.) How came the human mind to yield itſelf ſo tame a "captive" to thoſe ſeducing ſenſes? Not to aſk, (4.) Why the ſenſes themſelves were originally indued with that " weakneſs, and treachery," and power of "ſeduction," which the doctor ſo freely places to their account ?—I think myſelf warranted to conclude, that this maſterly allegorizer has not " clearly explained," nor ſo much as thrown the leaſt glimmering of explanation upon, " the true cauſes of man's fall and degeneracy." What, then, do we gain, by reading Moſes through the doctor's allegoric ſpectacles ? So far from gaining, we loſe the little we had. The man who pulls down my houſe, and builds me a better in its place, deſerves my thanks. But the man who takes down my dwelling, under pretence that it is not ſufficiently ample and elegant for a perſon of my dignity to inhabit ; and, after all this parade, leaves me to ſleep in the open air, unſheltered by any roof at all, does me a material injury. When infidels can raiſe a more commodious fabric (i. e. propoſe a more unexceptionable ſyſtem of principles), than that the Bible preſents us with ; we will chearfully remove from our old houſe. But, until then, let theſe gentlemen ſleep ſub dio by themſelves.

the

the charge of Manichæiſm, from themſelves, to other folks.

Nay, were I diſpoſed to make the moſt of my argument, I might add, and very fairly too, That the the old Manichæiſm was a gentle impiety, and a ſlender abſurdity; when contraſted with the modern Arminian improvements on that ſyſtem. For, which is worſe? To aſſert the exiſtence of two independent beings, and no more; or, to aſſert the exiſtence of about one hundred and fifty millions of independent beings, all living at one time, and moſt of them waging ſucceſsful war on the deſigns of him that made them?

Moreover, if ſo very minute a crumb of the creation, as this terraqueous planet, which we at preſent occupy, can furniſh out ſuch a formidable army of independent principles (i. e. of ſelf - determiners: in which number, infants and children themſelves muſt be virtually included, which will ſwell the catalogue with about ſeventy millions more); the aggregate number of independent and poſſibly-conflicting agents, contained in the univerſe at large, may exceed the powers of all the angels in heaven to compute. But, even confining ourſelves to our own world; it will follow, that Arminian Manichæiſm exceeds the paltry oriental duality, at the immenſe rate of 150000000 to 2! And this, at the very loweſt and moſt favourable computation, i. e. without taking infants into the account; and without reckoning the adult ſelf-determiners of paſt generations, nor of thoſe generations which are yet to come.

Poor Manes! with how excellent a grace do Arminians call thee an heretic! And, above all, ſuch Arminians (whereof Mr. John Weſley is one) as agree with thee, in believing the attainability of ſinleſs perfection here below: or, to uſe the good old Manichæan phraſe, who aſſert that the evil principle

may

may be totally ſeparated from man in the preſent life !

" Oh, but Manes held neceſſity alſo." But what ſort of neceſſity ? Such a neceſſity as a child would be under, if the Dragon of Wantley was pulling him by one arm, and Moore of Moore-hall by the other. Chriſtianity and philoſophy have nothing to do with this neceſſity, except to laugh at it.

4. Mr. Weſley ſeems much diſpleaſed with a brace of gentlemen, whoſe names he has not communicated to the public ; but who appear, from his account of them, to be in no very fair way toward ſinleſs perfection.

One of theſe, we are told, delivered his mind, to this effect ! " I frequently feel tempers, and ſpeak many words, and do many actions, which I do not approve of. But I cannot avoid it. They reſult, whether I will or no, from the vibrations of my brain, together with the motion of my blood, and the flow of my animal ſpirits. But theſe are not in my own power. I cannot help them. They are independent on my choice." Thus far, I totally agree with the gentleman unknown. Every one of his premiſes is true. But the concluſion limps, moſt miſerably. Which concluſion (if Mr. Weſley have repreſented it fairly) is this : " Therefore I cannot apprehend myſelf to be a ſinner." And pray, what does the gentleman apprehend himſelf to be ? A ſaint, I preſume. Should this tract ever fall into his hands, let me intreat him to cry mightily to God, for that ſupernatural influence of grace, which alone is able to convince him of his ſinnerſhip; to bring him to Chriſt; and to ſave him from the evil effects, which muſt, otherwiſe, continue to reſult from " the vibrations of his brain, the motion of his blood, and the flow of his animal ſpirits."

The other anonymous gentleman, according to Mr. Weſley's hiſtory of him, believes the omnipotence, but doubts the wiſdom, and flatly denies the

goodneſs, of God. From the peculiar complection
of this creed, I ſhould have imagined, that its compiler had picked up the two laſt articles of it at the
Foundery : but Mr. Weſley precludes this ſurmiſe,
by giving us to underſtand, that the gentleman is not
a free-willer. For thus the creed goes on : " All
the evil in the world is owing to God.   I can aſcribe
it to no other cauſe.   I cannot blame that cur; for
barking or biting : it is his nature : and he did not
make himſelf.   I feel wrong tempers in myſelf.   But
that is not my fault : for I cannot help it.   It is my
nature.   And I could not prevent my having this
nature : neither can I change it."

No man in the world is more prone to put things
in people's mouths, which they never ſaid, or thought
of, than Mr. J. W.   I therefore lay very little ſtreſs
on the teſtimony, which ſupports the authenticity
of this creed.   It may be genuine.   But it is more
probable, that it was forged, and dreſſed up, for the
occaſion.

However, I will beſtow a few conciſe annotations
on this confeſſion of faith, be it real, or be it fictitious.

" All the evil in the world is owing to God."
Nothing can be more falſe.   For, as the great and
good * Mr. Edwards obſerves, " It would be ſtrange
arguing

---

* Viz. the late Rev. Mr. Jonathan Edwards, of North America.
Whoſe Enquiry into the Freedom of the Will is a book which God
has made the inſtrument of more deep and extenſive uſefulneſs (eſpecially among Deiſts, and perſons of ſcience), than almoſt any other
modern publication I know of.   If ſuch of my readers, as have not
yet met with it, wiſh to ſee the Arminian ſophiſtry totally unravelled
and defeated ; let them add that excellent performance to their literary treaſures.   A more nervous chain of reaſoning it would be extremely difficult to find, in the Engliſh language.   Conſequently, it
is not one of thoſe treatiſes, that can be run through in an hurry.
It muſt be read deliberately, and weighed with attention : elſe, you
will loſe half the ſtrength of the connection.———A ſpruce Mac-
caroni was boaſting, one day, that he had the moſt happy genius in
the world.   Every thing, ſaid he, is eaſy to me.   People call Euclid's Elements an hard book : but I read it, yeſterday, from beginning

arguing indeed, becauſe men never commit ſin, but only when God leaves them to themſelves, and neceſſarily ſin, when he does ſo; that therefore their ſin is not from themſelves, but from God: and ſo, that God muſt be a ſinful being. As ſtrange, as it would be, to argue, becauſe it is always dark when the ſun is gone, and never dark when the ſun is preſent; that therefore all darkneſs is from the ſun, and that his diſk and beams muſt needs be black." (Enquiry, p. 364, 365.)

Mr. Weſley's neceſſitarian adds: "I cannot blame that cur for barking and biting." But did the gentleman never, ſo much as once in his life-time, beat a cur for barking and biting; I dare ſay, he has: and would again, if a cur was to fly at him with open mouth. It ſhould ſeem, therefore, that a cur, though he bark and bite neceſſarily, is liable ſtill to blame: elſe, how could he be juſtly entitled to blows?

"It is his nature." Moſt certainly. And yet you will beat him for it!

"He did not make himſelf." Who thinks he did?

"I feel wrong tempers in myſelf." I dare ſay, you do.

ning to end, in a piece of the afternoon, between dinner and tea-time. "Read all Euclid," anſwered a gentleman preſent, "in one afternoon? How was that poſſible?" Upon my honour, I did: and never read more ſmoother reading in my life. "Did you maſter all the demonſtrations, and ſolve all the problems, as you went?" Demonſtrations! and problems! I ſuppoſe you mean the a's, and b's, and c's; and 1's, and 2's, and 3's; and the pictures of ſcratches and ſcrawls. No, no. I ſkipt all they. I only read Euclid himſelf; and all Euclid I did read; and in one piece of the afternoon too.—Mr. Edwards muſt not be read ſo genteely.

There are, it ſeems, two eminent defences of neceſſity, which I have never yet ſeen: viz. Dr. Hartley's Obſervations on Man; and an anonymous Eſſay on Liberty and Neceſſity, publiſhed, ſome years ſince, at Edinburgh. I hope, I have a feaſt, of pleaſure and inſtruction, in reſerve. And it ſhall not be my fault if I do not ſoon enjoy it.

H 2 "But

"But that is not my fault." Certainly, the fault is in yourſelf; and conſequently, the fault is your's. How you came by it, is another matter: and belongs to the queſtion of original ſin.

"I cannot help it." Right: you cannot. But there is one that can. Apply to him.

"It is my nature." Very true.—"And I could not prevent my having this nature." I never imagined you could.—"Neither can I change it." I am very clear, you cannot. The Æthiopian might as ſoon change his ſkin, or the leopard his ſpots, Jer. xiii. 23. And yet, what will become of you, if you die unchanged? May the Almighty put that cry into your heart, Turn thou me, and I ſhall be turned! for thou art the Lord my God. Jer. xxxi. 18. Then will you know what this meaneth: we all, with open face, beholding, as in a glaſs, the glory of the Lord; are changed into the ſame image, from glory to glory, by the ſpirit of the Lord. 2 Cor. iii. 18.

5. Mr. Weſley's wrath is not confined to the two gentlemen abovementioned. It ſtrides back into the laſt century, and proſecutes "the aſſembly of divines who met at Weſtminſter." For what offence, are they thus dug out of their graves? For ſaying, that "Whatever happens in time, was unchangeably determined from all eternity."—— I beg leave to acquaint the court, that there is a flaw in the charge. Mr. Weſley cannot quote even a ſingle propoſition, without mangling and altering!

In the confeſſion, drawn up by thoſe divines, they expreſs the matter thus: God, from all eternity, did, by the moſt wiſe and holy counſel of his own will, freely and unchangeably ordain whatever comes to paſs. Yet ſo, as thereby neither is God the author of ſin, nor is violence offered to the will of the creatures, &c. *.—In their larger catechiſm, they phraſe

* Humble Advice of the Aſſembly, &c. p. 10, 11. Edit. Lond. 1658. Quarto.

it,

it, with no alteration of fenfe, as follows : God's
decrees are the wife, free, and holy acts of the
council of his will ; whereby, from all eternity, he
hath, for his own glory, unchangeably fore-ordained
whatfoever comes to pafs in time : efpecially, concerning angels and men.—In the fhorter catechifm,
they fay : The decrees of God are, his eternal purpofe according to the counfel of his will ; whereby,
for his own glory, he hath fore-ordained whatever
comes to pafs. God executeth his decrees, in the
works of creation and providence.—I fhall only obferve, concerning all and each of thefe paragraphs,
that if they be not true, the whole Bible is one
grand ftring of falfehood, from the firft verfe to
the laft.

While Mr. Wefley's hand was in, I wonder he did
not arraign another affembly of divines ; fome of
whom were mitred. I mean, the famous affembly
of bifhops and others, who met together, not many
bow-fhots from Weftminfter, on the Surrey fide of
the Thames, in the year 1595, at a certain place of
rendezvous, called Lambeth Palace : where, fays
Dr. Fuller, " archbifhop Whitgift, out of his
Chriftian care to propagate the truth, and fupprefs
the oppofite errors, caufed a folemn meeting of
many grave and learned divines." Among whom,
befides the good archbifhop himfelf, were Bancroft,
bifhop of London ; Vaughan, bifhop of Bangor ;
Tindal, dean of Ely ; Whitaker, Divinity Profeffor
of Cambridge ; &c. Which faid affembly of divines
drew up the celebrated Lambeth articles : whereof
I fhall here cite but one, for a fpecimen ; having
treated, at large, of this affembly, and its determinations, * elfewhere, " *Prædeftinatorum præfinitus et cer-
tus eft numerus : qui nec augeri, nec minui, poteft.*" i. e.

---

* In a Tract, entitled, The Church of England vindicated from
the Charge of Arminianifm ; and in my Hiftoric Proof of the Doctrinal Calvinifm of the Church of England.

The

The number of the predeſtinated is fore-determined, and certain: ſo that it can neither be increaſed,
nor diminiſhed.

There have alſo been ſtill larger aſſemblies of divines: compoſed of all the biſhops, deans, and de-
legates of the clergy, in England. Witneſs the aſſembly, who drew up the 39 articles, to which Mr.
Weſley has, indeed, over and over again, ſat his
hand: but with the ſame ſimplicity and godly ſin-
cerity (2 Cor. i. 12.), which ſeem to have actuated
Dr. Reid, Dr. Oſwald, and Dr. Beattie, when they
ſubſcribed the confeſſion and catechiſm of the Weſtminſter aſſembly.

> There's ſuch a thing, as holy tricking.
> Teſts are but pie-cruſt, made for breaking.
> Our own conveniency, and gains,
> Are ſweetmeats, which that cruſt contains.
> To come at theſe, what man ſo fooliſh,
> But would a thouſand cruſts demoliſh?

Moreover, what ſhall we ſay, concerning that moſt
reverend, right reverend, aſſembly; who put that
woeful collect into the liturgy, beginning with, O
God, whoſe never-failing providence ordereth all
things, both in heaven and earth? Can any thing
breathe, more ſtrongly, the whole of what we mean
by neceſſity?—A providence—a never-failing providence—That ordereth not only ſome, but all
things—Yea, all things both in heaven and earth!
In that one paſſage (and the Church has very many
others, quite like unto it), " See neceſſity drawn at
full length, and painted in the moſt lively colours."

6. It is curious, to behold Arminians themſelves
forced, by ſtreſs of argument, to take refuge in the
harbour of that neceſſity which, at other times, they
ſo vehemently ſeek to deſtroy. " It is neceſſary,"
ſay they, " that man's will ſhould be free: for,
without freedom, the will were no will at all."

I pity

I pity the diſtreſsful dilemma, to which they are driven. Should they ſay, it is not neceſſary for man's will to be free; they give up their whole cauſe at once. If they ſay (and ſay it they do), that it is neceſſary, yea abſolutely neceſſary, for the will to be free; and that, in its very nature, it cannot but be free;—then, ſay I, upon that principle, theſe good people are free, with a liberty of neceſſity, and ſheer neceſſity itſelf is the root and ſap of all their boaſted free-agency. In other words, free-agency, themſelves being judges, is only a ramification of neceſſity!

7. Though I have mentioned the following anecdote, in a preceding publication; yet, by way of recompenſing Mr. Weſley, for the amuſement he has afforded me, in publiſhing the converſation of the two neceſſitarian gentlemen, whereof I have juſt given the reader an account; I alſo, in my turn, ſhall refer him to a very remarkable converſation, which paſſed between a free-will gentleman and myſelf, June 21, 1774, in the neighbourhood of London, and in the preſence of my friend, the Rev. Mr. Ryland.

" God does all he poſſibly can," ſaid the Arminian philoſopher, " to hinder moral and natural evil. But he cannot prevail. Men will not permit God to have his wiſh."—Then the Deity, anſwered I, muſt certainly be a very unhappy being.—— " Not unhappy in the leaſt."—What! meet with a conſtant ſeries of croſſes; thwarted in his daily endeavours; diſappointed of his wiſhes; diſconcerted in his plan of operations; defeated of his intentions; embarraſſed in his views; and actually overpowered, every moment of every day, by numberleſs of the creatures he has made; and yet be happy under all this inceſſant ſeries of perplexing and mortifying circumſtances?—" Yes: for he knows, that, in conſequence of the free-will, with which he has en-

dued

dued his rational creatures, he himſelf muſt be diſappointed of his wiſhes, and defeated of his ends ;
and that there is no help for it, unleſs he had made
us mere machines. He therefore ſubmits to necef-
ſity: and does not make himſelf uneaſy about
it *."

Can any thing be more ſhockingly execrable, than
ſuch a degrading and blaſphemous idea of the ever
bleſſed God? And conſequently, is not the doctrine
of human ſelf-determinability the moſt daring, the
moſt inconſiſtent, the moſt falſe, the moſt contemptible, and the moſt atheiſtical tenet, that
was ever ſpawned by pride and ignorance in
conjunction? A doctrine, which, in running away
from the true neceſſity, coins an impoſſible neceſſity
of its own inventing; and, while it repreſents men
as gods, ſinks God far below the level of the meaneſt man !

Is not the adorable Creator of the world, the
Governor of it too? Or has he only built a ſtage,
for fortune to dance upon? Does Almighty Providence do no more than hold the diſtaff, while contingency (i. e. while nothing) ſpins the threads, and
wreathes them into a line, for the Firſt Cauſe (very
falſely ſo called, if this be the caſe !) to wind upon
his reel, and turn to the beſt account he can? Arminians may affirm it. But God forbid, that I
ſhould ever believe it.

For my own part, I ſolemnly profeſs, before God,
angels, and men, that I am not conſcious of my being endued with that ſelf-determining power, which
Arminianiſm aſcribes to me as an individual of the
human ſpecies. Nay, I am clearly certain, that I
have it not. I am alſo equally certain, that I do not

* See a note, ſubjoined to p. 5. of a Sermon lately publiſhed by
me, entitled, Free-will and Merit brought to the Teſt; or, Men
not their own Saviours: where ſome of the horrible conſequences,
and of the gigantic inconſiſtencies, inſeparable from this gentleman's
theory, are briefly pointed out.

wiſh

wiſh to have it: and that, was it poſſible for my
Creator to make me an offer of transferring the determination of any one event, from his own will to mine ;
it would be both my duty and my wiſdom, to en-
treat, that the ſceptre might ſtill remain with himſelf, and that I might have nothing to do in the
direction of a ſingle incident, or of ſo much as a
ſingle circumſtance.

Mr. Weſley laments, that neceſſity is "The
ſcheme, which is now adopted by not a few of the
moſt ſenſible men in the nation." I agree with him,
as to the fact. But I cannot deplore it as a calamity. The progreſs, which that doctrine has, of
late years, made, and is ſtill making, in this kingdom, I conſider as a moſt happy and promiſing
ſymptom, that the Divine Goodneſs has yet abundant
mercies in reſerve, for a Church, the majority of
whoſe reputed members have long apoſtatized from
her eſſential principles; and for a country, whoſe *

---

* Take a ſpecimen of the vitiated ſtate, in which the free-will
gangrene has reduced the moral taſte of this Chriſtian and reformed
country, in the following admired lines, which are part of a very
applauded entertainment, lately introduced on the Engliſh ſtage :

"With ſport, love, and wine, fickle fortune defy ;
 Dull wiſdom all happineſs ſours;
Since life is no more than a paſſage, at beſt ;
 Let us ſtrew the way over with flow'rs."

Was a religious and ſenſible foreigner, whether a Proteſtant, or
Popiſh ; Jew, Mahometan, or Heathen; to be informed, that
ſuch equally deteſtable and deſpicable ſentiments, as thoſe, are heard
with rapture at the Britiſh theatres, and choruſed with delight in
numberleſs private companies in every part of the kingdom : would
he not be inclined to ſet us down, in general, for a nation of Epicurean Atheiſts, fit only to wallow in the Circean ſty ; quite loſt to all
religion, philoſophy, virtue, and decency; and no otherwiſe entitled to the name of man, than by perpendicularity of ſhape connected with the art of ſpeaking ?

"If prone in thought, our ſtature is our ſhame:
And man ſhould bluſh, his forehead meets the ſkies."

morals

morals have degenerated, in proportion to the cor-ruptions of its faith.

May the * ſet time be nigh at hand, for our national recovery to the goſpel and to virtue! Then ſhall God, even our own God, give us his bleſſing.

* Pſalm cii. 13.

A DISSER-

A

DISSERTATION

SENSIBLE QUALITIES

OF

MATTER:

MORE ESPECIALLY, CONCERNING

COLOURS.

Judge not (κατ᾽ ΟΨΙΝ) according to Sight. John vii. 24.

WHEN I wrote the foregoing chapters, it was my intention to have taken no notice of Mr. Wesley's weak and puerile objections to the well established doctrine of sensible qualities : partly, because what he observes (or, rather, what he has picked up from Dr. Reid and others) on this subject, is so contemptibly frivolous, as hardly to justify any serious animadversion ; and, partly, because I did not consider the subject itself as directly connected with the article of necessity.

But, on my reflecting, that the aptitude of perceivable bodies to impress our senses with certain motions, called sensations ; and that the sensations so produced, together with the correspondent ideas which those sensations impart to, or excite in, the mind : are, all, the result of necessary relation, and form an indissolubly combined chain of cause and effect : I determined to subjoin some enquiries, concerning a branch of knowledge, which, in this view of it, is not altogether foreign to the main argument of the preceding disquisitions.

By

By the ſenſes, I mean thoſe conduits or avenues to the brain, through which, the ſoul receives its ideas of objects extraneous to its ſelf. No perſon need be reminded, that theſe ſenſes are five, viz. thoſe of feeling, hearing, ſeeing, ſmelling, and taſting. It may, perhaps, be ſolidly affirmed, that, in abſolute ſtrictneſs, we have but one ſenſe, preciſely ſo called, viz. that of feeling, or perception at large; of which the remaining four are but ſo many exquiſite modifications, or affections. I acquieſce, however, in the popular diviſion of the ſenſes into five.

The ſenſible qualities of extraneous objects are, properly, no more than " powers," as Mr. Locke juſtly terms them, viz. powers of producing ſuch particular motions in our animal organs, as have a native tendency to occaſion correſpondent perceptions in the ſoul, through the mediation of the nerves and brain : that is to ſay, extraneous objects have this effect, when duly preſented to the ſenſes, and when the ſenſes are in ſuch a ſtate as duly to receive the impreſſions naturally ariſing from the preſence, or application, of thoſe objects.

Theſe powers, inherent in extraneous bodies, of producing ſuch ſenſations in us ; indiſputably reſult from the figure, ſize, arrangement, and motion, of the particles which conſtitute the bodies themſelves. Which appears, among other conſiderations, from hence : that the ſame body, under different modes of corpuſcular ſize, arrangement, motion, and figure, occaſions different ſenſations in our organs, and conveys different ideas to the mind.

Now, theſe modal differences of arrangement, &c. are undoubtedly reſident in their reſpective ſubjects: and may eaſily be conceived of, as exiſtable, independently on us ; i. e. they might be juſt what they are, whether the bodies themſelves, in which they obtain, were objected to our ſenſes, or not. But the effects of thoſe combined modes (as colour, ſound, flavour, ſcent, pleaſure, and pain) are things

purely

purely relative ; and abfolutely require the concur-
rence of fenfe, in order to their having any kind or
degree of pofitive exiflence. They are but poten-
tially in their peculiar fubjects, until thofe fubjects
become objects, by being actually expofed to, and
by actually operating upon, the organs of a perci-
pient being.

Thus, there might have been tremulations in the
atmofphere, through the impulfe of one mafs of
matter upon another (primarily fet in motion by the
divine will), if no animal, or fentient being, had
been created. But, in that cafe, it is utterly inconceivable, how thofe tremulations, though ever fo
violent, could have occafioned what we call, found.
Again.—The difpofition of certain furfaces to reflect, refract, and abforb, the incident rays of light ;
might have been juft what it now is, independently
on the optic nerves of animals : but then no furface,
however difpofed, i. e. be its texture, reflections,
refractions, or abforptions, what they will ; could
have occafioned that ideal refult, which we term colour, without being oppofed to the vifual organ of
an intelligent fubftance. And fo on, through every
fpecies of fenfible quality.

Hence ; there is nothing hyperbolic, or extravagant ; but all is no lefs ftrictly and foberly philofophical, than fublimely and elegantly poetical ; in
the following lines of Dr. Young :

" The fenfes, which inherit earth and heavens,
Enjoy the various riches nature yields :
Far nobler ! give the riches they enjoy.
Give tafte to fruits ; and harmony to groves ;
The radiant beams to gold, and gold's bright fire ;
Take in, at once, the landfcape of the world, -
At a fmall inlet, which a grain might clofe,
And half-create the wond'rous world they fee.
But for the magic organ's pow'rful charm,
Earth were a rude, uncolour'd chaos ftill.

Objects

Objects are but th' occafion : our's th' exploit.
Our's are the cloth, the pencil, and the paint,
Which nature's admirable picture draw,
And beautify creation's ample dome.
Like Milton's Eye, when gazing on the lake,
Man makes the matchlefs image, man admires."

This is provable, not only by reafon, but by numberlefs experiments. Do but artfully vary the medium through which you fee it, and you may make the furface of any body whatever affume, in appearance, any colour you pleafe : and that in the moft rapid fucceffion, and in every mode of poffible diverfity. A certain fign, that colour is only a fenfible quality, and not a real property, of matter.

But let us hear Mr. Wefley : who wildly thinks himfelf no lefs qualified to demolifh the fundamental axioms of natural philofophy, than to overturn the firft principles of natural and revealed religion.

" Colour," fays he, " is a real, material thing. There is no illufion in the cafe, unlefs you confound the * perception with the * thing perceived. And all other fecondary qualities are juft as real, as figure, or any other primary one." With regard to colour (for I have neither room nor leifure to run through all the other fecondary qualities), its non-exiftence is certain, not only from the preceding confiderations ; but, likewife, in general, from the natural darknefs of matter. Every atom (even thofe not excepted, which conftitute that exquifite fluid, called light ; though it is the moft attenuated and fubtil body with which we are acquainted) is, in-

** The plain, natural meaning of this, is, that " the thing perceived," viz. colour, confidered as refident in bodies, is " real :" but that our " perception" of that " real" colour is a mere " illufion !"—Without any "illufion" at all, may we not pronounce Mr. Wefley to be the lameft, the blindeft, and the moft felf-contradictory wafter of ink and paper, that ever pretended to the name of reafoner ? It is almoft a difgrace, to refute him.

trinfically,

trinfically, dark : and, confequently, colourlefs.
Light itfelf, by whofe intervention other bodies become vifible, feems to depend greatly, if not entirely, for that power, on the exility, the extreme
rarefaction, and on the incomparably rapid motion,
expanfion, and protrudibility, of its component particles : by which properties, it is peculiarly fitted, to
act upon the inftruments of animal fight ; as thefe
are likewife reciprocally fitted to admit that fenfation, which Providence defigned they fhould receive,
in confequence of being fo acted upon.

"All colours," fays Mr. Wefley, "do as really
exift without us, as trees, or corn, or heaven, or
earth." He is welcome to enjoy a delufion, which
(like moft of his other opinions) has not one found
argument for its fupport. But hear him again :
"When I fay, that cloth is of a red colour ; I
mean, its furface is fo difpofed, as to reflect the
red ; i. e. the largeft, rays of light. When I fay,
the fky is blue, I mean, it is fo difpofed, as to reflect the blue, i. e. the fmalleft, rays of light. And
where is the delufion here ? Does not that difpofition, do not thofe rays, as really exift, as either the
cloth, or the fky ? And are they not as really reflected, as the ball in a tennis-court ?"

What, in the name of wonder, could induce Mr.
W. to make thefe conceffions ? Conceffions, which
cut the throat of his own hypothefis from ear to ear !
For I appeal to any competent Reader, whether the
following conclufions do not neceffarily flow from
thofe premifes ?

1. That colour is the mere creature of fenfation : which fenfation is occafioned (not by any real
tinge inherent, either in the object, or in the rays of
light ; but occafioned) by the "difpofition," i. e.
by the texture, or configuration and connection, of
the fuperficial particles ; and by the "largenefs,"
or "fmallnefs," i. e. by the fize, of the "reflected
rays." This is all very right, fo far as it goes.

2. That

2. That " rednefs" and " bluenefs" (for inftance)
are mere ideas, refulting from the peculiarly " difpofed furfaces" of the reflecting bodies, and from
the magnitude, or minutenefs, of the " rays" which
thofe furfaces either ftrike back, or refract in various
directions. And what is this, but the very doctrine,
againft which Mr. Wefley profeffedly draws his
wooden fword? For,

3. As to the real exiftence of bodies, and their
furfaces, and rays of light; it is not queftioned by
any, I know of, except by the few followers of
bifhop Berkley; and they are very few indeed. Not
three dozen, I fuppofe, in the three kingdoms.

4. It follows, that Mr. Wefley's inconfiftent affertion cannot, even on his own principles, be true:
viz. that " colour is a real, material thing." No:
it is an ideal thing; generated in our minds by the
" difpofition" of " furfaces," and by the reverbera-
tion, &c. of " rays."

The Methodift goes on. " It is true, that, when
they" [i. e. when irradiated furfaces] " ftrike upon
my eye, a particular fenfation follows in my foul.
But that fenfation is not colour : I know no one
that calls it fo." Nor I neither. The fenfation only
gives at firft, and repeatedly excites afterwards, the
idea of colour. For, properly fpeaking, there is no
fuch thing as abfolute colour, either in the bodies
themfelves, or in the rays which they reflect, or in
the eye, or in the foul. Yet is the ideas founded on
a complication of realities. For both the bodies,
and the rays, and the eye, and the foul, have a
pofitive exiftence.

But Mr. Wefley has a dreadful peal of thunder in
referve; which he thus rattles over the head of natural philofophy. " Take it altogether" [i. e. believe the fenfible qualities to be no more than fen-
fible], " what a fuppofition is this! Is it not enough
to make one's blood run cold? The great God, the
creator of heaven and earth, the father of the fpirits

of

of all flefh, the God of truth, has encompaffed with falfehood every foul that he has made! Has given up all mankind to a ftrong delufion, to believe a lie! Yea, all his creation is a lie! You make God himfelf, rather than the devil, the father of lies!"— Mighty pious, mighty rhetorical, and mighty philofophical. I fhall leave the horrid criminality of this indecent paffage, to the cognizance of the adorable being it blafphemes: and only obferve, that Mr. Wefley's heat and prophanenefs (of which he has, elfewhere, given innumerable famples) are fuch, that he dares to fcold his Maker, with as little ceremony, and with as much fcurrility, as an enraged fifh-woman would be-din the ears of a 'prentice wench.

But let me afk: Is God (I tremble even to put the queftion!) therefore "the father of lies," becaufe he has not furnifhed us with acutenefs of fight, fufficient to take in the real magnitudes of the fun and other celeftial bodies? Or, can he be faid to "encompafs us with falfehood," becaufe we do not perceive the annual and diurnal motions of the earth? Our fenfes tell us (and the far greater part of mankind, upon the credit of their fenfes, live and die in the belief) that the fun is not fo large as a coach-wheel; that the moon is lefs than the dial of St. Paul's clock; that the diameter of the laigeft vifible ftar is inferior to that of a tea-cup; and that the earth is abfolutely quiefcent, inftead of conftantly travelling (as in reality it does) at the rapid rate of about 60,000 miles an hour, exclufively of its diurnal rotation round its own axis. The illufions of colour, tafte, and fmell, are nothing, when compared with the immenfe difference between appearances and facts, in thefe and other points of fo much greater confequence. And, hence, it becomes the office of reafon and fcience, to rectify, fo far as they can, the frequent miftakes of fenfe.

I fhall add, to thefe remarks, a fketch of what Mr. Locke has obferved, concerning the qualities, called fenfible. And I the rather do this with fome extent, becaufe that profound and mafterly genius has cultivated this part of fcience, with a perfpicuity and folidity, equalled, I believe, by few other writers on the fubject.

" It being manifeft, that there are multitudes of bodies, each whereof are fo fmall, that we cannot, by any of our fenfes, difcover either their bulk, figure, or motion, as is evident in the particles of the air and water ; and others, extremely fmaller than thofe, perhaps as much fmaller than the particles of air and water, as the particles of air and water are fmaller than peafe or hail-ftones : let us fuppofe at prefent, that the different motions and figures, bulk and number, of fuch particles, affecting the organs of our fenfes, produce in us thofe different fenfations, which we have from the colours and fmells of bodies. Let us fuppofe, for example, that a violet, by the impulfe of fuch infenfible [i. e. invifible] particles of matter, of peculiar figures and bulks, and in different degrees and modifications of their motions, caufes the ideas, of the blue colour and fweet fcent of that flower, to be produced in our minds. It being no more impoffible to conceive, that God fhould annex fuch ideas to fuch motions, with which they have no fimilitude ; than that he fhould annex the idea of pain to the motion of a piece of fteel dividing our flefh, with which that idea hath no refemblance.

" What I have faid, concerning colours and fmells, may be underftood alfo of taftes, and founds, and other fenfible qualities : which, whatever reality we by miftake attribute to them, are in truth nothing in the objects themfelves, but powers to produce various fenfations in us ; and depend on the primary qualities, viz. bulk, figure, texture, and motion of parts.

" Flame ·

" Flame is denominated hot, and bright ; fnow,
white, and cold ; manna, white, and fweet : from
the ideas they produce in us. ·Whoever confiders,
that the fame fire, which, at one diftance, produces
in us the fenfation of warmth, does, at a nearer approach, produce in us the far different fenfation of
pain ; ought to bethink himfelf, what reafon he has
to fay, that his idea of warmth, which was produced
in him by the fire, is actually in the fire ; and his idea
of pain, which the fame fire produced in him, is not
in the fire. Why are whitenefs and cold in fnow,
and pain not ; when it produces both one and the
other of thofe ideas in us, and can do neither, but
by the bulk, figure, number, and motion, of its
folid parts ?

" The particular bulk, number, figure, and motion, of the parts of fire or fnow, are really in thofe
bodies, whether any one's fenfes perceive them, or
no : and may therefore be called real qualities. But
light, heat, whitenefs, or coldnefs, are no more
really in fnow or fire, than ficknefs or pain is in
manna. Take away the fenfation of them ; let not
the eye fee light or colours, nor the ears hear founds ;
let the palate not tafte, nor the nofe fmell ; and all
colours, taftes, odours, and founds, as they are fuch
particular ideas, vanifh and ceafe, and are reduced
to their caufes, viz. bulk, figure, and motions of
parts.

" Let us confider the red and white colours in
porphyry [marble]. Hinder light but from ftriking
on it, and ts colours vanifh ; it no longer produces
any fuch ideas in us. Upon the return of light, it
produces thefe appearances again. Can any one
think, that any real alterations are made in the porphyry, by the prefence or abfence of light ; and that
thofe ideas of whitenefs and rednefs are really in
porphyry in the light, when it is plain it has no colour in the dark ? It has, indeed, fuch a configuration of particles, both night and day, as are apt,

by the rays of light rebounding from fome parts of that hard ftone, to produce in us the idea of rednefs, and from others the idea of whitenefs ; but whitenefs and rednefs are not in it, at any time ; but only fuch a texture, as has power to produce fuch a fenfation in us.

" Pound an almond, and the clear white colour will be turned into a dirty one ; and the fweet tafte into an oily one. What real alteration can the beating of a peftle make in any body, but an alteration in the texture of it ?

" He that will examine his complex idea of gold, will find feveral of the ideas, that make it up, to be only powers : as the power of being melted, but of not fpending itfelf in the fire ; and of being diffolved in aqua regia. Which are ideas, as neceffary to make up our complex idea of gold, as its colour and weight : which, if duly confidered, are nothing but different powers. For, to fpeak truly, yellownefs is not actually in gold, but is a power in gold to produce that idea in us, by our eyes, when placed in a due light. And the heat, which we cannot leave out of our idea of the fun, is no more really in the fun, than is the white colour which it introduces into wax. Thefe are both equally powers in the fun, operating by the motion and figure of its infenfible parts fo on a man, as to make him have the idea of heat ; and fo on wax, as to make it capable to produce in a man the idea of white.

" Had we fenfes, acute enough to difcern the minute particles of bodies, and the real conftitution on which their fenfible qualities depend, I doubt not, but they would produce quite different ideas in us, and that, which now [feems] the yellow colour of gold, would then difappear, and, in ftead of it, we fhould fee an admirable texture of parts of a certain fize and figure.

" This microfcopes plainly difcover to us. For what, to our naked eyes, produces [the femblance of] of] a certain colour, is, by thus augmenting the acutenefs of our fenfes, difcovered to be quite a different thing : and the thus altering, as it were, the proportion of the bulk of the minute parts of a coloured object to our fight, produces different ideas from what it did before.

" Thus fand, or pounded glafs, which is opake, and white, to the naked eye; is pellucid, in a microfcope. And an hair, feen this way, lofes its former colour, and is in a great meafure pellucid, with a mixture of bright, fparkling colours, fuch as appear from the refraction of diamonds, and other pellucid bodies. Blood, to the naked eye, appears all red : but, by a good microfcope, wherein its leffer parts appear, fhews only fome few globules of red, fwimming in a pellucid liquor. And how thofe red globules would appear, if glaffes could be found, that could magnify them yet 100), or 10,000 times more, is uncertain *."

No difhonour will accrue to this great man, now fo largely quoted, by obferving, that, in what he fo ably delivered concerning the fecondary or fenfible qualities of matter, he ftood on the fhoulders of his illuftrious fore-runner in fcience, Mr. Boyle.—Permit me, at once, to enrich the prefent appendix, with a few paragraphs from this laft-mentioned philofopher; and to confirm its general drift, by the fanction of fo exalted an authority.

" I do not deny, that bodies may be faid, in a very favourable fenfe, to have thofe qualities [potentially], which we call fenfible, though there were no animals in the world. For a body, in that cafe, may have fuch a difpofition of its conftituent corpufcles, that, if it were duly applied to the fenfory of an animal, it would produce fuch a fenfible [effect], which a body of another texture would not. Thus, though, if there were no animals,

---

* Locke's Effay, book 2. chap. 8, and chap. 23.

I 3

there

there would be no fuch thing as pain ; yet a [thorn] may, upon account of its figure, be fitted to caufe pain, in cafe it were moved againft a man's finger : whereas a blunt body, moved againft it with no greater force, is not fitted to caufe any fuch perception. So fnow, though, if there were no lucid body, nor organ of fight, in the world, would exhibit no colour at all (for I could not find it had any, in places exactly darkened); yet hath it a greater difpofition, than a coal, or foot, to reflect ftore of light outwards, when the fun fhines upon them all three. We fay, that a lute is in tune, whether it be actually played upon or no, if the ftrings be all fo duly ftretched, as that it would appear to be in tune, if it were played on.

" Thruft a pin into a man's finger both before and after his death. Though the pin be as fharp, at one time, as at another; and makes, in both cafes alike, a folution of continuity ; yet, in the former cafe, the action of the pin will produce pain : and not in the latter, becaufe, in this, the pricked body wants the foul, and, confequently, the perceptive faculty.—So, if there were no fenfitive beings, thofe bodies, which are now the objects of our fenfes, would be no more than difpofitively endued with colours, taftes, and the like : but actually with only the more catholic affections of bodies, as figure, motion, texture, &c.

" To illuftrate this yet a little farther. Suppofe a man fhould beat a drum, at fome diftance from the mouth of a cave, conveniently fituated to return the noife he makes. People will prefently conclude, that the cave has an echo : and will be apt to fancy, upon that account, fome * real property in the place,

to

---

* Real properties it undoubtedly has : and it is, impoffible that any portion of matter fhould be without them. But Mr. Boyle means, that the particular effect, which we term found, is not of the number of thofe real properties, but merely fenfitive and ideal ;

and

to which the echo is said to belong. Yet, to speak physically of things, this peculiar quality, or property, which we fancy to be in the cave; is, in it, nothing else but the hollowness of its figure, whereby it is so disposed, as when the air beats against it, to reflect the motion towards the place whence that motion began. And what passes on the occasion, is indeed but this: the drumstick, falling on the drum, makes a percussion of the air, and puts that fluid body in an undulating motion; and the aërial waves, thrusting on one another, until they arrive at the hollow superficies of the cave, have by reason of its resistance and figure, their motion determined the contrary way: namely, backward, towards that part where the drum was when it was struck. So that, in that which here happens, there intervenes nothing but the figure of one body, and the motion of another: though if a man's ear chance to be in the way of these motions of the air forward and backward, it gives him a perception of them, which he calls sound.

" And whereas one body doth often seem to produce, in another, divers such qualities as we call sensible; which qualities therefore seem not to need any reference to our senses; I consider, that, when one inanimate body works upon another, there is nothing really produced by the agent, in the patient, save some local motion of its parts, or some change of texture consequent upon that motion': but, by means of its effects upon our organs of sense, we are induced to attribute this or that quality to it. So, if a piece of transparent ice be, by the falling of some heavy and hard body upon it, broken into a gross powder that looks whitish; the falling body doth nothing to the ice, but break it into very small

and becomes so, when matter, under certain modes and circumstances of figure and motion, is objected to and operates upon the suitably disposed organ of a perceiving animal.

I 4 fragments,

fragments, lying confusedly upon one another: though, by reason of the fabric of the world and of our eyes, there does, in the day-time, upon this comminution, ensue such a kind of copious reflection of the incident light to our eyes, as we call whitenefs. And when the fun, by thawing this broken ice, deftroys its whitenefs, and makes it become diaphonous, which it was not before; the fun does no more than alter the texture of the component parts, by putting them into motion, and, thereby, into a new order: in which, by reason of the difpofition of the intercepting pores, they reflect but few of the incident beams of light, and tranfmit moft of them.

" When you polifh a rough piece of filver, that which is really done is but the depreffion of the little protuberant parts, into one level with the reft of the fuperficies: though, upon this mechanical change of the texture of the fuperficial parts, we men fay, that it hath loft the quality of roughnefs, and acquired that of fmoothnefs; becaufe, whereas the exftances did, before, by their figure, refift a little the motion of our finger, our finger now meets with no fuch offenfive refiftance.

" Fire will make wax flow, and enable it to burn a man's hand. And yet this does not argue in it any inherent quality of heat, diftinct from the power it hath of putting the fmall parts of the wax into fuch a motion, as that their agitation furmounts their co-hefion. But though we fuppofe the fire to do no more than varioufly and brifkly to agitate the infenfible parts of the wax, that may fuffice to make us think the wax endued with a quality of heat; becaufe, if fuch agitation be greater than that of our organs of touch, it produces in us the fenfation we call heat: which is fo much a relative to the fenfory which apprehends it, that the fame lukewarm water (i. e. water whofe corpufcles are moderately agitated by the fire) will feem hot to one of a

man's

man's hands, if that hand be very cold; and cold
to the other, in cafe it be very hot; though both of
them be the fame man's hands.——Bodies, in a
world conftituted as our's now is, being brought to
act upon the moft curioufly contrived fenforics of
animals, may, upon both thefe accounts, exhibit
many different fenfible phænomena: which, however we look upon them as diftinct qualities, are
but the confequent effects of the often-mentioned
catholic affections of matter, and deducible from the
fize, fhape, motion, (or reft), pofture, order, and
the refulting texture, of the infenfible parts of
bodies. And therefore, though, for fhortnefs of
fpeech, I fhall not fcruple to make ufe of the word,
qualities, fince it is already fo generally received;
yet, I would be underftood to mean it, in a fenfe
fuitable to the doctrine above delivered *."

But there is one confideration, which, in my view
of it, decides the queftion abfolutely and irrefraga-
bly. To wit, the effential famenefs of matter in all
bodies whatever.

The opinion, that what are commonly termed the
four elements, (viz. earth, water, air, and fire,) are
fo many fimple and effentially different principles,
or abfolute and firft rudiments; feems, to me, an
exceedingly erroneous fuppofition. For I take thofe
elements, as they are ufually ftyled, to be, themfelves,
but fo many various modifications of that fame fimple matter, whereof all body, or extended fubftance,
without exception, confifts †.

. Now,

---

* Boyle's Origin of Forms and Qualities, p. 31—38. Edit.
Oxf. 1667.

† Without entering either deeply, or extenfively, into the confiderations which determine me to this belief; I would barely offer
the following hints.

1. To imagine, that Infinite Wifdom would multiply effences,
without reafonable caufe, were to fofter an hypothefis directly
contrary to that beautiful fimplicity, which, fo evidently, and fo
univerfally, characterifes the variegated works of God. Nature
(i. e. omnipotence behind the curtain) is radically frugal, though

Now, if it be allowed, that all matter is essentially the same, under every possible diversity of appearance;

its phænomena exhibit almost an infinity of modal diversification. Two essences only (viz. spirit and matter) are fully sufficient, to account for every appearance, and to answer every known purpose, of creation, and of providence. What occasion, then, for five? or, as some suppose, for no fewer than seven; viz. earth, water, air, fire, light, æther, and spirit? Might we not, just as rationally, dream of seventy, or even seventy millions of essences?

Sir Isaac Newton's rule for philosophising, and the argument on which he grounds it, strike me with all the force of self-evidence: Causas rerum naturalium non plures admitti debere, quàm quæ et veræ sint, & earum phænomenis explicandis sufficiant. Dicunt utique philosophi: Natura nihil agit frustra; & frustra fit, per plura, quod fieri potest per pauciora. Natura enim simplex est, & rerum Causis superfluis non luxuriat. If this be just, the admission of more essences, than two, would be totally inconsistent with a first and fundamental principle of all natural knowledge.

2. The four classes of matter, commonly called Elements, are, in reality, not simple, but exceedingly compound, bodies; and partake very much of each other. Which circumstance forms no inconsiderable branch of that ἀταξία, or confusion, literally so termed; introduced by original sin. Thus,

Earth associates to itself all the solvable substances that are committed to its bosom. Which substances, after the time respectively requisite for their solution, and for their co-alescence with the earth, are not distinguishable from original earth itself.

Water is known to comprehend every species of earthy particles; as well as to include no small portion of air : and to be capable, by motion, of assuming that quality which we term heat; even in such a degree, as to be no less intolerable by animals, than flame itself.

Air is constantly intermingled with an immense number of dissimilar particles. With household dust (for instance), which is, in fact, the wearings of almost every thing. Not to mention the countless effluvia, with which the atmosphere is charged, incessantly flying off from animal bodies, both sound and putrescent; and from the whole world of vegetable substances, both fragrant and fœtid. These particles, through the continual attrition occasioned by their motion and interference with each other, and by the ambient pressure of the air upon them all, undergo, it is probable, a gradual atomic separation : and, when sufficiently comminuted, become, at last, a genuine part of that aerial fluid, in which they only floated before.——Could we breathe nothing but pure, unmixed air, human health and life would, probably, extend to an extreme length.

Fire, or more properly a fiery substance, will burn (i. e. communicate a portion of its own motion to), and assimilate, all other

contracting

ance; it will follow, that what we call ſenſible qualities are, rather, modal diſcriminations, than real ·
differences.

Let us apply this doctrine to colours.

Several

contracting bodies, whoſe corpuſcular co-heſion is not ſufficiently
cloſe and firm to reſiſt the ſubtil agency of that inſinuating power.
But, when its force is exhauſted (i. e. when the inteſtine agitation of
its parts has forced off all that was volatile; and ceaſes, in conſequence of having no more to do), what remains? A quantity of
particles, equally capable (for ought that appears to the contrary) of
being condenſed into earth, or expanded into water, or rarefied into
air.—Which reminds me,

3. Of the continual tranſmutation of one modified ſubſtance into
another, by the chemical proceſs of nature; ſometimes aſſiſted, but
oftener quite unaſſiſted, by art; which literal metamorphoſis ſeems
to be a grand and fundamental law of this lower world; and, if
admitted, furniſhes me with an additional argument for the ſame-
neſs of matter under all its vaſt variety of modes and forms.

We may, for example, aſk, with the poet:

" Where is the duſt, that has not been alive ?
The ſpade, and plough, diſturb our anceſtors.
From human mould we reap our daily bread.
" The moiſt of human frame the ſun exhales:
Winds ſcatter, through the mighty void, the dry:
Earth re-poſſeſſes part of what ſhe gave."

And thus the myſterious wheel of nature goes round; the vaſt
mechanic circulation is kept up; and, by a wonderful, but real,
εμπεριχωρησις, well-nigh every thing (I ſpeak of matter only) becomes every thing, in its turn.

So thoroughly perſuaded am I, in my own mind, that all the
atoms, particles, and larger portions, of matter, are primarily and
intrinſically and eſſentially homogeneous; that I make no doubt,
but a millſtone is phyſically capable of being rarefied into light, and
light phyſically capable of being condenſed into a millſtone.—By
the way, light is, perhaps, no more than melted air: and air is,
perhaps, the never-failing reſervoir, which ſupplies the ſun with
materials for its rays. Air is, incontestibly, a neceſſary pabulum of
ſublunary, and why not of ſolar, fire?

I ſhall conclude this excurſive note, with a pertinent paſſage from
Mr. Boyle: in which that profound and judicious naturaliſt informs
us, on the authority of an experiment made by himſelf, that even
water is ultimately convertible into oil, and into fire.

" Since the various manner of the coalition of ſeveral corpuſcles
into one viſible body, is enough to give them a peculiar texture,
and thereby fit them to exhibit divers ſenſible qualities, and
to become a body, ſometimes of one denomination, and ſometimes of another; it will very naturally follow, that,
from the various [but providential] occurſions of theſe innumerable

Several neceffary pre-requifites muft concur, to imprefs my mind, at firft, with an idea of colour. 1. There muft be the prefence of a vifible object : 2. The

merable fwarms of little bodies that are moved to and fro in the world, there will be many fitted to ftick to one another, and fo compofe concretions: and many (though not in the felf-fame place) disjoined from one another, and agitated apart. And multitudes alfo, that will be driven to affociate themfelves, now with one body, and prefently with another.

" And if we alfo confider, on the one fide, that the fizes of the fmall particles may be very various; their figures almoft innumerable ; and that if a parcel of matter do but happen to ftick to one body, it may give it a new quality ; and, if it adhere to another, or hit againft fome of its parts, it may conftitute a body of another kind ; or if a parcel of matter be knocked off from another, it may, barely by that, leave it, and become, itfelf, of another nature than before : if, I fay, we confider thefe things, on the one fide ; and, on the other fide, that (to ufe Lucretius's comparifon) all the innumerable multitude of words, which are contained in all the languages of the world, are made of the various combinations of the twenty-four letters of the alphabet ; it will not be hard to conceive, that there may be an incomprehenfible variety of affociations and textures of the minute parts of bodies, and confequently a vaft multitude of portions of matter endued with ftore enough of different qualities, to deferve diftinct appellations, though, for want of heedfulnefs and fit words, men have not yet taken fo much notice of their lefs obvious varieties, as to fort them as they deferve, and give them diftinct and proper names.

" So that, though I would not fay, that any thing can immediately be made of every thing; as a gold ring, of a wedge of gold ; or oil, or fire, of water ; yet fince bodies, having but one common matter, can be differenced but by accidents [i. e. by modes and circumftances not effential to their nature as parts of matter at large], which feem, all of them, to be the effects and confequents of local motion : I fee not, why it fhould be abfurd to think, that (at leaft among inanimate bodies), by the intervention of fome very fmall addition or fubtraction of matter (which yet, in moft cafes, will not be needed), and of an orderly feries of alterations, difpofing, by degrees, the matter to be tranfmuted, almoft of any thing may at length be made any thing.

" So, though water cannot, immediately, be tranfmuted into oil, and much lefs into fire ; yet, if you nourifh certain plants with water alone, as I have done, until they have affimilated a great quantity of water into their own nature, you may, by committing this tranfmuted water (which you may diftinguifh and feparate from that part of the vegetable you firft put in) to diftillation in convenient glaffes, obtain, befides other things, a true oil, and a black

combuftible

2. The furface of that object muft have a certain difpofition, texture, or conftruction, of parts :— 3. Rays of light muft fall towards, and be returned from, that furface :—4. My organs of fight muft (1.) be of fuch a ftructure, and, (2.) be in fo found a ftate, as duly to admit the impreffion naturally refulting from the above complication of circumftances. Who, that confiders all this, can doubt, a moment, whether the idea of colour, with which my mind is affected, on its perception of an object, depend, as abfolutely, on the ftructure and on the ftate of my eyes, as on the fuperficial difpofition and illumination of the object itfelf? Yea, it depends much more on the former, than on the latter. For, as it has lately been well argued, " If all mankind had jaundiced eyes, they muft have been under a neceffity of concluding, that every object was tinged with yellow : and, indeed, according to this new fyftem" [viz. the fyftem which fuppofes that bodies are of the colour they feem to be of], " it would then have been fo ; not in appearance only, but alfo in reality ! *"

Befides ; was it to be granted, that " colour is a real, material thing ;" fuch conceffion would naturally engender a farther miftake, viz. that at leaft thofe feven colours, which are denominated original ones, and which appear fo very different from each other, are in fact fo many different effences. But as this conclufion, though forcibly deducible from the premife, would be fraught with abfurdities neither few nor fmall, we may fairly fufpect the premife itfelf to be untrue.

combuftible coal (and confequently fire); both of which may be fo copious, as to leave no juft caufe to fufpect, that they could be any thing near afforded by any little fpirituous parts, which may be prefumed to have been communicated, by that part of the vegetable that is firft put into the water, to that far greater part of it which was committed to diftillation." Origin of Forms, &c. p. 61—63.

* Dr. Prieftley's Examination of Beattie, &c. p. 143.

An

An objection was lately ftarted in private company, againft the doctrine which maintains the univerfal famenefs of matter, as if, upon this hypothefis, it would follow, that " All bodies and all qualities of bodies, are equally eftimable." Nothing,
however, can be more frivolous than fuch a fuppofition. It might as plaufibly be alledged, that,
" Becaufe all actions, confidered, as actions, are exertions of power ; therefore, all actions are equally
good." Whereas the modes and effects of action
occafion fuch vaft relative differences in actions
themfelves : that a man of common underftanding
and virtue cannot long hefitate, what fpecies of
action to approve. Thus it is, with regard to bodies, and femblances. For,

> " Tho' the fame fun, with all-diffufive rays,
> Blufh in the rofe, and in the diamond blaze ;
> We prize the ftronger effort of his pow'r,
> And juftly fet the gem above the flow'r."

If a philofophic lady vifits a mercer's fhop with a
view to felect the brighteft filk it affords ; the fair
cuftomer will be naturally led to fix her choice on
that, whofe colourings appear, to her, the moft elegant and vivid : though fhe knows that thofe colourings are illufive, and that, in reality, there is no
fuch thing as abfolute colour at all.

In fhort, we are fo conftituted, as to receive much
more delectable idea, from fome femblances, and
from fome combinations of femblances, than from
others. And we, with very good reafon, like or
diflike accordingly. Though, were our organs
contrarily fabricated to what they are ; the fame
objects, which now give us pleafure, would be
fources of pain : and what we now relifh as de-
firable, and admire as beautiful, would ftrike us as
difguftful and deformed.

- How

How often are pleafures and pains generated by imaginary confiderations! And yet thofe pains and pleafures are as real, and fometimes ftill more poignant and exquifite, than if they were juftly founded.

Dr. Dodderidge has fome concife obfervations, on the fecondary qualities of bodies, much to the purpofe of my general argument. " The fame external qualities, in objects, may excite different ideas in different perfons.

" 1. If the organs of fenfation be at all different, the ideas of the fame object muft be proportionably fo, while the fame laws of nature prevail.

" 2. It is probable, there may be fome degree of difference, in the organs of different perfons. For inftance: in the diftance of the retina and chryftaline humour of the eye; in the degree of extenfion in the tympanum of the ear; in the acrimony of the faliva, &c. And the variety, which is obfervable in the faces, the voices, and the bones of men; and almoft through the whole face of nature; would lead us to fufpect, that the fame variety might take place here.

" 3. Thofe things, which are very pleafing to one, are extremely difagreeable to another.

" 4. Thofe things which are, at one time, very agreeable; are, at another, very difagreeable; to the fame perfon: when the organs of his body are indifpofed, or when other difagreeable ideas are affociated with thofe that had once been grateful *."

Thus, as Mr. Boyle remarks, " Some men whofe appetites are gratified by decayed cheefe, think it then not to have degenerated, but to have attained its beft ftate, when, having loft its former colour and fmell and tafte, and, which is more, being in great part turned into thofe infects called mites; it is both, in a philofophical fenfe, corrupted, and, in

---

* Dodderidge's Lectures, p. 15.

the

the eftimation of the generality of men, grown putrid *."

It is well-known, that fome perfons have, literally, fainted, not only at the continued fight of the above-mentioned viand, whether decayed or found; but (which evinces the antipathy to be unaffected) even when the offending fubftance has been totally concealed, from the view of the unfufpecting gueft, by thofe who have purpofely tried the brutal and in-hofpitable experiment.—Others will be convulfed, at the approach of a cat.—And I have heard of a gentleman, who would fwoon, at the prefence of a cucumber properly cut and prepared for the table.

Now, whence is it, that what eminently gratifies the fenfes of one individual, fhall thus have a re-verfe effect on thofe of another? Certainly, not from any difference in the object: for both the fubftance and the attributes of that remain precifely the fame, whether the perceptions, which they occafion in us, be pleafing, or offenfive. Confequently, if one and the fame object operate in fo contrary a manner on the fenfitive organs of various people; the diverfity of effect, where it really obtains, muft be owing to a modal variation in the mechanical ftructure of the fenfitive organs themfelves.

I confider it, therefore, as equally ungenerous and abfurd, when particular averfions, feem they ever fo odd, are haftily blamed and ridiculed. They may be, and very frequently are, conftitutional, and infuperable.

The elegant fex, efpecially, are often favagely cen-fured, on thefe accounts. If a lady turn pale, when it thunders; or ftart from a fpider; or tremble at a frog; or fhriek at the nigh appearance of a moufe; I cannot, in common juftice, laughingly exclaim, with Dean Swift,

* Origin of Forms, &c. p. 59.

" If

" If chance a moufe creep in her fight,
She finely counterfeits a fright :
So fweetly fcreams, if it come near her,
It ravifhes all hearts to hear her."

Such antipathies are not, always, to be claffed under
the article of affectation, nor even of prejudice.
They frequently arife, more particularly in females,
and in very young perfons, from the extreme delicacy of their nervous and organic fyftems.

I fmiled, indeed, on a lady's once faying to me,
I have juft payed a morning vifit to Mrs. G———;
and really thought I fhould have fainted away, on
feeing the cloth laid for dinner, at fo fhocking an
hour as one o'clock. This, I confefs, ftruck me, at
firft, as the language, not of real, but affumed, elegance : and I treated it accordingly; by hoping,
that "in all her future vifits to Mrs. G———, fhe
would previoufly arm herfelf with a fmelling-bottle,
for fear of confequences." I will not, however, be
too peremptory in denying, that the fight of a table-
cloth, difplayed at an hour deemed fo " fhockingly"
unfeafonable, might literally excite fome, though
not an infupportable, degree of painful vibration, in
the nerves of fo refined a perfon.

A few other familiar illuftrations of our main
point fhall clofe the prefent difquifition.

We will imagine a gentleman to be, as we commonly phrafe it, violently in love. That is : the
charms, or affemblage of fenfible qualities, in a particular lady, are exactly adapted to ftrike with rapture a fyftem of fenfes fo fabricated as his ; and, of
courfe, to fall in with his ideas of beauty, merit, and
accomplifhment.—What is the confequence ? He
becomes her captive; and can no more avoid becoming fuch, than an afpin leaf can refift the impulfe of zephyr. Hence, fhe is neceffarily confidered, by him, as an Helen, a Venus, a Panfebia.

" Grace is in all her fteps : heav'n in her eye :
In ev'ry gefture, dignity and love."

And yet this ſelf-ſame lady may appear far leſs at-
tracting; or but barely paſſable ; or, perhaps, in
ſome reſpects, even homely and diſagreeable ; to the
eyes of another man.—Why? Becauſe our ideas depend upon our ſenſes : and our ſenſes depend upon
their own interior conformation, for the particular
caſt and mode of every perception which is impreſſed
upon them from without.   Hence, it is a common
phraſe, concerning a man who has never been in
love, that he has not ſeen the right object.   And
nothing can be more philoſophically true.

A lady; too, may be totally and inextricably captivated.   When this is the caſe, the happy ſwain
ſhines, in her eſtimation, a Narciſſus, an Adonis, a
Phoebus.   Nor are the virtues of his mind diſtanced
by the charms of his perſon.   Other gentlemen may
have their moral excellencies : but he, the incom-
parable he, is

   " More juſt, more wiſe, more learn'd, more ev'ry
       thing."

While, perhaps, a great part of her acquaintances
ſhall unite to wonder, very ſeriouſly, what ſhe could
poſſibly ſee in this imaginary ſanſpareill ; and even
lift up their hands, at her monſtrous indelicacy of
taſte.

Parental affection, likewiſe, affords obvious and
ſtriking proof of the theory for which I have been
pleading.

   " Where yet was ever found a mother,
   Who'd give her booby for another ?
   No child is half ſo fair and wiſe !
   She ſees wit ſparkle in its eyes."

Very probably.   And it is alſo very poſſible, that
ſhe may be the only perſon in the world, who is able
to diſcern any ſuch thing.   An acquaintance, or an
occaſional viſitant, ſo far from agreeing with the en-
raptured parent, would, perhaps, cry out, if politeneſs

nefs did not prohibit, concerning the fweet little dear, who paffes for the " very image: of his papa and mamma."

> " Where are the father's mouth and nofe ?
> And mother's eyes, as black as floes ?
> See here a fhocking, awkward creature,
> That fpeaks the fool in ev'ry feature !"

Different people fee the fame things differently.— And thus, as Mr. Meimoth writes to his friend : " Though we agree in giving the fame names, to certain vifible appearances ; as whitenefs, for inftance, to fnow : yet it is by no means demonftration, that the particular body, which affeéts us with that fenfation, raifes the fame precife idea in any two perfons who fhould happen to contemplate it . together. I have often heard you mention your youngeft daughter, as being the exaét counter part of her mother. Now, fhe does not appear, to me, to refemble her, in any fingle feature. To what can this difagreement in our judgments, be owing ; but to a difference in the ftruéture of our organs of fight.* ?"

What fhall we fay of felf-love ? How many noble and delightful fenfible qualities does a man of this caft really believe himfelf to poffefs ; moft, if not all, of which, are abfolutely invifible to every other being !

What fine fingers I have ! faid a lady, once, in my hearing : how beautiful the joints are turned ! Undoubtedly fhe thought fo. But doétors differ. Not only the articulation of her fingers, but the conftruétion of her own hand, feemed, to me, rather clumfy than elegant. The fame lady (by the way) aétually thought herfelf finlefs. But herein, likewife, I could not help diffenting from her judgment.

---

* Fitz-Ofborne's Letters, Vol. 1. Let. 34.

A vain

A vain man is, generally, ftill vainer, than the vaineft female. Mr. John Wefley, for example, declares himfelf to be " the greateft minifter in the world." I do him the juftice to believe, that, in permitting this declaration to pafs the prefs, his avowed vanity was the honeft trumpeter of his heart. But how few others will fubfcribe to his opinion! There is more learning, in one hair of my head, faid the felf-enamoured Paracelfus, than in all the univerfities together. Who ever queftioned, herein, the fincerity of that pratling empiric? But who does not more than queftion the reality of thofe great qualities, on which he fo extravagantly and fo ridiculoufly valued himfelf?—When, a bookfeller, defirous to prefix an engraving of Julius Scaliger to one of that critic's publications, requefted him to fit for a likenefs; Julius modeftly anfwered, If the artift can collect the feveral graces of Maffiniffa, of Xenophon, and of Plato, he may then be able to give the world fome faint idea of my perfon. If Scaliger was in love with his own outward man, Dr. Richard Bentley was no lefs fo with his own intellectual improvements. Mr. Waffe (faid the doctor, very gravely) will be the greateft fcholar in England, when I am dead.—Peter Aretin had a medal ftruck, at his own expence, exhibiting his own profile; encircled with this humble infcription: *il divino Aretino*, i. e. the divine Aretin*. When I reflect on fuch inftances of felf-idolatry, as thefe, they remind me of Congreve's obfervation:

" If happinefs in † felf-content is plac'd,
The wife are wretched, and fools only bleft."

We

---

* In fetting Mr. Wefley at the head of thefe felf-admiring gentlemen, I by no means intend to infinuate, that he ftands on a level with the loweft of them, in any one article; that of vanity and conceit, alone, excepted. Miftake me not, therefore, as though I meant to put him, abfolutely, into the company of fuch men as Paracelfus, Scaliger, Bentley, and Aretin.

† True happinefs, however, is not placed in " felf-content:" but arifes from a comfortable apprehenfion of our reconciliation to God

We have taken a furvey of love, in more of its terminations than one. Let us, for a moment, advert to its oppofite.

In revolving the defcription, which the celebrated Dr. John Ponét, bifhop of Winchefter, has given us of his Popifh predeceffor in that fee, I have been prone to furmife, that the latter might really appear as hideoufly frightful, in the eyes of the former, as the following written picture reprefents him to have done. " This doctor," fays bifhop Ponet, fpeaking of Stephen Gardiner, " has a fwart colour, hanging look, frowning brows, eyes, an inch within his head ; a nofe, hooked like a buzzard ; noftrils like an horfe; ever fnuffing into the wind ; a fparrow mouth, great paws, like the devil's. Talons on his feet, like a gripe [i. e. like a gryphon], two inches longer than natural toes ; and fo tied to with finews, that he cannot abide to be touched, nor fcarce fuffer them to touch the ftones. And nature, having thus fhaped the form of an old monfter, gave him a vengeable wit, which, at Cambridge, by labour and diligence, he made a great deal worfe: and brought up many in that faculty*." Such was bifhop Gardiner, according to bifhop Ponet's view of him. Notwithftanding which, this identical Gardiner might feem, in his own eyes, and in the eyes of queen Mary and others of his friends, a portly, perfonable prelate.

To be ferious. Let me, by way of needful and fincere apology, for a difquifition which has extended to an unexpected length, obferve ; that, in fifting the queftion, it was neceffary to recur to firft principles, and to furvey the argument in various points of view. Let me, moreover, add ; that, in

---

God by the blood and righteoufnefs of his fon. Hence, a good man fhall be fatisfied [not with, but] from himfelf: Prov. xiv. 14. viz. from within : or from the inward teftimony of the Holy Spirit, witneffing to his confcience that he is a child of God. Rom. viii. 16.

* Biogr. Dict. vol. v. p. 307.———Article, Gardiner.

all

all I have delivered on the fubject, I do but exprefs
my own fenfe of it, without the leaft aim of dictàt-
ing to others : or of prefumptuoufly feeking to ob-
trude my philofophic (any more than my religious)
creed, on fuch perfons as may honour thefe pages
with perufal.

Upon the whole, I conclude, with Mr. Locke* ;
that " The infinitely wife Contriver of us, and of all
things about us, has fitted our fenfes, faculties, and
organs, to the conveniences of life, and to the bufinefs we have to do. Such a knowledge as this,
which is fuited to our prefent condition, we want
not faculties to attain. But, were our fenfes altered,
and made much quicker and acuter, the appearances
and outward fcheme of things would have quite
another face to us : and, I am apt to think, would
be inconfiftent with our being, or at leaft well-being,
in this part of the univerfe which we inhabit."

* Effay on Und. book ii. chap. 23.

· COLLECTION OF LETTERS.

THE following letters were written by the author without the leaft view to publication, but foon after 'his deceafe, by the advice of friends, fome of them were deemed proper to be printed. It fhould have been notified at the time, that they were fudden thoughts committed to paper without correction. For in a book that the rough draught of the letters were inferted, a memorandum was made, *verbatim*, as follows :

" In looking among fome old papers, I met with the copies of a few letters, which I had formerly written, and which I defigned to enter, either in this or fome other plain-paper book, by way of preferving them, for my own future fatisfaction, if Providence fhould pleafe to.preferve my life."

" The finding of thofe, fuggefted to me the hint of taking foul copies of fuch letters as are any way interefting. I may, hereafter, write to particular friends, before I draw them out fair for the poft. If I live, they may be of ufe to myfelf; if not, they can do me no hurt."

Broad Hembury,   A. T.
   Oct. 1, 1772.

The chief value of this collection, lies in the exhibition it gives of the diftinguifhed merit, and pious occupation that followed the writer of them in his private correfpondence. They are interfperfed with feveral obfervations on religion and human life, and fhew a heart penetrated with truth, endeavouring to perfuade others, accompanied with fprightlinefs of wit, folidity of judgment, extent of knowledge, and elegance of tafte, joined with all the undefineable eafe, and familiarity of the moft unreferved converfation, which takes off that infipidnefs of a laboured ftiffnefs that often attends the epiftolary intercourfe of many very fenfible perfons.   ' EDITOR.

LETTER I.

Mr. E.

EVER DEAR SIR,

WILL my honoured friend forgive me, if, from a kind impatience to be informed of his welfare, I take the liberty to enquire how he does? Though writing letters is one of the things, which, in general, I am leaft fond of, yet I cannot forbear, dear fir, to prefent you and Mrs. ——, with my refpects, and to wifh you the joys of believing, and the comforts of the holy fpirit. I have been returned into Devonfhire about a fortnight: Mr. —— is at London, attending the fervice of parliament; fo that I cannot, very readily, get my letter franked. I am glad, notwithftanding, that he is abfent, as he was one of the two hundred and fix members, who, this day fe'nnight, carried the vote for the reduction of the land-tax, in oppofition (as he writes me word) to one hundred and eighty-eight, who were for keeping it up to four fhillings. But, to come to matters of infinitely greater importance, I hope, fir, you are enabled to truft your foul to Chrift, and to caft your care on God. Satan, no doubt, will be ever ready to bring in the indictment, and confcience cannot help pleading guilty to a great part of the charge: but remember, that your judge is, at the very fame time, your advocate and Saviour. He is a lover of your foul, and was the propitiation for your fins; they cannot be too numerous, nor too heinous, for mercy like his to pardon, nor for merit like his to cover. Only flee to him for refuge, fly to the hiding place of his righteoufnefs, death and interceffion;

and

and then, the enemy can have no final advantage
over you, nor the fon of wickednefs approach to
hurt you, in your everlafting intereft. Affault
you he may, in your way to the kingdom of God;
overcome you he cannot, if you look, or defire
to look, to Jefus for fafety; lie at his bleffed
feet for protection; lay hold on his victorious
crofs for falvation; and then you fhall find him gracious to relieve, mighty to deliver, and faithful to
uphold. Caft anchor on his love, and be happy,
rely on his omnipotence, and be fafe. He knows
that you are very near my heart, that not a day
paffes, in which I do not befeech him on your behalf; may his holy fpirit diffufe his heavenly peace
throughout your foul; make you be joyful with his
holy vifitations; and while he comforts you from on
high, fanctify you to the uttermoft! In life, in
death, in eternity, may he be your light, your
ftrength, and your exceeding great reward! I know
that your health is fo bad, you cannot read much,
but you can pray; you can fend up your defires, as
incenfe, to the throne of God, almoft every moment. As you fit, as you walk, as you take an
airing, you may cultivate an intimacy with heaven;
you may carry on a correfpondence with God, you
may hold filent intercourfe with the fpirit of grace.
Every figh, if directed to him, is a prayer; every
tear fhed for fin, is a fort of oblation, acceptable to
him in Chrift, and fhall be noted in his book. Yet,
not the fighs we breathe, nor the tears we pour, are
our juftifying merit; but the figh, the tears, the
obedience, the death, of his co-eternal Son: his are
the propitiations; our's are the memorial, and the
proof of the work of grace, which his fpirit begins in
the foul. Refign yourfelf to his will, in every difpenfation; lie paffive in his hand, ftir not from his
footftool, take all your fpiritual diftreffes, as com-
miffioned from him. The cup, the medicinal cup,
is of his mixing; the chaftifement is the chaftifement of a father, who loves while he ftrikes, and
whofe

whofe feeming wrath is real mercy. May his everlafting arms be fpread beneath you; may his grace
(as I doubt not it will) be fufficient for you; may
his prefence be

with you, with yours, and with your
affectionate fervant in him,

Auguftus Toplady.

P. S. From my earneft defire, for to have you
manage every one of your affairs in fuch a way as
may moft conduce to the peace of your own mind,
and the welfare of your family; I cannot help requefting leave to fuggeft an hint, which, was my regard for you lefs than it is, I fhould certainly fupprefs: it is, my dear fir, in relation to Mrs. ———,
and your two youngeft fons: with refpect to Mrs.
———, God forbid that you fhould leave her dependent, either for habitation, or for maintenance,
on your children, or on any body elfe. If you are
not quite clear as to thefe two points, do let me
befeech you, to revife your papers; and if there is
any deficiency in either of thefe refpects, fet it
right, while Providence, by prolonging your life,
continues it, in your power. Indeed, and indeed,
you will not difcharge your duty without it; nor
can you expect to depart in peace, if you omit it.
With regard to your two youngeft fons, let me en-
treat you to leave them equally; they have both
the fame right to your affection, and to what you
may defign to give. Their aunt's kind intentions,
ought to make no difference as to this point: it is
incumbent on you, my dear fir, to do your duty;
and by that means, Mrs. ———, will be left (as fhe
ought to be) at full liberty to beftow her favours on
the moft deferving. Weigh what I have faid, and
may the Lord God give you a right judgement in
all things. It is not from motives of impertinence,
that I have prefumed to mention thefe particulars,
but from the fincere affections I have for you, and
your's.

your's. Adieu, my dear friend, and forgive me, if my regard has carried me too far. My best respects, when you write next to Bath, and my kind compliments to the young gentlemen. Do not neglect to take the air every day. Once more, adieu.

LETTER II.

To Mr. Morris,

Broad-Hembury, near Honiton, Devonsh. Sept. 2, 1768.

IT is, now, above eight years, since I saw, or heard from, my ever dear Mr. Morris. The Lord knows, you are near my heart, and are often present to my thoughts. God grant that this letter may find my valued friend as well in body, and as lively in soul, as when I saw him last!

I have been in orders, between six and seven years; and now write to you from my living. The spirit of God has kept me stedfast in his glorious truths, and given me much joy and peace in believing. I trust, too, that my labours, as a minister, have been owned from above, to the calling in of some chosen vessels, and to the consolation of others who were, before, quickened from their death in trespasses and sins: which I mention to the praise of the glory of his grace, who vouchsafes to make use of the meanest, the feeblest, and the unworthiest instruments, to accomplish his designs of love towards those he delights to save.—Whilst I am writing, the fire kindles in my soul: may it reach your heart, when this letter reaches your hands. I am, at present, high on the mount of divine love, and can sing with the Church, Isa. lxi. 10. "I will greatly rejoice in the Lord," &c.—How is it with you? Are you as

zea ous for Chrift, and for fouls, as when God made
you the means of my converfion twelve years ago ?
O that the Lord would rend the heavens, and come
down, and fet you all in a flame for himfelf! Permit your fpiritual Son to remind you of the fweet,
the memorable days and months that are paft.   Indeed, and indeed, I love you tenderly, in the bowels
of Jefus Chrift.   How has my heart burnt within
me, and how have my tears flowed, like water from
the fmitten rock, when I have heard you preach the
unfearchable riches of his grace, blood, and righteoufnefs! The word came with power, and with the
Holy Ghoft fent down from heaven.   And is it true,
can it be poffible, that you fhould ceafe from your
work of calling finners to repentance ? Do you withdraw your hand from the gofpel-plough, after God.
has made it profper fo long in your hands? I am
told fo; but I cannot believe it.   O man of God,
ftir up the gift that is in thee : let it not ruft and
moulder, by lying ufelefs.   The Lord hath often
fpoke to me by your mouth: Oh, that he would
now fpeak to you by my pen! Do, at my requeft,
meet the dear people of C and who knows, but there
may, once more, be fhowers of blefiing? Blow the
trumpet in Zion, as heretofore.   While life and
health and ftrength continue, let your feet ftand upon the mountains, and the law of gofpel-kindnefs
dwell upon your tongue, to the very laft : yea, let your
lips feed many.—Adieu.   I fcarce know how to
leave off, when I write to any of my brethren in the
faith.   If even the poor, feeble, mortal faints below, love one another fo well: no wonder that the
love of an infinite God to his own dear elect, fhould
be from everlafting to everlafting.—Electing, juftifying, regenerating, fanctifying, and perfevering
grace, have been, and are, the fubjects of my miniftry : and, I hope, will be, to my lateft breath.   If
a meffenger of Chrift is under the lively, experimental influence of thefe glorious truths; the word

of

of his mafter will be as fire in his bones: yea, he
will be in pangs, as it were, like a woman in travail,
until Chrift is formed in the hearts of them that
hear.   God Almighty pour out fuch a fpirit of fer-
vency on my dear Mr. Morris, and on his

ever affectionate friend,

Auguftus Toplady.

LETTER III.

To Mr. PHILIPS,

Broad-Hembury, Sept. 6, 1768.

SIR,

I Believe I fhall go to town by way of Salifbury; in
which cafe, I will certainly do myfelf the pleafure
of calling on you.   I wifh I could fulfil your requeft in the other particular, concerning which you
write: but the times will not allow it.   Every one,
that knows me, knows that I have the greateft and
moft cordial regard for the evangelical diffenters.   I
am exactly the fame, in that refpect, as when you
knew me firft: and moft heartily wifh that the wall
of partition was fo far pulled down, as to admit all
gofpel minifters to occupy each others' pulpits, without diftinction of party and denomination.   But, as
this is an happinefs we cannot expect to fee; I am
under a neceffity of foregoing the fatisfaction it would
give me to hold forth the word of life to thofe Chriftians who are beyond the pale of the eftablifhment:
except (which, in the courfe of my miniftry, many
hundreds have done) any of them are fo condefcending as to attend on me, who, they know, am
tied up from waiting on them.—I am well acquainted with Mr. Elliot; and an excellent man he is: but
he has fet himfelf more at liberty, than I can be, by

abfolutely

absolutely renouncing all connection with the Church of England; which, I freely own, conscience will not suffer me to do: and I am clear, moreover, that it would be going out of bounds, and over-leaping those limits which Providence hath prescribed me, was I to attempt it.

Pray make my affectionate compliments accept-able to your people, and let them know, that it is neither bigotry, want of respect, nor want of love, that hinders me from complying with the re-quest they have done me the favour to make. Law-ful, in itself, I am convinced, it would be: but, all things confidered, far from expedient.—As mat-ters at present stand, it is a great blessing, never to be sufficiently valued and acknowledged, that there are some faithful ministers of every Protestant deno-mination among us: so that no denomination, un-less particularly circumstanced, need go beyond their own tents, in order to gather the gospel manna: by which wise and gracious dispensation of things, God's elect, of every name, are fed and nourished up to life eternal, notwithstanding the nominal distinc-tions, which bigotry, prejudice, and human laws, have fixed.—I am concerned to hear of Mr. H——'s defection. If he was ever of us in reality, God will, in due time, bring him to us again. A truly gra-cious man, like a thorough good watch, may deviate, and point wrong, for a season; but, like the machine just mentioned, will, after a time, come round, and point right as before. In the mean while, let such instances teach us to be jealous over our own cor-rupt hearts; make us dependent, sensibly and in-creasingly dependent, on the power and faithfulness of the Holy Ghost: stir us up to prayer, that we may be kept from being carried away with the error of the wicked; and put a song of thanksgiving into our mouths, to that God, whose free, invincible grace hath enabled us to stand, when others (in appear-ance, stronger than we) have fallen, and become as

water

water that runneth apace.—You enquire about my ufefulnefs, acceptance, and number of hearers. My parifh is very large, and confiderably populous. My Church, I fuppofe, will hold fix hundred at leaft. Strangers, I apprehend, ufually make one third of my auditory : and the word has been fignally bleft to fome, both in the parifh and out of it. I have the greateft reafon to believe, that, within the courfe of the laft twelvemonth, God has owned my miniftry more than ever. May my Mafter's feet go on to found behind me; and may the laft works be, continually, more and greater than the preceding!

Auguftus Toplady.

LETTER IV.

To Mr. RUTTER,

Broad-Hembury, October 3, 1768.

REV. and WORTHY SIR,

SLENDER as our acquaintance is, I yet cannot forbear requefting leave to exprefs the real concern I feel, on being informed of the afflictive vifitation you lately experienced : if that may be termed afflictive, which is the refult of God's unerring providence, who does all things well. May he vouchfafe to fanctify this, and every fubfequent difpenfation which may yet befal you! May the light of his gracious countenance, the comforts of his fpirit, and the chearing intimations of his favour, be your ftrength, and your portion, when heart and flefh fail! You have, I truft, a merciful and faithful high-prieft above, who bears you on his heart, and is touched with the feeling of your infirmities. To him, let us look; on him, let the anchor of our reliance

liance be caſt. The merit of his blood and righteouſneſs, like the waving of Elijah's mantle, ſhall
ſmite the waters of death; ſo that the ſtream ſhall
part hither and thither, and open a way for his redeemed to paſs over on dry ground. Doubt not,
dear ſir, but he will ſend forth his light and his
truth, to lead you to his holy hill and to his dwell-
ing-place, that land of reſt, and that city of habitation, where the inhabitants ſhall no more ſay,
I am ſick. I beg an intereſt in your prayers, and
remain, with much reſpect and eſteem, Rev. Sir,
your affectionate brother,

and moſt humble ſervant,

Auguſtus Toplady.

L E T T E R V.

To Mr. Bottomley,

New-Way, Weſtminſter, Dec. 3, 1768.

Worthy Sir,

I HAVE read, attentively, the paper you condeſcended to put into my hands; and which I
return, becauſe I apprehend you meant I ſhould
only peruſe it. I not only approve, but admire, the
modeſty, with which you write. I pray God, I
may be enabled, more and more, to adopt the ſame
truly Chriſtian ſpirit. And I verily hope and believe, that that moſt gracious Being, who has led you
thus far, will go on to tranſlate you farther and farther into the light and liberty of his children.—As
I once took occaſion to tell you, it is much the ſame
with miſtakes in matters of judgment, as it was with
the two diſciples in the dungeon of Philippi: firſt,
the priſon ſhakes; and, next, the doors fly open. I

am

am heartily glad, that you are shaken, as to the system you have long embraced; and trust, that it is prelusive to your deliverance from it.—I do not trouble you with my thoughts on the substance of your paper: though I must own, there is not, in the whole of it, any single exception against the doctrine of predestination, which will not admit of a very easy solution. But I omit attempting this, as the person, to whom that letter was particularly addressed, is abundantly more capable, than myself, of obviating your doubts.—Suffer me, dear sir, to repeat, with all humility, the request I made to you some time ago. Be not hasty, in determining your judgment on this most important point. View the question on all sides. Chiefly, keep your eye fixed on the Scriptures; and derive, by humble, earnest, waiting prayer, all your light and knowledge from thence. One thing I am very clear in; that, if you reduce your ideas to the standard of Scripture, and make this the model of those; suffering the unerring word of revelation to have the casting vote, and turning your mind into the gospel mould; you must and will, eventually, throw the idol of Arminianism, in all its branches, to the moles and to the batts; you will no longer dwell with Mesech, nor have your habitation among the tents of Kedar. Having tasted the good old wine of distinguishing grace, you will no longer have any relish for the new scheme of grace without a plan, and of a random-salvation: for you will both know and acknowledge, that the old is better. Hoping to see that happy time, I remain, with great esteem, dear sir,

your affectionate brother in Christ,

Augustus Toplady.

LETTER VI.

Mr. N——.

Broad-Hembury, Oct. 5, 1772.

DEAR SIR,

YOU need not trouble yourfelf to fend me the pamphlet you mention, entitled, A Philofophical Survey of Nature. It is already in my poffeffion. 1 remember to have read it, feveral years ago, when it firft came to my hands: and, fince my receipt of your laft favour, I have given it a frefh perufal. The author is, undoubtedly, a profeffed materialift. His fyftem therefore is atheiftical, to all intents and purpofes. He is, I fhould imagine, a perfon of too much fenfe, to be an abfolute atheift himfelf: but he feems to wifh he could. The two grand principles, which enter into the very bafis of his fcheme, viz. That matter may have exifted from all eternity; and that matter may, by organization, be refined into intelligence : are pofitions, which, if admitted, would lay the axe to the very root of all exiftence purely fpiritual; and, confequently, render the being of God impoffible.

To fuch horrid lengths of abfurdity and impiety, are men, even thofe of the brighteft talents, liable; when they unhappily fhut their eyes againft that written revelation, which fo kindly holds the lamp to benighted reafon. One would almoft think, that writers of this caft are purpofely raifed up by Providence, to fhew mankind the neceffity of fuperior illumination; and to demonftrate the utter infufficiency of mere reafon, genius and philofophy, to guide us either to happinefs or truth. *

This is the only principle, on which I can account for the glaring inconfiftencies, which never fail to difgrace the reafonings of infidels. The very author, now under confideration, though he at-

tenuates

tenuates his theory to a very nice and plaufible texture, is yet guilty of departing from an axiom which
he profeffes heartily to adopt, and from which more
than a few of his own deductions are fpun.   The
axiom is, that every effect muft refult from fome
prior, producing caufe.   If fo (and, furely, if this
be not true, we have no evidence of any thing), how
is it poffible for matter to be eternal?   Matter muft
be either the firft caufe, or an effect.   Should the
ingenious writer affirm matter to be the firft caufe:
he would only beg the queftion, by taking for granted
what (I am bold to fay) he will never be able to
prove: and, on a point of this confequence, wherein
both religion and philofophy are fo effentially concerned, the bare opinion and unfupported affertion
even of this able fpeculator will never carry the force
of demonftration.—On the other hand, if matter, in
all its diverfity of modes, cannot be proved to be the
firft caufe (i. e. to have caufed its own exiftence);
unprejudiced reafon will immediately conclude, that
matter muft, originally, have been the effect of a
fuperior intelligent power: which intelligent power
could be no other than that adorable agent whom
we call God.

If the whole fyftem of material nature be (as this
author himfelf acknowledges) a regular fucceffion
of caufes and effects; will it not follow, that the eternity of matter is a matter of abfolute impoffibility?
Let us inftance in an horfe.   Who was Lightfoot's
father? Turk.—Who was father to Turk? Sweepftakes.—Who got Sweepftakes? Hazel.   Were we
capable of tracing back the pedigree of Lightfoot to
its original fource, we fhould not ftop until we
came to the very firft horfe that ever exifted.   Being
arrived fo high as that, another queftion would yet
remain: how came this firft horfe to exift at all?
Certainly, by the will and power of fome fuperior
being.

L 2

Would

Would not reafon laugh at the man who fhould affirm, that there never was a firft horfe, but that horfes exifted eternally?

There muft, therefore, in all our afcending enquiries, be fome *ultimatum*, fome given point, at which to ftop. This given point, this firft caufe, is God.—The fame analyfis, which has been applied to Lightfoot, will hold equally true, when applied to any material thing whatever. All muft terminate fomewhere : for there is "no effect without a caufe." Confequently, matter is not eternal.

" But may not matter be fo organized and refined, as to rife into what we call intelligence?" The plain Englifh of this queftion is, " May not matter, (fuch as a cabbage, a marble ftatue, a candle, or a cheft), be able to hear, fee, feel, tafte, fmell, reafon, fpeak, read, write, and walk ?" If any individual of the human fpecies can coolly and in earneft fuppofe this; let his next of kin (if the infane man's poffeffions will recompence the trouble) fue for a ftatute of lunacy, and tranfmit him to his proper apartment in Moorfields.

I confefs myfelf afhamed to encounter fuch a pofition, with any degree of ferioufnefs. Suffer me, however, to afk : Is there no effential, but only a modal difference, between the writer of the Philofophical Survey of Nature, and the pen with which he committed his ideas to writing?

A correfpondent, lefs polite than yourfelf, would tell me, perhaps, that, inftead of enquiring into the capacities of our author's pen, it is time I fhould lay down my own. I cannot, however, do this, without firft repeating the affection and refpect with which I am, yours, &c.

Auguftus Toplady.

LETTER VII.

To B. S. Esq.

Broad-Hembury, Nov. 9, 1772.

SIR,

ACQUAINTED as you are with the leading objects of my thoughts, you still would not easily conjecture on what speculation they lately turned.—I have been comparing my own situation (not as some philosophers advise, with persons of inferior rank to myself; but) with that of those whom the world calls great. Every great man I know, has passed before me in a kind of intellectual review: and the result is, that, if it were even in my power, I would not make an exchange of condition with any one of the twenty-seven.

To be happy, we must be virtuous: and, in order to our becoming truly virtuous, we must experience the grace of God which bringeth salvation.

Augustus Toplady.

LETTER VIII.

AMBROSE SERLE, ESQ.

Broad-Hembury, Nov. 20, 1772,

SIR,

CONTRARY to my wishes, and by a sort of fatality, for which I find myself unable to account, I am, usually, least regular, in writing to those, whom I most regard. Though incapable of forgetting them, experience proves that I am but

L 3   too

too capable of feeming to neglect them : and none has more reafon to be difpleafed with me, on this account, than my dear, my very dear friend, to whom I am now, after a long interval of filence, addreffing myfelf at laft.

How many defects have I, for your candour to excufe! Prove yourfelf candid indeed, by excufing them all. Thus will you lay me under ftill deeper obligation, and fhame me, by your condefcenfion, into a more punctual acknowledgement of your favours. —Your favours, dear fir, eminently deferve the name. They have followed me, at home, and abroad, ever fince I faw you : and if I had, by a deadnefs to all gratitude, been even difpofed to forget you, they would have conftantly reminded me of you, whether I would or not. In juftice, however, to myfelf, as well as to you, I muft repeat my long intermitted affurances, that the perfon does not breathe, whom I love and refpect more than yourfelf. If I do not tell you fo, as often as I ought ; impute the omiffion to any caufe, except the want of thofe two.

The goodnefs of God ftill continues to furround me on every fide. Oh, that my thankfulnefs, and improvements in grace, bore fome little proportion to his exuberance of mercies! But in vain do I look within myfelf, for that excellence, which I fhall never find there, until death is fwallowed up in victory. God enable me, in the mean while, to feel my own nothingnefs, more and more ; and to truft in that great fulfiller of all righteoufnefs, who

" Toil'd for our eafe, and, for our fafety, bled."

To thofe who believe, he is τιμη, precioufnefs, in the abftract. And the more we fee of his precioufnefs, the more humbling views we have of our own vilenefs. Indeed, felf-renunciation is the grand, central point of the fpiritual life. It is the *ratio formalis*, the very effence, of true religion. Oh, for a larger meafure of it! We are then happieft, and fafeft,

when

when we lie loweft, and feel that Chrift and grace are all in all.

But I am, unawares, almoft preaching, to one, at whofe feet I wifh to fit. May you take the beft revenge, and preach largely to me, in return. The longer your fermon, the better I fhall like it: like him, who thought the longeft of Demofthenes's orations, the beft. I greatly defire to hear from you : and hope, you are too forgiving, to follow the bad example of delay, which I have fet you.

Commend myfelf to the continuance of your affection, I need not. Commend myfelf to your prayers, I ought, and humbly do. Every bleffing be with you. Above all, the beft of bleffings, the peace and love of God in Chrift.

Auguftus Toplady.

L E T T E R IX.

To Mrs. G ———.

Broad-Hembury, Nov. 20, 1772.

WILL good Mrs. G. permit the moft unworthy, but not the leaft fincere, of her well-wifhers, to enquire after her health; and, at a confiderable diftance of place, and after a long interval of time, to repeat his thanks for her many inftances of politenefs and condefcenfion ?

Above all, Madam, how is it with your foul ? What are your views of God, and Chrift, and heaven ? Lively, I truft, and full of glory. Yet, if our views are dim and languid, ftill he abideth faithful, and cannot deny himfelf. Not upon our frames, but upon the adorable giver of them, is all our fafety built. If we cannot follow him in the light, God help us to follow him in the dark : and if we cannot

follow

follow him fo, to fall down at his feet, and fink into nothing, under the feelings of our own vilenefs. They, who are enabled thus to fall, fhall be raifed in due time.

I know not why, but I could no longer forbear writing to you. May the fpirit of the living God write his confolations on your heart, and caufe your triumphs in Chrift to abound more and more. Impute this liberty to refpeet and efteem: and believe me to be, with a great fhare of both, Madam,

your obliged and obedient fervant,

Auguftus Toplady.

LETTER X.

To Mr. SAMUEL NAYLOR,

[Extract.]   *Broad-Hembury, Nov.* 27, 1772.

I AM informed, that inveterate troubler in Ifrael, Mr. J. W——, has lately publifhed a fourth fquib againft Mr. Hill, I fhould be glad to fee it. What a mercy it is, that the enemies of the gofpel, amidft all their plenitude of malice, have little fkill, and lefs power! Mr. W——, confidered as a reafoner, is one of the moft contemptible writers, that ever fet pen to paper. O, that he, in whofe hand the hearts of all men are, may make even this oppofer of grace a monument of its almighty power to fave! God is witnefs, how earneftly I wifh it may confift with the divine will, to touch the heart and open the eyes of that unhappy man. I hold it as much my duty, to pray for his converfion, as to expofe the futility of his railings againft the truths of the gofpel.

Auguftus Toplady.

LETTER

LETTER XI.

To Mr. B. E———.

[Extract.]　　　　　*Broad-Hembury, Dec.* 4, 1772.

I AGREE with you, that the expreſſion [viz. That one drop of Chriſt's blood would have ſuf-ficed to the redemption of ſinners] has been uſed by ſome very pious and well-meaning perſons. Yet, I can by no means look upon the idea itſelf as true, or on the expreſſion as warrantable. If an individual drop had been ſufficient, we might indeed well aſk, Why all this waſte of ſufferings and of love? The overplus was, according to this ſuppoſition, abſolute-ly ſhed in vain. But I cannot bring myſelf to be-lieve, that any part of Chriſt's moſt precious humi-liation was ſuperfluous and unneceſſary. His in-effable dignity as God, and his abſolute innocence as man, forbid me to imagine, that the Father would inflict a ſingle grain of puniſhment, on his co-equal and immaculate Son, beyond what was abſolutely requiſite to the plenary payment of our infinite debt. If it be a rule even in the operations of nature, *fruſtra fit per plura, quod fieri poteſt per pauciora*; much more ſtrongly will it hold, in the preſent argument. What idea ſhould we have of that man's wiſdom, who ſhould laviſh a million of guineas, to procure what a ſhilling might purchaſe?

As to the ſecond queſtion, "Whether ſinners might not have been ſaved in ſome other way, than by the incarnation, righteouſneſs, and death of Chriſt?" I make no ſcruple to give it as my judg-ment, that there was no other poſſible way of ſalva-tion for the loſt ſons of Adam. If there had, Infi-nite Wiſdom and Goodneſs would certainly have fixed upon it, in preference to the ſorrows and agonies, the wounds and death, of him who had done no ſin, neither was guile found in his mouth. His own

prayer,

prayer, If it be poffible, let this cup (the cup of pain and death) pafs from me; would moft infallibly have been granted (for the Father heareth him always,) and Chrift could no more pray, than he could bleed, in vain, if any thing fhort of the oblation of himfelf could have obtained eternal redemption for the people of his love.—Ought not Chrift to have fuffered thefe things? Ουχι ταυτα ιδι παθειν; was there not a muft be, a neceffity for it? Yes: there was. And, upon any other hypothefis, I fee not how it could pleafe the Father to bruife the finlefs Meffiah and and put him to grief; without forfeiting every claim to juftice, wifdom, and goodnefs.

Neither is this, "fettering and limiting the omnipotence of God." It is a received maxim in metaphyfics, and no maxim can be more juft and reafonable, that an effential contradiction is no object of power. Now, the pardon of fin, without an adequate expiation; the juftification of finners, without a perfect righteoufnefs; and, in a word, the falvation of the guilty, without a complete redemption; would have effentially contradicted every attribute of God, and every declaration of his will. It is, therefore, putting no more limitation on the divine power, to believe that fallen men could not poffibly be reftored, but by the intervention of Chrift's obedience, atonement, and interceffion; than to believe, that God cannot poffibly ceafe to be wife and holy, juft and true. Infinite exemption from all poffible imperfection, is a proof, not of defective power, but of fuch inconceivable greatnefs, as more than dazzles the keeneft view of man, and utterly abfo;bs the moft extended comprehenfion of all created intellect.

I feel the overwhelming glory of the fubject, too forcibly to proceed.—May the adorable, the ever bleffed God, who only hath independent immortality, dwelling in the light which no man, in the prefent ftate of unfpiritualized nature, can approach unto;

may

may he, my dear fir, fhine into our hearts, and infpire us with " wonder, love, and praife!" Soon
will mortality be fwallowed up of life: and then,
with what 'holy contempt fhall we look back, and
look down, on the littlenefs, the comparative nothingnefs, of our puny reafonings when below! An
angel of light is not more fuperior, in knowledge,
dignity, and blifs, to an infant in the cradle; than
the fouls of the elect, when death tranfmits them
to the throne of God, differ from what they are
while plunged, I had almoft faid, while buried, in
the living fepulchre of a mortal body.

> Minors of yefterday we are;
> Nor into manhood rife,
> 'Till death pronounces us of age,
> And crowns us for the fkies.

Auguftus Toplady.

LETTER XII.

To RICHARD HILL, Efq.

[Extract.]   *Broad-Hembury, Dec.* 11, 1772.

THE farther my thread of life is extended, the
more clearly I fee, and the more deeply I feel,
the infinite importance of thofe ineftimable doctrines, of which God has made you fo able an affertor. Go on, fir, in the ftrength of him, who
hath placed you foremoft in this bleffed warfare;
and doubt not, that he will enable you to be more
than conqueror, through his love. Certainly, this
is not a time, for any, who have his caufe at heart,
to hold their peace. Fond as, I fuppofe, moft men
naturally are, of eafe and quiet; there is, ftill, a
bleffing, incomparably fuperior: even the honeft
and

and indefatigable avowal of thofe truths, which lie at the foundation of all that can render us happy in time and eternity; truths, in which, the glory of God, the confolation of his faints, and the interefts of holinefs, are fo eminently and effentially involved. I pray God, that you may never (as Dr. Young expreffes it) "unbuckle your armour, until you put on your fhrowd."

I have never feen Mr. W———'s Remarks on the *Farrago*, nor Mr. F———'s *Logica Genevenfis*. But, if I may conjecture of thofe, by what I have already feen in time paft, you have abundantly more, than even the goodnefs of your caufe, in your favour. May your fmooth ftones of the brook, flung by the hand of faith, continue to pierce thofe foreheads of brafs, which oppofe themfelves to the living God.

I admire and blefs his providence, which has put you on entering the lifts, not only againft the declared adverfaries of the gofpel, but alfo againft its pretended friends: who, under the mafk of fpirituality, affect to promote the religion of Jefus; while, in very deed, they are labouring to cut it up by the roots. Two or three years ago, you feemed to think, that I was rather exceffive, in forming fuch a judgmen of them. Themfelves have, fince, given you ample reafon to be of my mind.

May the Holy Spirit keep you lively, and humble, and richly comfortable in your own foul; while you wield the fpiritual fword, which, as matters now ftand, you cannot fheath without fin. And let me prefume to drop an hint, which, by the way, I need to have impreffed on myfelf; namely, confult not your own eafe, at the expence of God's caufe. Be not weary of, and God will keep you from being weary, in well-doing. Forgive my freedom, and know, that, if I had not the higheft opinion of your candour, I fhould not exprefs my wifh with fo little ceremony. Dr. Dodderidge was ftrengthened and
comforted,

comforted, at a time when he was greatly ſtraight-
ened in ſoul, by only hearing (as he was riding
through a country village) a child reading, at a
door, to his ſchool-miſtreſs, thoſe words, Thy
ſhoes ſhall be iron and braſs, and, as is thy day, ſo
ſhall thy ſtrength be. May this haſty ſcribble,
though coming from me, who am, in all things, a
child, except in years, be condeſcendingly accepted:
and may my utmoſt prayers and expectations, concerning you, be anſwered.—Believe me to be,

Ever your's, in him who died for us and roſe
again,   *Auguſtus Toplady.*

L E T T E R . XIII.

To Mrs. BACON,

Broad-Hembury, Dec. 11, 1772.

I HOPE I ſtand too fair in dear Mrs. B's opinion,
to be ſuſpected of levity in friendſhip, only becauſe I do not trouble her with my reſpects ſo often
as I ought and wiſh. However appearances may be
againſt me, realities are not. I ſhall always remember you, madam, with high eſteem: and conſider
myſelf more than a little intereſted, in whatever refers to your ſpiritual or ſecular happineſs.

For this reaſon, on my receipt of your laſt favour,
I deeply felt for the writer. That ſpirit of grief and
that turn of dejection, by which it was ſo ſtrongly
marked, made me, whether I would or no, ſigh on
your behalf at the throne of God.

Oh, let faith dry your tears: and know, that what
he wills and does, is, and muſt be, not only right
but beſt. Afflict not yourſelf with uneaſy appre-
henſions, concerning the ſtate of him, whom you
mourn as an huſband, and I regret as a friend:
                                                    Leave

Leave his foul with him, who, I humbly truft, redeemed it with his own moft precious blood: blood,
which cleanfes from all fin; and fprinkled with which,
any and every finner, who is enabled to truft in it,
may lift up his head, with boldnefs and joy, in the
prefence of him who chargeth even the angels with
folly.

Blefled be God, that dear Mr. Bacon pleaded
that availing blood, as the bafis of his fupplications
for mercy.—I have read, concerning good Mr. Fox,
the Martyrologift, that "he could never refufe giving pecuniary relief to any, who afked him in the
name and for the fake of Chrift." Much lefs will
the Great Father of mercies reject the petitions of
thofe, whom his blefled fpirit hath ftirred up (and
none can ftir us up, but his own fpirit) to intreat
his favour, on account of what the agonizing friend
of finners has done and fuffered for the unworthy,
the guilty, and the hell-deferving. It is a plea that
cannot fail, while God is God.—May the plea be
your's and mine, both in life and death.

Auguftus Toplady.

L E T T E R XIV.

To Ambrose Serle, Efq.

Broad-Hembury, Dec. 18, 1772.

DEAR Mr. Serle's moft obliging favour of the
28th ult. calls for an affectionate acknowledgement on my part. I muft, however, enter an exception to the ceremonious paffages which occur in
his much efteemed letter; and beg leave to file a
proteft againft all future declarations of that high
refpect, with which my valued friend vouchfafes to
honour

honour me. I know, my dear fir, that your politenefs is not a mere complaifance, like that of the
world. If I confidered it in fuch a view, I could
difpenfe with it, readily enough. But your tranf-
parent fincerity, which adds weight and ferioufnefs
to the elegance with which you write, is the very
circumftance that humbles and abafhes me. Certain I am, that you condefcend to allow me a place
in your regard : and, by that regard, I intreat you
to confider me, and to addrefs me, as (what indeed
I am) lefs than the leaft of all faints. The higheft
character, to which I afpire (God grant I may be
entitled to it,) is that of an elect finner, redeemed
with blood, and faved by grace.

I rejoice unfeignedly on your behalf, that you are
favoured with a calm and fettled comfort from on
high. I faid, from on high : for, that peace and joy,
which lay us in the duft, at the footftool of free
grace, do and muft come from God alone. To be
abforbed, and melted as into nothing, under the
over-whelming radiance of his unmerited love; to
fit in holy filence and ftillnefs of foul, beneath the
fhadow of the crofs ; to derive, by the miniftration
of his fpirit, all our hope, happinefs, and tranqui-
lity, from the ineftimable merits and interceffion of
the Lamb that is in the midft of the throne ; to caft
anchor on the covenant-favour, and covenant-
faithfulnefs, of Father, Son, and Spirit ;—are the
grand and only fources of holinefs and joy.

I admire your excellent motto. It is more than
a motto: it is a maxim, an axiom, certain as certainty itfelf. *Deo duce, omnia bona*; is the language
of reafon, no lefs than of faith. It is a text, on
which, eternity itfelf will be an everlafting comment.
God enable us to live under the chearful influence
of that great principle, until mortality is fwallowed
up of life.

I did not apprehend, that your knowledge of——
amounted to an intimacy. I thank you for informi-
ing

ing me of it, as it gives me a double pleafure. You may eafily guefs, that I mean the pleafure of congratulating you on fuch a connection; and the pleafure of knowing, that fo worthy a perfonage has the happinefs of fo valuable a friend. Had I the honour of being acquainted with his ——, I fhould felicitate him on his acquifition: an acquifition, which rarely falls to the portion of the great. God, I doubt not, will enable you to wait, with implicit confidence, and with the moft paffive ferenity, the iffue of his own all-wife purpofes. He that believeth fhall not (at leaft, he fhould not) make hafte.

You condefcend to enquire after my projected life of archbifhop Laud. I cannot fay, that I have not began it. But I am in doubt, whether I ought to proceed in it. Ecclefiaftical matters wear a very different afpect among us, from what they did when I firft formed the defign. We bid fair, at prefent, not for having an high Church, but for having no Church at all. A review of the life and times of that prelate, pregnant with the moft horrid detail of civil and religious tyranny, would hardly be feafonable at prefent, when every unfledged ignoramus has a ftone to fling at the eftablifhment. I may, perhaps, feem to fpeculate too minutely: but, I affure you, it is a fpeculation which has confiderable weight with me.

It is time, however, that my fpeculations fhould ceafe to intrude on the attention and valuable moments of my dear friend: elfe, he may be induced to fuppofe, that my motto is,

Scriptus & in Tergo, necdum finitus, Oreftes.

I fhall, therefore, with affectionate compliments to Mrs. S. and your family in general, fubfcribe myfelf, dear fir,

Your obliged and obedient fervant,

Auguftus Toplady.

LETTER XV.

To the Rev. Dr. B. of *Saliſbury.*

Broad-Hembury, Feb. 4, 1773.

YOUR late favour, dear ſir, arrived in due courſe: and as your letters never fail to be fraught with friendſhip, politeneſs, and good ſenſe, I cannot but lament that ſo few of them find their way hither. If you had my excuſe to plead, I could not, with any tolerable propriety, expect you to write oftener to me, than I to you. But, as you have hitherto found no employment for the printers, you are the more at leiſure to entertain and improve me by manuſcript.

Accept my condolences, on your loſs of your uncle at Bulbridge: the qualities of whoſe heart rendered him more truly amiable and reſpectable, than, without them, the brighteſt talents could poſſibly have done.

Your account of your own health is ſuch, as I wiſh ever to receive. Next to the pleaſure of enjoying your converſation, I value every information that aſſures me of your welfare. As to myſelf, in conſequence of being well, I have, for ſome months paſt, been far from idle: though, that induſtry might not make me ill, I keep (as you rightly conjecture) to my old cuſtom of intermixing labour with occaſional relaxation. I could wiſh, indeed, to be ever on the wing, ever on the ſtretch: but it is impoſſible, in the preſent ſtate. We muſt wait, for every ſpecies of perfection, until we enter a ſuperior world.

What think you, concerning the archi-epiſcopal ſcheme of " reforming" the liturgy and articles? Such a plan is certainly on the carpet; and it, as certainly, originated at Lambeth. The oftenſible pretext is, to expunge ſome exceptionable paſſages, which are "offenſive to thinking men, and hurtful to tender conſciences." The new Lambeth-articles (if Providence do not render the deſign abortive) will be of a very different caſt, from the old ones of 1595.

I am much obliged to you, for your kind invitation, in my way to London, if I ſhould have occaſion to go thither. The truth is, I ought to have ſeen the capital, long ago. But I really dread to do ſo. The ſight of places, and the converſation of perſons, where and with whom I have enjoyed ſo many happy hours in the company of my late honoured parent, will naturally recall her ſo ſtrongly to my remembrance, that, I fear, my nerves will hardly bear it. I am thankful, that ſhe never accepted any of my invitations into Devonſhire; as it would, now, have only tended to revive thoſe ideas, which I ſhould be happier never to recollect. The higher a departed ſatisfaction has been, the more painful (ſuppoſing the departure to be final) is its remembrance. Philoſophy may cenſure theſe feelings, as a weakneſs; but they are ſuch a weakneſs, as I cannot help. Reſignation is one thing, inſenſibility is another.

I have, unawares, extended theſe reflections to too great a length. If I was not writing to a friend, I ſhould certainly, on a review, cancel this letter, and ſubſtitute a more reviſed half-ſheet. But, as the caſe ſtands, I will avail myſelf of your candour. Believe me to be,

Rev. and dear ſir, ever your's,

Auguſtus Toplady.

LETTER XVI.

To Mrs. S. H.

Madam, · *Broad-Hembury, Feb.* 5, 1773.

MY parifhioner, Mrs. H. H. defires me to prefent you with her moft refpectful and affectionate thanks, for your late kind and obliging letter. Indeed, as the good woman told me, with
tears of gratitude, your many inftances of friendfhip
and regard are fuch, as plainly indicate the particular hand of Providence, which alone could raife up
fo valuable and difinterefted a fupporter of her old
age. She is inexpreffibly fenfible of the kindnefs of
your offer, refpecting your readinefs to fend her fome
additional affiftance, on account of her prefent ill-
nefs. But fhe defires, moft thankfully, to decline
putting you to that trouble: as, through the goodnefs of God, fhe can hitherto defray the expences of
her ficknefs, by means of your ftated fupply. I
hope fhe recovers, though flowly, her pain and fee-
blenefs continuing very great.

She requefts me to inform you, that any advantages of outward fituation, which might attend her
removal to Columpton, would not, in her judgment,
compenfate for the fpiritual want of fuch a miniftry,
as fhe could fit under with comfort.

Permit me now, madam, to apologize, for my
taking upon myfelf to acquaint you with thefe particulars. The truth is, Mrs. H. has now no near
neighbour, in whom fhe can venture to confide, but
myfelf. She knows I love her dearly ; to which I am
induced, by the grace which is given her of God. I
may fafely exprefs myfelf fo unrefervedly, of one who
cannot be lefs than ninety. And, I own, there are
very few in my parifh, large as it is, whom I fo tenderly efteem. Her many doubts and fears, refpect-

ing

ing the fafety of her foul, and the certainty of her
acceptance with God, are, to me, fo many proofs,
that fhe is indeed chofen, redeemed, and juftified.
And I am perfuaded, that the Lord will not take her
hence, until he has fhone her doubts and fears away.
At leaft, it is a remark, to which I never remember
to have met with a fingle exception, that fuch of
God's people, as are moft exercifed with fear and
trembling on their journey through life, are the
moft comfortable and triumphant in the hour of
death.　Like Mr. Ready-to-halt, in the Pilgrim's
Progrefs, they are ufually the firft to fling away
their crutches, when they actually come in view of
Jordan.

It would be needlefs to inform you, that Mrs. H.
begs you to accept her beft refpects and moft grateful acknowledgements.　To which I add the fincere
compliments of, &c.

Auguftus Toplady.

P. S.　If Providence fhould prolong all our lives
until fummer, and you fhould have leifure and inclination to fee Mrs H. before fhe goes to Heaven,
I have a part of the vicarage houfe at your fervice.

L E T T E R　XVII.

To Ambrose Serle, Efq.

Broad-Hembury, March 5, 1773.

Ever Dear Sir,

GOD, I truft and believe, will, himfelf, be the
giver of that fupport and confolation, which
I, with all my fympathy, can only wifh and pray
that you may experience. Having premifed my
hope,

hope, permit me to thank you for your letter: the only one of your's, that ever gave me pain.

With melting heart, and lifted eye, I blefs the Lord, for his having pointed the late providential fhaft with gold: in other words, for his having foftened your unfpeakable lofs of dear Mrs. Serle (dearer, as an angel, than when only a faint) with fuch undoubted and juft affurance of her eternal reft in Chrift. May thofe foretaftes of the joy that fhall be revealed, with which fhe was fo eminently favoured, be our ftrength and fong, during the appointed courfe of our remaining pilgrimage, until the fpirit of God have matured us for the inheritance of the faints in light.

I have long obferved, that fuch of his people, as are leaft on the mount, while travelling to Heaven; are higheft on it, and replenifhed with the richeft difcoveries of divine love, in the clofing fcene of life. When they come in actual view of that river, which parts the Church below from the Church above, the celeftial city rifes full in fight. The fenfe of intereft in the covenant of grace becomes clearer and brighter. The book of life is opened to the eye of affurance. The holy fpirit more feelingly applies the blood of fprinkling, and warms the foul with that robe of righteoufnefs which Jefus wrought. The once feeble believer is made as David. The once trembling hand is enabled to lay faft hold on the crofs of Chrift. The fun goes down without a cloud.

Thofe lines of Dr. Watts are as weighty, as they are beautiful.

" Juft fuch is the Chriftian. His race he begins,
Like the fun, in a mift, while he mourns for his fins,
And melts into tears. Then he breaks out and
    fhines,
And travels his heavenly way.
But, as he draws nearer to finifh his race,
Like a fine, fetting fun, he looks richer in grace;
And gives a fure hope, at the end of his days,
    Of rifing in brighter array,"

On

On occasions of this kind, I never offer to condole. I would wish to conceal even my own feelings.
Officious lenitives generally operate as corrosives,
when tendered to an heart that bleeds under so ex-
quisite a loss; and do but irritate the wound, they
are meant to assuage. Rather, let me wish you to take
down your harp from the willows, and to adore the
unerring wisdom of him, who is daily " accom-
plishing the number of his elect, and hastening his
kingdom."

You have my thanks, dear sir, for your polite
and obliging invitation. Should business force me
to London, this year, I certainly shall, were it only
for my own sake, pay my respects to you, as usual;
though I shall hardly prevail with myself to take full
advantage of your kind and friendly offer.

Our meeting together again, on earth, is, humanly speaking, precarious. Not so, our meeting in
Heaven. We are, by no means, sure of the former;
but I am fully assured of the latter.

Grace, mercy, and peace, be with you and your's.
So prays, from the inmost of his heart, dear sir,

Your obliged, &c.

Auguftus Toplady.

L E T T E R   XVIII.

To Richard Hill, Efq.

[Extract.]   *Broad-Hembury, March* 12, 1773.

I AM told, that Mr. Fletcher has it in contemplation
to make an attack on me too. He is welcome.
I am ready for him. Nor shall I, in that case, altogether imitate the amiable examples of yourself
and your brother; unless Mr. Fletcher should treat me
with

with more decency, than he has, hitherto, obferved towards others.   Tendernefs, it is very evident, has no good effect on Mr. Wefley, and his pretended family of love.   Witnefs the rancour, with which Mr. Hervey's memory and works are treated by that lovely family.   For my own part, I fhall never attempt to hew fuch millftones with a feather.   They muft be ferved as nettles : prefs them clofe, and they cannot fting.—Yet have they my prayers, and my beft wifhes, for their prefent and future falvation. But not one hair's breadth of the gofpel will I ever (God being my helper) offer up at their fhrine, or facrifice to their idol,

Auguftus Toplady.

LETTER XIX.

To Mr. RYLAND, Junior.

London, April 30, 1773.

MANY and beft thanks to dear Mr. R. for his two valuable and much efteemed letters : as alfo for the feveral pamphlets, with which the latter of his two favours was accompanied.   Mr. Richard Hill had fhewn me Wefley's fecond remarks, immediately on my coming to town : I am, however, greatly obliged to you for forwarding it.

Heartily I wifh, that I could avail myfelf of your dear father's invitation to Northampton.   But it is a pleafure, which my time, at prefent, will not fuffer me to enjoy. I muft, *volente Deo,* leave town next week. Should life be fpared, and opportunity granted, in future, I know not the family, with whom I could fpend a week or two, more profitably and agreeably, than your's.

The

The word of God runs and is glorified in London. Cobler Tom laments, it feems, publicly from his preaching-tub (mif-named, a pulpit), that fuch an Antinomian as myfelf fhould have crouded auditories, while the preachers of the pure gofpel (by which, you know, he means free-will, merit, and perfcc on) are fo thinly attended.

The envy, malice, and fury of Wefley's party, are inconceivable. But, as violently as they hate me, I dare not, I cannot hate them in return. I have not fo learned Chrift.—They have my prayers and my beft wifhes, for their prefent and eternal falvation. But their errors have my oppofition alfo : and this is the irremiffible fin, which thofe red-hot bigots know not how to forgive.

You defire to be informed of the title to my intended publication, now in the prefs. It runs thus. "Hiftoric Proof of the doctrinal Calvinifm of the Church of England : including, a brief Account of fome eminent Perfons, famous for their Adoption of that Syftem, both before and fince the Reformation ; with Specimens of their Teftimonies."

I fear, it will extend to a four or five fhilling volume. But the facts and evidences are fo numerous, and drawn from fuch a multiplicity of fources, that I could not poffibly bring it into lefs compafs. Acquaint your good father, that his grand favourite and mine, archbifhop Bradwardin, makes a very eminent figure, in the chapter which relates to our own Englifh heroes.

Though I have, for fifteen years paft (i. e. for very near half my life), been folidly and clearly convinced of the original and intrinfic Calvinifm of the eftablifhed Church ; ftill, I did not know, that the fubject was fupported by fuch a vaft confluence of pofitive authorities, until the furious oppofition of the Methodifts forced me to take a nearer and more exact view of the argument. Thus far, at leaft, I am obliged to that virulent fect. And, on a retro-

fpective

spective survey of the whole matter, I myself stand
astonished at that profusion of evidence, which pours
from every quarter, in favour of the main point.
My own collections (to go no farther,) viewed in
the aggregate, absolutely surprise me. And yet,
the argument is far from being exhausted.—But, if
that is not exhausted, my paper almost is. I must
therefore conclude: having but just room to salute
you and your family; to commend me to your
prayers; and to subscribe myself, ever dear sir,

Your's most affectionately,

Augustus Toplady.

L E T T E R XX.

To the Rev. Mr. P.

[Extract.]   *London, May* 3, 1773.

YOU was not mis-informed, as to my having
had an interview with Thomas Oliver. It
happened thus:

On Saturday, the 8th of last month, I was going
to see good Mr. Hitchin, of Hoxton. On my way,
passing by the Foundery, it occurred to me, that I
had now an opportunity of gratifying my curiosity,
by purchasing Wesley's last printed Journal. I
therefore went in, and found a man reading, in what
is called the Book-room, i. e. the room where
Wesley's publications are sold. The man, on my
telling him what I wanted, answered, "Sir, I am
not the person that sells the books; but I will step
and call him." He left me, for two or three
minutes; and returned with (I think) two other
men and three women. Having paid for the Journal and taken my change, I was coming away:
when one of the men, who proved to be Mr. Joseph
Cownley, asked me, "whether my name was not
Toplady?"

Toplady?" My anfwer was, " Yes, fir, at your fervice." All prefent immediately affumed an air of much
civility. I ftopped and chatted with them for, I believe, ten minutes. In the courfe of my ftay, I took
out my fnuff-box. Mr. Cownley afked for a pinch. As
I held it to him, I faid, with a fmile, " Is not it againft
the law of this place, for a believer to take fnuff?"
Mr. Cownley huddled the matter up, by alledging,
that he was troubled with the head-ach. Immediately on which, one of the good women (whom I
afterwards found to be the wife of Mr. Thomas
Oliver) faid, directing herfelf to me, " O fir, Mr.
Wefley has no objection to people's taking fnuff me-
dicinally." I anfwered, " I am glad you are allowed
fome latitude : I thought you were tied up by an
abfolute prohibition, without any loop-hole of exception." Our chat (which, though humorous,
was extremely civil on all fides) being over, I took
leave of the company.—I fhould have told you before, that, no fooner was my name authenticated,
than one of the women flipped out of the room.
Who fhe was, I know not : but fhe was fufficiently
corpulent : as broad, comparitively, as fhe was long.
The reafon of her decampment, I fuppofe, was, to
announce the tidings to cobler Tom, of the unexpected vifitant in the Book-room.

As I was going out of the faid room, the fat lady
ftood on the right hand, and a man in black on the
left, without fide the door. In paffing, I moved my
hat. Sir, cried the corpulent fifter, pointing to the
other fide of me, " that is Mr. Oliver."—I faid,
fmiling, " what, my famous antagonift?" Oliver
fmiled and bowed. " Mr. Oliver," added I, " give me
your hand : cudgel-players fhake hands, though
they mean to break each others' heads." He made
me no verbal anfwer, but, repeating his bow, fhook
me by the hand; and feemed pleafed. As I was
not willing to have quite a filent meeting on his
part, I began afrefh : " Your complexion, Mr,
Oliver,

Oliver, feems to indicate too clofe an intenfenefs of thought. Do not ftudy too hard, left the fword be too fharp for the fheath." He then began to open: " Oh, fir, I do not ftudy too clofely. I do not hurry myfelf. I take my time." On which I told him, " As you are thrown in my way, I fhould be glad of a quarter of an hour's converfation with you, if you are at leafure." He anfwered, " with all my heart, fir: I fhall be very glad:" and calling for a key, up ftairs we went to his apartment.

On entering it, I faw a fmall table covered with printed pamphlets and written papers. Among the pamphlets, was Mr. Hill's *Logica Wefleïenfis.*—To avoid the frequent repetitions of faid I, and faid he; I fhall throw as much of our converfation as I can recollect, dialogue-wife, under the initials of our refpective fur-names. Premifing one remark, viz. that he ftrove much to draw me into a pitched debate on the Arminian points, which I was as much determined to avoid; and that for this reafon, becaufe, as none were prefent but himfelf and his wife, what I might have faid, would have lain at the mercy of their mifreprefentation afterwards. I therefore parried him at arm's length, and was rather an hearer than a fpeaker.

After reconnoitring his table at my firft going up, I obferved to him, " So, here is the whole polemical apparatus, ready to fire off. When do you intend to publifh againft us?

O. It feems, fir, that you too are going to publifh a book againft Mr. Sellon.

T. Perhaps fo: and I will give you a friendly hint. Do not be too hafty in printing your next attack. If you will have patience to wait, you may have an opportunity of killing two or three birds with one ftone. You know, if we write a folio, it is but your printing a penny fheet, and we are anfwered at once. Nay, write but a fingle page, and call it an anfwer, and we are knocked down flat.

O. Mr.

O. Mr. Richard Hill is a very bitter abufive
writer.

T. If you knew him, you would pronounce him
as amiable a man as lives.

O. We once thought you the bittereft of Mr.
Wefley's oppofers : but, upon my word, Mr. Hill's
fcurrilities exceed every thing.

T. How partial are moft men to themfelves and
to their own party ! Had Mr. Hill written for Mr.
Wefley, inftead of writing againft him; he would
have been cried up, by the gentlemen on your fide
of the queftion, as one of the meekeft and moft
candid authors that ever put pen to paper, had he
written ten times more fmartly than he has.

O. I believe the time will come, when both you
and Mr. Hill will be grieved in your minds, for what
you have publifhed againft Mr. Wefley.

T. Mr. Wefley, if you pleafe, has abundant reafon to be grieved for what he has publifhed againft
the truths of God. I hope, for his own fake, that
divine grace will make him grieve foon and grieve
deeply.

O. Mr. Wefley is a very good man, and a very
honeft one.

T. He has amply fhewn himfelf fo. Forgery, for
inftance, is honefty all over.

O. He only drew fuch plain inferences from Zanchy, as neceffarily flow from Zanchy's principles.

T. He ought to have given the inferences as his
own: and not to have fathered them upon another man.

O. Do you not think I have demonftrated that
thofe inferences are juft ?

T. Do not you think that I have refuted every
one of them ?

O. Mr. Wefley is certainly an honeft man.

T. Mr. Wefley's honefty, Mr. Fletcher's meeknefs, and Mr. Sellon's politenefs, are very fit to go
together.

O. O fir,

O. O fir, furely you will not talk about meeknefs!

T. Certain I am, that your writers have no more
title to arrogate meeknefs to themfelves, than many
of your preachers and perfectionifts have to fet up
for a monopoly of holinefs.

O. Sally, [or Nanny; I am not fure which]—
do fetch a bottle of wine. Mr. Toplady, perhaps,
will drink a glafs.

Mrs. Oliver went, and returned in half a minute.

T. To fhew you that I bear you no enmity, I
will drink your health in a fingle glafs.

O. I have read logic, and I have read metaphyfics, and I have read natural philofophy.

T. Doubtlefs, your reading has been very extenfive.

O. Oh fir, I am no more than a cobler, you know.
You have bid me get away to my ftall.

T. Certainly you are a Crifpinian, though not a
Crifpian. Do you remember one William Gay, of
Uffculme, in Devonfhire?

O. Gay? Gay? Let's fee. What is he?

T. A mafter mafon. He remembers you, if you
do not remember him. You lodged at his houfe,
fome years ago; and like St. Paul, preached and
worked at your trade by turns.

O. It is a good many years fince I was at h's
houfe.

T. I beg pardon for breaking the thread of metaphyfics.

O. Why, fir, I was going to fay, that fome metaphyfical writers think the will takes the lead of
the underftanding. Others fuppofe the underftanding leads the will.

T. You have read logic too.

O. Yes, indeed.

T. Mr. Wefley's three-penny cut?

O. O, much more than that. I have read feveral
fyftems.

T. The

T. The poor predeſtinarians had need look about them.

O. Before I would be a predeſtinarian, I would ſuffer myſelf to be tied hand and foot, and carried through this window to yonder mad-houſe

T. Should you ſtand in need of confinement, there would be no occaſion for removing you out of your preſent quarters. The Foundery would anſwer all the purpoſes of a mad-houſe, without conveying you out at the ſaſh. I ſhould vote for keeping you where you are.

O. Ha, ha, ha! Well: But ſmartneſs is not argument.——Pray, ſir, have you read the Aſſembly's Catechiſm?

T. Yes, ſir.

O. The poſition with which it ſets out, is, that " God hath from all eternity unchangeably ordained whatever comes to paſs." I ſuppoſe, ſir, you agree with thoſe learned divines as to this particular.

T. You may poſſibly have ſeen ſome of my pamphlets: and, as you are remarkably pat at drawing inferences, you may from my writings infer pretty nearly, how far I do or do not agree with thoſe learned divines.

O. But, ſir: their doctrine deſtroys all free-agency.

T. What may your idea of free-agency be?

O. Why—why—free-agents are them that can act or not act, juſt as they pleaſe.

T. You do not ſuppoſe that men are free, with a freedom of independency?

O. I acknowledge, that men are dependent on God, as creatures. He made them, and he can put an end to their lives whenever he thinks fit.

T. But are man's volitions independently free?

O. Moſt undoubtedly.

T. Men, in determining their own wills, are independent on their Maker himſelf?

O. They

O. They muſt be ſo: or the will would ceaſe to be free.

T. Do not let me miſ-underſtand you. You hold, that men are abſolutely independent on God, ſo far as relates to the management and actings of their own wills?

O. I believe it firmly.

T. You are honeſt, and conſiſtent: but I cannot call you orthodox. You ſuppoſe man to poſſeſs a degree of independence and ſelf-command, which not an angel in heaven can dare lay claim to.—Abſolute, independent ſelf-determination is an attribute truly and properly divine. If I thought you poſſeſſed of it, I ſhould immediately fall down and worſhip you as a God.

O. You have it, and I have it, and every man has it, except he ſins away his day of grace.—If I ſhould ſay to this cane, [taking up my walking cane, which happened to lean near him] O cane, repent, believe, and obey the goſpel; would not you think me out of my ſenſes?

T. That I ſhould indeed.

O. If man has not free-will, to what end are exhortations?

T. Among other uſeful ends, they are made inſtrumental, under the influence of God's ſpirit, to convince men that they have, by nature, neither will nor power to do what is good.

O. I have many ſtrong objections againſt that doctrine.

T. Then put your ſtrong objections into the book you are going to publiſh, and we will conſider them at leaſure. In the mean while, let me put one queſtion to you, which a valuable friend, now with God, once put to me.—When I was a lad of 15 or 16 years old, I was haranguing, in company, on the doctrine of free-will, as you are now. A good old gentleman roſe from his chair, and coming

to

to mine, held me by one of my coat buttons, while he spoke as follows: " My dear fir, you have been talking largely in favour of man's free-agency. Allow me to leave argument, and come to experience. How was it with you, when God firſt laid hold on you by effectual grace? had you any hand in procuring it? Nay, would you not have reſiſted and baffled God's ſpirit, if he had left you to your will?" I was more embarraſſed with this queſtion, than I was willing to ſhew. Yet I had then too much pride to confeſs how much I was *non-pluſt* by this calm and ſingle interrogation. However, before I was eighteen, God was gracious̄ly pleaſed to enlighten me into that precious chain of truths which, through his good hand upon me, I ſtill abide by.— Permit me, Mr. Oliver, to put the above queſtion to you. I truſt, you have experienced ſomething of a work of God, upon your heart. What ſay you? Did you chuſe God, or did God chuſe you? Did he lay hold on you, or did you lay hold on him?

O. I muſt own to you, that, before my converſion, I was one of the moſt abandoned ſwearers and drunkards in England. I received my ſerious impreſſions from Mr. Whitefield. On the day of the evening in which I firſt heard him preach, I ſuppoſe I had not ſworn ſo few as forty prophane oaths.

T. Then it is very clear that your converſion, at leaſt, was not conditional.

O. I will not ſay, that I procured grace, of myſelf. Nor will I ſay, how far I might have reſiſted it.

T. I plainly perceive, that you are not diſpoſed to return a direct anſwer to my firſt queſtion. But, if you will not anſwer it to me, let me requeſt you to take an early opportunity of anſwering it on your knees before God in prayer. Go to your cloſet, and pour out your heart in his preſence : and beg him to ſhew fhew you, whether you was converted by free-will, or by free-grace alone.——To this he gave little or no reply.

At my coming away, I faid: "I am going to mention a circumftance, of no importance in it-felf, but of fome confequence to your own reputa-tion as a man of integrity. I fhould have deemed it no fort of blot, had I been, what you have rafhly reprefented me in print, a native of Ireland. Thou-fands have been born in that country, whofe fhoes latchet I am unworthy to loofe. With regard to myfelf, however, your conjecture was a miftaken one. If you doubt it, confult the regifter-book at Farnham, in Surrey. My fole motive, for fetting you right in fo infignificant a particular, is, that you may, for the time to come, be more cautious of pub-lifhing uncertain anecdotes.

He very civilly attended me down ftairs, to the Foundery door. As we paft through the preaching-place, 1 obferved, " This, I prefume, is looked upon as your cathedral." He anfwered, " We have lately had it repaired. We are not without thoughts of building it anew." " A good fcheme," faid I : " new doctrines deferve a new place."—" Our's," he rejoined, " are the true old doctrines." I added, " There we differ; but let it be our mutual prayer, that we may experience the efficacy of God's word in our hearts, and evidence the power of it by the holinefs of our lives." On which, we fhook hands, and parted.

Upon the whole, this was a curious interview. To fay the truth, I am glad I faw Mr. Oliver: for he appears to be a perfon of ftronger fenfe and better behaviour, than I imagined. Had his underftand-ing been cultivated by a liberal education, I believe he would have made fome figure in life.

What pleafed me moft, was that appearance of honefty, by which he is fo greatly diftinguifhed from the old fox, Mr. John Wefley.—In perfon, he is rather low of ftature, of a full make, pale and broad faced, and confiderably disfigured by the fmall-pox. His wig was fitter for a bifhop, than for a fhoe-maker.

I am not without hope, that God will lead him into the way of truth. He is, I believe, extremely fincere ; and the promife runs, " them that are up-right will he learn his way." Not that I fuppofe man's uprightnefs, or fincerity, is conditional of di-vine guidance ; but where God has given fincerity, I look upon it as a token for good, and am in hopes of his gracioufly giving fomething more. As I told Mr. Oliver, in the courfe of our chat, " I have known as ftubborn freewillers as he brought to lick the duft at God's footftool."

The Wednefday after this converfation, his curi-ofity led him to hear me preach at Black-friars. My text was, Matth. xii. 21. I thought I glimpfed him ; but, being near-fighted, was not certain.— However, left it fhould be he, I threw out fome things, in the courfe of my fermon, which I fhould not have mentioned, if I had not thought him pre-fent. A friend of mine, Mr. Flower, of Cannon-ftreet, happened to fit in the fame pew with him. When fermon was ended, Oliver turned to Mr. Flower, and faid, with much rancorous emotion, " Believe this, and be damned." Mr. Flower an-fwered, " No, fir ; believe this, and be faved." Mr. Flower himfelf was the perfon, from whom I after-wards learned this particular. He added, that, during fermon-time, Oliver was in fuch uneafinefs and agitation, that he feemed hardly able to contain his rage. Poor, dear man, if God has a fet time for opening his eyes, the enmity of his freewill fhall not be able to fteel him againft the gofpel, when the fet time comes.

Another intimate friend of mine went, fhortly after, to hear Mr. Oliver preach at one of Wefley's meeting-houfes. The preacher had not forgot the penance

penance he underwent at Black-friars, in hearing a whole fermon on free grace and finifhed falvation. "I went," faid he to his auditory, "laft Wednef-day morning, to a famous Antinomian Church in the city, to hear one of the Antinomian clergymen. I expected to have feen but very few people there. But, alas! though it was on a week-day, and a rainy morning, and though the Church is large, the Church was quite full. What a fhame is it, my brethren, that an Antinomian preacher fhould have fo many people to hear him, when I, who preached the pure gofpel, was forced, but now, to wait a con-fiderable time for my congregation; and, after wait-ing long, to begin to eighteen or twenty people! I never talked to you about election, and perfeverance, and imputed righteoufnefs. I never tell you of a finifhed falvation. I preach the pure gofpel. And yet, how backward are you to hear it! You dif-courage your minifters. I cannot omit one paffage in the fermon, which was as follows: "My brethren, if man's free-will is nothing, there can be no room for praife or blame. If I ftick a candle into this focket" (pointing to the fconce at or near the preach-ing defk) "am I to thank the fconce for receiving and holding the candle; nay, verily, for the focket, not being a free agent, cannot help admitting the candle that is thruft into it: and it is the fame with man and grace, if grace be given irrefiftibly."

And fo fay I. Man is no more to be thanked, for the grace which is given him of God, than a fconce is to be thanked for the taper which it holds. But here lies the difference; man in regeneration, is made willing to receive grace, and made happy by receiving it, neither of which can be faid of Oliver's fconce.

I wifh, my dear fir, you may not be as tired, with reading this long letter, as the enraged fhoe-maker was with hearing what he calls my Antino-mian fermon. I muft, however, do myfelf the juftice

to

to say, that I have not written so prolix an epiſtle, theſe many years; nor are there many perſons, in the three kingdoms, to whom I would have written a letter of half this length. I wiſh you would make retaliation, and revenge yourſelf in kind.

Every bleſſing be with you and your's.

Auguſtus Toplady.

LETTER XXI.

To Mrs. MACAULAY.

Broad-Hembury, June 11, 1773.

DEIGN to accept my beſt acknowledgements, madam, for your very obliging letter, which, you told me, awaited me in Devonſhire; and which I, accordingly, found on my return. You do me infinitely too much honour, in condeſcending to ſo-licit my opinion of the merits of your laſt publica-tion. But, as my judgement is aſked, I will give it, without reſerve. I think its merits are unſpeakable, both as to ſubſtance and compoſition. That ſedulous attention to truth, that undeviating zeal for the rights of mankind, and that nervous refinement of thought, which ſo eminently mark and adorn your character and writings, ſhine, with full force, in your fifth volume. Be it ſo, that your political theory is too ſublimely virtuous, to be univerſally adopted by an age, of ſuch a caſt as the preſent; yet are you ſecure of the affections and the admira-tion of the honeſt and diſcerning: who, though they have, in all periods of times, conſtituted far the ſmaller part of ſociety; yet is their eſteem of more

weight

weight and value, than the difgraceful applaufe of the weak or the interefted multitude.

As greatly, madam, as I revere your uncommon talents; and as fincerely as I regard your public and private virtues, there are two or three minutiæ, on which I refpectfully diffent. It is not, for inftance, clear to me, that the levellers were a " brave and virtuous party :" nor that Cromwell was fo utterly deftitute of confcience and principle, as, to you, he feems to have been. That he was a traitor to the liberties of his country, can admit of very little difpute. Yet can I perceive, in various features of his mental character, fome ftriking fymptoms of magnanimity and virtue, which leave me in fufpenfe, as to the total corruption of his heart. You, who have penetrated into the receffes of hiftory, with more attention than I have had opportunity of applying, and with far greater judgement than I am capable of exerting, may wonder, perhaps, at the freedom, with which I venture to mention any thing relative to a province fo peculiarly your own. But you muft place the liberty, madam, which I have prefumed to take, to the account of your own condefcenfion, which commanded me to prefent you with my genuine thoughts.

I wifh my honoured friend may, in her turn, prove as obedient to my requeft, as I have to her command. If fo, you will not fail to re-vifit Devonfhire, in the courfe of this fummer. My neighbours, Mr. and Mrs. Northcote, long, impatiently, for the happinefs of enjoying your company again. And, for myfelf, I hope I need not affure you, that I reap too much pleafure and improvement from the privilege of your converfation, to be diftanced, in the defire of feeing you, by the warmeft of your admirers. Though this is a fpecies of avarice, which I deem it an honour to avow; I have ftill another argument to urge, infinitely fuperior to any motive deduced from my own felf-intereft as an in-

N 3   dividual.

dividual. I faw, with pain, when laft in London, that the clofenefs of that over-grown town, your want of exercife, and your intenfe literary applica- tion, appear to have had an unfavourable effect on your health. Confider, madam, that, notwithftand- ing all your paft meritorious fervices, you are ftill a debtor to fociety. You owe yourfelf to your coun- try. If you do not take care of its beft citizen, you will be guilty of the higheft injuftice to the public. Say not, " How does this advice comport with your doctrine of predeftination?" For I hope, you are predeftinated to take the advice; and that a pre- deftinated old age will be the refult. Our friend, Mr. Northcote, fometimes fays, " Mr. Toplady be- lieves abfolute predeftination; and yet he is loth to ride on horfeback, for fear of breaking his neck." I anfwer, " True :" and, perhaps, that very fear may be an appointed means of preferving my neck un- broken. The corollary from the whole, is; let Mrs. Macaulay, by coming down foon into Devonfhire, confult her health, gladden her friends in the weft, and fhew herfelf juft to the community. We fet too high a value on the productions of your pen, to wifh you to lay it afide entirely, while you are with us. We will allow you to devote your mornings to ftudy; and I am pretty certain, that Mr. N. and myfelf together, can furnifh you with moft, if not with all the books which you may wifh to confult, relative to the period on which you are now employ- ed. If invitation will not prevail, I fhall have re- courfe to threats. I told you, when I faw you laft, that I would fo pefter you with letters, that you fhould be glad to vifit us, in your own defence : and I mean to be as good as my word. The pre- fent piece of prolix expoftulation is a difagreeable fample of what you have to expect, from, madam,

your's, &c.

Auguftus Toplady.

LETTER XXII.

To Mrs. MACAULAY.

Broad-Hembury, July 13, 1773.

LET a lady alone for dexterity. The king has loft by you. Your late much efteemed favour, madam (doubly valuable, for being double in fize), was fo ingenioufly folded, as to elude the vigilance of the poft-office, and be charged only as a fingle letter. The circumftance, however, of poftage, is an article that I fhall never think of, when Mrs. Macaulay's improving favours are the freight. It is in obedience to your own defire, that I trouble you with an incident, in all other refpeéts, too trivial for notice. But, as I am on the fubjeét, I muft requeft you, once for all, never to let a deficiency of franks lay the fhorteft embargo on your correfpondence hither. I imagine them to be (what, confidered in this relation, they indeed are) mere things of nought.

Of all the letters, madam, with which you have vouchfafed to honour me, I fet the higheft value on your laft. Should you afk why? My anfwer would be, becaufe it is the longeft. That a perfon of your eminence, and engaged by fo many avocations of ufefulnefs and importance, fhould oblige me with fo much of your time and attention, is an inftance of condefcending friendfhip, which refleéts as much honour on your own politenefs, as I can receive from its effeéts.

Doubtlefs, the charaéter of Cromwell, when contrafted with the fhining benevolence and exemplary difintereftednefs of Antonius Pius; or with that gentlenefs, yet fteadinefs of wifdom, that felf-denying fimplicity, that difcreet but noble liberality, that

N 4 *unrelaxing*

unrelaxing adherence to juſtice, truth, and equity, which (ſtill more than even his writings) have ſtamped greatneſs and immortality on the name of Marcus Aurelius; the maxims and conduct of the Engliſh uſurper, when weighed againſt ſuch characters as thoſe, cannot but appear, on the compariſon, black as darkneſs, and lighter than emptineſs itſelf. Much leſs will Cromwell's meaſures bear to be paralleled with the humane, the juſt, the wiſe, the improving adminiſtration of our own Alfred: who, perhaps, both as an individual, and as a chief magiſtrate, came the neareſt to moral and political perfection, of any regal character, which adorns the page of ſecular hiſtory. I know of but one prince who would, probably, have out-ſhone Alfred; I mean, Edward VI.

Yet, after all, I queſtion if it be ſtrictly fair, to bring Cromwell to the teſt of ſuch very exalted ſtandards. Antoninus Pius, Antoninus the philoſopher, Nicocles of Salamis, Alfred and Edward VI. of England, Louis XII. of France, and (perhaps) one or two more individuals, who were formed for the good of mankind, and for the honour of monarchy; are examples, too ſeverely bright, for Cromwell's competition. Inexcuſable, as many of his principles ſeem to have been, and unjuſtifiable as the main of his conduct undoubtedly was; the peculiar exigencies of his ſituation might ſtill, in ſome degree, oblige him to avail himſelf of maxims he deteſted, and to purſue a courſe of action which his heart might diſapprove. In ſhort, much allowance muſt be made for the times in which he lived; much for the ſituation, in which he was gradually placed; much for that teeming train of events, which appear to have drawn him in ſtep by ſtep; much for the embarraſſment ariſing from thoſe diſtreſſing alternatives, to which public perſons are ſometimes reduced, and which frequently poſe the ſhallowneſs of human wiſdom; and much for the depravity of human nature itſelf, which it is ſufficiently plain, was

not

not lefs operative in Cromwell, than in the reft of the fpecies. To which we may add, that perfons who are actually parties in the bufy fcenes of political tranfaction, are often hurried and perplexed into meafures, which the cool fpeculative politician would juftly condemn; and at either the profpect or the retrofpect of which, the delinquents themfelves would fhudder. But to clofe this amicable controverfy, with a fingle queftion. What a figure would the generality of Englifh hiftorians (though many of them have great merit) make, if fet in competition with Mrs. Macaulay's noble and fpirited performance? Or, to vary the query; how fhould I dwindle to a fpan, to an inch, to a point, to nothing, if compared with a Witfius, a Turretin, a Spanhemius, a Gurnall, a Hervey! Think on this, when you are for contrafting Cromwell with the two Antoninus's and Alfred.

Sorry I am to learn, that your health is not improved, fince I had the honour of feeing you in the fpring. But, though deeply concerned, I cannot wonder. The heat of the feafon, for fome time paft, has been intenfe, even at Broad-Hembury. At London, it muft be fcarce fupportable. You, whofe conftitution is almoft as delicate as your mind is elegant, muft have fuffered much by it, aided as, I fear, it has been, by confinement, and application. Would to God, you would receive, with your ufual attention in other matters, the hint I took the liberty to give you, at our laft interview, viz. Write little, that you may write much.

If no entreaties can prevail with you to fee the weft this fummer; yet be fo kind to your friends and to the world, as to fpare yourfelf all you can. When you perceive fatigue and languor approaching, lay down your pen for that day; and imagine that I am at your elbow, requefting and adjuring you, with all the earneft importunity of refpectful friendfhip, to be tender of that exquifite machine which Providence

dence has formed into the diftinguifhed tenement of fo much exalted reafon and virtue. Nothing exhaufts the fpirits, and impairs the health, more, than the continued labour of deep hiftorical refearches. It engages, for the time, all the powers of the foul, and engroffes the whole collective force of the nerves. What can be more dangerous, what more pernicious to the human fabric? Timotheus, the Athenian, is juftly admired for having faid, that, "being at the head of an army, he took care not to expofe himfelf rafhly to danger: for the life of a general is of too much confequence, to be needlefsly thrown away." Valuable as your hiftory is, it is not of equal value with the hiftorian. Befides: fhould the hiftorian fail, what would become of the remainder of the hiftory? I fear, I fhould be the means of detaining you too long from the exercife and relaxation I recommend, were I not to cut fhort this free lecture, by fubfcribing myfelf, with great refpect,

Madam, your obliged and moft obedient fervant,

Auguftus Toplady.

LETTER XXIII.

To the Rev. Dr. GIFFORD.

Broad-Hembury, July 14, 1773.

I AM often reminded of my much valued and refpected friend, by the highly efteemed plates of Englifh coins, with which he favoured me. I confult them very frequently: and, partly, on their own account, but more on his, I defervedly number them amongft my choiceft literary κιμηλια.

I hope, dear fir, you have, long fince, received the Danifh fword (for Danifh it more probably was),

which

which I left for you, at Mr. R's, when I was laft in London. It was given me, the firft time I was in Ireland, in the year 1755, by counfellor Harding, on whofe eftate (in the county of Limerick, if I rightly remember) that, and fome hundreds more of the fame make, were dug up. I have, firft and laft, fhewn it to many virtuofi: not one of whom could form any judgment of the metal it is of. It certainly is a very antient weapon: and if admitted to be Danifh, or Norwegian, it cannot be lefs than 8 or 900 years old. But you, who are fo confummate an hiftorian, know, much better than I can pretend to do, about what period thofe Northern plunderers ceafed to infeft Ireland.

Permit me to enquire into a matter of incomparably greater importance. How is your health? Have you got rid of your cough? Is your appetite returned? I expect a full and diftinct anfwer to each of thefe queftions.

May our gracious covenant God in Chrift caufe you to renew your ftrength, in every fenfe of that promife. Remember me in your petitions: Let me hear from you, without delay: and believe me to be, what, *ab imo pectoris*, I am,

dear and Rev. fir,

your affectionate and obedient fervant,

Auguftus Toplady.

L E T T E R XXIV.

To the Rev. Mr. B. P. of *New York.*

Broad-Hembury, Sept. 6, 1773.

DEAR and REV. SIR,

YOUR very obliging favour, of July 17, arrived here by the laft poft. Accept my thanks, for the regard it breathes; and permit me to fhew

my

my fenfe of it, by fincerely befeeching God to crown you with thofe important mercies, which you fo affectionately wifh to me, the unworthieft of his meffengers.

It gives me unfpeakable pleafure, to perceive, that you are a clergyman of the Church of England. I fhould have received fo valuable a letter, as your's, with refpect, and with joy, of what denomination foever the writer had been. But, I confefs, I am fo far partial to our own hill, in Sion, as to rejoice peculiarly, when I hear of faithful, fpiritual, well-principled watchmen being ftationed on her walls. I know not, how it is in America; but fure I am, that, here, their number is, comparatively, exceeding few. Yet has God favoured us, of late years, with a manifeft revival: and I had the fatisfaction, when laft in London (viz. about three months ago) of feeing fix or eight evangelical clergymen, lately ordained, whom I had not, until then, fo much as heard of. May the little leaven, in God's due time, leaven the whole lump!

Your idea of Mr. J. W. and his affociates, exactly tallies with mine. Abftracted from all warmth, and from all prejudice, I believe him to be the moft rancorous hater of the gofpel-fyftem, that ever appeared in this ifland. I except not Pelagius himfelf. The latter had fome remains of modefty; and preferved, in the main, fome appearances of decency: but the former has outlived all pretenfion to both.—Have two pieces, written by my learned and religious friend, Mr. Richard Hill, found their way to America? The one is entitled, "A Review of all the Doctrines taught by Mr. J. W." The other, "*Logica Wefleïenfis.*" If you have not yet feen them, they will give you unfpeakable fatisfaction.

I am glad, for the truth's fake, to hear, that my tranflation of Zanchius was fo well received, and has been re-printed, on your fide of the Atlantic. God blefs it there, as he has gracioufly vouchfafed to do

to

to many in England.—It was quite a juvenile exercise; accomplished, about a year and half before I entered into orders, by way of filling up a few supernumerary hours. I remember shewing the manuscript, one day, to the late Dr. Gill, when he did me the favour of a visit. He advised me to publish it : but, to say the honest truth, I was then not sufficiently delivered from the fear of man: and•it slumbered by me, from 1760, to 1769. I literally fulfilled Horace's direction (though from a motive, not at all allied to that for which he recommends it)

———— nonumque prematur in annum.

I can never sufficiently bless God, for giving me to see the day, when I can truly affirm, that I care not whom I displease, when the inestimable truths of his gospel are at stake. His providence has rendered me independent on any but himself; and his grace enables me to act accordingly.—I must likewise add, as a still further motive to my gratitude, that, the bolder I am in his cause, the more he gives me the affections of those to whom I minister, and with whom I am connected. Where I have lost one friend, by standing up for Christ; I have gained a multitude.

The anonymous pamphlet, to which you refer, is the production of one Mr. W———— S————; who was, originally, it seems, a baker, by trade : he then became a lay-preacher of Mr. W's : and, in process of time, lady Huntingdon got him into orders. She is now extremely sorry that she did so : for her ladyship is convinced, at last, that her tenderness for Mr. W———— was sadly misplaced.

Though, as you justly observe, Mr. S————'s low libel is not, in any respect whatever, a real answer to my Vindication of the Church of England from Arminianism; yet have I taken the opportunity which his virulence has afforded me, of setting the essential and absolute Calvinism, of the Church established, in a

still

ftill fuller and ftronger point of view. My piece, which is now far advanced in the prefs, is entitled, Hiftoric Proof of the Doctrinal Calvinifm of the Church of England. If Providence fpare me to fee it out of the prefs, I will direct my bookfeller, purfuant to your requeft, to leave a copy for you with our friend Mr. Gardner: and which I fhall defire your acceptance of, as my prefent.

There is but one paragraph, dear fir, in your much efteemed letter, which gave me uneafinefs. I mean, the paffage relating to your ftate of health. I cannot help feeling a moft tender concern, that fo valuable a perfon, as you appear to be, fhould labour under the difadvantages of too delicate a machine.—And yet, why do I permit fuch a remark to efcape my pen? God beft knows what he has to do with us. If brotherly affection compels me to fympathize with you; faith, on the other hand, bids me leave you, without fear, and without complaint, to the paternal, the unerring difpofal of him who does all things well.

Be fo kind as to indulge me with a line, by the firft opportunity, after your receipt of this. One reafon for which requeft is, that I may know what pamphlets of mine you have met with; which I beg the favour of you to enumerate: that I may, by the channel you have pointed out, fend you fuch of them as are in print, and which you may not already have feen.

Grace be to you, fir, and love, with faith, from God our Father, and from our Lord Jefus Chrift. May the enlightening, the comforting, the fanctifying, the fealing influences of the eternal fpirit be your ftrength, your fong, and your ever-prefent portion, all through the courfe of your pilgrimage.— Excufe this inaccurate accknowledgement, written *currente calamo*; and believe me to be

your obliged, &c.

Auguftus Toplady.
P. S. Why

P. S. Why do you exprefs fo much diffidence of publicly taking up your pen in the caufe of God? He feems to have ftrongly breathed the defire into your heart: and your letter fully convinces me, that he has endued you with abilities for fuch a work. I hope (and, I affure you, it will be, in the mean while, an article in my prayers to God) that you may be effectually inclined, and powerfully enabled, to bear your teftimony againft error, in a day of fuch rebuke and blafphemy as this.—Up, then, and be doing: and the Lord crown your endeavours with his bleffing. Adieu.

Pray for me, as I alfo for you.

LETTER XXV.

To the Rev. Mr. ROMAINE, (now at *Tiverton*).

Broad-Hembury, Sept. 11, 1773.

MANY thanks to dear and honoured Mr. Romaine, for his obliging favour of to-day, juft received from Tiverton. I blefs God, for bringing him fafely thither; and for the expectation of hearing him at my Church, both parts of the day, on the 19th inftant: of which I fhall, gladly, give notice, to-morrow.—Mrs. R. and yourfelf will, I hope, give me the pleafure of accommodating you both, as well as my batchelor's houfe will permit, as many days, next week, as you conveniently can, antecedently to the Sunday above-mentioned. For which purpofe, I fhall take care to be at home; or, at the utmoft, within call.

God's Holy Spirit come with you, and fpeak by you, and blefs you to this people. You will fow on ploughed ground: and cannot offend the generality

of

of my hearers, preach free and finished falvation as ftrongly as you will. May you be enabled to reach their hearts.

With affectionate refpects to dear Mrs. Romaine, I fubfcribe myfelf, *ex animo* (as all my fubfcriptions are) ever your's,

Auguftus Toplady.

LETTER XXVI.

To Ambrose Serle, Efq.

Broad-Hembury, *Oct.* 1, 1773.

MY having fpent part of the week at Exeter, will account for this late acknowledgement of dear Mr. S's favours, which I found at my return.

You have my particular thanks, ever valued fir, for the tranfmiffion of your learned and ingenious manufcript concerning the Origin of the Human Soul *. I waited, with fome degree of impatience, for this completion of your kind promife, made when we were travelling together from Honiton to Exeter: and I muft own, that, though I am not profelyted, I am confiderably ftaggered, by the arguments you bring. The ftrongeft of which, in my idea, is, that, drawn from the eternal generation of God the Son. This, certainly, if any thing, bids faireft for turning the fcale in favour of the hypothefis, you fo heartily adopt, and fo ingeniously de-

---

* The manufcript, here alluded to, has fince been publifhed in a feries of fome of the firft numbers of the Theological Mifceilany, by the ingenious and refpectable gentleman unto whom this letter is addreffed; who is held in high eftimation for his integrity, piety, and benevolence, but particularly for his profound and critical refearches evinced in his exhibition of divine truth. Editor.

fend.

fend. Nor can I anſwer to the inference you deduce from that topic.

I muſt, however, with all the reſpect and tenderneſs ſo juſtly due to my excellent friend, ſuſpend my judgment concerning the whole matter · as I have, hitherto, been always forced to do ; and as no leſs a man, than St. Auſtin, did, to the end of his life. Yet, though not determined to either ſide of the queſtion *(non noſtrûm eſt tantas componere lites)* I own myſelf inclinable to believe that ſouls are of God's own immediate creation and infuſion. Difficulties, both many and great, do, without doubt, clog the wheels of this opinion. But thoſe, which embarraſs the ψυχοſοια, ſeem, at preſent, to me, both more and greater. I know not, for inſtance, how to reconcile it to ſuch Scriptures as Eccles. xii. 7. Zech. xii. 1. Heb. xii. 9. Nor can I conceive how ſoul can generate ſoul, without ſuppoſing the ſoul to have *partes extra partes :* and if we once grant its diviſibility, what becomes of its abſolute immateriality, together with its eſſential incorruptibility, and its intrinſic immortality ? Neither can my dear friend aſcertain, from which of the two parental ſouls a third is educed : whether from the father's only, or from the mother's only, or by a *deciſione utriuſque.*

—— As little can it be explained, how one, or two ſouls, can produce many. The uſual ſimile, of " candle being lighted by candle," will here give us no light at all. One candle, it is true, is able to light up an hundred others : but not *ſine interciſione materiæ propriæ.* It actually communicates ſome of its own luminous particles to the candle or candles which it enflames. But can we ſay this of the ſoul, and at the ſame time maintain its ſpirituality ? Theſe, my dear ſir, are a ſpecimen of the difficulties which will not allow me to adopt the ψυχογονια; and which induce me to conſider the ψυχοκλιſις as the leſs exceptionable ſcheme of the two.

After all, it may, perhaps, be beſt, for us, as humble Chriſtians, not to launch too far into the immenſe ocean of too curious ſpeculation. God's word is the believer's chart. God's ſpirit is the believer's pilot. Where the former ceaſes to deſcribe our path, and the latter to ſhape our courſe, it will moſt conduce to the ſimplicity and joy of faith, to limit our enquiries, to leave with God the ſecret things which belong to him, to keep within ſight of land, and wait for all unneceſſary ecclairciſſements until our diſ-impriſoned ſouls ſhall aſcend on angels' wings to the preſence of him whoſe are all the treaſures of wiſdom and knowledge.

And yet, I wiſh to ſee your modeſt and elegant diſquiſition in print. I hope you will give it to the public : for, whether the hypotheſis it aſſerts be intrinſically right or wrong, you treat the argument with ſuch purity of diction, with ſuch refinement of reaſon, and with ſuch tranſparent piety, that it muſt pleaſe the philoſophic, and cannot poſſibly offend the Chriſtian reader.—Permit me to detain it from you a week or two longer : as I am very deſirous of giving it ſeveral peruſals more.

After putting your patience to ſo long a trial, I muſt not aggravate my prolixity, by apologizing for it. Nor can I conclude, without reminding you, that you are ſtill my debtor, by promiſe, for a ſight of thoſe compoſitions in verſe, in which (by the few ſamples you have formerly indulged me with) I know you to poſſeſs ſo refined a taſte. Lay me, ſoon, under this obligation alſo : though no obligations, which even you are able to confer, can make me, more than I already am,

your affectionate and devoted,

Auguſtus Toplady.

LETTER XXVII.

To Mr. M. POLLARD.

Broad-Hembury, Oct. 1, 1773.

DEAR SIR,

I FEAR you have, long ago, set me down for little less than a monster of incivility, on account of my permitting your letter to lie so long unacknowledged. I am really ashamed to review its date. You wrote it, Oct. 1, 1772. I am answering it, Oct. 1, 1773. Such a seeming failure, in common decency, needs much candour, in you, to excuse it; and requires a very sufficient apology, from me, to extenuate it.

The truth is, your favour was, by some means or other, mislaid: and was not retrieved, until a few days ago, when I was hunting among my papers. I often recollected, with pain and regret, that I was your epistolary debtor: but was forced to continue so, until, by recovering your address, I could know, with certainty, how to direct my answer.

I read that rancorous and paltry libel on the Church of England, compiled by Cornish, of Culliton, which you was so obliging as to send me: a performance, raked together from a variety of antient and modern dunghills; and exhibiting such a jumble of scurrility, as was never, I believe, before, crowded into so small a compass.

I cannot agree with you, that it deserves a public animadversion. It is, moreover, by this time, dead and buried, in great measure. It was pity to recall it into life. Let it sink, and be forgotten. The Church has nothing to fear, from the efforts of such an indecent scribbler, who has started nothing new; but deals in stale, borrowed cavils, which have been refuted, again and again, times without number.

Besides:

Befides : an anfwer would only conduce to render both the man and his pamphlet confpicuous. It would fet the former, on a pedeftal; and diffufe the latter into a greater number of hands.

Mr. Addifon fomewhere obferves, there are in-fects, fo exceedingly minute, that we cannot examine them, without magnifying them : and compares per-fons, who enter the lifts with contemptible writers, to the traveller, in the fable ; who, being incommoded with the noife of grafshoppers, " alighted from his horfe, in great wrath, to kill them all. Which was troubling himfelf, to no purpofe : for, had he pur-fued his journey, without taking notice of them, they would have died, of themfelves, in a very few weeks."

This is my chief reafon for declining the tafk you wifh me to undertake. To which I muft add, that my bufinefs, for feveral years paft, has lain in another department. My call from Providence feems to be, not the affailing of thofe who honeftly feparate from a Church which (unhappily) they do not approve ; but to expofe the treachery, and to obviate the interefted fophiftry, of too many among us, who, for caufes fufficiently notorious, pretend to revere the Church, and actually live by her breafts, while they hate her doctrines in their hearts, and labour, with all their might, to ftab her under the fifth rib.

With affectionate wifhes for your welfare both here, and ever, I remain,

Sir, your obedient fervant,

Auguftus Toplady.

LETTER

LETTER XXVIII.

Tò Mr. Burgess.

[Extract.]   *Broad-Hembury, Oct. 22, 1773.*

I HAVE feen fo much of the religious world, and have fo largely experienced how little ftrefs is to be laid on fair appearances; that I prize, with re-doubled efteem, the graces and the friendfhip of the genuine few : in which number, I am thoroughly fatisfied, my valued Mr. B. ftands. I am led to this remark, by the recent conduct of a very flaming profeffor (R——, of Lyme) who has at length dropt the mafque, and, with equal difhonour to the gof-pel and himfelf, proves (I fear) no other than a whited wall and a painted fepulchre.—In fhort, one hardly knows, whom to truft, or of whom to enter-tain a good opinion. But the great Head of the Church knows them that are his; and bleffed be the riches of his faithful love, he will take care of his own to the end.

Mrs. W. I am afraid, will think my filence a mark of difrefpect. But I am fo thoroughly cer-tain, that all Zion's children fhall be taught of the Lord; that I am the lefs folicitous to obviate her fcruples, refpecting the doctrines of grace. God has, already, began to do great things for her. He will, doubtlefs, go on, to make her path brighter and brighter. There is no need of my holding a lan-tern to her fteps. She is in a fair way for the king-dom : and I would have as little of human teaching enter into her experience, as poffible.—Pray, prefent her with my Chriftian falutations : and affure her of an intereft in my unworthy addreffes at the throne of our common Father.

The bleffings of Providence, and of grace, continue, through mercy, to furround my path. I have no

O 3   caufe

caufe of perfonal uneafinefs, but the remains of unbelief and unthankfulnefs And even thefe fhall be
done away, totally and for ever, when mortality is
fwallowed up of life.

The richeft bleffings of God's covenant love be
with you. I affectionately falute our friends in general: particularly, good captain T. Mr. and Mrs.
S———r, Mr. and Mrs. S———y, and Mifs B.
Write to me, as often as you can. And though my
many engagements may not always permit me to
return you letter for letter; yet believe me to be,
what I moft fincerely am,

Your affectionate brother in the Lord our righteoufnefs,

Auguftus Toplady.

L E T T E R XXIX.

To AMBROSE SERLE, Efq.

[Extract.] *Broad-Hembury, Oct.* 22, 1773.

I FEEL my utter inability to debate fo abftrufe a
point, with fo potent and mafterly an antagonift.
We are, however, both agreed, that we have fouls.
And bleffed be God, for giving us caufe to believe,
that they are redeemed to himfelf, by the precious
blood of his co-equal Son.

Allow me, dear fir, to repeat my requeft, relative to the publication of your thoughts on a fubject, which has exercifed fo few pens of eminence,
and which your own is fo peculiarly qualified to difcufs. In fhort, I fhall never ceafe teazing you,
until my wifh is granted.

You are too generous, to blame me, for the flow-
nefs, with which I recede from my own opinion concerning the queftion in difpute: or, rather, for my
fufpenfe

'fufpenfe between the two opinions. I well remember, that, in 1758, when I firft began to difcern
fomething of the abfurdities and impieties of Arminianifm, my mind was in a fimilar ftate of fluctua-
tion, for many fucceeding months. Dr. Manton's
Sermons on the 17th of St. John were the means,
through which my Arminian prejudices received
their primary fhock : a blefling, for which an eternity of praife will be but a poor mite of acknowledgement to that God, whofe fpirit turned me from
darknefs to light. But it was a confiderable time
(and not until after much prayer, and much reading
on each fide of the argument) ere my judgment was
abfolutely fixed.—I fhall, when in heaven, remember the year 1758, with gratitude and joy : as I,
doubtlefs, fhall the year 1755, in which I was firft
awakened to feel my need of Chrift.

The origin of the foul, though not of equal importance with the doctrines of grace, yet requires
much difquifition, in order to our coming at any
fatisfactory and folid ground whereon to reft the
fole of our foot. At leaft, I find it extremely difficult. I fee not any thing, by intuition. *Veritas
in puteo.* It, moft times, requires much labour, to
draw it up : and, very frequently, eludes our utmoft fkill and pains, at laft. It is a comfort, after
all, that the foul may be happy here, and faved
forever; though ignorant, at prefent, of her own
immediate fource.

Augufus Toplady.

L ET T E R XXX.

To Mrs. MACAULAY,

Broad-Hembury, Oct. 22, 1773,

AS we live at a period, when to be in debt, and to be in the fashion, are almost inseparable ideas ; I offer no apology, for the length of time, during which, my honoured friend's obliging letter has passed without acknowledgement.

I will go farther still : and even value myself on an omission, which has, perhaps, contributed something to the public benefit. In writing to me, you please and improve a grateful individual. But, as an historian, you convey pleasure and instruction to multitudes. Was I to return you an immediate answer to the favours I receive, your friendship and politeness would not fail to balance the epistolary account with equal exactness. A consideration, which induces me, now and then (contrary to the general maxim of the age), to consult my country's advantage, though at the occasional expence of my own.

With regard, madam, to Oliver Cromwell, on whom our correspondence has, of late, chiefly turned, I find myself silenced, though not entirely convinced, by the force of your observations. I must resign my client, to your better judgement and superior powers : unless you will permit me to compromise matters, in the language of Lord Lyttleton. " By an uncommon appearance of zeal, by great address, and great valour, Cromwell first enflamed the spirit of liberty into extravagance; and, afterwards, duped and awed it into submission. He trampled on the laws of the nation, but he raised the

the glory of it : and it is hard to fay, which he moft deferved ; an halter, or a crown."

From a perfon, whofe public merits were thus ᷂equivocal, I revert, with pleafure, to one, whofe patriotic deferts no honeft and capable judge can difpute. To be informed, and from fo good authority as your own, that your health and ftrength are improved, give me far greater and folider joy, than any other information you were able to convey. I hope to be an eye-witnefs of their continuance, if, as I have fome thoughts of doing, I fhould fpend a fortnight in London, during the enfuing winter.

I learned another piece of good news, a few days fince, at H——, where our friend Mr. N——, acquainted me, on Mr. D—'s authority, that your 6th volume will appear, early in the fpring. This will be the moft valuable amends you can make us, for depriving us of your company, this year, in the Weft.

Your old acquaintance and admirer, Mr. H. has, I am told, received fome difguft at L——, and is very feldom there. Lord C. however, ftill profeffes to affect that romantic fea-port; though it does not promife to yield him (as, if fame fay true, he once hoped it would) a fecond Sir W. P. it were pity a fecond fhould ever fall to his fhare.

With every wifh of happinefs, and with the utmoft fincerity of refpect, I remain, Madam, your moft obliged and obedient fervant,

Auguftus Toplady.

LETTER XXXI.

To Ambrose Serle, Efq.

Broad-Hembury, Nov. 23, 1773.

WHEN favours, received, diftance all power of equal return, the receiver can but barely acknowledge his receipt of them, and confefs his incompetency to repay them. Your inftances of friendfhip, to me, are of the above kind, both as to number and value. My returns, to you, are, and muft ever be, as laft defcribed.

Allow me, dear fir, fo far to revive our late amicable conteft, as to intreat you not to fupprefs the ,publication of your Thoughts *De Origine Animæ.* Were they to appear, they might open a way for other learned and ingenious perfons to ventilate the fubject : which is one reafon why I take the liberty to urge the requeft.—If I have detained your valuable manufcript, too long, you may draw on me, for it, whenever you pleafe ; though, the longer I am indulged with it, the more your debtor I fhall be. —Pray, have you feen Mr. Charles Crawford's Remarks on Plato's Phædon ? I am told, that performance is not deftitute of fire and genius, though very excentric from the point of orthodoxy. Poffibly, the perufal of it might give you occafion to enlarge your papers, on the fubject we have debated, fhould you be prevailed with to give them to the public : in which cafe, the random fhots of the fanguine and romantic Weft Indian may be of fervice to the Church of God, by being turned into a contrary direction. Do think of this, ferioufly.

I reckon myfelf fo interefted in whatever relates to you, that I cannot help intimating a wifh, which dwells much upon my mind, concerning the treatife,

tife, you have in hand, on the proper divinity of our adorable High Priest and Saviour. My wish is, that you would take occasion, in the course of that work, to vindicate and establish the personality and divinity of the Holy Spirit: points, which were never more necessary to be asserted and elucidated, than at present; when the poison of *sabellianism* begins to pour in, as a flood, even among some spiritual professors themselves.

Let me teaze you, with yet another request. It is, that I may be indulged with a sight of those compositions, which you mentioned on our way between Broad-Hembury and Honiton. You see, I am already so deeply in your debt for obligations received, that, like a professed bankrupt, I care not how many fresh debts I incur. Nay, I wish to sink, deeper and deeper.

God give us to sink deeper into his love, and to rise, higher and higher, into the image of his holiness! Thoroughly persuaded I am, that, the more we are enabled to love and resemble him, the more active we shall be, to promote his glory and to extend his cause, with our lips, our pens, our lives, our all. Be this our business, and our bliss, on earth. In heaven, we shall have nothing to do, but to see him as he is, to participate his glory, and to sing his praise; in delightful, in never-ending concert with angels, with saints who are got home before us, and with those of the elect whom we knew and loved below. I would hardly give six-pence for a friendship, which time and death are able to quench. Our friendship is not of that evanid species. I can, therefore, subscribe myself,

ever and forever your's,

Augustus Toplady.

LETTER XXXII.

To Ambrose Serle, Efq.

Broad-Hembury, Dec. 8, 1773.

I Cannot but fmile, at the eafe and readinefs, with which we cut our work for each other. My dear friend's politenefs, in fo condefcendingly hearkening to my folicitations for the public appearance of his mafterly thoughts, fhould induce me, by every tie of refpectful gratitude, to meet his wifhes, with equal facility. But I am really unqualified for the department affigned me by his partiality of efteem. My acquaintance with the fathers is too flender, and my general compafs of reading far too contracted, for the undertaking you recommend. I fhould be mafter of at leaft, Irenæus, Epiphanius, and Auftin, to write, in a manner tolerably fatisfactory, on fo complicated a fubject, as a review of heretics and herefies. I have, it is true, many fubfidiary helps; but I ever wifh, where the nature of the cafe will poffibly admit, to derive my informations, not at fecond hand, but from the fountain's head. Allow me, dear fir, to recommend the propofal, to the propofer himfelf. The work would be as compleat, as any human performance can be, if you was to oblige and improve the world with the projected looking-glafs for heretics.

Glad I am, to be informed, that your defence of the Meffiah's divinity is almoft finifhed. My admiration is fure to be excited, by every thing you write: nor fhall my moft facred wifhes be wanting, that God would ftamp general ufefulnefs on all your attempts for the glory of his name.

Your defign, of honouring and gratifying me with the firft perufal of your treatife, calls for more acknowledgement than I am able to exprefs. Next

to

to your converfation, I can receive no higher intellectual feaft, than that which refults from a perufal
of your writings. Though felf intereft, therefore,
operates, in this matter, too ftrongly on my mind,
to admit of my declining fo decifive a proof of your
affectionate friendlhip; yet, that I may not be too
greatly indulged at the public expence, I cannot
help intimating a defire, that my enjoyment of the
firft fruits may not prejudice the harveft: I mean,
that the advanced parts of your work may be tranfmitted hither, fo feafonably, as not to delay the
publication of the whole.

Accept my thanks, likewife, for the promifed
fight of what you are pleafed to ftile the *Verfus iner-
tes*. If they " give me the head-ach," I will let
you know it: and, by the fame rule, if they charm
me into admiration, your delicacy muft difpenfe
with my telling you fo.

- - - - - - - - - - - -
- - - - - - - - - - - -

The fubject of ordination, revives my wifh, that
you would fubmit to the impofition of hands. The
Church would then (a very uncommon thing in this
age) be a gainer at the expence of the ftate.

LETTER XXXIII.

To Mrs. MACAULAY.

Broad-Hembury, Jan. 11, 1774.

LAST Saturday, I returned from a fhort excur-
fion to Dorfetfhire. Though you can be no
ftranger to the lofs, which the public have fuftained,
in the deceafe of Mr. Hollis; yet, it is poffible, you
may not have been apprifed of the particulars, by
an authentic hand.

That

That friend of the British empire and of mankind was, early in the afternoon of New Year's Day, in a field, at some distance from his place of residence at Corscombe, attended by only one workman, who was receiving his directions, concerning a tree, which had been lately felled. On a sudden, he put one of his fingers to his forehead; saying, "Richard, I believe the weather is going to change: I am extremely giddy." These words were scarce off his lips, when he dropped. He fell on his left side: and, being near an hedge, his head was received by the subjacent ditch. The man (I know not, whether a carpenter, or a common labourer) sprung to his assistance; and, raising him from that sad situation, administered what little relief he could. The expiring patriot was still sufficiently himself, to say, " Lord, have mercy on me; Lord, have mercy on me; receive my soul:" which were the last words he was able to pronounce. His lips moved, afterwards; but no sound was formed. In a few seconds more, his spirit was dis-imprisoned.

The frighted assistant lost no time. Leaving the corpse on the grass, he hastened away, for superior help. But in vain. The lancet, when applied, was without effect.

It seems, Mr. Hollis always wished, that his death might be sudden. Providence was pleased to grant his request.—Was I qualified to chuse for myself, and were it lawful to make it a subject of prayer, I would wish for the same indulgence, whenever my appointed change may come. It is, I think, the most desirable mode of departure, where the person is in a state of grace. How happy, to be surprised into heaven! And, to surviving friends, it is but a single shock, once for all.

At the time of his decease, Mr. Hollis was ready booted; intending to ride that day to Lyme Regis. When I was there, it was my melancholy lot to occupy the chamber in which he always slept, during

his

his occafional ftay in that town, and which had been prepared for his reception, two or three nights before. It was at the Three Cups: an inn, which he purchafed a few years ago.

How black is the ingratitude of human nature! Though this valuable man lived entirely to the benefit of others, and may be claffed with the moft public-fpirited worthies that ever breathed; yet I have feldom known a death fo little regretted by the generality. An eminent foreigner was of opinion, that " there is no fuch thing as friendfhip in the world." Had he faid, " there is not much," he would have hit the mark.

" With fame, in juft proportion, envy grows:
The man, that makes a character, makes foes."

Very exalted virtue is often admired: but not often loved. What is the reafon? Becaufe, few are truly virtuous. And we muft have fome virtue, ourfelves, ere we are capable of loving it in others, or of loving others for it.

You knew and efteemed Mr. Hollis's virtues; nor (which is one of the higheft encomiums his memory can receive) was he unworthy even of your friendfhip.

Allow me, madam, to exprefs my wifh, that the precious blood and the imputed righteoufnefs of the adorable Meffiah, who lived and died for finners, may prefent you, in the hour of death, and in the day of judgement, faultlefs and complete before the uncreated Majefty. But, for the fake of thofe whom, in virtue and in knowledge, you fo greatly furpafs; may you be long detained from receiving that crown of life, to which (I truft) the Son of God has redeemed you by the atonement of his ineftimable death.——

Auguftus Toplady.

LETTER

To Ambrose Serle, Efq.

Broad-Hembury, *Jan.* 11, 1774.

I WAS in Dorfetſhire, when dear Mr. S—'s favour, of the 4th inſtant, arrived here: elſe,
my thanks had waited on him, much earlier than
they now do, for his repeated obligations. I never
was maſter of fo uſeful a pocket-book, as that,
which your laſt packet conveyed. Nor have I often
met with compofitions, fo pleafing, and fo profit-
able, as thofe, which your friendſhip was fo good
as to communicate, under the fame inclofure. But
how could my dear friend (whofe judgment rarely
fails, unlefs when his own pieces are the objects of
its criticifm) ever think of fubmitting fuch finifhed
performances to my corrections? No. To preferve
their excellence, they muſt continue as they are. I
muſt fay of them, as Handell faid concerning the
old tune of the 100th Pfalm, when he was afked to
improve that confummate piece of noble mufic:
" was I to alter a note, I fhould fpoil the whole."—
Make your obligation complete, by favouring me
with more of thofe elegant and devout productions.
If you have copies, of thofe already fent, I fhall beg
leave to keep them. If not, I fhall folicit your permiffion to tranfcribe them, before they are returned.

I was once in company with Mr. M'Gregor, of
Woolwich; whom you have honoured with your
pious, benevolent, and judicious animadverfions.
I believe him to be a good man: but he is, certainly, a very ignorant one. If you fuffer yourfelf to be
at the beck of every conceited nibbler, who dreams
himfelf qualified to conteſt the plaineſt truths, you
will

will have work enough upon your hands.——My beft thanks are due, for your valuable tract. Though, perhaps, it may conduce to render both your antagonift, and his antecedent fcrawlation (for-give an homely Devonfhire term), more confpicu-ous, than they might otherwife have been.

I am happy, in the expectation of foon receiving your introduction to your great work. Do not fuf-pect me of complaifance, for ftyling it great, before I have feen it. I give it that epithet, on account of the unutterable confequence of the fubject on which it treats. What my unworthy judgement may be, of the manner, in which you have treated the argu-ment; fhall, as ufual, be tranfmitted to you, *ex animo*, when I have had the long wifhed-for indul-gence of perufing the welcome pacquet.

Some confiderable time ago, I requefted my ever dear friend, to reftrain the overflowings of his kind partiality toward, not the leaft grateful, but the leaft important, of his obliged confidence. Talk no more, of a " giant" and a " dwarf," unlefs you will allow me to affume all title to the latter denomi-nation. If you love me, treat me as (what I am) an ignorant, feeble, dying finner. And, if you are fo benevolent, as to entertain a favourable idea of my wifhes for the caufe of God, keep that favourable idea to yourfelf, in time to come.

The holidays, I fuppofe, will hardly be expired, when this reaches your hands. Commend me, therefore, to your dear little folks. And may the children of my ineftimable friend be the children of the living God.

Mr. Fletcher may fire off, as foon as he pleafes. The weapons of his warfare can never wound the truths of God, any more than an handful of feathers can batter down my Church tower. I fhall, how-ever, be glad to fee his performance, when it ap-pears. Mr. Shirley told me, when I was laft at Bath, that Fletcher is to fucceed pope Wefley, as commander in chief of the focieties, if he fhould furvive his holinefs. No wonder, therefore, that the cardinal of Madely is fuch a zealous ftickler for the caufe. One would think, that the Swifs were univerfally fated to fight for pay. Adieu.

Auguftus Toplady.

L E T T E R XXXV.

To the Rev. Mr. ROMAINE.

Broad-Hembury, Jan. 11, 1774.

ACCEPT my thanks, honoured and valued fir, for the welcome prefent of your three precious volumes. May the life of faith be more and more operative in my heart; and may the walk of faith be difplayed in every part of my converfation; until the great author and finifher of faith give me an abundant entrance into the land of fight and of glory.

I wifh it was in my power, to render you an acknowledgement, adequate, in worth, to the kind favour you have conferred. When the printer will give my intended publication leave to appear, a copy of it, fuch as it is, will folicit your acceptance.

The God, whofe you are, and whom you ferve, lend you long to his Church; multiply his mercies toward you, and caufe your path to fhine, with increafing brightnefs, to the perfect day. You give me your friendfhip; give me alfo your prayers, and confider me as

your affectionate and obliged,

Auguftus Toplady.

My beft remembrance waits on dear Mrs. Romaine. Mifs L——— exprefles much concern and furprize,

furprize, at your having paffed through Welling-
ton, without calling on her; and wifhes to know
the reafon.

LETTER XXXVI.

To Mr. ———.

Broad-Hembury, Feb. 9, 1774.

DOCTOR Young has an obfervation, which
difcovers, as much as any he ever made, his
knowledge of human nature: "It is dangerous," I
think he fays, "to dive, into moft men, deeper than
the furface; left clofer acquaintance fhould abate
our good opinion of them."

You, my deareft friend, are *primus è paucis,* eminent among the rare exceptions to that rule. The
perfon, who knows you beft, will be fure to value
you moft: and, the longer he has the happinefs of
knowing you, the more muft he regard and refpect
you. His efteem will refemble the progreffive en-
largements of a river, which widens and increafes as
it flows. I am led to this remark, by a repeated
perufal of your valuable manufcript. Pardon the
delay, if no part of it wait on you by the prefent
pacquet. Were your papers lefs excellent, they would
be difmiffed from hence with greater expedition.

I did not doubt of your approving Gale's Court
of the Gentiles. It is indeed a treafure. Though,
I think, in fome cafes, the learned and devout author winds up his darling hypothefis too high, in
fuppofing, that the Jews, during the very infancy of
their nation, were the fole *lumina terræ,* or the foun-
tains from whom the Egyptians and other eaftern
literati derived the fubftance of their erudition. I

likewife

likewife agree with you, that he might have difplayed more judgement, in arranging his materials:
which (like what Mr. Addifon obferves concerning
Solomon's Proverbs) refemble a fuperb amaffment
of pearls, rather piled into a magnificent heap, than
regularly ftrung and artificially difpofed. However,
it is eafy to criticife. But, to compile fuch a performance, was not attended with equal facility:
hic labor, *hoc opus*.

Did you ever meet with a tract, written by Witfius, and entiled (to the beft of my remembrance)
De Trinitate Judaïca? It is the only part of his Latin
works, which I have never been able to procure. I
dare believe, it would be worthy of your perufal: as
every thing of his is peculiarly learned, elegant and
judicious. Poffibly, if you enquire among your
literary friends, fome of them may get you a fight of
that very fcarce differtation. Markius mentions it,
in his Oration at Witfius's interment.

Thanks to you, dear fir, for the news-paper extraordinary; which contained feveral particulars, deferving of attention. The anecdotes, related of
Richard III's illegitimate fon, are fo curious, and
wear fuch an afpect of probability, that I thought
them worth cutting out; and have pafted them to
a blank leaf of Walpole's Hiftoric Doubts. The
minutes of doctor Samuel Johnfon's Tour to Scot-
land are perfectly in character. He is the very original, there delineated. I have fome perfonal
knowledge of him: and, however I diffent from various of his principles, nor can avoid fmiling at fome
of his not-unpleafing oddities: he ftill paffes with
me, for one of the ableft and honefteft men, who
now adorn the republic of letters. Mr. Hollis's
character is, I think, prodigioufly overcharged; and
the panegyric beyond meafure exceffive; though he
certainly was a very valuable member of fociety;
and his deceafe awakened, in me, much of that
painful fenfibility, which I heartily wifh I could
divest

diveſt myſelf of. I ſtood obliged to him, for a number of ſcarce and curious tracts, relative to the time of Charles I. and he would have favoured me with incomparably more ſolid tokens of his eſteem, had I been capable of feigning myſelf a republican, and of diſſembling my ſincere attachment to the Scriptures and to our eccleſiaſtical eſtabliſhment.

I tremble, with you, for the event of things in America. But the kingdom of Providence rules over all. This is as much of politics, as I almoſt ever ventured to write. *Vox audita perit: Litera Scripta manet.* Adieu.

Auguſtus Toplady.

LETTER XXXVII.

To Mrs. MACAULAY, *now at Bath.*

Broad-Hembury, Feb. 18, 1774.

HAD I not lived long enough in the world, to ceaſe from wondering at any thing, I ſhould have more than wondered at the incident, of which you ſo juſtly complain. If almoſt any pen, except your own, had informed me of Mr. ———'s ingratitude and injuſtice, I ſhould have queſtioned the reality of the fact. I am ſorry, ſtill more for his ſake, than for your's, to find it ſo authentically atteſted. Well may Scripture (a book which you, madam, are too wiſe and too virtuous to deſpiſe) ſay, What is man !

Pity it is, that, on ſuch occaſions as the preſent, you are not diveſted of that exquiſite ſenſibility, which, at your own expence, adds too much honour to the remembrance of a ſocial delinquent. Forget it all ; and, as you are more than female, in underſtanding ; be more than maſculine, in fortitude.

Triumph

Triumph over the irritating favageneſs of the cyni-
ciſm which has requited you fo ill, by oppoſing to
it the iron apathy of the portico.

Do more. Riſe into a ſtill nobler revenge.—
Namely, by centering your expectations in him,
who never diſappoints thoſe defires, of which his
fpirit is the gracious inſpirer.

> " Lean not on earth; 'twill pierce thee to the
>   heart :
> At beſt, a broken reed ; but, oft, a ſpear.
> On it's ſharp point, peace bleeds, and hope ex-
>   pires."

Only the experienced favour and the felt poſſeſſion
of God in Chriſt can fill the vaſt capacities of a foul
like your's. Enjoy his communicated ſmile :

> " Then bid earth roll ; nor feel the idle whirl."

May Bath have an happy effect on the health of a
perfon fo important to the community. You tell
me, your ſtay there will be of confiderable duration.
I think to fee London, fome time in April. Should
you continue at the Weſtern Betheſda, until the
latter end of that month, or until the beginning of
May, I will take Bath in my return to Devonſhire,
by way of feeing how the waters have agreed with
you.

Let me fubmit a fingle caution to your candour,
viz. Be careful not to renew your acquaintance with
the dapper doctor ; and, above all, beware of being
feen with him in public.

————— *Hic niger eſt : hunc tu, Romana, caveto.*

He would derive luſtre from you ; but, like a piece
of black cloth, he would abforb the rays, without
reflecting any of them back. The world is very ma-
licious : and a character, fo eminently confpicuous
as your's, is a mark, at which envy and cenfure de-
                                        light

light to feize every opportunity of difcharging their arrows.

As you give me hopes of feeing you in this coun-try, during the courfe of the enfuing fummer; who knows, but I may have the honour of efcorting you hither, through the whole length of Somerfetfhire? But I mutt not detain you from the Pump-room, by my tedious fpeculations. So, for the prefent, farewel. God give you good fpirits; for, where they lead the van, good health generally brings up the rear.

Auguftus Toplady.

P. S. I could wifh you acquainted with Mrs. Derham, of Green-ftreet, Bath. You would find her one of the moft fenfible and amiable women in that city. She has all the genuine eafe, without any of the affected grimace of politenefs, her hufband is a wine-merchant, and fhe has a lovely daughter, nearly the age of your's.

L E T T E R XXXVIII.

To the Rev. Mr. DE COETLOGON.

Broad-Hembury, April 5, 1775.

DEAR SIR,

I Received your late favour; and am much your debtor, as well for your obliging partiality to my humble efforts in behalf of God's truths; as for the politenefs, with which you exprefs it.

Were I fituate near the capital, I fhould, with much readinefs, accede to your requeft, by con-tributing my affiftance toward carrying on the Gofpel Magazine: but I find it fo very inconvenient, to

have

have any concern with printing, at fo remote a diftance, that I fhall, probably, in future, publifh no more, in any way whatever, than abfolute occafion may require. With beft remembrance to your moft amiable bride,

I remain, your affectionate fervant,

Auguftus Toplady.

L E T T E R XXXIX.

To Mr. G. F.

Broad-Hembury, April 8, 1774.

LONGER time is ufually allowed, for the payment of large debts, than of trivial ones. By parity of argument, a delay of correfpondence, on the fide of him who has received great epiftolary obligations; is the more venial, on that very account. If my valuable and valued friend will not admit this reafoning to be fair, I muft own, that I have nothing better to urge, in extenuation of my having fo long omitted to thank him for his laft welcome and much efteemed favour. Yet, as fome degree of imperfection is connected with every thing human : I muft likewife confefs, that I cannot extend my thanks, for thofe ftrokes of undue panegyric, with which, dear fir, your kind partiality fo profufely honours me. Sincerely I fay it (and it may be faid, once for all) that I would much rather be told of my real faults, than of thofe fuppofed excellencies which the extreme benevolence of my friends is fo ready to place to my account. Candour and politenefs, like your's, firft illuminate every object, on which they fhine ; and then afcribe, to the object itfelf, thofe communicated rays, of which it is no more than the humble and obliged receiver.

Let

Let me now advert to a superior subject: and thank you for the improving particulars, so kindly forwarded, concerning the lamented decease of our honoured and deserving friend, the late truly excellent Mr. Hitchen ; that amiable and precious man of God, whose grace was as solid, as his parts were shining. His steady faith, and his calm, unruffled departure, amidst such circumstances of bodily pain, can only be attributed to that everlasting love, and to that atoning blood, which made him more than conqueror. Looking, the other day, into my book of occasional collections, I found two remarks, which dropped from Mr. Hitchen, in a conversation I had with him, July 18, 1769; and which were well worthy of being preserved from oblivion. They run, *verbatim*, thus :

" The greater our sanctification is, and the more advanced we are in holiness, the more we shall feel our need of free justification."

" An architect cannot say, to his rule, to his line, or other instrument, " Go, build an house." He must, first, take them into his own hand, ere the wished for effect will follow. What are ministers of God, but mere instruments? And, if ever they are useful in building up the Church of Christ, it is his own hand must make them so."

Such improving observations as these ; such valuable reliques, of saints indeed ; are too precious, to be lightly forgot. May they be engraven on our hearts !

I rejoice to hear of dear Mr. Ryland senior's liberty and sweetness, in his ministrations to Mr. H——'s widowed flock. Our Northampton friend is an Israelite without guile ; and he is among those, who stand highest in my regard. He blames me for seldom writing to him : but, was I to correspond regularly, even with my first rate favourites, I should do nothing more than write letters from morning to night. In heaven, we shall be all together, for ever and ever.

Make

Make my affectionate respects acceptable to dear Mrs. F——, &c. &c. Grace, mercy, and peace; bright evidences, sweet experiences, and growing holiness; be your portion, their portion, and the portion of

your affectionate servant in Christ,

Augustus Toplady.

LETTER XL.

To Mr. H.

[Extract.] *Titchfield-street, London, May* 23, 1774.

YESterday afternoon, being Whitsunday, curiosity led me to hear Mr. Theophilus Lindsey, who lately resigned the vicarage of Catterick. I took care to be there, before any of the service began, in order to hear, what that gentleman calls, the reformed liturgy: but what may more truly be termed, the liturgy deformed. It is a wretched skeleton of the old Common Prayer, shorn and castrated of all its evangelical excellencies.

He preached, or rather read, a poor, dry, ungraceful harangue, on Matt. xxv. 14, 15. So wretchedly was he tied and bound by the chain of his notes, that, if, by accident, he happened to take his eye from his papers (and it happened several times) he was sure to blunder; and endeavoured, in an exceedingly confused and embarrassed manner, to gather up the broken thread as well as he could. He is a palpable Arian, in his ideas of Christ's person; and appears to be a thorough-paced Socinian, as far as concerns the doctrine of atonement. Yet, God forbid that I should judge and condemn him. To his own master he must stand or fall. But I must observe two things: 1. I bless the grace of
God,

God, for giving me eyes to fee, and an heart to value, the ineftimable truths of his holy gofpel: 2. I
never prized our good old liturgy, and the precious
doctrines of the reformation, more, than on hearing
Mr. Lindfey's liturgy and fermon yefterday. No
man (as our Lord obferves) having drank old wine,
ftraightway defireth new: for he faith, the old is
better.

Mr. Lindfey's Arian meeting is held in Effex-
ftreet, up one pair of ftairs, in the houfe called
Effex-houfe. It is a long narrow room (which, if
filled, would hold about two hundred people) where
auctions (particularly for books) ufed to be held.
He feems to be a man of much perfonal modefty and
diffidence; and, I verily believe, acts upon principle.
But he has no popular talents: no pathos, no dignity, no imagination, no elegance, no elocution.
He muft, unavoidably, foon fink into obfcurity,
when the novelty of his fecefion begins to fubfide,
ard when his Arian friends are weary of puffing him
off in the news-papers. Take my word for it (and
I am very glad I can truly have it to fay) the Church
of England has nothing to fear from a gentleman of
Mr. Lindfey's flender abilities. He can neither
thunder nor lighten; but crawls on, quite in the
hum-drum way; and is no more qualified, either
by nature or attainments, to figure at the head of a
party; than I am, to undertake the command of a
navy. One of my company (for a whole coachful
of us went) faid to me, after fervice was over;
" Well, I fuppofe you will call Mr. Lindfey's dif-
courfe a piece of arrant Lindfeywolfey." No, indeed, replied I: it was mere Lindfey throughout:
abfolute Arianifm, Socinianifm, and Pelagianifm,
without one thread of the contrary from firft to
laft.

Auguftus Toplady.

L E T T E R

LETTER XLI.

To Mrs. Macaulay.

[Extract.]   *Broad-Hembury, July 8, 1774.*

I Arrived here, from London, no longer ago, than this day se'nnight ; and though I was not able to take Bath in my way home, through the unavoidable length of my stay in town, I hope, madam, to be, soon, amply recompensed for that loss, by seeing you, safe and well, in this part of the world. Favour me with a line : and God grant it may import these two things : 1st, That all your complaints are completely annihilated by the Bath waters; and, 2dly, That you have begun to take the previous measures for your intended two months excursion to Devonshire.

I left good Mr. Ryland behind me in London. He desired his best remembrance to you : and wishes (in his lively manner), " that you may be a perfect idiot once in every twenty-four hours, and incapable of writing, reading, thinking, or conversing, viz. from ten at night, until six or seven in the morning :" that you may not impair your health by sitting up late. No friend, I verily believe, has more respect and esteem for you, than he : not even your obliged and obedient

Augustus Toplady.

P. S. One day, when Mr. Ryland and I went to Islington, to dine with Mrs. Bacon, he took that opportunity of introducing me to Mr. Burgh, author of the " Political Disquisitions." I saw him to great disadvantage, as he was in much pain, and in a very ill humour. The interview, on the whole, was a curious one. I was hardly seated, when he said to

Mr.

Mr. Ryland, concerning me, " This gentleman, I apprehend, is an antagonift of Mr. Lindfey's." I anfwered, for myfelf, no, fir ; I am not, indeed, of Mr. Lindfey's principles, but I look upon him, with all his miftakes, to be an honeft man : and I refpect an honeft man, be his opinions what they will. By degrees, our converfation grew rather engaging : and Mr. Burgh feemed, for a while, to feel a truce from the torments of the ftone, and afiume fome degree of good-nature. But I fhould have had a fharp onfet, if he had been in perfect health. Even as it was, he could not forbear feeling my pulfe, on the article of freewill. In the courfe of our debate, I drove him into this dreadful refuge, viz. that " God does all he poffibly can," [thefe were Mr. Burgh's own words] " to hinder moral and natural evil, but he cannot prevail : men will not permit God to have his wifh." Left I fhould miftake his meaning, I requefted him to repeat thofe terms again ; which he did. Then the Deity, faid I, muft needs be a very unhappy being. " Not in the leaft," replied Burgh. " What (rejoined I,) difappointed of his wifhes, embarraffed in his views, and defeated of his fchemes, and yet not be unhappy ?" " No," rejoined Burgh : " for he knows that he muft be fo difappointed and defeated, and that there is no help for it : and therefore he fubmits to neceffity, and does not make himfelf unhappy about it." A ftrange idea this, of the Supreme Being ! At coming away, I told Mr. Burgh, that however he might fuppofe God to be difappointed of his will, I hope the public would not be difappointed of the remaining volumes of the Political Difquifitions yet unfinifhed. And, in very truth, madam, your friend Burgh is much better qualified for political difquifitions, than either for theological or for metaphyfical ones. Adieu.

Auguftus Toplady.

L E T-

L E T T E R XLII.

To the Rev. Mr. Madan.

[Extract.]　　　　　*Broad-Hembury, July 8, 1774.*

ENOUGH of bufinefs. Now for chit-chat.
My few *horæ fubficivæ*, fince my return hither,
have been devoted, chiefly, to the perufal of lord
Chefterfield's Letters. I fhould think the better of
my own judgment, if it fhould be fo happy as to
coincide with your's. Mine is, in general, that they
are not only, what his lordfhip terms, "letters written from one man of the world to another;" but,
many of them, fuch as might well be expected from
a decent civilized fornicator, to his favourite
baft—d. Do you not alfo complain of a negligence,
in point of ftyle, compofition, and connection;
really to be wondered at, in even the running productions of fo mafterly an hand? It is true, letters
are but converfation committed to paper: yet, I
believe, the generality of well-bred people would
blufh to converfe in a ftyle equally inaccurate and
defultory, with that, in which lord Chefterfield
fometimes wrote.

I own, myfelf, however, on the whole, extremely
entertained and improved, by this publication. There
are almoft an infinity of rules and remarks, refpecting both men and *les manières*, founded on, the
deepeft worldly wifdom and truth: yet, fo inter-
mixed with drofs and refufe, that, had I the care of
a young perfon, I would not venture to put thofe
letters into his hands, without the precaution of an
index expurgatorius.

But was any thing ever like his portrait of the
female fex, in letter 129? Where he traduces them
all, without making a fingle exception. I know but

one

one way to bring him off : and that, I fear, will be far from doing it effectually : viz. by suppoling, that, when he sketched that caricature, his mind was acidulated by a recent fracas with lady Chesterfield : and that, in revenge, he instantly libelled the whole sex.

I never heard of Mr. Wesley's Sinai-covenanters, until you was pleased to mention them. Poor creatures ! to meet once a year, and solemnly bind themselves to keep the whole law ! I wish I had known this particular, some months ago. Can you tell, whether they have a written form of covenanting, or whether it be all *ore tenus ?* and, if the former, whether it be possible to procure a sight of it ? This is a matter, well worth enquiring into.

You once favoured me with a more critical explication of Pet. i. 19, than I had before met with. I wish you would condescend to give it me in writing.

Augustus Toplady.

LETTER XLIII.

To the Rev. Mr. ROMAINE.

Broad-Hembury, July 8, 1774.

Rev. and DEAR SIR,

AS it is possible that our valuable and valued friend, Mr. ———, may not hitherto have had an opportunity of acquainting you with the polite manner in which lord ——— received your late favour ; and as Mr. ——— has been so good as to communicate to me, in a letter received here yesterday evening, the substance of what passed ; permit me, without delay,

1. To

1. To inform you, in general, that your kind application appeared to have a very favourable effect: and that his lordſhip was ſo obliging as to ſay, he would "try the ground" with the lord chancellor.

2. To thank you, under Providence, for the very friendly intervention of your good offices: which, whether crowned with ultimate ſucceſs, or not, I ſhall, ever, moſt affectionately remember.—And,

3. To requeſt an exertion of your intereſt with that bleſſed and only potentate, who has all power both in heaven and earth; that he would gracioufly give ſuch an event to this whole matter, as he will be pleaſed to bleſs moſt to the glory of his own name.

I returned hither, from London, this day ſe'nnight: and, laſt Tueſday, attended the biſhop's viſitation at Tiverton. The ſermon was preached by Mr. Land: and upon the whole, a very excellent one it was. Among its few flaws, was, the claſſing of Hutchinſon, with Clarke, Shafteſbury, and Hume: the former of whom, if living, would have been very ſorry at being put among ſuch company. The Strand divines were, rather ſeverely, than ſmartly, taken to taſk: and, as I was afterwards told, old Whitter and young Wood held down their heads in ſome confuſion.

The epiſcopal charge, though extremely conciſe (i. e. diſpatched in about 12 or 14 minutes), was the very beſt I ever heard. It chiefly turned, on the excellency of the 39 articles; the expediency of ſubſcription; and the peculiar duties, more than ever, at this time, incumbent on the clergy, relative to their morals, manners, dreſs, and abſtractedneſs from the world. The whole of his lordſhip's behaviour, both in the Church, and afterwards at dinner, gave much ſatisfaction to the generality, and peculiar pleaſure to me.

Adieu,

Adieu, honoured and dear fir. Kindeſt reſpects
to yourſelf, and to Mrs. Romaine, from
your obliged and affectionate
Auguſtus Toplady.

L E T T E R XLIV.

To Ambrose Serle, Eſq.

Broad-Hembury, July 8, 1774.

SHALL I attempt to thank my ever dear and
ever reſpected friend, for his polite and obliging
favour of the 30th ult. or for the kind ſervices,
which preceded that favour, and to which it refers?
No. It is a duty, to whoſe performance I feel myſelf unequal. Your friendſhip, therefore, like what
ſome ſay concerning virtue at large, muſt be its own
reward. Yet, think me not inſenſible. My ſenſibility is the very cauſe of the omiſſion. Were the
obligations, under which you lay me, more moderate,
I could with eaſe, thank you for them: but, as the
caſe ſtands, I muſt follow Horace's direction, *con-
ſule quid valeant humeri*; and not aim at impoſſibi-
lities.

Sure I am, that God will incline the ſcale (and
not this only, but every other, to the end of time,)
ſo as ſhall conduce to his own glory, and to the accompliſhment of his own purpoſe. It is our's, to
uſe the means, in a dependance on his abſolute providence; to bleſs the means uſed, is his. With him,
all events muſt be ultimately reſted: and I truſt, I
can ſay, *ex animo*, with him I ever wiſh and deſire to
reſt them; nor would I have a ſingle incident removed
out of his hand, were I poſſeſſed of all power both
in heaven and earth.

You kindly remind me, " To ſtrike while the iron is warm." In anſwer to which, I muſt obſerve, that I have written, to-day, to Black-heath, and to Epſom. Can you ſuggeſt any other adviſable ſteps? You will find, not only my ear, but my heart, ever open to the leaſt hint ſuggeſted by a friend of your wiſdom and faithfulneſs, whether the ſubject relate to my own intereſt, or not.

You are ſo good as to enquire after my ſafe return into the Weſt. I bleſs God, my journey was both ſafe, and pleaſant. The ſlighteſt mercies ought to be thankfully received and noticed: for they are as abſolutely undeſerved, as the greateſt. We can no more merit a moment's eaſe, or ſafety, or happineſs, in our going out and coming in, or on any other occaſion whatever, than we can merit the kingdom of heaven.

I travelled with a very old (or rather, with a very early) acquaintance: an officer, of the 21ſt regiment: with whom, at our firſt ſetting off in the coach from London, I had an hour or two's controverſy, concerning the lawfulneſs of duelling. Your friend was on the negative ſide of the queſtion: the captain, on the affirmative. During the amicable ſkirmiſh (a duel againſt duelling,) and for many hours after, we were quite ignorant of each others names. And no wonder; for we had not met, ſince the year 1757, when we were both lads: and time has made ſuch alteration in each, that neither knew the other. We travelled to Bridport (i. e. 138 miles) before we found out who was who: and I have ſeldom known an ecclairciſſement which gave more pleaſure on both ſides. The captain, very politely, invited me to ſee him, if I ſhould ever go to Plymouth: and, on my aſking, for whom I ſhould enquire, the diſcovery was made.

On a review, I am really aſhamed of treſpaſſing on your patience and time, by ſuch petty chit-chat It is high ſeaſon for me to apologize; not by pro 1.

excuſe

excufes, but by cutting matters fhort at once. Only obferving, that, if the unexpected fight of an old and valued friend, on earth, gives an heart-felt joy, which none, but a breaft formed for friendfhip, can experience; what far more exceeding and exalted bleffednefs muft refult from that " Communion of faints" made perfect which will obtain in the kingdom of glory!—Until then, and when there, I am, and fhall ever be,

your affectionate friend,

Auguftus Toplady.

LETTER XLV.

Mr. O——.

Broad-Hembury, July 29, 1774.

BEST thanks to you ever dear fir, for your kind and obliging letter, of the 19th inftant. From what I felt, in reading it, I cannot help believing, that your foul was much alive to God, when you wrote it. May your holinefs and comforts refemble the flow of fome mighty river, which widens and enlarges, more and more, in proportion as it advances nearer the ocean into which it falls.

I rejoice at what you fay, concerning the happy frame of foul, in which the reverend Mr. Green afcended to Abraham's bofom. It is delightful, to live and walk in the fhinings of God's countenance: but to die in the light and confolations of his prefence, is (next to heaven itfelf) the crowning mercy of all. How gracious is the Holy Spirit of promife, thus to fhine away the doubts and fears of his people, and put them to bed by day-light! O may we

tafte

tafte the fweetnefs of his love, rife into a nearer conformity to his image, enjoy clofer communion with
him both in and out of ordinances, and experience
an increafing fenfe of his never failing faithfulnefs;
till we receive the end of our faith, even the full and
ultimate falvation of our fouls. I blefs the Lord,
I cannot doubt of his making all this our portion.
He fometimes enables me to look as it were, into his
heart of everlafting love ; and to catch a glimpfe of that
page-in the Book of Life, where he has written my
unworthy name : and in the ftrength of that comfort;
I can travel many days.

I am very glad, that dear Mr. ———— has broken
the ice, at Weftminfter. Would to God, that the
nafty party walls, which feparate the Lord's people
from each other below, were every one of them
thrown down. Sure I am, that, in heaven, all God's
houfe will be laid into one. Ephraim fhall, then,
no more envy Judah ; nor Judah vex Ephraim.

I am greatly indebted to Mr. M ————, for what
he did me the honour to fay of me, and of my late
publication, in the pulpit. But I defire, at the
fame time, to be (and, I blefs God, I am) humbled
and abafhed, inftead of elevated and puffed up, by
the unmerited obligations which I continually receive from the excellent of the earth. Not unto
me, O Lord, not unto me, but to thy name, be
the undivided glory of every gift, and of every
grace afcribed.

Prefent my affectionate refpects to dear Mrs.
————: who, I hope, has, by this time, added to
your family, without danger to herfelf. Let me
know this particular : for I bear her much upon my
heart.

While your dear little daughter continues as little
as fhe is, I may venture to fend my love to her. And
I wifh, alfo, to be kindly remembered to all in your
houfe, who love your Lord and mine.

How

How is mifs ———! Chriftian falutations to her
and all that family; and to as many as condefcend
to enquire after,

Dear fir, your obliged and very affectionate
fervant,   *Auguftus Toplady.*

LETTER XLVI.

To Mr. ———.

Broad-Hembury, Sept. 30, 1774.

EVER DEAR SIR,

THOUGH your kind politenefs has defired
me, never to thank you by letter, for the many
inftances of the regard with which you are continually
obliging me; yet, I muft, for once, violate the
prohibition, by acknowledging my fafe receipt of
the ———, &c. which you have lately added to
my ———, and for which I requeft you to accept my
cordial thanks. I wifh, that you and dear Mrs. ———
were here, to help to ufe them.

I greatly admire the elegant —— and ——, in
particular, and I pray the Father of mercies, that
the fweet fentences, with which the former is deco-
rated and infcribed, may be written, indelibly, on
the hearts both of the donor and of the receiver.

Next, let me thank you for your much efteemed
letter of the 15th inftant, and for the kind trouble,
you were fo good as to take, in calling on Mr. ———.
Whatever courfe the Northamptonfhire affair may
take, it will be in confequence of that "never failing Providence, which orders all things, both in
heaven and earth." Bleffed be God, for enabling
me, in fome meafure, not only to acquiefce, but to
rejoice, in the unerring difpofals of his will; and to
adore, with thankfulnefs, that Infinite Wifdom,

'Q 3'   which

which alone is able to chufe our heritage and our lot.

I have not been on the mount, for some days, until now. The Lord warm your heart with a ray of that fire, which, through the free grace of his fpirit, he, at prefent, gives me to experience. Oh, what treafures are in the blood of Chrift, what fafety, in his righteoufnefs! what fweetnefs in his fellowfhip! Lord, enlarge our fouls to receive of his fullnefs more and more. If the fcanty veffel of imperfect faith can draw fuch water of comfort from the wells of falvation; what will be the bleffednefs of God's elect, when they are taken up into glory, and there walk with him,

" High in falvation and the climes of blifs!"

The clearer views God gives us, of intereft in his covenant, and in the unfearchable riches of Chrift; the deeper we fink into an humbling fenfe of our own vilenefs and unfruitfulnefs. The fame candle of the Holy Spirit, which fhews us God's love, and our part in the Book of Life, difcovers to us the exceeding hatefulnefs of fin, and convinces us that we are hell deferving finners. It alfo fires us with an inextinguifhable wifh and thirft for conformity to Chrift in holinefs, and effectually caufes us to cry out, with David, " Make me to go in the path of thy commandments, for therein is my defire."

Doubt not, my dear fir, but the Lord will go on to take care of us, in all thefe refpects, and in every other; even beyond the utmoft we are able to afk or think.

My beft remembrance wait on the amiable and deferving partner of your heart: and I do, with truth and love in Chrift Jefus, fubfcribe myfelf, her and your

affectionate fervant in him,

Auguftus Toplady.

P. S. Be

P. S. Be fo good as to prefent my refpectful falutations to Mr. ———: whom I requeſt to accept my thanks for the intended 'token of his eſteem, which, when it arrives, I hope ever to preferve and value, for the fake of the giver.

I fhall be happy, to hear from you, as often as you can find leiſure. Is Mrs. ——— hour of danger paſt? She has my earneſt prayers. Adieu.

LETTER XLVII.

To Mrs. B———.

Broad-Hembury, Nov. 11, 1774.

ON my receiving a letter, franked by lord Sandwich, I immediately conjectured, to whom I ſtood indebted for the contents: and on breaking the feal, found my hope moſt agreeably realized. Your friendſhip and politeneſs, dear madam, are great indeed: which not only induced you to forgive my omiſſions; but even prevailed on you to be yourſelf, the renewer of that correfpondence, which both your merit, and my own promife, required me to recommence. Happy in the continuance of your eſteem, and fignally obliged by the accumulated favours you confer, I fhould be totally inexcuſable, were I to perſiſt in putting your condefcenſion to thoſe trials, whereof our truly valuable friend, Mr. Ryland, fo loudly complains.

But what can I fay, relative to the profufe encomiums, with which you deign to honour my late publication? Your probity is unqueſtionable. Your diſcernment, in every other inſtance, unimpeachable. I am thankful, for not having difpleafed fo refined a judge. May that adorable Being, whofe fpirit, alone, is able to enlighten the darkneſs of the human mind, command his gracious bleſſing on every attempt, which has his glory, and the illuſtration of his truths, for its objects!

Q 4

A per-

A perfon, whom we both deſervedly admire, has
juſt left Devonſhire, after a reſidence in it of no leſs
than three months. I mean Mrs. Macaulay; who
wiſely intermitted her hiſtorical purſuits, for the ſake
of purſuing that, without which the former would
ſoon come to a final period; namely, health. I left
her very weak and languid (as, I believe, I told you),
when I parted from her, laſt May, at Bath, on my
way to London. But ſhe has quitted this part of
the Weſt, in all the vigour and alacrity of health.
She is returned to Bath, where ſhe has taken an
houſe on St. James's Parade; and where, if buſineſs
or inclination ſhould call you to that city, ſhe will
be, I doubt not, extremely glad to ſee you. I have
promiſed to make an excurſion thither, for a month
or two, before winter is over, provided my ſtudies
will any way give leave: and ſhould be happy, if
you could, with convenience to yourſelf, contrive to
viſit Bath at the ſame time.

You tell me, you have been amuſed at London,
or rather ſhocked, by thoſe vehement exertions of
female zeal, which, in peereſſes, are no leſs violations
of law, than of delicacy. I too was, laſt Wedneſ-
day, amuſed, here in my own pariſh, by a ſcene,
much humbler than that which your electioneering
ladies exhibited; viz. by what is called, in this country, a Skimmington. A proceſſion, which is very
accurately deſcribed in Hudibras, and not with more
humour than the real fight conveys. A moſt uneaſy pair, whoſe conſtant jarrings, and whoſe frequent ſkirmiſhes (in which, however, the heroine,
not the hero, generally came off victorious), have
long been the talk of the pariſh, and a nuiſance to
their immediate neighbours, were mimicked, and
ridiculed, to the life, in this ruſtic exhibition: but
accompanied with much better and ſofter muſic,
than the ſquabbles of the original couple uſually
afford.

I have

I have heard you remark, and no remark was ever more juft, that, let me be where I will, I am fure to meet with inftances of connubial infelicity. They really occur to me, on every hand; juft as "the graces" bolt, from every corner, on the purfuers of lord Chefterfield's Letters. And yet (you will fmile, if not triumph, at fuch a declaration from me), I am, really and literally, tired of being a batchelor: not unwilling, to try a certain hazardous experiment; though half afraid to venture.

After giving fuch a voluntary and decifive proof of my fincerity, I cannot be fufpected of duplicity, if I fubfcribe myfelf, what in very truth I am,

dear madam, your obliged friend and moft obedient fervant,

Auguftus Toplady.

P. S. Good Mrs. Ch. has my refpectful and affectionate remembrance. God loves her; and will take care of her, even to the end, and without end. —Adieu.

LETTER XLVIII.

To the Rev. Dr. B. of *Sarum.*

Broad-Hembury, Nov. 18, 1774.

AS I fuppofe you are, by this time, returned from Frefhford; it is incumbent on me, dear fir, to acknowledge your favour of the 9th ult. which arrived here, a day or two after my laft to you was forwarded to Sarum. I fhould have been extremely happy to have enjoyed your and Mrs. B's company in Devonfhire: but cannot wonder at my difappointment, when I confider the fuperior attractions, of which Frefhford and its environs have to boaft. Another year, I hope, will make me amends.

Mrs.

Mrs. Macaulay has lately left us, in a more vigorous state of health and spirits, than I ever yet remember to have seen her enjoy. Notwithstanding the many local and social charms of Freshford, you have really sustained a loss, by not being here, during her long residence in this neighbourhood.

I shall be extremely obliged to you, for communicating the Jamaica epitaph on Bradshaw. Though, before I see it, I must inevitably set it down for a mere *lusus ingenii :* the person, from whom you had it, being most egregiously mis-informed, if he in earnest believes that the subject of it died in that island where the epitaph was born. Certain it is, that Bradshaw died at London, in November, 1657, the year before Cromwell expired: and that he [Bradshaw] was interred in Henry 7th's chapel; Mr. Rowe, the famous Puritan minister, preaching his funeral sermon, in Westminster Abbey, from that text in Isaiah, The righteous perisheth, and no man lays it to heart. Moreover, Bradshaw's remains were, soon after the Restoration, dug up, and buried under the gallows, with those of other partizans in the same cause. So that your West Indian correspondent is totally mistaken, in every point of view. But, pray, let me see the epitaph : which is no more the worse for the mis information with which it was introduced to your acquaintance, than the intrinsic merits of Mr. Drelincourt's excellent Treatise on Death, are impaired, by the fabulous legend, prefixed to it, concerning Mrs Veal's apparition.

Augustus Toplady.

LETTER

LETTER XLIX.

To the Countefs of HUNTINGDON.

Broad-Hembury, Dec. 9, 1774.

MADAM,

I WAS, in due courfe, honoured with your ladyfhip's letter, of Nov. 24; and, had its contents
been lefs weighty, fhould have fooner acknowledged
my receipt of it.

After fo condefcending, and fo explicit, a difplay
of your views of divine things; I fhould be crimi-
nally inexcufable, were I not, with all poffible refpect, but yet with the moft naked and undifguifed
fimplicity, to fubmit the refult, both of my prayers
and of my reflections, to your ladyfhip's judgement
and candour.

I confider the true minifters of God, as providen-
tially divided into two bands: viz. the regulars,
and the irregulars.

The former may be compared to centinels, who
are to keep to their ftations: or to watchmen, whofe
attention is immediately confined to their refpective
diftricts.—The latter, like troops of light-horfe, are
to carry the arms of their fovereign, wherever an
opening prefents, or occafional exigence may require.
—Both thefe corps are ufeful, in their diftinct departments; and, in my opinion, fhould obferve the
fame harmony with each other, as obtains among the
ftationary and planetary ftars, which are fixed and
erratic in the regions above us.

Hitherto, I have confidered myfelf as a regular:
and have been very cautious, not to overftep that
line, into which, I 'am perfuaded, Providence has
thrown me; and in which, I can thankfully affirm,
divine grace has been pleafed to blefs me.   Ought

I not

I not to fee the pillar of divine direction moving before me, very vifibly, and quite incontcftibly, ere
I venture to deviate into a more excurfive path?

I remember, that, in one of my laft converfations
with dear Mr. Whitefield, antecedently to his laft
voyage to America, that great and precious man of
God faid as follows: " My good fir, why do not
you come out? why do not you come out? You
might be abundantly more ufeful, were you to
widen your fphere, and preach at large, inftead of
reftraining your miniftry to a few parifh churches."
My anfwer was to this effect: that "The fame Providence, which bids others roll at large, feems to have
confined me to a particular orbit." ·

And, I honeftly own, I am ftill of the fame mind.
If there be, for me, a yet more excellent way, God,
I truft, will reveal even this unto me. I hope I
can truly fay, that I defire to follow his guidance,
with a fingle eye.

As to the doctrines of fpecial and difcriminating
grace, I have thus much to obferve: that, for the
four firft years after I was in orders, I dwelt, chiefly,
on the general out-lines of the gofpel, in the ufual
ccurfe of my public miniftry. I preached of little
elfe, but of juftification by faith only in the righteoufnefs and atonement of Chrift; and of that perfonal holinefs, without which, no man fhall fee the
Lord. My reafons for thus narrowing the truths of
God, were (with humiliation and repentance I defire
to fpeak it,) thefe two: 1. I thought thefe points
were fufficient to convey as clear an idea, as was abfolutely neceffary, of falvation. And, 2. I was
partly afraid to go any further.

God himfelf (for none but he could do it) gradually freed me from that fear. And as he never, at
any time, permitted me to deliver, or even infinuate, any thing contradictory to his truths; fo has he
been gracioufly pleafed, for between feven and eight
years paft, to open my mouth to make known the

entire

entire myftery of his gofpel, as far as his fpirit has enlightened me into it.—The confequence of my firft plan of operations was, that the generality of my hearers were pleafed: but very few were converted.—The refult of my latter deliverance from worldly wifdom and from worldly fear (fo far as the Lord has exempted me from thofe fnares), is, that multitudes have been very angry: but the converfions, which God has given me reafon to hope he has wrought, have been, at leaft, three, for one before. Thus, I can teftify, fo far as I have been concerned, the ufefulnefs of preaching predeftination: or, in other words, of tracing falvation, and redemption, to their firft fource.

Your ladyfhip's goodnefs will pardon the unreferved freedom and plainnefs, with which I have taken occafion to open my mind. Nor will you, I hope, difbelieve me, when, with the fame fimplicity and truth, I affure your ladyfhip, that I love and revere you, for what God has made you, and for what he has effeéted through you. Let me have, as you kindly promife, an intereft in your prayers.

Should I vifit my Bath friends, this winter, as I have fome thoughts of doing, I will avail myfelf of your ladyfhip's invitation, by paying my refpeéts to you; and the rather, as it is, now, between ten and eleven years, fince I had an opportunity of prefenting you with them in perfon. Whenever I have been in Bath, during this long period, your ladyfhip never happened to be there.

Wifhing you, not the compliments of the enfuing feafon, but an encreafing enjoyment of the realities, which it brings to our remembrance, I remain, madam,

Your ladyfhip's moft obedient, and moft humble fervant,

Auguftus Toplady.

P. S. May I take the liberty, to wifh, that, when you next write to lord Moira, your ladyfhip would conde-

condèfcend to make my refpects acceptable to him.
Mr. Shirley, if at Bath, has my affectionate falutations.

L E T T E R   L.

To the Rev. Dr. Priestley.

Rev. Sir,   *Broad-Hembury, Dec.* 23, 1774.

COndefcend to accept the thanks of a perfon,
who has not the honour of being acquainted
with you, for the pleafure and improvement, recently received, from a perufal of your fpirited (and,
for the moft part, juft) Animadverfions on the three
Northern Doctors.   Allow me alfo to thank, in an
efpecial manner, the good providence of God, which
has raifed up no lefs a man, than yourfelf, to contend, fo ably, for the great doctrine of neceffity : a
doctrine, in my idea, not only effential to found and
rational philofophy ; but, abftracted from which, I
could not, for my own part, confider Chriftianity itfelf as a defenfible fyftem.

Greatly as I admire the main of your performance,
I fhould, probably, not have taken the liberty to
trouble you with my acknowledgements, but for the
following circumftance.

In your fuccefsful affault and battery of the new
Scotch fortification, you have, occafionally, fired
fome random fhot on a very numerous fet of men,
who, fo far as concerns the article of neceffity, are
your actual friends, and your natural allies.   Permit
me, therefore, fir, to offer you, in this private manner, a few plain, but not intentionally difrefpectful,
ftrictures on fome rafh and exceptionable paffages ;

which

which ferve, as foils, to render your penetration and candour, on fome other occafions, the more confpicuous.

I fhall confine myfelf to your Introduction.

1. Are you certain that " The common Arminian doctrine of freewill is founded on Scripture, and prefuppofed by the philofophic doctrine of neceffity?" Is it not very poffible, and often actually matter of fact, that men have not " the power of doing what they pleafe, or will" to do? The triumvirate of doctors (for inftance) are, I doubt not, very willing to beat you off from their intrenchments, and to give you a total defeat. But I am much miftaken, if they have " the power of doing it."

2. Why are " Calvin's notions" reprefented as " gloomy?" Is it gloomy, to believe, that the far greater part of the human race are made for endlefs happinefs? There can, I think, be no reafonable doubt entertained, concerning the falvation of very young perfons. If (as fome, who have verfed themfelves in this kind of fpeculations, affirm) about one half of mankind die in infancy; and if, as indubitable obfervation proves, a very confiderable number, of the remaining half, die in early childhood; and if, as there is the ftrongeft reafon to think, many millions of thofe, who live to maturer years, in every fucceffive generation, have their names in the Book of Life : then, what a very fmall portion, comparatively, of the human fpecies, falls under the decree of preterition and non-redemption! This view of things, I am perfuaded, will, to an eye fo philofophic as your's, at leaft open a very chearful vifta through the " gloom;" if not entirely turn the imaginary darknefs into fun-fhine. For, with refpect to the few reprobate, we may, and we ought to, refign the difpofal of them, implicitly, to the will of that only King who can do no wrong : inftead of fummoning the Almighty, to take his trial at the tribunal of our

own

own fpeculations, and of fetting up ourfelves as the judges of Deity.

3. I muft confefs, I fee nothing "wonderful," nor to be gazed at "as a ftrange phenomenon;" in the co-incidence of "philofophic neceffity" with the Calviniftic theology and metaphyfics. I fhould rather "wonder," if they did not co-incide: fince (according to the ideas formed by me, who live in a Chriftian country, and believe the Chriftian revelation) they mutually fuppofe and fupport each other. For, what is Calvinifm, but a fcriptural expanfion of the philofophic principle of neceffity? or, if you pleafe, a ramification of that principle into its religious parts? It is poffible, indeed, for a perfon to be a grofs Neceffitarian, or a Neceffitarian at large, without being, fully, a Calvinift (witnefs many of the antient, and fome modern, philofophers:) but it feems impoffible, to me, that any perfon can be, fully, a Calvinift, without being a Neceffitarian.

Moreover, every Chriftian Neceffitarian is, fo far, a Calvinift. Have a care, therefore, Dr. Prieftley: left, having fet your foot in the Lemaine lake, you plunge in, *quantus quantus*. A cataftrophe, which, for my own part, and for your own fake, I fincerely wifh may come to pafs; and of which I do not wholly defpair.

4. There is, I apprehend, no fhadow of reafon, for fuppofing, that, had the great and good Mr. Edwards "lived a little longer, he would have been fenfible, that his philofophy was much more nearly allied to Socinianifm, than to Calvinifm." That deep and mafterly reafoner would, rather, have rejoiced, at feeing fo important a branch of the Calviniftic philofophy, (viz. the doctrine of neceffity) fo warmly adopted by a Socinian divine.

Serioufly, I think you have admitted a Trojan horfe into your gates; whofe concealed force will, probably, at the long run, difplay the banner of

John

John Calvin on your walls, and mafter your capital, though at prefent garrifoned by the confederate forces of Pelagius, Sozzo, and Van Harmin.

5. Nor was it any " piece of artifice, in Mr. Edwards, to reprefent the doctrine of philofophical neceffity, as being the fame thing with Calvinifm ; and the doctrine of philofophical liberty, as the fame thing with Arminianifm." This fuggeftion, fir, (which, by the way, is more than a little ungenerous, when we confider how upright and valuable a man Mr. Edwards, by all accounts, proved himfelf, in every part of his conduct) feems to have been ftarted, merely, as a falvo for yourfelf. You are, on the article of neceffity, the reverfe of an Arminian. And you are terribly afraid of being dubbed a Calvinift. I muft own you are in fome little danger. But, chear up. Your cafe is not yet defperate. Poor Janffenius was in a fituation, fomewhat fimilar to your's. He, indeed, fwam farther into the Geneva lake, than you have ventured to do : and, to elude the name of heretic, affured as many good people, as would believe him, that he was, all the while, bathing in the Tiber.

So far as I can judge, Mr. Edwards gave the naked and genuine fentiments of his heart to the public. And I am, likewife, of opinion, that the fact ftands, fimply and literally, juft as he reprefents it. Arminianifm, when ftripped of its fophiftical trappings, contends for fuch an abfolute and inviolable freedom, εν αμφισρεπες, as is independent, in its exercife, on any thing but the will itfelf. Confequently, the Arminian fcheme is no lefs incompatible with the religion of reafon, than with the religion of the Bible : and directly contravenes the whole current, both of natural and of revealed truth.

6. It is, certainly, a very unguarded affertion, that " the modern queftion of liberty and neceffity" is what the Calvinian divines, " never underftood, nor, indeed, fo much as heard of." The contrary is

evincible, from their writings. The queftion, fo far from being purely " modern," has exercifed fome of the ableft Proteftant pens, from the reformation, quite down to the prefent day. It has been agitated, with no little zeal, *pro & contra*, even among the Papifts, long before, but more frequently fince, the Proteftant æra. And it was the fubject of no fmall debate, among fome of the heathen philofophers themfelves.

7. Mr. Edwards, therefore, was not the " firft Calvinift who ever hit upon the true philofophic doc-trine of neceffity." A vaft number of the greateft reformed divines, both foreign and Englifh, touched the felf-fame key. And it is extremely evident, that Mr. Edwards, himfelf, received much light, from them, into the fubject; and even availed himfelf, very frequently, of phrafes, diftinctions, and argu-ments, which thofe grand luminaries had, with fuc-cefs, made ufe of, before him.

8. " Zealous Calvinifts," you tell us, " regard your writings with abhorrence." It would have been candid, fir, to have expreffed this, with more re-ftriction, and with lefs vehemence. Many very " zealous Calvinifts" regard your writings, on fome fubjects, not only without " abhorrence," but with honour and admiration. Dark and " gloomy" as you have reprefented us; we ftill have fufficiency, both of eye-fight and of day-light, to difcern the luftre of your genius, and the improvements which your equally profound and refined refearches have added to the ftock of philofophic knowledge.

9. Nervous (and, I think, irrefragable) as Mr. Edwards's treatife is; you ftill are much too fan-guine in afferting that the Calvinifts " boaft of it, as the ftrongeft bulwark of their own gloomy faith." We never boafted of it, under any fuch character. We have, in my apprehenfion, fome hundreds of " bulwarks," no lefs " ftrong" than this American one, whofe towers I concur with you in defervedly admiring.

admiring. Exclufively of which numerous bulwarks, we have a citadel (the Bible,) againft which, no weapon can poffibly prevail. I pafs over your favourite epithet "gloomy," which you fo repeatedly prefix to Calvinift.c "faith." When you have attended, as minutely, to the philofophy of Scripture-vifion, as you have to that of animal optics ; you will perceive the diftrict of Calvin to be, not a Cimmerian region, but a very land of Gofhen.

10. You think proper, fir, to fuppofe, that " zealous Calvinifts will be furprifed to hear" (it is well we are not deaf and blind too) " you fo full and earneft in the recommendation of Mr. Edwards's book." I much queftion, whether their wonder will mount to " furprife." There are fo many weakneffes, contradictions, and inconfiftencies, in philofophers, as well as in ordinary men, that few people, who know much of the world, and of human nature, will be greatly " furprifed" at any thing.

11. You, however, are of a different opinion. Perhaps, becaufe " zealous Calvinifts," like moles and bats, live in a thick and perpetual gloom, with hardly a fingle ray of truth, or of common fenfe, to gild their midnight darknefs. People, in fo melancholy a fituation, are, doubtlefsly, very apt to take fright. If your charity will not pour day-light on our gloomy abodes, it would at leaft be compaffionate in you, to mitigate the woeful " furprife," with which you think your treatife calculated to imprefs us.

No! You will no more deign to alleviate our " furprife," than to diffipate our gloom. It is rather cruel, though, firft to fhut us up in the dark ; and, then, to fcare us. It feems, we " muft ftill continue to wonder." Wherefore? Becaufe " It would be to no purpofe for you to explain, to" the zealous Calvinifts, " Why they ought not to wonder at the matter. What I fhould fay on that fubject," adds the high and mighty doctor, " would not be intelligible to them." Inexpreffibly candid and polite! The plain Englifh of the compliment is this:

"Every zealous Calvinift is a fool; or a dunce, at beft. I will therefore wafte no time on fuch incurable affes. All my philofophic apparatus itfelf would not afford them a gleam of knowledge : nor all my confummate fkill in language and in reafoning make them comprehend the loweft of my fublime ideas. I therefore leave them, to ftumble on, in their impenetrable gloom : and to knock their blockifh heads againft tables, doors, walls, and pofts, amid the tremor of their furprife."

Our cafe is pitiable indeed. But why will not, the illuminated and illuminating doctor direct a few of his rays, by way of experiment, toward our dark and dreary habitations? Be honeft, good fir : and fairly tell us, that your reafon, for huddling the matter up, and for not defcending to particulars, was not our ftupidity, but your fear of the confequences that would refult to yourfelf, had you gone to the bottom of the fubject, and unfolded all that was in your heart. To fcreen yourfelf, you affect to give us over, as incurable, before you have fo much as tried what you can make of us. If you fet about it, who can tell, but, ftupid as we are, fome of us may recover our fight and fenfe, and be emancipated from our gloom and from our furprife together? Electricity, under your aufpices, may work miracles.

However lightly I may, occafionally, have expreffed myfelf; I affure you, on the word of an honeft man, that I have the honour to be, with ferioufnefs and truth,

Reverend fir,

your admirer,

and very humble fervant,

Auguftus Montague Toplady.

P. S. On

P. S. On reviewing this letter, I deem myself obliged, in some meafure, to apologize for that vein of freedom, into which, the fupreme and infulting contempt, you exprefs of the Calvinifts, has, unwarily, betrayed me. Your laft-quoted paragraph, fir, appears to carry an implication of extreme prejudice, and of fovereign pride. Nothing can be more fupercilious, more rude, and more unjuft, than the letter and the fpirit of that whole paffage. I would willingly, if I were able, frame an excufe for you: by fuppofing, that it efcaped you, *volante calamo*; and that it is to be imputed, not fo much to malice, to haughtinefs, or even to your unacquaintednefs with the people you traduce; as to the hurry and precipitation, with which your treatife was apparently written.

Believe me to be, fir,

moft refpectfully, your's.

LETTER LI.

To Mr. * * * * *.

Broad-Hembury, Dec. 29, 1774.

NO congratulations wait on my ever dear friend, from Broad-Hembury, on account of his new connection. The reafon is, becaufe no change of ftate, on his part, can make me love and wifh him better, than I did before. Nor do I tranfmit you thofe compliments, which ufually reverberate, from friend to friend, at this particular feafon of the year: becaufe you have my very beft wifhes, without intermiffion, all the year round. And fo, I doubt not, will the new partner of your heart, when I have the honour and the pleafure of knowing her. In the mean while, I requeſt you to inform her, that ſhe has my reſpectful ſalutations.

I take the liberty to trouble you with the incloſed pacquet, for Mr. M. It contains only the ſermoh on Pſalm cxv. 1 ; which owes its tranſmiſſion to the preſs, entirely, to your condeſcending deſire, ſignified when I was laſt in London. You ſee, I am not all diſobedience to your commands ; though I muſt, for once, run counter to ſome of them : I mean, ſo far as concerns the principal ſubject of your laſt kind and obliging letter. Some nephritic complaints, to which I have long perceived myſelf liable, warn me, to ply my pen no more than neceſſity may require.

I am, with great affection and reſpect, &c.

Auguſtus Toplady.

P. S. I loſt poor Mr. Lane, about a fortnight ago : who, at the age of ſeventy-ſix, preſerved all the ſtrength and gaiety of a boy at ſixteen, until within a few days of his deceaſe. He was the ſecond of my domeſtics, whom God has removed by death, in the compaſs of two months. Mrs. Lane (who, by the way, continues as lively at ſeventy-ſeven, as ſhe could be at thirty) ſtill keeps my houſe ; and ſupports the loſs of her huſband, not only philoſophically, but heroically. An eſtate, however, of twenty-five pounds *per annum*, which died with him, is, I believe, very ſincerely, though not inconſolably, regretted. Mr. Lane had not been dead a quarter of an hour, when his relict addreſſed me thus : " Sir, I have been thinking, that it will be to no purpoſe to lay out money for a fine ſhroud, to be hid in a coffin ; nor for a fine coffin, to be hid under the earth." This was natural philoſophy, literally ſo called. It is, really, an happineſs, on irremediable occaſions, to have little or no feeling. I envy inſenſible people ; becauſe they are ignorant of mental pain, the keeneſt ſpecies of any. Adieu.

LETTER

LETTER LII.

To the Rev. Mr. RYLAND.

Broad-Hembury, Dec. 29, 1774.

WHEN my dear friend's letter (whose date I am quite ashamed to recollect) arrived, our valuable Mrs. Macaulay was present. Her countenance brightened, at learning from whom it came. She, on all occasions, testifies a singular esteem of you : which is, in other words, saying, that she really has you in very great estimation ; for she is too magnanimous, and too upright, to dissemble. She gives your name, as a favourite toast of your's and mine, in public and mixed companies. And she has, moreover, so high an opinion of your judgement, in physic, no less than in metaphysic, that she makes it a constant rule, and did so, during the whole of her three months stay in Devonshire, to retire to her chamber at ten o'clock.

Though I love and respect you, as much as that extraordinary lady can do ; still, I cannot say, that I have carefully followed your advice, relating to that early hour of repose, with the same implicit obedience. We often regard the physician, and yet transgress his prescriptions. I am, however, reforming, very fast, in this particular. As a proof of which, I must tell you, that, if I prolong my studies, at any time, until two or three in the morning, I begin to think I am setting up late. For the most part, I rarely exceed twelve or one.

Had the Northamptonshire living fallen to my lot, I should have been a very troublesome neighbour to you. Not a sixpenny pamphlet would I have sent to the press, without previously soliciting your corrections and amendments. You may be

thankful,

thankful, that I am only your friend, and not your neighbour. Let me, in a religious view, ferioufly add, that I myfelf am thankful, and very thankful, that I cont'nue where I am. And I fay this, not becaufe I fhould not have preferred your county to this; but becaufe it was the will of God, as the event has clearly proved, that I fhould remain in this county, and not be tranfplanted to your's.

Your thoughts, concerning the " Directions to young Divinity Students," are fo juft, fo forcible, and fo vivid, that I muft, abfolutely, lay afide all view, of engaging in fuch a book, myfelf. The department is eminently, and exclufively, your's. Let Homer, therefore, write his own Iliad. As to me, I feel my incompetence to fo difficult and important a tafk; and muft follow the old, fenfible advice: *Confule, quid faleant*, &c.

My beft thanks attend you, for that valuable paper, tranfmitted to me, fome time ago, from Wells, under Mr. Tudway's enclofure; enumerating the paffages, in the Old Teftament, wherein Chrift is ftiled Jehovah. You may judge how poorly qualified I am, to accommodate young divines with rules for ftudy; when I affure you, that I did not know, until you informed me, that the bleffed Mediator, between God and man, is called Jehovah, almoft two hundred times, in the courfe of the firft Teftament.

If you wifh your letters to Mr. S—— may arrive free of poftage, you muft inclofe them to ——. Mr. S—— is one of the moft learned, moft devout, and moft valuable men I know. With all his choir of refpectable and of amiable qualities, he poffeffes this crowning one, viz. an heart, like your's, capable of friendfhip.

Auguftus Toplady.

L E T T E R

LETTER LIII.

To Ambrose Serle, Efq.

Broad-Hembury, Jan. 25, 1775.

Ever Dear Sir,

I Write, to requeft, that you will condefcend to prefent Mr. M. with my thanks, for his pacquet, lately fent : and to inform him, that, though I was by no means well, when it arrived ; yet, the perufal of Mr. Wefley's " Thoughts upon Neceffity" (which were part of the pacquet's contents) put my fpirits into fuch a pleafing flow, that I inftantly refolved to attack thofe thoughts, and, in half an hour afterwards, actually fet about it. 1 have, at three fittings (or, rather, ftandings ; for I generally write upon my feet), got mid-way through my intended pamphlet ; which will, if Providence pleafe to continue health and leifure, be a Defence of Chriftian and Philofophical Neceffity.

I defign writing to Mr. M. myfelf, fo foon as I have finifhed my tract : and thanking him for the kind conveyances, with which he has favoured me. But, to fay the truth, I am, at prefent, fo abforbed in the fubject on the tapis, that I am willing to purfue it, while my ideas are warm ; and warm ideas, if not fpeedily feized and arrefted, are very fugitive.

Every happinefs be your's,

' *Auguftus Toplady.*

LETTER LIV.

To Mrs. MACAULAY.

Broad-Hembury, Feb. 10, 1775.

DEAR MADAM,

YOUR favour, of Jan. 27, arrived in due courfe. Had you defered penning it, but three days longer, it would have borne the date of a certain anniverfary, on which no perfon living is fo well qualified to write as yourfelf.

I have had too much ill health, this winter, to be, as you fuppofe me to have been, very affiduoufly engaged " in deep refcarches after philofophical and religious truth." The principal refult of my few refearches in that way, has been a tract (begun and finifhed within a fortnight) in explication and defence of Chriftian and philofophic neceffity. But, I believe, I fhall not commit it to the prefs, until I go to London : the printers being a very teafing fet of people, to be concerned with at fo great a diftance from the fcene of action.

As I know not how much longer my fuppofed " refearches" may be impeded, by want of health ; I muft beg, that you will not, in time to come, forbear writing hither, from an imaginary fear of " interrupting" refearches which have little or no exiftence.

I will reduce you to a dilemma, on the occafion. Either I am, or I am not, engaged in the faid refearches. If the former, then do you write by all means ; and the oftener, the better : for I know no pen, more capable of affifting a philofophic enquirer, than your own. If the latter, ftill write : for, in that cafe, the very reafon, under which you fhelter yourfelf, ceafes to exift.

To tell you the truth, I am quite of opinion, that by your polite apology for being fo bad a correfpondent,

dent, you have only wedged yourfelf faſt in a cleft
ſtick : from which, nothing can extricate you, but
your directing as many letters to Broad-Hembury
as poſſible.   .

I have not been at Honiton, ſince I took leave of
you there.   But your hoſt, Mr. N. I have ſeen
twice; once at my own houfe, and once at Mr.
Drewe's.

Many thanks to you, dear madam, for the purſe,
which, you tell me, you have condefcended to knit
for me.   I would rather, however, defer receiving it,
until I have the pleaſure of ſeeing you at Bath:
which I hope will be within thefe two months;
either in my way to, or in my return from, London.

I have a very extraordinary letter to ſhew you ; ſent
me by my refpectable friend, Dr. Baker, vicar of
St. Martin's, in Salifbury : relative to Bradſhaw's
interment in Jamaica.   I own, I am partly ſtagger-
ed, though not profelyted, as to that matter.   I ſet
it down under the clafs of " Hiſtoric doubts."

But, without any ſhadow of doubt at all, I have
the honour to be,

   madam,

     your much obliged

      and very obedient ſervant,

        Auguſtus Toplady.

P. S.   Compliments to Miſs Macaulay.———— I
obferve, you do not ſay a ſyllable, concerning our
common favourite, Mr. Lytton.——On ſecond
thoughts, I will not (as I at firſt defigned) defer
ſhewing you Dr. B's letter until we meet : but ſhall
inclofe it in this.   The circumſtance, of double
poſtage, is not to be confidered.   Adieu.

To Mr. L. C——.

[Extract.]   *Broad-Hembury, Feb.* 13, 1775.

IT is Dr. Samuel Johnson, whom lord Chesterfield terms "a respectable Hottentot:" and whom his lordship, by a caricature abundantly too severe and over-charged, represents as the living essence of aukwardness, and ill-breeding. I can testify, upon my own knowledge, that the shades are too deepened, and the lines too distorted. But the doctor is pretty even, it seems, with the noble defamer: and styles those letters, "A system of morals for a whore, and a system of manners for a dancing-master." I totally agree with the doctor, as to the morals: and partly agree with him, as to the manners. Seriously, poor Mr. Phil. Stanhope was greatly to be pitied, for falling under the management of such a father: a father, who was at once capable of guiding a son into the ruinous paths of vice; and of pretending, at other times, to give him a few squeamish cautions against it. Like some hypocritical prostitute, who entices with an air of affected modesty; and assumes that air of modesty, only to render her enticements the more effectual. Moreover, after all his lordship's attention to the "graces" of his disciple; the poor young gentleman lived and died almost as great a stranger to the graces of politeness, as to those of the Holy Spirit. So that the disappointed father had the mortification of perceiving, that he had only been raining upon a rock. Few men of education and high connection were ever more clumsy and ungainly in their devoir, than Mr. Stanhope.

I take the true original of lord Chesterfield's disgust against Dr. J—— to have been, the doctor's having

having too much Christianity for his lordship's taste.
Not but what Johnson has, on some occasions, a
great deal of positiveness about him: and lord
C——— was so much of the fine gentleman, as to
think, that nothing, either in religion or philosophy,
was worth contending for, in opposition to whatever
genteel company a person might happen to be with.
It would be committing an act of hostility " on the
graces," were a man not to swim implicitly with the
current, whether good or bad. Johnson, I believe,
was never guilty, so much as once in his life, of such
mean, cowardly dissimulation. And I honour him
for it. If he likes his company, no man is more
affable and communicative. If he meets with a
coxcomb, he is sure of taking him down without
mercy. Or, if people of sense affront him, he dis-
covers very great and quick sensibility, and generally
makes them pay dear for their temerity: for his re-
proofs are weighty with sentiment, and his repartees
cuttingly smart. It must have been pleasant, to
have seen him and lord Chesterfield together.

The smooth dissimulation of the latter, extended, in some measure, even to me. The year after I
was in orders (viz. 1763), I asked his lordship for a
scarf. "I am extremely sorry, sir," replied he,
" that you did not mention it early enough, Had
you asked me two days sooner a scarf should have
been at your service: but, no longer ago than
yesterday, I gave away my only vacant one." I
answered, that I should be glad to hope for the honour of the next that fell. He replied, " The very
next is already promised: but you shall certainly
have the next after that." You can discern, without my pointing it out, the flat self-contradiction of
these two plausible speeches.—I never asked him
again: but looked upon him, as a finished courtier,
from that day forward. When I was a boy, he used
to give me a guinea now and then: and generally
prefaced his donation (which to me, was then a ca-

pital

pital fum) with fome fuch proper advice as this: "Now, do not buy too many apples, or nuts, or oranges, to make yourfelf fick." He certainly had a great fund of good nature, at bottom: though it was half fmothered and corrupted by art and fineffe.

Have you read Mrs. Macaulay's Addrefs to the People? I am greatly pleafed with the ftrength of fenfe, which appears in that concife, but folid performance. Alas, too folid! Would to God, that the facts, which it cenfures, were ill founded. But his Providence governs and orders all. No thanks to them, that they are, involuntarily and unknowingly, accomplifhing the decree of heaven. "Leaches," as a good man fomewhere obferves, "when they draw blood of a patient, do it to gratify themfelves: they know nothing of the wife end, for which the phyfician ordered them to be applied."

The mention of my valuable friend, Mrs. Macaulay, reminds me of the aforefaid Dr. Johnfon: whofe high principles, both political and ecclefiaftical, are very different from thofe of the fair hiftorian. A few years ago, Mrs. M. and the doctor (who never had a very cordial efteem for each other) met at the houfe of a third perfon, who had invited them to fpend the day. Before dinner, the converfation turned on the nature of civil government. Johnfon, as ufual, declared, in very ftrong terms, for monarchy. Mrs. M. for a republic. Some fparring paft on both fides: and Johnfon happening to cite fome paffage of Scripture, which he thought fpoke in favour of his own fyftem; Mrs. M. undertook him on the fcriptural fcore, and (as I was told, for I was not prefent) was rather more potent and pertinent, in her quotations, than he. Johnfon, who does not eafily digeft contradiction, grew rather four: and he well knows, that he acquits himfelf better in a political, an hiftoric, or a philofophic war, than in an holy one. The annunciation of dinner

dinner occafioned a truce to debate. But the doctor, with more ill manners than I ever heard authentically placed to his account, except in this inftance, took occafion, when the company were all feated at table, to renew hoftilities with his amiable antagonift. Mrs. M's. footman was ftanding, according to cuftom, at the back of his lady's chair; when Johnfon addreffed him thus: "Henry, what makes you ftand? Sit down. Sit down. Take your place at table with the beft of us. We are all Republicans, Henry. There's no diftinction here. The rights of human nature are equal. Your miftrefs will not be angry, at your afferting your privilege of peerage. We are all on a level. Do, take your chair, and fit down." This was very indelicate, and rude. Nor was it arguing fairly: for a mafter or miftrefs (let the natural rights of mankind be, originally, ever fo equal) has not only a juft claim to fuperiority, but a title to the fervices of every perfon, who, by voluntary ftipulation, engages to render thofe fervices for a confideration agreed upon. Mrs. Macaulay, it feems, coloured a little, and drew up her head, but made no anfwer. If I had been there, I fhould not have let the doctor off fo eafily, for this favage piece of fpurious wit. It is true, his great parts are entitled to proper refpect: but, as Mrs. Macaulay was obferving to me, when fhe was laft in Devonfhire, with reference to this very doctor Johnfon, "A learned man is not fo miraculous a phenomenon in this kingdom, that he fhould expect to be honoured with divine worfhip." Though, it muft be owned, there are very few Johnfon's, in any kingdom, or in any age.

It is, however, this great man's foible, to look for more homage and attention, than every body will give him. How little he brooks oppofition, may be inferred from the droll (but which might have been a very ferious) adventure, between him and Ofborne, the Lincoln's Inn bookfeller. Ofborne called upon him

him one morning, foon after the publication of his
Dictionary. The particulars of the converfation I
have forgot: but, in the courfe of it, fome reference was had to a paffage in that work. The doctor was for confulting the particular place itfelf: and,
afcending a fet of moveable fteps, reaching down his
Dictionary from one of the higher-moft fhelves,
while Johnfon was thus mounted, and holding the
Dictionary in his hands, Ofborne, who was ftanding
beneath, happened to fay fome faucy thing that the
doctor did net relifh: on which, without farther
ceremony, he hurled the maffy folio at the poor
bookfeller's head, who fell to the floor with the
blow, but foon recovered his feet again. " An im-
pertinent puppy;" faid Johnfon to him, " I will
teach you to behave with infolence to me; I will."
But, furely, this was not acting very philofophically.

One more anecdote while my hand is in: and
then I will releafe you. I knew this Ofborne; and,
by the way, a very refpectable man he was. In the
fpring of 1762, a month or two before I took dea-
con's orders, I was cheapening fome books of him.
After that bufinefs was over, he took me to the far-
theft end of his long fhop, and, in a low voice, faid
thus: "Sir, you will foon be ordained. I fuppofe,
you have not laid in a very great ftock of Sermons.
I can fupply you with as many fetts as you pleafe.
All originals: very excellent ones: and they will
come for a trifle." My anfwer was, " I certainly
fhall never be a cuftomer to you, in that way: for
I am of opinion, that the man, who cannot or will
not make his own Sermons, is quite unfit to wear
the gown. How could you think of my buying
ready made Sermons? I would much fooner, if I
muft do one or the other, buy ready-made cloaths."
His anfwer fhocked me: "Nay, young gentleman,
do not be furprifed at my offering you ready-made
Sermons: for, I affure you, I have fold ready-made
Sermons to many a bifhop in my time." My reply
was:

was: " Good Mr. Ofborne, if you have any concern
for the credit of the Church of England, never tell
that news to any body elfe, from henceforward,
forever."

Auguftus Toplady.

L E T T E R LVI.

To Francis Toplady, Efq.

Broad-Hembury, March 19, 1775.

Very Dear Sir,

YOU are one of the laft perfons on earth, in
whofe breaft I would wifh to occafion pain.
Confequently, it gives me much concern to find,
from your favour of *Feb.* 21, that the fubject, mentioned in my laft, "touched you to the quick." Let
it refemble a drawn ftake, on each fide; and let
both of us confider the matter, as if it had never
been ftarted.

· Your kind folicitude for my health, merits my
affectionate acknowledgements. Though I cannot
entirely agree with you, in fuppofing that intenfe
ftudy has been the caufe of my late indifpofitions;
I muft yet confefs, that the hill of fcience, like that
of virtue, is in fome inftances, climbed with labour.
But, when we get a little way up, the lovely profpects, which open to the eye, make infinite amends
for the fteepnefs of the afcent. In fhort, I am
wedded to thofe purfuits, as a man ftipulates to take
his wife : viz. for better for worfe, until death us do
part. My thirft for knowledge is, literally inextinguifhable. And, if I thus drink myfelf into a
fuperior world, I cannot help it : but muft fay, as

some report Ariftotle to have faid, when he threw himfelf into the fea (if it be true that he did fo throw himfelf,) *quod non capere poffum, me capiet.*

Since I wrote· to you laft, my complaints have been crowned, or rather fhod, with a fhort, but fmart, touch of the gout. On this occafion, I have been congratulated, until I have loft all patience. Therefore I do, by thefe prefents, enter an exprefs caveat againft your wifhing me joy.—I am glad, however, that I know at laft, what is the matter with me : for I have not been right well thefe two years; and was unable, until feized by the foot, to afcertain the radical caufe. It is really one of the laft diforders, to which I fhould have fufpected myfelf liable. If the ftricteft temperance could have faved me from the gout, I moft certainly had been exempted : for I never knew what it was to be the reverfe of fober, fo much as once, in my whole life.

On a review, I am quite afhamed to perceive, that I have made myfelf the fole hero of my letter. But, notwithftanding the felf-important pronoun I, has already occurred too often, I muft yet repeat it again; by affuring you, that I am, with tender and refpectful compliments to yourfelf, to my aunt, and to my coufin Charlotte,

Dear fir, your affectionate nephew,

Auguftus Toplady.

L E T T E R LVII.

To the Rev. Mr. ———.

Broad-Hembury, April 5, 1775.

VERY DEAR SIR,

I AM, both literally and figuratively, your debtor, for the welcome packet, with which you favoured me toward the clofe of laft January.

Friendfhip

Friendſhip and politeneſs, leſs indulgent and extenſive than your own, would tell me, that I ought to bluſh, for having delayed my acknowledgements ſo long.—The truth is, I had been extremely ill, for ſeveral weeks, before the parcel arrived; and continued ſo, for ſome weeks afterwards: which, added to the numerous avocations, that have, ſince, demanded my attention, obliged me to poſtpone, until now, the pleaſure of tendering my affectionate thanks to your condeſcending acceptance.

I have not been able to devote many hours to the peruſal of Lilly's Aſtrology. But I muſt frankly own, that I have read enough, to deter me from falling very deeply in love with that real or ſuppoſed ſcience. Judge, my dear ſir, how exalted an idea, I muſt needs entertain, of your candour, ere I could preſume to teſtify, in ſuch blunt terms as theſe, my opini n of a ſtudy, which, in the eyes of your ſuperior eſtimation, appears to be recommended by ſo many ſolid and alluring charms.

Among others, two obſervations, in particular, ſtrike me, with great force, on this occaſion.

1. Either we can, or we cannot, learn, from the ſtars, the train of future events.—If we cannot, the whole buſineſs evaporates, at once, into a laborious deluſion and an ingenious nothing.—If we can, it ſeems unwarrantable to pry into "the times and ſeaſons, which the Father hath put in his own power," and which, the higheſt authority aſſures us, "are not for us to know." The leaſt that can be ſaid, is, that it is more humble, and more ſafe, to leave the evolution of futurity to Providence: to pray, inſtead of erecting a planetary figure: and, inſtead of conſulting the ſtars, to caſt all our care on him that made them.

2. Without doubt, many different infants are born into the world, at the ſame preciſe point of time; and, conſequently, under the ſelf-ſame aſpects of the heavenly orbs. From which leading

S 2　　　　　　circum-

circumftance, it would follow, on aftrological principles, that the caft of mind, the actions, the felicities, the adverfities, and, in fhort, the whole lives
and deaths, of perfons fo born, fhould, exactly, in
every punctilio, refemble thofe of each other. Their
nativities being common, their fates would be the
fame.—But are there any two men upon the ftage
of the earth, though they entered it at the fame inftance, whofe minds and fates are perfectly fimilar
and uniformly correfpondent throughout?

Notwithftanding thefe free, fceptical remarks, I
value Lilly's Book, as a very curious one: and fhall,
with many thanks, reimburfe my dear friend for
its coft.

Though you have not fet me to work, as an
aftrolbger; you have as a polemic. Mr. Wefley's
Thoughts on Neceffity, which made a part of your
obliging pacquet, determined me to reprefent that
grand theological and philofophic article in its true
point of view. Though I was then fo ill, that I could
fcarcely hold my pen, Providence enabled me to
begin my Effay almoft immediately on my receiving
Mr. John's Tract, and to finifh it within a fortnight. I fhould not, however, have made fuch
hafte; had I not apprehended, that, if I did not
avail myfelf of the prefent hour, I might, probably,
be in another world, before my treatife was com-
pleated.—But God has extended my reprieve. May
I live, and fpeak, and act, to his glory!

May I congratulate you, on your fuccefs, as candidate for the lecturefhip of St. * * * * * *? If not,
I fhall ftill wifh you joy. You, and all your concerns, are in the hand of him, whofe will is wifdom,
whofe heart is love, and whofe providence is omnipotence itfelf.

Auguftus Toplady.

LETTER LVIII.

To the Rev. Dr. GIFFARD.

Broad-Hembury, April 6, 1775.

Dear and Rev. SIR,

IN obedience to your wifh, I fhall, concifely, prefent you with my extemporaneous thoughts, concerning the Arminian cavil, againft perfonal election
and reprobation, drawn from that relationfhip of
God to men, by which he is denominated and confidered as the Father of the whole human race.

Properly fpeaking, paternity and filiation are cor-
relates, refulting from the production of a fimilar
intelligent being, *ex effentiâ productoris.* Where this
agency and effect obtain, the producer is, ftrictly,
ftyled, a Father; and the produced is, ftrictly,
ftyled, the offspring of that Father.

Confequently, when any of mankind, or when all
of them together, are termed fons, or children of
God, the phrafe is, neceffarily and apparently, figu-
rative. For, no being, lefs divine than God himfelf, can, according to the precife ideas of paternity
and filiation, be literally, termed his Son.

Hence, when this predicate, fons of God, is affirmed, concerning angels or men; the affirmation
neither is, nor can be, philofophically ftrict. Becaufe,
there is no communicated famenefs of effence, from
the producing party, to the party produced.

Over and above which metaphyfical obfervation,
holy Scripture explicitly afcertains the fenfe, in which
God is reprefented as the Father of men.—Have we
not, all, one Father? Hath not one God created us.

Mr. Toulmin therefore, in his controverfy with
Mr. Rooker (a controverfy, by the way, whofe
merits I have not looked into,) fhould have ftated

his

his objection thus: "Can the common maker of mankind put an arbitrary difference between the men he has made, consistently with infinite goodness and justice?"

However, we will let Mr. Toulmin have his own way, and cloath his argument in his own terms.

He observes,

1. That "Our Lord has taught us to argue from the paternal character" of God.—True. And that paternal character is neither less nor more, than the creative character. The passage, Matt. vii. 11. to which Mr. Toulmin refers, plainly establishes this remark: for it is tantamount to saying, How much more shall your Maker, who is in heaven, &c. [Let me digress, *en passant*, by observing, that, in the 21st verse of the above chapter, Christ uses the word, Father, in its true and absolute signification. For the first person in the Godhead is, properly, literally, and physically, the Father and the immediate source of the second, *per communicationem essentiæ.*]

2. Mr. T. asks Mr. R. "Would you, sir, who are a parent, secretly resolve, before your children were born, and could have done either good or evil, to disinherit any of your children?"

On which I observe,

(1.) That Mr. Rooker may, in his turn, ask Mr. Toulmin, And would you, sir, after your children are born, actually permit any of them to be very wicked and very miserable, if it was in your power, by a single nod of your will to make them good and to render them happy? Now, God certainly is able to endue all mankind, and the very devils themselves, with holiness and felicity. He could both have saved them from falling; and can still reclaim them, though fallen. And yet he, knowingly and willingly, permits many of the former, and the whole number of the latter, to be the subjects of sin and pain. And, if the real, positive, continued permission of this be not inconsistent with the "paternal character;"

ter;" why fhould that "character" be fuppofed to
reftrain God from fecretly refolving, beforehand, on
that permiffion? For, furely, the refolution to do,
or to permit, a thing; can no more clafh with the
"paternal character," than the actual doing, or the
actual permitting, of the thing itfelf.—But, after all,

(2.) God, and an earthly parent, are not parallels,
in any one refpect whatever. When an human father becomes poffeffed of the fame numerical nature
and attributes as God is, in all their infinity and
perfection; it will then (but, until then, it cannot)
be an admiffible pofition, that the Deity is and muft
be fuch an one as ourfelves, and ought to regulate
his conduct, by the example we fet him.—I remember, in the year 1759, while I was a ftudent at college, a gentleman afked me (with reference to this
very doctrine which Mr. T. oppofes,) would you, if
you was God, create any being to mifery? My anfwer was, when I am God I will tell you.—Surely,
Arminians muft be at a difmal lofs, ere they could
thus think of fetting up the human paffions, and
parental affection in particular (which is, ufually,
the blindeft affection of any,) as the ftandard, and
model, and archetype, from which God himfelf muft
form his eftimate of right and wrong, and in conformity to which he his bound, (for the plea fuppofes
this, if it fuppofes any thing) to accommodate his
purpofes and fhape his moral conduct! As if his
ways were not higher than our ways, and his thoughts
than our thoughts!

(3.) The cavil is very unhappily ftated. For,
the moft material part of it is phrafed in the very
words of Scripture. With this effential difference,
however: that the faid Scripture phrafes pofitively
affirm the identical propofition, which the cavil is
framed to deny. So directly and totally contrary is
the judgement of Mr. T. to that of St. Paul!

(4) It is monftroufly inaccurate, to infinuate,
that God has "Secretly refolved to difinherit fome

of

of his children." We utterly reject the very fhadow of fuch an idea, as involving in it both a religious and a philofophical impoffibility. To difinherit is, to cut off, from fucceffion to a patrimony or other property, one, who, before, was actual heir. Men may do this: becaufe men are liable to change, and to miftake, and to be chagrined or difgufted by un-forefeen incidents. But this can never be the cafe with God. Confequently, he cannot be faid to dif-inherit the reprobate, who never were heirs. And, for the elect, he will never difinherit them : feeing, nothing fhall be able to feparate them from that un-changeable love, which hath gracioufly made them heirs of God, and joint-heirs with Chrift himfelf.

(5.) I fuppofe, Mr. Toulmin meant to afk : " Would God refolve, not to invest fome of his creatures with a title to the heavenly inheritance ?" To which I anfwer, Yes. God not only juftly might, but he actually has fo refolved : unlefs the Bible is falfe from end to end. But, as to difinheriting, the Bible knows nothing of that. It is Arminianifm, which reprefents the immutable God as the capricious difinheritor of his children ; not we, who be-lieve, that whom he did predeftinate,—them he alfo glorified.

(6.) To make the objection fquare with the thing objected to, the objection fhould run thus : " Would you, Mr. Rooker, who are a creator, fecretly refolve, before your creatures were formed, to exclude any of them from felicity, for wife and juft reafons beft known to yourfelf ?"——But this phrafeology, which alone comes up to the point in debate, would not fuit Mr. Toulmin's fallacious views. It would not fuffice to raife a fophiftical mift before the eyes of the unwary, which are apt to be caught by fu-perficial appearances, and to be dazzled by the trappings of undue metaphor artfully put on. To make a ftrait ftick feem crooked, you muft look at it, through a denfer medium than air : i. e. hold it

flantingly

flantingly under water, and the bufinefs is done. Unguarded fpeƈtators may be feduced by the ftratagem : but careful obfervers perceive the trick.

In one word : the queftion, as ftated and phrafed by Mr. Toulmin, argues *à diverfo ad diverfum :* and, confequently, is totally illogical, and proves nothing.

I am, with great efteem, &c.

Auguftus Toplady.

L E T T E R   LIX.

To Meffieurs VALLANCE and SIMMONS.

Plymouth, July 7, 1775.

GENTLEMEN,

I AM here, on a fhort vifit, previoufly to my fetting out for Bath and London : and now write to you, on occafion of a report, which prevails here, that Mr. J. W—— died, lately, in Ireland.

You, who dwell at the mart of intelligence, know, probably, the real ftate of that matter, with more certainty, than I can yet attain to at this diftance. But, fhould my information be true, I muft fignify to you my hearty wifhes, that my Effay on Neceffity, if not yet actually publifhed, may be fuppreffed for the prefent : until I can throw it into a new form, by cancelling all the paffages, which have any perfonal reference to my old antagonift ; and by retaining only fo much of the Treatife, as relates to the naked argument itfelf.

I hope, this intimation will reach you, time enough, to anfwer the defired purpofe. If it be too late, I cannot help it. But I do not wifh to profecute my war with that gentleman, if he be really

summon'd

summoned to the tribunal of God, and unable on earth to anfwer for himfelf.   In that cafe, let my remembrance of his mifdemeanors die and be buried with him.

Direct your anfwer, to me, at Mr. D———'s, in G—— ftreet, Bath.   I have only time to add, that I am, with efteem,

Gentlemen, yours, &c.

Auguftus Toplady.

L E T T E R LX.

To Lady HUNTINGDON.

Brighthelmftone, Sept. 22, 1775.

MADAM,

BEST thanks to your dear ladyfhip for the honour of your much efteemed letter from Briftol, of the 8th inftant.   You was fo ill when I left you there, that the receipt of a letter which carries in it the evident traits of your recovery, was peculiarly welcome, and furnifhed me with additional matter of thankfgiving to that God, who, in mercy to his Church, has been gracioufly pleafed to protract a life fo tranfcendently ufeful and valuable.   It would be far better for your ladyfhip to be diffolved and to be with Chrift: but it is more needful for his people below that you remain in the body.   On their account, may it be very long ere you exchange your coronet for a crown.

It would have given me much joy, to have been prefent, on a late happy occafion, at Briftol; our friends Mr. and Mrs. ———, when they had the honour of waiting on your ladyfhip there, prefented my meffage, I fuppofe, and affigned the reafon; 1 blefs the Father of mercies, that the power of the fpirit was experienced,

perienced, and that he continues to fpeed your gofpel plough.

I have been at this place a week to day; and
mean, if the Lord pleafe, to overftay the 1ft Sunday
in October: here is a very confiderable gathering of
people to the ftandard of the crofs. I have found
much union with them, and the unction of the Holy
One has given me much comfort and enlargement
among them hitherto, in our public approaches to
God. By a letter from dear Mr. P——, who is
now at Chichefter, I find that a new chapel at Pet-
worth, and another at Guildford, are to be opened
the 1ft of October. May they receive that true
confecration which arifes from the prefence and
power of the Great Shepherd and Bifhop of fouls.
I truft God will enable me and the people here,
who are now of the moft clearly enlightened, moft
judicious, moft harmonioufly united, and moft
lively congregations I ever was with, to pour out
our fouls in prayer on that day, for a bleffing on your
ladyfhip's labour of love in general, and on thofe
two new encampments in particular.

I am informed, that lady M——'s zeal for God,
has been confiderably bleft to many of her neighbours at or near Ealing. She has frequent preaching in her houfe; and it feems there is good hope,
that lord R—— himfelf begins to have the
hearing ear and the feeling heart.

Has your ladyfhip feen the corrected copy of dear
Mr. R——'s Treatife on Pfalmody? If you have,
you muft have perceived that the very exceptionable paffages, which laid that great and good man
open to fuch juft reprehenfion, are happily expunged.
I afked him for a copy, foon after my arrival in
London. He anfwered, that in its prefent ftate, he
did not acknowledge it for his: but, I fhould have
one as foon as publifhed. He was as good as his
word, and fhortly after gave me his book. I examined it very carefully, and find that the faulty

pages have been cancelled. We now no longer read of Watts's Hymns being Watts's whims, nor of the Holy Spirit's being always prefent where the Pfalms are fung; and never being prefent where hymns are fung. I am glad that my valuable friend was under a neceffity of ftriking out thefe and fuch like violent and unguarded pofitions. I never met with fo much as one fpiritual perfon who did not cenfure them moft feverely; but as he has been fo humble, and fo juft to truth, as to difplace them from his Effay, I hope he will meet with no farther flight and mortification on their account.

God go with your ladyfhip into Cornwall, and fhine on all your efforts for the glory of his name, and for the transfufion of his falvation into the hearts of finners. Open your trenches, and ply the gofpel artillery. And may it prove mighty, through God, to the demolition of every thought and every error, and every work, which exalts itfelf againft the knowledge, the love, and the obedience of Chrift!

Your affectionate fervant in him,

A. M. Toplady.

LETTER LXI.

To Mr. L———,

Brighthelmftone, Sept. 25, 1775.

DEAR SIR,

PERMIT me to condole with you, and with dear Mrs. ——, on the lofs of our valuable and va-lued friend, Mrs. ——: the oldeft, and one of the moft efteemed acquaintance, I had on earth. I re-joice, however, that, through the precious blood and the imputed righteoufnefs of Chrift, fhe is exalted

to

to that place of glory and of reft, where the inhabitants fhall no more fay, I am fick.

Let me give you the true apology, for my having no fooner acknowledged the receipt of your obliging letter, which you will not wonder at, when I inform you, that I was five or fix weeks in travelling from Broad-Hembury to London, occafioned by the many interjacent friends I had to vifit : and by their condefcending importunities, which detained me much longer with each of them, than I expected or defigned.

On my arrival in town, I found your letter, and would have anfwered it while there, but for the multiplicity of engagements, in which the affection of my London friends involved me. I had not been long in the capital, when I received a preffing invitation to this place, where I have ftayed near a fortnight, and from whence I return to London next week.

May the late affecting breach, which Providence has made in your domeftic connections, be fanctified to you both, and excite you to feek an intereft in that Saviour, who is the certain and only deliverer of his people, from the wrath to come.

In him I remain, dear fir, your and Mrs. ——'s, very fincere friend and fervant,

A. M. Toplady.

———————

L E T T E R   LXII.

To Mr. N——,

Brighthelmftone, Sept. 26, 1775.

IF you fhould ever ftand in peculiar need of very violent exercife, come down hither, by way of Ryegate and Cuckfield ; and before the prefent
ftage

ftage coach is worn out. The road, from the former of thefe towns to this, is the rougheft; the country, the coarfeft, and the vehicle the uneafieft, that can well be imagined. I never yet had fo complete a fhaking: and, though much ufed to travelling, was literally fore from head to foot, for twenty-four hours after my arrival here; occafioned by fuch a feries of concuffions, (I had almoft faid contufions), as I really thought it impoffible for any carriage to impart. But I have had ample amends, at my journey's end. For though, in my opinion, our weftern fea-ports have generally, many local charms, greatly fuperior to thofe of this; yet, the inhabitants here, feem to have received a much higher polifh, from their intercourfe with ftrangers. But, above all, the ferious people of Brighthelmftone, are, fo far as I can hitherto judge, peculiarly amiable and eftimable; extremely judicious, and well informed in things of God; and all alive to him. In fhort, I know of no congregation, any where, who feem to be more entirely after my own heart. Their union, likewife, and fellowfhip with each other, are uncommon, confidering their number. The great mafter of our affemblies, God the Holy Spirit, has given us fome comfortable opportunities in public; and deigned, I truft, feveral times, to be eminently prefent. To free and covenant grace, be all the praife.

I am as well, as I ufually find myfelf, when implunged in a fea air. The falts, I apprehend, with which thefe kind of atmofpheres are charged; together with the large quantity of vapour, exhaled by fo great an expanfe of water; by confiderably increafing the weight of the element we breathe, make it, at once, more externally compreffive, and require a ftronger force of interior effort and refiftance, to refpire with due vigour.

Laft Wednefday we were faluted by a continued feries of lightening, from eight at night until one in the morning. Not a moment's interval obtained

between.

tween the flashes; which formed absolute sheets of the moft vivid flame, fucceeding each other with a rapidity I never was witnefs to before. As it played on the fea (for I fpent the evening at a gentleman's, who lives on the Eaft Clift) it refembled a grand, regular cafcade of fire, falling on a vaft reflecting mirror. There was rain, during a fmall part of the time; and fome audible thunder. I have heard louder claps; but never fuch long extended peals. How happy is it, to feel, that the God of nature is alfo the God of all!

I am,

your affectionate fervant in him,

A. M. Toplady.

LETTER LXIII.

To Dr. WILLIAM DODD.

REV. SIR,

BELIEVE me, when I affure you, that the liberty, which I now take, refults neither from want of tendernefs, nor of refpect; but from an humble wifh of being ferviceable to a perfon, who is recommended to me, as a very deferving individual; and whofe circumftances are, it feems, confiderably narrowed and embarraffed, through the unfufpecting confidence, which fhe repofed on your veracity, juftice, and honour.

The lady, to whom I allude, is Mrs. G——, I need not ftate the merits of a cafe, with which you, fir, are fo thoroughly acquainted. Only, permit me to conjure you, by every facred and moral confideration, and by all your feelings, as a man of fenfibility, not to depart this world, without repaying as much of that iniquitous debt, as you poffibly can.

I fay,

I say, before you depart this world. For it is but too indubitable, that there is not a single ray of hope, from any one quarter whatsoever, of your avoiding the utmost effect of the terrible sentence which impends. Let me, therefore, importune you, for God's sake, and for your own, to devote the remainder of your time to more important employ, than that of writing notes on Shakespeare. Indeed, and indeed, your situation is such, as should confine your attention to objects of infinitely greater moment. The Searcher of hearts knows, that I thus plainly address you, from motives of absolute humanity, and from an anxious solicitude for your everlasting welfare.

I am, with undissembled sympathy and respect,

SIR,

your well-wisher in time, and eternity,

New-street,
March 17, 1777.

Augustus Toplady.

You will oblige me, sir, if you favour me with a line (by the gentleman who delivers this to your hands) relative to the business respecting Mrs. G———.

L E T T E R   LXIV.

To the Rev. Mr. BERRIDGE.

DEAR SIR, *New-street, March* 19, 1776.

THE paper, to which you refer, in your favour of to day, is, I apprehend, the Public Ledger, of the 5th instant. As you inform me, that you have not seen it, I inclose it to you, for
your

your perufal, under the prefent cover : together with a fubfequent ledger, of the 9th, containing my an-fwer. When you have read them, I requeft you to return them, fo foon as convenient: for I referve every thing, of this kind ; left it may prove neceffary, to appeal to them in future.

It I was not certain, that the glorious and gracious Head of the Church orders all things for the good of his myftic body; and that not an hair can fall, with-out his leave ; I fhould deeply lament the continu-ance of your cough. But, when I recollect, who it is that fits at the helm ; I can, in a fpirit of prayer and of faith, commit you, and all that relates to you, to the unerring difpofal of infinite wifdom, love, and power. In whofe covenant-bonds I re-main,

dear and rev. fir, &c.

Auguftus Toplady.

L E T T E R LXV.

To Mr. T——.

London, April 4, 1776.

SIR,

IT gives me unfpeakable pleafure, to find, that you defign to republifh the Abridgment of Fox's Martyrology : which I confider as a faithful and ju-dicious compendium of the moft valuable eccle-fiaftical hiftory extant in our language.

We live at a time, when the generality of profeffed Proteftants appear to have loft fight of thofe grand and effential principles, to which the Church of England was reformed, and in defence of which her martyrs bled.

Religious ignorance, and a general unconcernedness about divine things, together with the most profuse dissipation, and a growing disregard of moral virtue, are the reigning characteristics of the present age.

In a country thus circumstanced, Popery (ever on the watch for advantages) will, and must, and does, gain continual ground. Ignorance, infidelity, and licentiousness, naturally terminate in superstition, as their ultimate refuge: and Rome too often reaps, what profaneness and immorality have sown.

To stem so dangerous a torrent, no means are more likely (under God), than the re-publication of such a work as this: a work eminently calculated to display, and to guard us against, the principles and the spirit of Popery; to perpetuate the holy lives, the faithful testimonies, and the triumphant deaths, of those evangelical worthies, who resisted error, even unto blood; to exalt the standard of Christ; to exhibit the loving-kindness of the Holy Ghost, who gave such grace and power unto men; and to stand as the best commentary on those inestimable truths, which (through the good hand of God upon us) still continue to shine in the liturgy, articles, and homilies, of our established Church.

I wish this performance much success, in the name of the Lord. May its diffusion be very extensive, and its usefulness very great. May it prove mighty, through God, to make the Protestant Churches in general, and our own national Church in particular, remember from whence they are fallen; stir them up to doctrinal and practical repentance; and bring them back to their first principles, and to their first works! With this prayer, breathed from the inmost of my heart,

I remain, sir,

your affectionate well-wisher,

Augustus Montague Toplady.

L E T T E R   LXVI.

To Mr. Hussey.

Broad-Hembury, Sept. 9, 1776.

Very dear Sir,

A Student of Lady Huntingdon's, whose name is Cottingham, and from whom I parted at Briftol, on my return from Wales, promifed me to wait on you and Mrs. Huffey in London, to inform you, how gracious the Lord has been to me, ever fince I faw you laft.

The night I left town, the Worcefter coach, in which I went, broke down : but not one of us received the leaft injury. I have a ftill greater deliverance to acquaint you with : even fuch as, I truft, will never be blotted from my thankful remembrance. On the Anniverfary Day, in Wales, the congregation was fo large, that the chapel would not have contained a fourth part of the people; who were fuppofed to amount to three thoufand. No fewer than one thoufand three hundred horfes were turned into one large field, adjoining the College; befides what were ftationed in the neighbouring villages. The carriages, alfo, were unufually numerous. A fcaffold was erected, at one end of the College-court, on which a book-ftand was placed, by way of pulpit : and, from thence, fix or feven of us preached, fucceffively, to one of the moft attentive, and moft lively congregations I ever beheld. When it came to my turn to preach, I advanced to the front; and had not gone more than half through my prayer before fermon, when the fcaffold fuddenly fell in. As I ftood very near the highermoft ftep (and the fteps did not fall with the reft,) Providence

T 2

enabled

enabled me to keep on my feet, through the affiftance of Mr. Winkworth, who laid faft hold on my
arm. About forty minifters were on the fcaffold and
fteps when the former broke down. Dear Mr.
Shirley fell undermoft of all; but received no other
hurt, than a very flight bruife on one of his
thighs. A good woman, who, for the conveniency
of hearing, had placed herfelf under the fcaffold, received a trifling contufion on her face. No other
mifchief was done. The congregation, though
greatly alarmed, had the prudence not to throw themfelves into outward diforder : which, I believe, was
chiefly owing to the powerful fenfe of God's prefence,
which was eminently felt by moft of the affembly.

Such was the wonderful goodnefs of the Lord to
me, that I was not in the leaft difconcerted on this
dangerous occafion : which I mention, to the praife
of that grace and providence, without which, a much
fmaller incident would inevitably have fhocked every
nerve I have. About half a minute after the interruption had commenced, I had the fatisfaction to
inform the people, that no damage had enfued : and
removing for fecurity, to a lower ftep, I thanked the
Lord, with the rejoicing multitude, for having fo
undeniably given his angels charge concerning us.
Prayer ended, I was enabled to preach : and great
grace feemed to be upon us all.

If God permit, I hope to be with you, in London, foon after the middle of this month. I deem
it one of the principal felicities of my life, that I
have the happinefs and the honour to minifter to a
praying people. We fhould not have had fo much
of the Lord's prefence in Orange-ftreet, if he had
not poured upon us the fpirit of fupplication. Go
on to pray, and God will go on to blefs. Remember me, moft refpectfully and moft tenderly, to as
many of our dear friends in Chrift, as you are acquainted with. And, particularly, inform Mr. and
Mrs. Willett, and Mr. and Mrs. Stokes, that I have

not

not forgot my promife to write to them; and that I will perform my promife, unlefs they are fo kind as to difpenfe with it: which, I am very fure, they would moft willingly do, if they knew how little time I have to myfelf.

Farewell. Grace be with you, and with dear Mrs. Huffey. Grace comprehends all we want, in time, and in eternity.

I remain, my valuable friend, ever, ever your's,

Auguftus Toplady.

P. S. I had the happinefs to fee dear lady Huntingdon (who is the moft precious faint of God I ever knew) well, both in body and foul.

The Lord, I truft, ftill continues with you at Orange-Chapel. I fhall be much obliged to you, for informing me how things go on; by a line directed to me, at Mr. Derham's, in Green-ftreet, Bath: for which place I intend to fet out, from Devonfhire, on Monday next, the 16th inftant.

I have the unutterable fatisfaction to find feveral more awakened people at Broad-Hembury, than I formerly knew of. The Lord never fends his gofpel to any place, in vain. He will call in his own people; and will accomplifh his own work. There is really a very precious remnant, in and about this parifh. Thanks to free grace for all.

LETTER LXVII.

To Mr. ———.

MUCH LAMENTED SIR,

IN confequence of your defire, communicated to me by Mr. ———, I fignified my intention of waiting on you: but, on reflection, I more than

fear,

fear, that I have not fufficient firmnefs of nerves, to
fuftain fo trying an interview. My feelings are (unhappily for myfelf) fo terribly keen, that I fhould
only receive material injury, without being able to
render you the leaft good. My tears can be of no
fervice to you. My prayers are frequently afcending
to God for you, both in public and in private. May
the uncreated angel of the covenant take them,
warm as they rife from my unworthy heart and lips ;
and make them his own, by prefenting them with the
much incenfe of his ever effectual interceffion !

If I am rightly informed, you have, formerly, fat
under the found of the gofpel. Let me befeech
you, fir, to cry mightily to him who is able to fave,
that the Holy Ghoft may realize, to your departing
foul, thofe precious truths of grace, which have, it
feems, been often brought to your ears. Nothing,
fhort of experimental religion, will ftand you in any
ftead. The Lord Jefus enable you, by the operation of his fpirit, to come to him, as a loft finner ;
throwing yourfelf on the righteoufnefs of his life,
and on the atonement of his death, for your free
pardon and full juftification with God ! In which
cafe, though your tranfgreffions be as fcarlet, they
fhall be white as fnow ; and, though deep as crimfon, they fhall be made as wool.

I have too much reafon to apprehend, that all
application in your behalf, to the powers of this
world, will be, totally, without avail. Confider
yourfelf, therefore, dear fir, as abfolutely a dying
man.

My earneft fupplications fhall not ceafe to be
poured out at the footftool of the throne of grace,
until death fets you beyond the reach of prayer.—
Several congregations of God's people bear you,
deeply, on their hearts.

Jefus blefs you with the manifeftations of his favour ; and grant you to fing his praifes, for ever and
ever, in concert with that innumerable affembly of

fallen

fallen finners, whom he has loved, and wafhed from their fins in his own blood. So prays, with bended knees and weeping eyes, he who is, fir,

> Your unknown,
>> but not lefs affectionate well-wifher,

Oct. 31, 1776.   *Auguftus Toplady.*

L E T T E R LXVIII.

To A. B———.

Knightfbridge, Aug. 12, 1777.

IF A. B's favour, of June 16, had not been miflaid, it would have been anfwered, long before. I hope, the polite and ingenious writer will pardon the delay.

In reply to the queftion ftated, I am moft deeply and clearly convinced, that the faints in glory know each other: and more particularly, thofe with whom they took fweet counfel when on earth, and with whom they walked in the houfe of God as friends. Our Lord himfelf, I apprehend, gives us to underftand as much, where he tells us, that the elect fhall be, in the future ftate, ισαγγελοι, or equal to the angels. Now, it feems impoffible, that the unfallen angels, who have lived together, in heaven, or (at leaft) very near 6000 years, fhould not be perfectly acquainted with each other. And the fame privilege is requifite in order to our being, in every refpect, on an equality with them.—The departed foul of the rich man knew Lazarus, when he beheld him afar off· and likewife, at fight, knew Abraham, whom he could never have feen in the prefent life. Much more do Abraham and Lazarus, and all the glorified family

T 4   above,

above, rejoice in that communion of faints, which obtains in their Father's houfe.—St. Paul, fpeaking of the fpiritual children whom God had given h'm among the Theffalonians, fays, that they would be his " glory and crown of rejoicing, in the day of the Lord Jefus." But how could this be, and how could they mutually congratulate each other on the grace beftowed upon them below, if all perfonal acquaintance was to ceafe? Surely, there are no ftrangers, in that land of light and love!

The three apoftles, who attended our bleffed Lord on the Mount of Transfiguration, knew Mofes and Elijah, when they appeared in glory.——To add no more: that remarkable text, I think, fully eftablifhes the point, where our adorable Saviour bids us make to ourfelves friends, by the mammon of unrighteoufnefs; that, when we fail, they may receive us into the everlafting habitations. As if he had faid: " While you are on earth, take care to conciliate the affections of my indigent difciples, by beftowing on them a proper portion of the wealth which God has lent you, and, which is too often perverted to purpofes of unrighteoufnefs, by them that know not me. So, when your bodies die, and when your fouls afcend to heaven, the fouls of thofe poor afflicted faints, whom your bounty relieved below, and who were got to glory before you, fhall be among the firft exulting fpirits, who fhall meet you on your arrival above, and congratulate you on your fafe and triumphant entrance into the world of joy." But they could not do this, unlefs they knew us, and we them.

May the precious blood and righteoufnefs of our Incarnate God, and the faithful leadings of his eternal fpirit, bring you and me to that general affembly and Church of the firft-born! where we fhall both fee him, as he is; and likewife know each other, even as we fhall then be known. With this prayer, and
in

in this hope, I beg leave to' fubfcribe myfelf, who-
foever you may be,

Your affectionate well-wifher in Chrift,

Auguftus Toplady.

LETTER LXIX.

To the Rev. Dr. B. of *Sarum.*

Knightfbridge, Auguft 12, 1777.

YOU pay me a compliment I do not deferve, in
fuppofing, that I am induftrioufly employed
on fome ufeful work. For a long while, I have been
unufually idle, both as a preacher, and as a writer.
But my indolence was and is the refult of obedience
to medical prefcription. I have been, at beft, in a
moft fluctuating ftate of health for a year and half
paft: and, feveral times, was in a near view of land-
ing on that coaft, where the inhabitant fhall not fay,
I am fick. At thefe times, I blefs God, my chearfulnefs never forfook me; and, which calls for ftill
infinitely greater thankfulnefs, my fenfe of perfonal
intereft in his electing mercy, and in the great falvation of Jefus, was never darkened by a fingle
cloud. For the laft two months, I have been abundantly, and almoft miraculoufly, better. Whether
my remaining days be few or many, I only pray and
wifh that they may be confecrated to the glory of
the great Three-One.

And now to defcend to the affairs of this world.
The accounts of the extravagant and ridiculous
manner, in which, as you obferve, my friend Mrs.
M——'s birth-day was celebrated at Bath, gave me
extreme difguft; and have contributed to reduce
my opinion of her magnanimity and good fenfe.
Such contemptible vanity, and fuch childifh affectation of mock-majefty, would have difgraced a much
inferior underftanding; and have funk even the
meaneft

meaneſt character lower, by many degrees. If I live to ſee her again, I will rally her handſomely.

I muſt agree with you, in feeling for the advancing miſeries of our unhappy country. We are already become the jeſt, and the contempt, of all Europe. Never, ſurely, was a great and important empire ſo wantonly thrown away; and never was nation ſo infatuated before! However, when we recollect who it is that preſides, inviſibly, at the helm of all human affairs (ſee Daniel iv. 32, 35.) we are reconciled to every appearance, melancholy as appearances may ſeem; and adore the infinite wiſdom, which, ſecretly, but irreſiſtibly, over-rules even the vices, and follies, and the madneſs of men, to the accompliſhment of its own deſigns.

I am happy, to hear that yourſelf and family are well; and, if you was not a very particular friend, I ſhould almoſt have grudged you the felicity you muſt have enjoyed, in your late excurſion .to our much eſteemed friends at Freſhford.

More than compliments to you and your's, conclude me

your affectionate ſervant,

Auguſtus Toplady.

L E T T E R LXX.

To Mrs. A. G———.

Knightſbridge, Lord's-Day Evening, Nov. 2, 1777.

MADAM,

YOUR letter quite diſtreſſes me: becauſe it places excellencies to my account, which I feel myſelf to be totally unpoſſeſſed of. Among all the weak and unworthy ſervants of Chriſt, I am the unworthieſt

unworthieſt and the weakeſt. If you knew me, as well as I know myſelf, you would be entirely of my mind.

For the Lord's ſake, let us look to Jeſus only, and learn to ceaſe from man. Chriſt is all in all. Every other perſon and thing are vile, and wretched, and hateful, but ſo far as he deigns to ſmile and bleſs. " Leſs than nothing and vanity ;" is the only motto that belongs to me. If he vouchſafe to waſh me in his blood, and to ſave me by his infinitely free and glorious redemption ; a more worthleſs and helpleſs ſinner will never ſing his praiſes in the land of glory.

Inſtead of commending me, pray for me ; that I may be kept from evil, and devote my few days (in humble and earneſt attempt at leaſt) to the honour of his name.

If I wiſhed you to retain your exalted opinion of me, I ſhould, in my own defence, wave the honour of your acquaintance, which you ſo politely offer me. But, as I deſire to undeceive you, and to appear juſt what I am ; I ſhall be extremely happy to ſee you here, any day, in the forenoon, after the preſent week is elapſed ; which latter, viz. the remainder of the preſent week, I am to paſs at the houſe of a friend, who lives nine miles from hence.

God have you in his keeping, and make you a partaker of the graces and conſolations of his ſpirit.— I am, with much reſpect,

Madam, &c.

Auguſtus Toplady.

LETTER

LETTER LXXI.

To Mr. E. K———.

Knightſbridge, Nov. 22, 1777.

My Friend and Brother in Chriſt,

BY a letter, which I have this moment received from Mr. Lake, I am informed, that you are apprehenſive of the ſpeedy approach of death: and that you are particularly deſirous of ſeeing me; or, if that cannot be, of at leaſt hearing from me; before the great change comes.

As I am not certain of being able to wait on you, ſo ſoon as I could wiſh, conſidering the long extent of way that interpoſes between us; and being willing to loſe no time in aſſuring you how much I love you, and how earneſtly I commend you to God; I ſeize the immediate opportunity of writing to you. Nor ſhall I ceaſe to remember you in my worthleſs addreſs at the throne of grace, both publicly and in private.

The time, however, is perhaps arrived, which eminently calls upon you to ceaſe entirely from man. Forget me; forget even your family; forget all your earthly friends, ſo far as to loſe ſight of them: and look only to Jeſus, the glorious author and faithful finiſher of ſalvation. Repoſe your confidence on his alone blood, righteouſneſs, and interceſſion. He repreſented you, on the croſs; he bears your name, on his breaſt, and on the palms of his hands, in heaven; he ſympathizes with you, in all your pains and ſorrows; and will take care of you, unto death, through death, and to all eternity. May his comforting ſpirit make theſe bleſſings clear to your view, and powerfully ſeal upon your heart a ſenſe and enjoyment of your perſonal intereſt in them.

Leave

Leave Providence to take care of your wife and children. And leave the covenant-grace of Father, Son, and Spirit, to take charge of you. Nor do I doubt, that, whether we meet again, or not, in this valley of tears, we shall sing together, for ever, in the Jerusalem above. So believes, and so prays, your old friend and ransomed fellow-sinner,

Augustus Toplady.

P. S. I shall hold myself greatly indebted to Mr. Lake, for informing me, from time to time, how the Lord deals with you.

LETTER LXXII.

To Mr. F——.

Knightsbridge, Nov. 27, 1777.

DEAR SIR,

IF I rightly understood you yesterday, the case of conscience, proposed by your friend, is this:

" He lives in a part of England, where the gospel is not preached, by the clergy of the established Church. But the gospel is preached, in a neighbouring congregation of dissenters. He is compelled therefore, either not to hear the gospel preached at all; or to hear it at a dissenting meeting-house. —Query: Is it his duty to communicate with the dissenters, as well as to hear them? Or may he with a safe conscience, continue only to hear them, and still maintain his communion, with the Church of England ?"

For my own part, I am most clearly of opinion, (1.) That, if he cannot hear the Church of England doctrines preached in a parish-church

(which

(which is terribly the cafe in fome thoufands of places;) he is bound in confcience to hear thofe truths, where they can be heard: was it in a barn, in a private houfe, in a field, or on a dung-hill.——But,

(2.) I am no lefs clearly convinced, that he is not under the fmalleft neceffity of breaking off from the communion of the Church eftablifhed.

Some of my reafons are thefe:

1. Your friend's love to the Church-doctrines (i. e. to the gofpel of grace,) is the very thing that forces him to forfake the Church-walls, as an hearer. But this need not force him from communicating there. It fhould rather bind him, more clofely and firmly, to a Church whofe doctrines and facraments are holy, harmlefs, and undefiled; and alike remote from error, fuperftition, and licentioufnefs.

2. Our bleffed Lord, himfelf, communicated with the eftablifhed Church of Judea; though its minifters and people were as deeply degenerated from the purity and power of God's truths, as the prefent minifters and people of the Church of England are, for the moft part, now.—That our Lord actually did thus communicate in the Jewifh church (fallen as its pro-feffors were,) is evident, from his celebration of the Paffover, antecedently to his inftitution of the Holy Supper, in the evening of the very night wherein he was betrayed.

3. The goodnefs, or badnefs, of a parifh minifter, neither adds nor detracts from, the virtue and value of the facraments he difpenfes. Judas appears to have preached the gofpel, and to have wrote mira-cles. Was the gofpel, or were thofe miracles, at all the worfe on his account? No: in no wife.—" But the minifter of my parifh does not preach the gofpel." Be it fo.—You do right, therefore, in not hearing him. Neverthelefs, though (in this refpect) he out-fins Judas himfelf; why fhould that unhap py circumftance make you quarrel with, and abfent

yourfelf

yourfelf from, the communion-fervice of the Church?

4. I can fet my own *probatum eft*, to the conduct I am now recommending. For feveral years after I was made acquainted with the grace of God, I chiefly refided in a place, where I was obliged, either to ftarve my foul, by never fitting under the miniftry of the word; or to go for it, to a diffenting meeting-houfe. I made not a moment's hefitation, in chufing the latter; and would again purfue the fame line, if Providence was again to place me in fimilar circumftances. But, though I heard the gofpel, conftantly, at meeting (becaufe I could hear it no where elfe,) I, conftantly and ftrictly, communicated in the Church only. I know that this was pleafing to God, by the many happy foul-feafons I enjoyed, both at the Lord's table, and in the feparate affembly. And yet, (as you may judge from my leaving them as preachers,) the clergymen, at whofe hands I received the memorials of Chrift's dying love, knew no more of the gofpel, than fo many ftocks or ftones.

5. Let a parifh-minifter be ever fo fpiritually blind and dead, the liturgy remains the fame. Bleffed be God, the clergy are forced to read it; and to adminifter the Lord's fupper, and other offices, according to its admirable and animating form of found words.

6. While your friend communicates in the Church of England, he is at full liberty to hear the gofpel elfewhere: But,

Should he communicate with a diffenting-church, he muft, firft, fo far become one of them, as to hear the gofpel, in great meafure, if not entirely, among them only. Such a transfer of communion, therefore, would refemble tying himfelf by the leg (or, rather, nailing himfelf by the ear) to a fingle tree; in preference to enjoying the full range of God's garden. I have feen fo very many inftances of this, in

a courfe

courfe of more than two and twenty years obfervation, that no antecedent promifes, profeffions, or
proteftations, to the contrary (made to a new convert by any of thofe religious affemblies,) would
have the leaft weight on my judgement of this
matter.

Thus I have, agreeably to your defire, fignified a
few of thofe reafons, which have long had great influence in determining my own mind. Influence fo very
great and decifive, that I am thoroughly perfuaded,
was the glorious company of apoftles to live again
on earth, at this very time, and to live in England;
not one of them, I very believe, would be a diffenter
from our eftablifhed Church: though they would
all deeply lament the dreadful ftate of fpiritual, of
doctrinal, and of moral declenfion, to which the
greateft part of us are reduced.—May God inform
and teach your friend, the way in which he ought to
go; and, forever, guide him with his eye! With
which prayer, for him, for you, and for myfelf,
I remain,

Sir, your fervant in Chrift,

Auguftus Toplady.

LETTER LXXIII.

To Mr. VALLANCE.

Knightfbridge, Dec. 1, 1777.

DEAR SIR,

ON the cover of laft month's magazine, I read
the following notice: " Thanks to Minimus,
for his pious Meditation." Now, as I am the only
perfon, who ever appeared, in your magazine, under
the

the fignature of Minimus; and as I never fent you any meditation, whether pious or impious, fince I furrendered my editorfhip of the faid magazine [in July laft], and as it is generally known, that the papers figned Minimus, were written by me : ——It will be both ufing me extremely ill; and alfo look like a defire, on your part, to palm a deception on your readers, if you permit any future paper, of which I am not the author, to bear the fignature above-mentioned.

Not doubting, that, on further confideration, you will fee the juftice and propriety of this hint, and act accordingly; I remain, fir,

your affectionate friend and fervant,

Auguftus Toplady.

L E T T E R LXXIV.

To J. W———, Efq.

Knightfbridge, Dec. 30, 1777.

Sir,

I THROW myfelf on your candour and politenefs, for your pardon of the prefent freedom, taken by a perfon who has not the honour of being known to you. The favour which I prefume to folicit, is, that you would be fo obliging as to communicate to me fuch leading particulars, as you may recollect, concerning a late friend of your's; who was one of the greateft, and yet (by a fate peculiarly ftrange) one of the obfcureft men, whom this ifland ever produced : I mean, Mr. Baxter, the metaphyfician, who dedicated the 3d volume of his

chief

chief work to you. I have a very cogent reaſon,
for wiſhing to acquire authentic and exact information of the times and places of his birth and death;
and of ſuch other principal circumſtances, as may
merely ſuffice to perpetuate the out-lines of his perſonal hiſtory: which, in point of diffuſiveneſs, need
not be more prolix, than is the letter I now addreſs
to you. I am, &c.

Auguſtus Toplady.

L E T T E R LXXV.

To the Rev. Dr. PRIESTLEY.

Knightſbridge, Jan. 20, 1778.

I AM much your debtor, ſir, for your late polite
favour from Calne: but, eſpecially, for the obliging
preſent of your Diſquiſitions concerning Matter and
Spirit; and of the Appendix, concerning Neceſſity.
I have read them, with great attention: and, as you
condeſcend to requeſt my opinion of thoſe ingenious
pieces; you ſhall have it, with the moſt tranſparent unreſerve.

I need not ſay any thing, as to the article of neceſſity: becauſe you well know, that I have the honour to coincide, almoſt entirely, with your own
view of that great ſubject. Permit me, however, to
aſk, *en paſſant*, in what part of any printed work of
mine, I " ſeem to think that the torments of hell
will not be eternal?" You yourſelf, dear ſir, I doubt
not, will, on a calm review, be the firſt to condemn
your own temerity, in having publicly advanced a
conjecture totally unwarranted on my part: and I
am equally diſpoſed to believe, that this will be the
laſt liberty of the kind, which you will venture to
take

take either with me, or with any other man.   You
muſt be ſenſible, that not a word, on the nature or
the duration of future puniſhment, ever paſt between you and me, either in writing, or in perſonal
converſe.   Conſequently, you muſt be entirely un-
acquainted with my ideas of that awful ſubject:
and, as ſuch, was totally unqualified to advance the
inſinuation, of which I have ſuch juſt reaſon to
complain.

With regard to your "Diſquiſitions," &c.   I
would obſerve,

1. That I can ſubſcribe to no more than to one
moiety of them.   I ſtill conſider materialiſm, as
equally abſurd in itſelf, and atheiſtical in its tendency.

But, 2. The peruſal of your book gave me no ſurpriſe ; becauſe I have, for a conſiderable time paſt,
viewed you as a ſecret materialiſt : whoſe favourite
principle, like the workings of a ſubterraneous fire,
would, at laſt, break forth into open birth.

3. Nor has this publication leſſened, in the ſmalleſt degree, my reſpect and eſteem for its author.
You have a right, to think for yourſelf; and to
publiſh the reſult of your thoughts, to the world.
If my own brother was of a different judgment, as
to this point, I ſhould ſet him down for an enemy
to the indefeaſible prerogatives of human nature.

4. I revere and admire real probity, wherever I ſee
it.   Artifice, duplicity, and diſguiſe, I cannot away
with.   Tranſparency is, in my opinion, the firſt and
the moſt valuable of all ſocial virtues.   Let a man's
principles be black as hell, it matters not to me, ſo
he have but integrity to appear exactly what he is.
Give me the perſon, whom I can hold up, as I can
a piece of chryſtal, and ſee through him.   For this,
among many other excellencies, I regard and admire
Dr. Prieſtley.

5. I muſt acknowledge, ſir, that, in the foregoing
part of your "Diſquiſitions," you throw no ſmall

quantity of light on the nature of matter at large.
My apprehensions, concerning visible substance, are,
in several important respects, corrected and improved, by your masterly observations on that subject. I wish you had stopt at matter, which you
evidently do understand, and better, perhaps, than
any other philosopher on earth; and not meddled
with spirit, whose acquaintance, it is very plain, you
have not cultivated with equal affiduity.

6. Bishop Berkeley tells me, that I am all spirit,
without a single particle of matter belonging to me.
Dr. Priestley, on the other head, contends, that I
am all body, untenanted and unanimated by any
immaterial substance within. Put these two theo-
ries together, and what will be the product? That
my sum total, and that of every other man, amounts
to just nothing at all, I have neither body, nor soul.
I have no sort of existence whatever.—Here it may
be alledged, "That the two systems cannot be thrown
together, as being totally incompatible." I answer: Why may not bishop Berkeley's word go as
far as Dr. Priestley's; and the doctor's as far as
the bishop's? Though, when all is done, the best
way, in my opinion, is, to cease from both, and
to believe neither.

7. The arguments, for absolute and universal ma-
terialism, drawn (or, rather, pretendedly drawn)
from rational and philosophic sources, appear, to
me, prodigiously forced, lame, and inconclusive.
And, if we take Scripture into the account, not all
the subtilty nor all the violence of criticism will ever
be able to establish your system on that ground.
What wretched work do you yourself make, with
those few texts, which you venture to quote and
strive to obviate, wherein *plenâ* & *primâ facie*, man is
spoken of, as a being compounded of matter and
spirit!

Can you bear this plain dealing? If you can, give
me your hand. And I most heartily wish, that all,
who differ from you, and especially that all who

may

may commence your public antagonifts, may treat you, as I ever defire to do, with the refpect due to your virtues and your talents.

How is your health ? Beware of too clofe application, and of too intenfe exertions of mind. I, for my own part, can moft heartily fubfcribe to thefe remarks of the apocryphal writer : " The thoughts of mortal men are miferable, and our devices are but uncertain. For the corruptible body preffeth down the foul, and the earthy tabernacle weigheth down the mind that mufeth on many things. Hardly do we guefs aright, at things that are upon earth ; and with labour do we find the things that are before us : but the things which are in heaven, who hath fearched out ? And thy counfel who hath known, except thou give wifdom, and fend thy Holy Spirit from above ?"—May that Holy Spirit, fhining on his written word, and fhining into our hearts, be a light to the paths of the much-efteemed friend, to whom I am writing ; and the paths of his

obliged and moft obedient fervant,

Auguftus Toplady.

L E T T E R LXXVI.

To Mrs. FOWLER.

Knightfbridge, Feb. 20, 1778.

DEAR MADAM,

KNOWING that the officious zeal of numerous vifitants, however well-meant, occafions more trouble than relief, during the firft impreffions that refult from fo trying a difpenfation, as that, under which God is now exerciling you; I, for this reafon, wave prefenting you with my perfonal condolences,

and

and requeſt yourſelf and your amiable family to accept my written reſpects.

You and your's are deeply on my heart, before the mercy-ſeat. Has the Holy Spirit yet brought you to that point, whither faith invariably tends, and in which it will always ultimately reſt? viz. " It is the Lord. Let him do, as ſeemeth him good." That your huſband's God is and will be your God, even to the end, and without end, I believe, with the fulleſt aſſurance. May he likewiſe be the God of all your offspring! It is a great, an unſpeakably great thing, to be born again. How far that moſt momentous work has taken place on their ſouls, I know not. But may they ever tread in the religi- ous footſteps of their deſervedly honoured father; and never forget, that the ſame bleſſed and triumph- ant conſolations which enlivened his laſt hours, will alſo felicitate their lives, and brighten their deaths, if effectual grace render them partakers of like pre- cious faith, with him, in the righteouſneſs of our God and Saviour.

The preſence of our Lord Jeſus Chriſt be with you all. Remember, that " Your Maker is your huſband:" an huſband, who never dies, and who changes not.—My kindeſt and moſt ſympathiſing reſpects attend the two young ladies, and both the gentlemen. Adieu, until I have an opportunity of aſſuring you, by word of mouth, how much

I am, &c.

Auguſtus Toplady.

LETTER

LETTER LXXVII.

To Mr. Hussey.

Broad-Hembury, March 19, 1778.

VERY DEAR SIR,

THE hofpitable kindnefs of my old friend at Salifbury, detained me in that place, until Monday laft; in the afternoon of which day I fat forward for my own parifh, and arrived here on Tuefday.

I cannot boaft of any great effects, produced by the journey and by change of air. If my hoarfenefs abates, my cough comes on, with redoubled violence; and, if my cough grows favourable, the hoarfenefs returns. But welcome, ten thoufand times welcome, the whole will of God. I truft, his fpirit has begun to render me paffive in his bleffed hand, and to turn me as clay to the feal. I am enabled to be more than refigned: I am thankful for his every difpenfation, knowing them to be all ordered in faithfulnefs and love.

I was unable to preach, while at Salifbury; and begin to apprehend, that I muft not attempt to preach at my own Church, here, next Sunday. But though fuch abfolute ufeleffnefs is the moft afflictive part of my prefent vifitation; yet, even this I can leave with God my Saviour, who is the governing head of his family, both in heaven and earth, and orders all things well.

It is ftill my hope, and my intention, to return to town, in the courfe of next week. I am to have a fale of my furniture in my houfe here on Monday and Tuefday next; and, I truft, the whole of that bufinefs will be accomplifhed in thofe two days, without detaining me longer. But, if otherwife, may I not venture to defer my return, until Monday the 30th, or Tuefday the 31ft, of this prefent month? I.

am

am never fond of worldly bufinefs, and am now particularly difqualified for managing it well : but when
once undertaken, I deem it my duty to go through
with it, in the beft manner I am able.

Dear Mrs. Huffey, yourfelf, and all the flock of
Chrift who worfhip with us at Orange-ftreet, are
much and deeply on my heart. And if I, a finful
dying worm, feel fuch glowing affection for the
people of God : oh, with what intenfenefs muft the
Almighty Father love thofe whom he ordained to
eternal life, before all worlds ; and whom he gave to
his Son to fave, and for whom he gave up the Son
himfelf to the death of the crofs ! How aftonifhingly,
alfo, muft Jefus have loved his people, when he con-
fented to difcharge their two-fold debt of perfect
obedience and penal fuffering ! And how are they
loved by the moft holy and bleffed fpirit of grace,
who converts, comforts, fanctifies, and feals them to
the day of redemption !

May that three-fold love, the three-fold cord that
can never be broken, be the prefent and eternal rejoicing of my much valued Mr. and Mrs. Huffey,
and of their

Obliged and affectionate fervant,

Auguftus Toplady.

P. S. I hope you had my letter from Sarum,
dated the 11th inftant. It would rejoice me to have
one from you.

L E T T E R LXXVIII.

To Mr. Hussey.

Ever dear Sir,

GOD's good providence brought me hither, yefterday, early in the afternoon, quite unfatigued
by my journey, and rejoicing in fpirit before him.

It

It can hardly be expected, that fo fhort a time fhould have any very falutary effect, on complaints fo fixed as mine: my voice, however, has been much better to-day, than for three weeks paft.

My mind is quite at reft. All my affairs, refpecting both this world and a better, are completely fettled. My falvation was provided for, in the covenant of grace, from all eternity, and fealed by the finifhed redemption of my adorable Saviour. My temporal bufinefs is all fettled to my fatisfaction, by the completion of my laft will and teftament, before I left London. So that I have, at prefent, nothing to do, but to fing in the ways of the Lord, that great are the glory and the goodnefs of the Lord.

I am uncertain, whether I fhall fee Broad-Hembury, late in this week, or early in the next. When you favour and oblige me with a line, be fo good as to direct to me, fimply, at Broad-Hembury, Honiton.

As an old friend, whom I have not feen for many years, has, juft now, called at Dr. Baker's, in order to fee me, I am obliged to be very concife. I fhall depend, if the Lord permit, on hearing from you, when I am in Devonfhire. And it gives me great happinefs, to be able to inform you, that I fully defign, with the leave of my heavenly Father, to be in town again, before the laft Sunday in this month. God only can tell, how deeply my Chriftian friends, and the dear people at Orange-ftreet, in particular, dwell upon my heart. May they pray for me, as I alfo for them. Remember me, moft kindly and refpectfully, to dear Mrs. Huffey, Mr. and Mrs. Ward, of Weftminfter, and all others who condefcend to enquire after the meaneft of my Lord's redeemed finners. I have not room to mention a quarter of the perfons, by name, whom I love in the Lord: but all our names are written on his breaft.

Adieu, dear fir,

I am, deeply and ever your's,

Auguftus Toplady.

AN ANSWER

" Whether popular Applause can yield solid Satisfaction to a truly great Mind ?"

REAL greatnefs of mind includes whatever is noble, worthy, and exalted: of courfe, independency is effential to it. If the poftulatum be granted (and I fee not how it can be denied) the next inquiry will be, whether a perfon, whofe fatisfaction, in whole or in part, is fufpended on the applaufe of others, can be called an independent man ? If he may, it would follow, that greedinefs of popularity does not infer dependence ; if he cannot, it will follow, that a perfon, who drudges for popular applaufe, is not poffeffed of a truly great mind. Add to this, that all motives to public ufefulnefs, which arife from principles merely felfifh, are very far from being indicatory of magnanimity. This exalted quality, foaring fuperior to all the little arts of felf-recommendation and perfonal aggrandizement, fhuts felf out of the queftion : and regards only the welfare of others, not their praife. Thus, for inftance, a truly patriotic ftatefman, or a truly confcientious minifter of Chrift, aims, not at the evanid applaufe, but at the folid benefit, of thofe for whom he labours : nay ; one, actuated by thefe elevated views, would, to ferve mankind fubftantially, even run the rifque of doing good to them againft their wills, though he was fure of fuffering in their eftimation for doing it. Such difinterefted benevolence, and fuch heroic beneficence, are as fhining and conclufive marks, as can be given, for a mind truly great.

Befides,

Befides, it puts a truly magnanimous man on too low and defpicable a footing, to fuppofe him capable of finking into the meaneft of all purfuits, by commencing an angler for fame, and building any part of his mental happinefs on the unftable bafis of popular breath. A really great perfon, does not live, as the cameleon has been vulgarly fuppofed to do, on air: but on that which will yield fure and folid fupport, when every exterior happinefs fails. The fenfe of divine favour; univerfal and difinterefted love to mankind; uncorrupt intention; and integrity of action; in a word, the men's *confcia recti*; are what conftitute the felicity of one who deferves the name of man. Add to this, that real magnanimity is abfolutely inconfiftent with pride. Of all vices, pride is the meaneft, and the moft truly contemptible. But pride is the very bafis of that wretched ambition which terminates in the affectation of applaufe; confequently, a mind truly great, cannot degenerate into this inverted ambition; unlefs meannefs and magnanimity are terms fynonymous. That juft praife, which ufually attends characters and actions truly great and good, is a deferved confequence of thofe actions, but ought not to be the motive to performing them. Depraved as mankind are, I yet hope and believe that we have many ufeful perfons, both in the learned, civil, and religious world, who difdain fo bafe a principle of action: and that the love of fame is a paffion not quite fo univerfal as a late ingenious fatirift imagined. The love of truth, the love of beneficence, and the love of juftice; or, in other words, the love of God, and the love of man; are the predominant and exciting principles, in every breaft, which genuine greatnefs warms. I would mention one argument more.

The mind, whofe fatisfaction is at all founded on popular eclat, muft be, in itfelf, extremely fickle; and a mere Proteus, ready, on every occafion, to vary its determinations, and to fhape its meafures, according to the mutability of the multitude, in or-

der to preferve the applaufe already gained. A perfon under the unhappy influence of fo bafe and paltry a paffion, muft alter with the times, and fwim
with the ftream, right or wrong; and, like the
cameleon juft mentioned, affume any colour next
him; for fear of lofing that eftimation, which his
paft compliances had acquired him. Now, a truly
great man can never be a voluntary flave: but the
man whofe leading paffion is love of praife, makes
himfelf a voluntary flave for life: therefore, it is impoffible for one, under fo defpicable a bias, to be a
truly great man. To defcend from argument, to
plain matter of fact. If any perfon doubts whether
popular applaufe be that unfatisfactory thing which
I have defcribed it, he need only go a few miles out
of town, to a place called Hayes: and there he will
fee, with his own eyes, that popular applaufe, however it may tickle a man's vanity for a while, will,
if he has not fomething more folid for his mind to
feed on, leave him, fooner or later, miferable, contemptible, and unfatisfied. I know but of one truly
great man, who was a profeffed lover of popular applaufe; and that was the illuftrious Cicero: but it
fhould be remembered, that that confummate ftatefman, patriot, and philofopher, flourifhed in the very
dregs of the Roman commonwealth; when public
virtue, and public liberty (which will always, at the
long run, ftand or fall together) were expiring. At
fuch a time, to love Cicero, and to love virtue, to
love Cicero and to love liberty, were the fame thing.
Of this, that moft accomplifhed man could not but
be confcious: and it may be, he was ambitious of
popular eftimation, at the critical time, in hopes of
being able, by the credit he fought and deferved, to
give an happy turn to the public affairs, and make
the fcale preponderate in favour of his finking country: all wnich, he well knew, it would be impoffible
for him to effect, by any counfels he could give, or
any meafures he could take, unlefs he could previoufly fecure the approbation of the people he wifhed

ed to fave: fo that Cicero's unbounded thirft of
praife feems to have arifen purely and folely from
the love he bore to the nobleft republic that ever
fubfifted : and he coveted popularity, not for his
own fake, or for any folid fatisfaction it yielded to
himfelf as an individual ; but, as matters then ftood,
he confidered the acquifition of univerfal efteem, as
the medium to his country's welfare, and the only
poffible expedient which could retrieve it from the
ruin which then threatened, and with which it was
foon after actually overwhelmed, notwithftanding
the manifold and almoft fupernatural efforts of that
great man to avert the blow.—Or, even fuppofing
that Cicero, with all his philofophy and virtue, had
fome remains of vanity in him, which he fought to
gratify, by ftanding a perpetual candidate for praife,
(which, however, his character and conduct in all
other refpects, forbid us to believe) ; yet, even on
this hypothefis, it would not follow, that " popular
applaufe can yield folid fatisfaction to a truly great
mind." For the gratification of vanity is one thing ;
fatisfaction of mind is another. Vanity may be qualified, and yet the mind go unfatisfied : and *vice
verfa*. Befides, were it otherwife, we are not to
adopt the foibles even of a great man, for they are
foils and blemifhes, in what character foever they
are found. Though, for reafons already hinted, I
cannot perfuade myfelf, that Cicero's was mere love
of praife : it had the nobleft of motives, and was directed to the beft of ends. It was founded on love
to his country, and a paffionate ardour for her pre-
fervation. But, admitting the reverfe to be probable, it would not follow, that becaufe Cicero, the
moft fhining perfon heathen antiquity has to boaft
of, deferved, and, from confcioufnefs of that defert
(which we could not juftly wonder at, in one who
had not the advantage of gofpel revelation to humble him) coveted applaufe ; that therefore others
have a right to claim the fame privilege, fince,
Cicero was fo tranfcendent and peculiar a character.

that what was lawful for him to confpire to, would be inexcufable in the reft of mankind. For though fucceeding ages will, without doubt, give many millions of men to the world; yet, poffibly, no age nor country will ever produce a fecond Cicero.

―――――――

AN ANSWER

To the following Question.

" Whether an Highwayman or a cheating Tradefman, is the honefter Perfon ?"

I Suppofe, moft perfons will allow, that plain deal-ing is one very important branch of honefty. Taking this for granted, the next enquiry will be, who is the plain dealer? The highwayman, who openly avows his defign, and fays to you, frankly and above-board, your money or your life! Or the fharking, fhuffling tradefman, who, in a fly clan-deftine manner, abufes the confidence you repofe in him, and cheats you, under the fictitious appear-ance of a fair dealer? Is not fuch a perfon, as much a robber, to all intents and purpofes, as the man who privily fteals any part of your property out of your dwelling-houfe, or takes it from you by force on the highway?

Mutual confidence, fuch as is fuppofed to obtain between buyer and feller, is one main band of fo-ciety: and every illicit practice, that tends to render that confidence precarious, is a ftep to-war... ...olving thofe focial connections, of which confidence is the bafis. Here, again, I the fcale turns in favour of the high-Then he prefents his piftol at the coach-'t may be, fomething that looks like infpire terror, without even a poffibi-lity

fity of doing real mifchief), he gives you your alter-
native ; he lets you know what you have to expect,
in cafe of refufal. You are not betrayed under a
pretext of honefty, but exprefsly left to your own
option, whether you will refign your purfe, or ftand
to the confequence. I grant this to be a breach of
the peace, and a breach of integrity : but then it is
an open, declared one ; and you know what you have
to do. And, let it be a breach of what it will befide, it is plainly no breach of truft : confidence is
utterly difavowed on both fides : and therefore,
though forced to part with fome of your money, in
order to fecure your perfonal fafety (and he, I
think, is a fool who would not), yet you are not
cheated of it. And though force of this kind, if
univerfal, would be no lefs fubverfive of fociety, than
fraud ; yet, fince, by the care of the legiflature, inftances of the former are infinitely fewer than inftances of the latter ; going on the highway is not, upon
the whole, and as matters now ftand, either fo general an evil, or fo pernicious to the community, as
cheating behind a counter.

Add, to all this, that, when I exchange my money for fome certain commodity in lieu of it, I juftly
expect, and my tradefman profeffes to let me have,
an equitable equivalent for the money fo paid. But,
if, inftead of fuch an equivalent, there is, in reality,
no due proportion between the price I pay, and the
article I purchafe ; I am as much robbed by that
infiduous falefman, as if he was to ftop me on Houn-
flow Heath. 1 mean not to juftify the gentlemen
of the road. I am truly fenfible, that before a perfon can take that defperate and unlawful method of
repairing his fortune, he muft have bid adieu to
virtue and be loft to principle ; we are not now ex-
culpating villainy, but only weighing and comparing it.

In common life, it is ufual to diftinguifh between
theft and robbery. But I apprehend, thefe, though
nominally

nominally and circumstantially different, are, in fact, one and the same.

The man, who unjustly deprives another of his property, robs him: and there are but two ways of doing this; either privately or publicly. But, in this case, the thing itself suffers very great alteration, from the mode of doing it. I therefore set down the unfair tradesman, and the profest highwayman, for robbers. Only, one conducts his scheme in an open manner; the other adds treachery to dishonesty. Robbery is robbery, either way: if there is any difference, it seems to consist in this: that robbery on the public road, is robbery barefaced; whereas, robbery in a shop, is robbery disguised: which only makes it a worse species of the same genus.

One thing more deserves consideration. There have been instances of men who have robbed others on the highway, and, some years after, sent the persons, they robbed, anonymous letters, including Bank bills to more than the amount of what they took: thus repaying, with interest, what they had formerly borrowed on the Heath. But I never yet heard of a cheating tradesman who made the same return to the customers he had defrauded: and, indeed, if a tradesman of that stamp was, afterwards, to act on this noble principle of recoiling integrity, he would have enough to do, and, after all his unjust gains, have little or nothing to bequeath to his own family. However, as the instances, of reimbursing the party robbed are rare; and as general conclusions cannot be formed from particular premises, I lay no great stress on the last observation: but for the reasons alledged before, I must, and do give it as my opinion, that though the cheating tradesman, and the highway robber are both rogues, and great ones; yet that, upon the whole, the highwayman is the honester rogue of the two. And as, of two evils, prudence bids us chuse the least; so, of two villains, justice tells us, that the least is to be preferred.

POEMS

P O E M S

o.w

SACRED SUBJECTS,

WHEREIN THE

Fundamental Doctrines of Christianity,

WITH

MANY OTHER INTERESTING POINTS;
are occasionally introduced.

Written between Fifteen and Eighteen Years of Age.

En, fanctos Manibus punfet fumeret
Ignes Veftatem fe Mufa facit; bene libera
Curis Libera Deliciifque, Jocifque & Amore profano,

The PREFACE.

THE following Pieces are not recommended to the patronage of the Public, on account of any excellency in themselves, but merely for the importance of their subjects: for, however defective the superstructure may be, its foundation is unquestionably good. All the doctrines here advanced, deducing their authority from the Sacred Scriptures, and their faithful epitome, the Homilies, and Articles of the established Church.

That the dignity of truths so momentous, might be impaired as little as possible by the manner of expressing them, they are often introduced in the very words of the inspired Writers, and our venerable Reformers; as every reader, who is intimate with the invaluable Books just mentioned, cannot fail of observing.

Since all the essentials of religion are comprised in these two, found faith, and a suitable course of obedience, every thing that may give offence to Christians dissenting from each other in points merely indifferent, is studiously avoided, and no particular tenets any where struck at, except one or two, which apparently tend to invalidate the authority of Revelation, and, by consequence, to subvert the whole system of Christianity.

The Author wishes it was in his power to do justice to the sublime doctrines here treated of; but, until death is swallowed up in victory, the glorious privileges and ineffable benefits redounding to believers from the manifestation of God in the flesh, cannot be perfectly conceived, much less properly expressed.

Lest a continued sameness should pall, and want of method confuse the reader, the metre is occa-

sionally

fionally varied, and the whole prefents itfelf to his view, digefted as follows:

    I. Petitionary Hymns.

    II. Hymns of Praife.

    III. Paraphrafes on fome Select Portion of Holy Writ.

    IV. A few Pieces occafioned by the Death of Friends. And,

Laftly, feveral Pieces, not properly referable to any of the preceding Heads, thrown together by way of Appendix.

PETITIONARY

PETITIONARY HYMNS.

Te Mente purâ & fimplici
Te Voce te Cantu pio,
Rogare curvato genu,
Flendo & canendo difcimus.   PRUDENTIUS.

" Oratio eft Oris Ratio, per quam intimæ Cordis
Noftri manifeftamus Deo."

POEM I.

1 REFINING Fuller, make me clean,
 On me thy coftly pearl beftow:
Thou art thyfelf the pearl I prize,
 The only joy I feek below.

2 Difperfe the clouds that damp my foul,
 And make my heart unfit for thee:
Caft me not off, but feal me now
 Thine own peculiar property.

3 Look on the wounds of Chrift for me,
 My fentence gracioufly reprieve:
Extend thy peaceful fceptre, Lord,
 And bid the dying traitor live.

4 Tho' I've tranfgrefs'd the rules prefcrib'd,
 And dar'd the juftice I adore,
Yet let thy fmiling mercy fay,
 Depart in peace, and fin no more.

POEM II. *At entering into the Church.*

1 FATHER of love, to thee I bend
 My heart, and lift mine eyes;
O let my pray'r and praife afcend
 As odours to the fkies.

2 Thy pard'ning voice I come to hear,
 To know thee as thou art:

Thy

Thy minifters can reach the ear,
   But thou muft touch the heart.
3 O ftamp me in thy heav'nly mould,
   And grant thy word apply'd
May bring forth fruit an hundred fold
   • And fpeak me juftify'd.

POEM III. *When Service is ended.*

1 LORD, let me not thy courts depart,
   Nor quit thy mercy-feat,
Before I feel thee in my heart,
   And there the Saviour meet.
2 Water the feed in weaknefs fown,
   And ever more improve:
Make me a garden of thine own,
   May ev'ry flow'r be love !
3 O fend my foul in peace away ;
   For both my Lord hath bought:
And let my heart, exulting, fay,
   I've found the pearl I fought !

POEM IV. *For the Morning.*

1 JESUS, by whofe grace I live,
   From the fear of evil kept,
Thou haft lengthen'd my reprieve,
   Held in being while I flept.
With the day my heart renew ;
Let me wake thy will to do.
2 Since the laft revolving dawn
   Scatter'd the nocturnal cloud,
O how many fouls have gone,
   Unprepar'd, to meet their God !
Yet thou doft prolong my breath,
Nor haft feal'd my eyes in death.
3 O that I may keep thy word,
   Taught by thee to watch and pray !
To thy fervice, deareft Lord,
   Sanctify th' prefent day :

                         Swift

Swift it's fleeting moments hafte :
Doom'd, perhaps, to be my laft.
4 Crucify'd to all below,
    Earth fhall never be my care;
Wealth and honour I forego,
    This my only wifh and care,
Thine in life and death to be,
Now and to eternity.

POEM V. *For the Evening.*

1 GOD of love, whofe truth and grace
    Reach unbounded as the fkies,
Hear thy creature's feeble praife,
    Let my ev'ning facrifice
Mount as incenfe to thy throne,
On the merits of thy Son.
2 Me thy Providence has led
    Through another bufy day :
Over me thy wings were fpread,
    Chafing fin and death away :
Thou haft been my faithful fhield,
Thou my footfteps haft upheld.
3 Tho' the fable veil of night
    Hides the cheering face of heav'n,
Let me triumph in the fight
    Of my guilt in thee forgiv'n.
In my heart the witnefs feel,
See the great invifible.
4 I will lay me down to fleep,
    Sweetly take my reft in thee,
Ev'ry moment brought a ftep
    Nearer to eternity :
I fhall foon from earth afcend,
Quickly reach my journey's end.
5 All my fins imputed were
    To my dear, incarnate God ;
Bury'd in his grave they are,
    Drown'd in his atoning blocd :

Me

Me thou wilt not now condemn,
Righteous and compleat in him.

6 In the Saviour's right 1 claim
   All the bleffings he hath bought ;
For my foul the dying Lamb
  . Hath a full redemption wrought ;
Heaven through his defert is mine ;
Chrift's I am, and Chrift is thine !

POEM VI. *There is Mercy with Thee.*

1 LORD, fhould'ft thou weigh my righteoufnefs,
Or mark what I have done amifs,
   How fhould thy fervant ftand ?
Tho' others might, yet furely I
Muft hide my face, nor dare to cry
   For mercy at thy hand.

2 But thou art loth thy bolts to fhoot ;
Backward and flow to execute
   The vengeance due to me :
Thou doft not willingly reprove,
For all the mild effects of love
   Are center'd, Lord, in thee.

3 Shine, then, thou all fubduing light,
The powers of darknefs put to flight,
   Nor from me ever part :
From earth to heaven be thou my guide,
And O, above each gift befide,
   Give me an upright heart.

POEM VII. *In Sicknefs.*

1 JESUS, fince I with thee am one,
   Confirm my foul in thee,
And ftill continue to tread down
   The man of fin in me.

2 Let not the fubtle foe prevail
   In this my feeble hour :
Fruftrate all the hopes of hell,
   Redeem from Satan's pow'r.

3 Arm

3 Arm me, O Lord, from head to foot
 With righteoufnefs divine;
My foul in Jefus firmly root,
 And feal the Saviour mine.

4 Proportion'd to my pains below,
 O let my joys increafe,
And mercy to my fpirit flow
 In healing ftreams of peace.

5 In life and death be thou my God,
 And I am more than fafe:
Chaftis'd by thy paternal rod,
 Support me with thy ftaff.

6 Lay on me, Saviour, what thou wilt,
 But give me ftrength to bear:
Thy gracious hand this crofs hath dealt,
 Which cannot be fevere.

7 As gold refin'd may I come out,
 In forrow's furnace try'd;
Preferv'd from faithleffnefs and doubt,
 And fully purify'd.

8 When, overwhelm'd with fore diftrefs,
 Out of the pit I cry,
On Jefus fuffering in my place
 Help me to fix mine eye.

9 When * marr'd with tears and blood and fweat,
 The glorious fufferer lay,
And in my ftead, fuftain'd the heat
 And burthen of the day.

10 The pangs which my weak nature knows
 Are fwallow'd up in thine:
How numberlefs thy pond'rous woes!
 How few, how light are mine!

11 O might I learn of thee to bear
 Temptation, pain and lofs!
Give me an heart inur'd to prayer,
 And fitted to the crofs.

* Referring to his Agony in the Garden.

12 Make

12 Make me, O Lord, thy patient fon;
    Thy language mine fhall be:
  "Father, thy gracious will be done,
    I take the cup from thee."
13 While thus my foul is fixt on him
    Once faften'd to the wood,
  Safe fhall I pafs through Jordan's ftream,
    And reach the realms of God.
14 And when my foul mounts up to keep
    With thee the marriage feaft,
  I fhall not die, but fall afleep
    On my Redeemer's breaft.

POEM VIII. *John* xiv. 17. *He dwelleth with you,*
               and fhall be in you.

1 SAVIOUR, l thy word believe,
    My unbelief remove;
  Now thy quick'ning fpirit give,
    The unction from above;
  Shew me, Lord, how good thou art,
    My foul with all thy fullnefs fill:
  Send the witnefs, in my heart
    The Holy Ghoft reveal.
2 Dead in fin 'till then I lie,
    Bereft of pow'r, to rife;
  'Till thy fpirit inwardly
    Thy faving blood applies:
  Now the mighty gift impart,
    My fin erafe, my pardon feal;
  Send the witnefs, in my heart
    The Holy Ghoft reveal.
3 Bleffed Comforter, come down,
    And live and move in me;
  Make my ev'ry deed thine own,
    In all things led by thee:
  Bid my ev'ry luft depart,
    And with me O vouchfafe to dwell;
  Faithful witnefs, in my heart
    Thy perfect light reveal.

4 Let

4 Let me in thy love rejoice,
  Thy fhrine, thy pure abode;
Tell me, by thine inward voice,
  That I'm a child of God:
Lord, I chufe the better part,
  Jefus, I wait thy peace to feel;
Send the witnefs, in my heart
  The Holy Ghoft reveal.

5 Whom the world cannot receive,
  O manifeft in me:
Son of God, I ceafe to live,
  Unlefs I live in thee.
Now impute thy whole defert,
  Reftore the joy from which I fell:
Breathe the witnefs, in my heart
  The Holy Ghoft reveal.

POEM IX. *On War.*

1 GREAT God, whom heav'n and earth and fea,
With all their countlefs hofts, obey,
Upheld by whom the nations ftand,
And empires fall at thy command:

2 Beneath thy long fufpended ire
Let papal Antichrift expire;
Thy knowledge fpread from fea to fea,
'Till ev'ry nation bows to thee.

3 Then fhew thyfelf the prince of peace,
Make ev'ry hoftile efforts ceafe;
All with thy facred love infpire,
And burn their chariots in the fire.

4 In funder break each warlike fpear;
Let all the Saviour's liv'ry wear;
The univerfal Sabbath prove,
The utmoft reft of Chriftian love!

5 The world fhall then no difcord know,
But hand in hand to Canaan go,
Jefus, the peaceful king ado
And learn the art of war no more.

POEM X.

POEM X. *Defiring to be given up to God.*

1 O THAT my heart was right with thee,
   And lov'd thee with a perfect love!
O that my Lord would dwell in me,
   And never from his feat remove!
·Jefus remove th' impending load,
And fet my foul on fire for God!

2 Thou feeft I dwell in awful night
   Until thou in my heart appear;
Kindle the flame, O Lord, and light
   Thine everlafting candle there:
Thy prefence puts the fhadows by;
If thou art gone, how dark am I!

3 Ah! Lord, how fhould thy fervant fee,
   Unlefs thou give me feeing eyes?
Well may I fall, if out of thee;
   If out of thee, how fhould I rife?
I wander, Lord, without thy aid,
And lofe my way in midnight's fhade.

4 Thy bright, unerring light afford,
   A light that gives the finner hope;
And from the houfe of bondage, Lord,
   O bring the weary captive up;
Thine hand alone can fet me free,
And reach my pardon out to me.

5 O let my prayer acceptance find,
   And bring the mighty blefling down;
With eye-falve, Lord, anoint the blind,
   And feal me thine adopted fon:
A fallen, helplefs creature take,
And heir of thy falvation make.

POEM XI. *Mat.* viii. 25. *Lord, fave us, we perifh.*

1 PILOT of the foul, awake,
   Save us for thy mercies fake;
Now rebuke the angry deep,
Save, O fave thy finking fhip!

2 Stand at the helm, our veffel fteer,
  Mighty on our fide appear;
Saviour, teach us to defcry
  Where the rocks and quickfands lie.

3 The waves fhall impotently roll,
  If thou'rt the anchor of the foul:
At thy word the winds fhall ceafe,
  Storms be hufh'd to perfect peace.

4 Be thou our haven of retreat,
  A rock to fix our wav'ring feet;
Teach us to own thy fov'reign fway,
  Whom the winds and feas obey.

POEM XII. *O that my Ways were made fo direct, &c.*

1 O THAT my ways were made fo ftrait,
    And that the lamp of faith
  Would, as a ftar, direct my feet
    Within the narrow path!

2 O that thy ftrength might enter now,
    And in my heart abide,
  To make me as a faithful bow
    That never ftarts afide!

3 O that I all to Chrift were giv'n,
    (From fin and earth fet free)
  Who kindly laid afide his heav'n,
    And gave himfelf for me!

4 Not more the panting hart defires
    The cool refrefhing ftream,
  Than my dry, thirfty foul afpires
    At being one with him.

5 Set up thine image in my heart;
    Thy temple let me be,
  Bid every idol now depart
    That fain would rival thee.

6 Still keep me in the heav'nly path;
    Beftow the inward light;
  And lead me by the hand till faith
    Is ripen'd into fight.

POEM XIII.

POEM XIII.

1 FATHER, to thee in Chrift I fly,
What tho' my fins of crimfon dye
 For thy refentment call?
My crimes he did on Calv'ry bear,
The blood that flow'd for finners there
 Shall cleanfe me from them all.

2 Spirit divine, thy pow'r bring in,
O raife me from this depth of fin,
 Take off my guilty load:
Now let me live through Jefus's death,
And being juftified by faith,
 May I have peace with God!

3 Foul as I am, deferving hell,
Thou can'ft not from thy throne repel
 A foul that leans on God:
My fins, at thy command, fhall be
Caft as a ftone into the fea——
 The fea of Jefu's blood.

POEM XIV.

1 SUPREME high prieft, the pilgrim's light,
 My heart for thee prepare,
Thine image ftamp, and deeply write
 Thy fuperfcription there.

2 Ah! let my forehead bear thy feal,
 My arm thy badge retain,
My heart the inward witnefs feel
 That I am born again!

3 Thy peace, O Saviour, fhed abroad,
 That ev'ry want fupplies:
Then from its guilt my foul, renew'd,
 Shall, phœnix like, arife.

4 Into thy humble manfion come,
 Set up thy dwelling here:
Poffefs my heart, and leave no room
 For fin to harbour there.

5 Ah! give me, Lord, the fingle eye,
  Which aims at nought but thee :
I fain would live, and yet not I——
  Let Jefus live in me.

6 Like Noah's dove, no reft I find
  But in thy ark of peace :
Thy crofs the balance of my mind,
  Thy wounds my hiding-place.

7 In vain the tempter fpreads the fnare,
  If thou my keeper art :
Get thee behind me, God is near,
  My Saviour takes my part !

8 On him my fpirit I recline,
  Who put my nature on ;
His light fhall in my darknefs fhine,
  And guide me to his throne.

9 O that the penetrating fight,
  And eagle's eye were mine !
Undazzled at the boundlefs light,
  I'd fee his glory fhine !

10 Ev'n now, by faith, I fee him live
  To crown the conqu'ring few ;
Nor let me linger here, but ftrive
  To gain the prize in view.

11 Add, Saviour, to the eagle's eye,
  The dove's afpiring wing,
To bear me upwards to the fky,
  Thy praifes there to fing !

POEM XV. *Self Dedication.*

1 JESUS, my Saviour, fill my heart
  With nothing elfe but thee ;
Now thy faving pow'r exert,
  And more than conquer me :
Each intruding rival kill,
  That hinders or obftructs thy reign ;
All thy glorious might reveal,
  And make me pure within.

2 Through

2 Through my foul in mercy fhine,
   Thine holy fpirit give ;
Let him witnefs, Lord, with mine,
   That I in Jefus live ;
Set me free from Satan's load,
   The gift of liberty difpenfe,
In my heart O fhed abroad
   Thy quick'ning influence.

3 Let the gifts beftow'd on me,
   Live to thy praife alone ;
Lord, the talents lent by thee
   Are thine, and not my own :
May I in thy fervice fpend
   All the graces thou haft given,
Taken up, when time fhall end,
   To live and reign in heav'n.

POEM XVI. *In Temptation.*

1 COMPASS'D by the foe, on thee
   Feebly I prefume to call ;
Get thyfelf the victory,
   Hold me and I fhall not fall :
On thy creature mercy fhew,
  Thine I am by purchafe too.

2 Guard of my defencelefs heart,
   Wherefore hideft thou thy face ?
Mercy's fountain head thou art,
   Ever full of truth and grace :
Quell the roaring lion's pow'r,
Father, fave me from this hour.

3 Sun of righteoufnefs arife,
   Shed thy blifsful rays on me ;
Kindly liften to my cries,
   Try'd by him who tempted thee :
Thou my helplefs foul defend,
Keep me blamelefs to the end.

4 Rife in vengeance from thy feat,
   Jefus, Lord, make hafte to fave ;
Me, to fift my foul as wheat,
   Satan hath defired to have : '

Let him not too far prevail,
Suffer not my faith to fail.
5 Try'd, afflicted, and diftreft
   By temptation's fearching flame,
Tho', beneath its load oppreft,
   Now in heavinefs I am;
I fhall foon at freedom be,
More than conqueror in thee.
6 This affliction fha'l work out,
   (Light and tranfient as it is)
When I am to Sion brought,
   Everlafting joy and peace:
Here but for a moment try'd,
There for ever glorified.

POEM XVII.

1 O MAY I never reft
   'Till I find reft in thee;
'Till of my pardon here poffeft,
   I feel thy love to me!
Unfeal my dark'ned eyes,
   My fetter'd feet unbind;
The lame fhall, when thou fay'ft " arife,"
   Run fwifter than the hind.
2 O draw the alien near,
   Bend the obdurate neck,
O melt the flint into a tear,
   And teach the dumb to fpeak:
Turn not thy face away,
   Thy look can make me clean;
Me in thy wedding robe array,
   And cover all my fin.
3 Tell me, my God, for whom
   Thy precious blood was fhed;
For finners? Lord as fuch I come,
   For fuch the Saviour bled:
Then raife a fallen wretch,
   Difplay thy grace in me;
I am not out of mercy's reach,
   Nor too far gone for thee.

4 Thou quickly wilt forgive,
　　My Lord will not delay ;
　Jefus, to thee the time I leave,
　　And wait th' accepted day :
　I now rejoice in hope
　　That I fhall be made clean :
　Thy grace fhall furely lift me up
　　Above the reach of fin.

5 Haft thou not dy'd for me,
　　And call'd me from below ?
　O help me to lay hold on thee,
　　And ne'er to let thee go !
　Though on the billows toft
　　My Saviour I'll purfue :
　A while fubmit to bear his crofs,
　　Then fhare his glory too.

POEM XVIII.

1 FROM Juftice's confuming flame,
　　Saviour, I fly to thee :
　O look not on me as I am,
　　But as I fain would be.

2 Deferted in the way I lie,
　　No cure for me is found ;
　Thou good Samaritan, pafs by,
　　And bind up ev'ry wound.

3 O may I, in the final day,
　　At thy right-hand appear !
　Take thou my fins out of the way,
　　Who did'ft the burthen bear.

4 What though the fiery ferpent's bite
　　Hath poifon'd ev'ry vein——
　I'll not defpair, but keep in fight
　　The wounds of Jefus flain.

5 My foul thou wilt from death retrieve,
　　For forrow grant me joy ;
　Thy pow'r is mightier to fave
　　Than Satan's to deftroy.

POEM XIX.

POEM XIX. *After being surprised into Sin.*

1 AH! Give me Lord myself to see,
    Against myself to watch and pray,
  How weak am I, when left by thee,
    How frail, how apt to fall away;
  If but a moment thou withdraw,
  That moment sees me break thy law.

2 Jesus, the sinner's only trust,
    Let me now feel thy grace infus'd;
  Ah! raise a captive from the dust,
    Nor break a reed already bruis'd!
  Visit me, Lord, in peace again,
  Nor let me seek thy face in vain.

3 O gracious Lord, now let me find
    Peace and salvation in thy name;
  Be thou the eye-sight of the blind,
    The staff and ancles of the lame;
  My lifter up whene'er I fall,
  My strength, my portion, and my all.

4 Let thy meek mind descend on me,
    Thy holy spirit from above:
  Assist me, Lord, to follow thee,
    Drawn by th' endearing cords of love;
  Made perfect by thy cleansing blood,
  Completely sav'd and born of God.

POEM XX. *Christ the Light of his People.*

1 I LIFT my heart and eyes to thee,
    Jesus, thou unextinguish'd light:
  My lanthorn, guide, and leader be,
    My cloud by day, my fire by night.

2 Glory of Israel, shine within,
    Unshadow'd, uneclips'd appear;
  O let thy beams dispel my sin,
    Direct me by a friendly star.

3 The world a maze and lab'rinth is,
    Be thou my thread and faithful clue;
  Thy kingdom and thy righteousness
    The only objects I pursue.

4 Light

4 Light of the gentiles thee I hail !
    Essential light, thyself impart !
  Spirit of light his face reveal ;
    And set thy signet on my heart.
5 Thy office is to enlighten man,
    And point him to the heav'nly prize ;
  The hidden things of God t' explain,
    And chase th' darknefs from our eyes.
6 Shew me I have the better part,
    The treafure hid with Chrift in God ;
  Give me a perfect peace of heart,
    And pardon through my Saviour's blood.

POEM XXI.

1 CHAIN'D to the world, to fin ty'd down;
    In darknefs ftill I lie ;
  Lord, break my bonds, Lord, give me wings,
    And teach me how to fly.
2 Inftruct my feeble hands to war,
    In me thy ftrength reveal,
  To put my ev'ry luft to death,
    And fight thy battles well.
3 Rend ev'ry veil that fhades thy face,
    Put on thine helmet, Lord ;
  My fin fhall fall, my guilt expire,
    Beneath thy conqu'ring fword.
4 Thou art the mighty God of hofts,
    Whofe counfels never fail ;
  Be thou my glorious chief, and then
    I cannot but prevail.

POEM XXII.

1 O WHEN will thou my Saviour be,
    O when fhall I be clean,
  The true, eternal fabbath fee,
    A perfect reft from fin !
  Jefus, the finners reft thou art,
    From guilt, and fear, and pain ;
  While thou art abfent from my heart
    I look for reft in vain.

2 The confolations of thy word,
   My foul hath long upheld,
The faithful promife of the Lord,
   Shall furely be fulfill'd :
I look to my incarnate God,
   'Till he his work begin ;
And wait 'till his redeeming blood
   Shall cleanfe me from all fin.

3 His great falvation I fhall know,
   And perfect liberty :
Onward to fin he cannot go,
   Whoe'er abides in thee ;
Added to the Redeemer's fold,
   I fhall in him rejoice :
I all his glory fhall behold,
   And hear my fhepherd's voice.

4 O that I now the voice might hear,
   That fpeaks my fins forgiv'n ;
His word is paft to give me here
   The inward pledge of heav'n :
His blood fhall over all prevail,
   And fanctify the unclean ;
The grace that faves from future hell,
   Shall fave from prefent fin.

POEM XXIII.

1 JESUS thy light impart
   And lead me in thy path ;
I have an unbelieving heart,
   But thou can'ft give me faith.

2 The work in me fulfil,
   Which mercy hath begun ;
I have a proud rebellious will,
   But thou can'ft melt it down.

3 Sin on my heart is wrote,
   I am throughout impure ;
But my difeafe, O Lord, is not
   Too hard for thee to cure.

Y 3

4 The

4 The darkneſs of my mind,
  Lies open to thy ſight;
Jeſus, I am, by nature, blind,
  But thou can'ſt give me light.

5 Send down thy Holy Ghoſt,
  To cleanſe and fill with peace;
For O, mine inward parts thou know'ſt
  Are very wickedneſs.

6 Thy love all power hath,
  Its power in me exert;
And give me living active faith,
  That purifies the heart.

7 Unrival'd reign within,
  My only ſovereign be,
O crucify the man of ſin,
  And form thyſelf in me.

8 Thy blood's renewing might,
  Can make the fouleſt clean;
Can waſh the Ethiopian white,
  And change the leopard's ſkin.

9 That, Lord, can bring me nigh,
  And wipe my ſins away;
Can lift my abject ſoul on high,
  And call me into day.

10 Fulfil thy gracious word,
  And ſhew my guilt forgiv'n;
Bid me embrace my dying Lord,
  And mount with him to heav'n.

POEM XXIV. *The Chriſtian's Wiſh.*

1 EMPTY'D of earth I fain would be,
The world, myſelf, and all but thee;
Only reſerv'd for Chriſt that dy'd,
Surrender'd to the crucify'd.

2 Sequeſter'd from the noiſe and ſtrife,
The luſt, the pomp, and pride of life;
For heav'n alone my heart prepare,
And have my converſation there.

3 O may

3 O may I the Redeemer trace,
  Invefted with his righteoufnefs !
  This path, untir'd, I will purfue,
  Nor flack while Jefus is in view.

4 Nothing fave Jefus may I know,
  My Father and companion thou !
  Lord, take my heart, affert my right,
  And put all other loves to flight.

5 My idols tread beneath thy feet,
  And enter'd, once, maintain thy feat ;
  Let Dagon fall before thy face,
  The ark remaining in its place.

6 O lend me now a two-edg'd fword,
  To flay my fins before the Lord ;
  With Abraham's knife, before thine eyes,
  Each favourite Ifaac facrifice.

POEM XXV. [*Before Meat*] 1 *Cor.* x. 31.

1 LORD, we invite thee here,
    Vouchfafe to be our gueft ;
Jefus, do thou appear
    The mafter of the feaft :
Thy quick'ning prefence let us prove,
And banquet on thy hidden love.

2 With manna from on high
    Feed thine inheritance,
And come and fanctify
    Our outward fuftenance :
With it the inward food be giv'n,
The bread of life, the wine of heav'n.

POEM XXVI. *For the Morning.*

1 MY foul, can'ft thou no higher rife,
    To meet thy God, than this ?
Yet, Lord, accept my facrifice,
    Defective as it is.

2 Tune all my organs to thy praife,
    And pfalmift's mufe impart ;
And, with thy penetrating rays,
    O melt my frozen heart.

3 Give me thyfelf the only good,
 And ever with me ftay;
Whofe faithful mercies are renew'd,
 With each returning day.

4 Ah! guide me with a Father's eye,
 Nor from my foul depart;
But let the day-ftar from on high
 Illuminate my heart

5 This day preferve me without fin,
 Unfpotted in thy ways;
And hear me, while I ufher in
 The welcome dawn with praife.

6 Far as the Eaft from Weft remove
 Each earthly, vain defire,
And raife me on the wings of love,
 'Till I can mount no higher.

POEM XXVII. _For the Evening._

1 THOU unexhaufted mine of blifs,
 From whence all comfort flows;
Infpire me with that perfect peace,
 Which only Chriftians knows.

2 The curtains of thy love extend
 Around my calm abode,
As I began, fo may I end
 My ev'ry day with God.

3 My life unhurt thine hand hath kept,
 Accept the praife I pay;
For all the dangers I've efcap'd,
 And mercies of the day.

4 Far, far away the tempter chace,
 My foul from terror keep;
Let angels fill this hallow'd place,
 And guard me as I fleep.

5 O wafh out ev'ry fin whereby,
 This day, I have tranfgrefs'd;
And feal my pardon ere I give
 My flumb'ring eye-lids reft.

6 Prepare

6 Prepare me for the bed of death,
   Be that my hourly thought,
  That when I yield my lateſt breath,
   I may be found with God.

POEM XXVIII. *He is the Propitiation of our Sins.*

1 O THOU that hear'ſt the prayer of faith,
  Wilt thou not fave a foul from death
   That caſts itſelf on thee ?
  I have no refuge of my own,
  But fly to what my Lord hath done
   And ſuffer'd once for me.

2 Slain in the guilty ſinner's ſtead,
  His ſpotleſs righteouſneſs I plead,
   And his availing blood :
  Thy merit, Lord, my robe ſhall be,
  Thy merit ſhall atone for me,
   And bring me near to God.

3 Then ſnatch me from eternal death,
  The ſpirit of adoption breathe,
   His conſolations fend ;
  By him ſome word of life impart,
  And ſweetly whiſper to my heart,
   " Thy Maker is thy friend."

4 The King of terrors then would be,
  A welcome meſſenger to me,
   That bids me come away ;
  Unclog'd by earth or earthly things,
  I'd mount upon his ſable wings
   To everlaſting day.

POEM XXIX. *Hab.* ii. 14. *For the Earth ſhall be filled, &c.*

1 BRING the kingdom, Lord, make haſte,
  Bring on the glorious day,
  From the greateſt to the leaſt,
   When all ſhall own thy ſway :

When

When the convert world, with grief,
    Shall fee the error of their ways,
Lay afide their unbelief,
    And yield unto thy grace.

2 In thy gofpel-chariot, Lord,
    Drive through earth's utmoft bound ;
Spread the odour of thy word
    Through all the nations round :
Fill the darken'd earth with light,
    Thine own victorious caufe advance;
Take the heathen as the right
    Of thine inheritance.

3 In our day expofe to view,
    The ftandard of the Lamb ;
Bid the nations flock thereto,
    Who never knew thy name :
Let them quit the downward road,
    Compell'd thy gofpel to receive ;
Turn'd from Satan unto God,
    With one confent believe.

POEM XXX.

1 REDEEMER, whither fhould I flee,
    Or how efcape the wrath to come ?
The weary finner flies to thee
    For fhelter from impending doom :
Smile on me, gracious Lord, and fhew
Thyfelf the friend of finners now.

2 Beneath the fhadow of thy crofs,
    The heavy-laden foul finds reft :
. Let me efteem the world as drofs,
    So I may be of Chrift poffefs'd !
I borrow ev'ry joy from thee,
For thou art life and light to me.

3 Clofe to my Saviour's bloody tree,
    My foul, untir'd, fhall ever cleave ;
Both fcourg'd and crucified with thee,
    With Chrift refolved to die and live.
My pray'r, my grand ambition this,
Living and dying to be his.

4 O nail me to the facred wood,
　There hold me by the fpirit's chain,
There feal me with thy faft'ning blood,
　Nor ever let me loofe again :
There may I bow my fuppliant knee,
And own no other Lord but thee !

POEM XXXI.

1 LORD, ftand not off, come nearer ftill,
　Illuminate my darken'd foul,
Renew my heart, correct my will,
　Make the polluted leper whole.
2 Behold my ftruggles, Lord, and fet
　My fin-bound foul at liberty :
Give me thine hand to break the net,
　And bid the fetter'd flave be free.
3 My own defert I cannot plead,
　My pureft filver is but drofs :
Let Jefus' merits intercede,
　O nail my errors to the crofs.
4 Fain would I mount to thee my crown,
　And gain the realms of endlefs light ;
But fett'ring earth ftill keeps me down,
　And fin impediates my flight.
5 Father to me impart thy bread,
　To me thine healing manna give ;
On life eternal let me feed,
　That my difeafed foul may live.
6 Unworthy to intreat thy grace,
　Unworthier ftill thy grace t' obtain,
I plead my furety's righteoufnefs,
　Nor fhall my plea be urg'd in vain.

POEM XXXII. *Where two or three are gathered*
together in my Name, &c.

1 JESUS, God of love attend,
From thy glorious throne defcend ;
Anfwer now fome waiting heart,
Now fome harden'd foul convert :

To

To our advocate we fly,
Let us feel Emanuel nigh ;
Manifeſt thy love abroad,
Make us now the ſons of God.

2 Hover round us, King of kings,
Riſe with healing in thy wings ;
Melt our obſtinacy down,
Cauſe us to become thine own :
Set, O ſet the captives free,
Draw our backward ſouls to thee ;
Let us all from thee receive
Light to ſee and life to live.

3 Proſtrate at thy mercy ſeat
Let us our beloved meet ;
Give us in thyſelf a part,
Deep engraven on thine heart :
Let us hear thy pard'ning voice,
Bid the broken bones rejoice ;
Condemnation do away,
O make this the happy day !

4 Father, Son, and Holy Ghoſt,
Join to ſeek and ſave the loſt :
Raiſe ſome ſinner to thy throne,
Add a jewel to thy crown !
Are we not, without thy light,
Darken'd with Egyptian night ?
Light of light, thy pow'r exert,
Lighten each benighted heart !

5 Prayer can mercy's door unlock ;
Open, Lord, to us that knock !
Us the heirs of glory ſeal,
With thy benediction fill :
Holy Spirit, make us his,
Viſit ev'ry ſoul in peace ;
Give our vanquiſh'd hearts to ſay,
Love divine has won the day !

6 Give the heavy-laden reſt,
Chriſt make known in ev'ry breaſt ;
Void of thee we quickly die,
Turn our ſackcloth into joy :

Witneſs

Witnefs all our fins forgiv'n,
Grant on earth a glimpfe of heav'n ;
Bring the joyful tidings down,
Fit us for our future crown.

7 Let us chaunt melodious hymns,
Loud as thofe of cherubims ;
Join with heart and tongue to blefs
Chrift our ftrength and righteoufnefs :
All our praife to him belongs,
Theme of our fublimeft fongs;
Object of our choiceft love,
Thee we laud with hofts above.

8 Thee we hail with joint acclaim,
Shout the glories of thy name ;
Ever may we feel thee thus,
Dear Immanuel, God with us !
Prince of peace, thy people fee,
All our thanks we aim at thee ;
Deign our tribute to receive,
Praife is all we have to give.

POEM XXXIII.

1 COME from on high, my King and God,
My confidence thou art ;
Difplay the virtue of thy blood,
And circumcife my heart.

2 From heav'n, thy holy place, on me
Defcend in mercy down;
Water of life, I thirft for thee,
To know thee for my own.

3 Rend, O rend the guilty veil,
That keeps me from my God ;
Remove the bar, and let me feel
That I am thine abode.

4 O might this worthlefs heart of mine
The Saviour's temple be !
Empty'd of ev'ry love but thine,
And fhut to all but thee !

POEM XXXIV.

POEM XXXIV. *I know that in my Flesh dwelleth no good Thing.*

1 LORD, is not all from thee ?
  Is not all 'fulnefs thine ?
  Whate'er of good there is in me,
  O Lord, is none of mine.
2 Each holy tendency
  Did not thy mercy give?
  And what, O Saviour, what have I
  That I did not receive ?
3 I cannot fpeak a word,
  Or think a thought that's good,
  But what proceedeth from the Lord ;
  And cometh forth from God.
4 Jefus, I know full well,
  What my beft actions are ;
  They'd fink my grievous foul to hell,
  If unrefin'd they were.
5 Myfelf and all I do,
  O fprinkle with thy blood ;
  Renew me, Saviour, ere I go,
  To ftand before my God.
6 I of myfelf have nought,
  That can his juftice pleafe ;
  Not one right word, nor act, nor thought,
  But what I owe to grace.

POEM XXXV. *Refuge in the Righteoufnefs of Chrift.*

1 FROM thy fupreme tribunal, Lord,
  Where juftice fits fevere,
  I to thy mercy feat appeal,
  And beg forgivenefs there.
2 Tho' I have finn'd before the throne,
  My advocate I fee :
  Jefus, be thou my Judge, and let
  My fentence come from thee.
3 Lo, weary to thy crofs I fly,
  There let me fhelter find :

Lord,

Lord, when thou call'ft thy ranfom'd home,
  O leave me not behind!
4 I joyfully embrace thy love
  To fallen man reveal'd;
My hope of glory, deareft Lord,
  On thee alone I build.

5 The law was fatisfy'd by him
  Who flefh for me was made:
Its penalty he underwent,
  Its precepts he obey'd.

6 Defert and all felf-righteoufnefs
  I utterly forego;
My robe of everlafting blifs,
  My wedding garment thou!

7 The fpotlefs Saviour liv'd for me,
  And dy'd upon the Mount:
Th' obedience of his life and death
  Is plac'd to my account.

8 Can'ft thou forget that awful hour,
  That fad, tremendous fcene,
When thy dear blood on Calvary
  Flow'd out at ev'ry vein?

9 No, Saviour, no; thy wounds are frefh,
  Ev'n now they intercede;
Still, in effect, for guilty man
  Inceffantly they bleed.

10 Thine ears of mercy ftill attend
  A contrite finner's cries,
A broken heart, that groans for God,
  Thou never wilt defpife.

11 O love incomprehenfible,
  That made thee bleed for me!
The Judge of all hath fuffer'd death
  To fet his prifoner free!

POEM XXXVI. *For Pardon of Sin.*

1 JESUS, thy feet I will not leave,
  Till I the precious gift receive,
    The purchas'd pearl poffefs:

Impart

Impart it, gracious Lord, while I
  With fupplications humbleft cry,
    Inveft the throne of grace.
2 Baptize me with the Holy Ghoft;
  Make this the day of Pentecoft,
    Wherein my foul may prove,
  Thy fpirit's fweet renewing pow'r,
  And fhew me, in this happy hour,
    The riches of thy love.
3 Thou canft not always hide thy face,
  Thou wilt at laft my foul embrace,
    Thou yet will make me clean :
  My God, is there not room for me?
  I'll wait with patience, Lord, on thee,
    'Till thou fhalt take me in.
4 Remember, Lord, that Jefus bled,
  That Jefus bow'd his dying head,
    And fweated bloody fweat :
  He bore thy wrath and curfe for me
  In his own body on the tree,
    And more than paid my debt.
5 Surely he hath my pardon bought,
  A perfect righteoufnefs wrought out
    His people to redeem :
  O that his righteoufnefs might be
  By grace imputed now to me :
    As were my fins to him.

POEM XXXVII.

1 THOU Sun of righteoufnefs arife,
    Shine glorious morning ftar,
  Enlighten my benighted foul,
    And make the Ethiop fair.
  Confus'd and blind tho' now I am,
    And prone to go aftray,
  Bid me receive my fight, and I
    Shall clearly fee my way.
2 The captive, at thy word, fhall be
    From ev'ry chain releas'd ;

The broken heart, fhall fing for joy,
　　The troubled fea fhall reft:
Enflame me with a ray of heav'n,
　　Pure, fervent love infpire;
And let thy dove-like fpirit aid
　　And fan the holy fire.

3 Be thou my light, for light thou art,
　　O crucify each doubt;
Sweep ev'ry corner of my heart,
　　And turn the tempter out:
Let not my hopes be over-caft
　　With fhadows of defpair;
Dart through my foul thy quick'ning beams,
　　And build an altar there.

4 Redeem me from temptation's rage,
　　Break down the holds of fin;
Give me to ftand in crooked ways,
　　And keep my garments clean:
Tranfplant me, Saviour, from my felf,
　　And graft me into thee;
Then fhall the grain of muftard-feed
　　Spring up into a tree.

POEM XXXVIII. *Phil.* ii. 5. *Let this Mind be in*
　　you which was alfo in Chrift Jefus.

1 LORD I feel a carnal mind
　　That hangs about me ftill,
Vainly tho' I ftrive to bind
　　My own rebellious will;
Is not haughtinefs of heart
　　The gulf between my God and me?
Meek Redeemer now impart
　　Thine own humility.

2 Fain would I my Lord purfue,
　　Be all my Saviour taught,
Do as Jefus bid me do,
　　And think as Jefus thought:
But 'tis thou muft change my heart,
　　The perfect gift muft come from thee:

Meek Redeemer now impart
Thine own humility.

3 Lord, I cannot, muſt not reſt,
'Till I thy mind obtain,
Chaſe preſumption from my breaſt,
And all thy mildneſs gain ;
Give me, Lord, thy gentle heart,
Thy lowly mind my portion be :
Meek Redeemer now impart
Thine own humility.

4 Let thy croſs my will controul ;
Conform me to my guide ;
In thine image mould my ſoul,
And crucify my pride ;
Give me, Lord, a contrite heart,
An heart that always looks to thee :
Meek Redeemer, now impart
Thine own humility.

5 Tear away my ev'ry boaſt,
My ſtubborn mind abaſe ;
Saviour, fix my only truſt
In thy redeeming grace :
Give me a ſubmiſſive heart,
From pride and ſelf dependance free ;
Meek Redeemer, now impart
Thine own humility.

POEM XXXIX. *For all the Mind of Chriſt.*

1 HAIL, faultleſs model, ſinleſs guide,
In whom no blame was ſeen !
Able thou were, and none beſide,
To ranſom guilty men.

2 I want my happineſs below
In thee alone to find ;
Surely thou wilt on me beſtow
Thy pure, thy heav'n'y mind !

3 Active for God I fain would be,
And do my work aſſign'd :
Jeſus, look down, implant in me,
Thy zealous, fervent mind !

4 While

4 While here, it was thy conftant aim
To benefit mankind :
O give me, dear redeeming Lamb,
Thy loving, gracious mind !

5 Stiff is my neck, and proud my heart,
Unbroken, unrefign'd :
When wilt thou, bleffed Lord, impart
Thy patient, humble mind !

6 My fins how flowly do I leave,
To earthly things inclin'd !
But wean me, Lord, and let me have
Thy felf denying mind !

7 O might I walk with faithful heed,
And look no more behind,
Poffefs'd of what I chiefly need,
Thy ferious fteady mind !

8 Still may my ev'ry grace increafe,
'Till' I in heaven appear :
On earth like thee in holinefs,
Like thee in glory there.

POEM XL. *For Pardon.*

1 NOW, Lord, the purchas'd pardon give,
Nor e'er the grant revoke,
But bend my ftiff obdurate neck
Beneath thine eafy yoke.

2 O might I, as a faithful fheep,
My fhepherd ne'er forfake !
O might I now for heav'n fet out,
And never more turn back !

3 Chrift, in his refurrection's pow'r,
Within my heart reveal :
Forgive my deep revoltings, Lord,
And my forgivenefs feal.

4 Thou only haft the words of life,
My fpirit upward draw,
Me to thy kingdom, Lord, inftruct,
And teach me in thy law.

3 Apollo's.

5 Apollo's water's but in vain,
　　Paul plants without fuccefs ;
　The prophets labours fruitlefs are
　　Except thou give increafe.

POEM XLI. *The Same.*

1 SHOULD'ST thou be ftrict to mark our faults,
　　Who could acquitted be ?
　Who, unrenewed, could ftand the fearch,
　　Or bear the fcrutiny ?

2 Lord, at thy feet I meekly fall,
　　Held in contrition's chain :
　Thy gracious hand that caft me down,
　　Shall raife me up again.

3 O fpeak the word, thy fervant hears,
　　Pronounce me pardon'd now :
　Lord, I believe, encreafe my faith,
　　And let me know thee too.

4 Thou only, Saviour, haft the key,
　　Unlock the prifon door !
　Tho' yet I cannot fly to thee,
　　I'll fend my heart before.

5 The blood of fprinkling now apply,
　　And that fhall make me clean ;
　Weigh not my worthlefs works, O Lord,
　　But O forgive my fin !

6 Take now away whate'er obftructs
　　Thine intercourfe with me :
　And may I cheerfully leave all
　　I have, to follow thee !

POEM XLII.

1 JESUS, thy pow'r I fain wou'd feel,
　　Thy love is all I want :
　O let thine ears confider well
　　The voice of my complaint.

2 Thou feeft me yet a flave to fin,
　　And deftitute of God ;
　O purify and make me clean
　　By thine all-cleanfing blood.

3 Far

3 Far off I ftand, O bring me nigh,
   And bid me fit up high'r :
Immanuel, now in love pafs by,
   And anfwer my defire.

4 O Jefus, undertake for me,
   Thy peace to me be given :
For while I ftand away from thee,
   I ftand away from heav'n.

5 I will not my offence conceal,
   I will not hide my fin,
But all my crimes with weeping tell,
   And own how vile I've been.

6 Lord, will thy wrathful jealoufy
   As fire for ever burn ?
And wilt thou not a fuccour be,
   And comfort thofe that mourn ?

7 Reject not Lord my humble pray'rs,
   Nor yet my foul deftroy :
Thine only Son hath fown in tears
   That I might reap in joy.

EUCHARISTIC

EUCHARISTIC HYMNS.

" Immenfa Beneficia Laudibus immenfis celebranda."

PRIMAS.

————————————O thou Patron God,
Thou God and Mortal, thence more God to Man,
Man's Theme eternal, Man's eternal Theme!
Thou canſt not 'ſcape injur'd from our Praiſe.

NIGHT THOUGHTS. NIGHT IX.

HYMNS OF THANKSGIVING.

HYMN I. *Praiſe for Converſion.*

1 NOT to myſelf I owe
    That I, O Lord, am thine,
Free grace hath all the ſhades broke thro',
    And caus'd the light to ſhine.
Me thou haſt willing made
    Thy offers to receive ;
Call'd by the voice that wakes the dead,
    I come to thee and live.

2 Why am I made to ſee,
    Who am by nature blind ?
Why am I taken home to thee,
    And others left behind ?
Becauſe thy ſov'reign love
    Was bent the worſt to ſave,
Jeſus, who reigns inthron'd above,
    The free ſalvation gave.

3 Tho' once far off I ſtood,
    Nor knew myſelf thy foe,
Brought nigh by the Redeemer's blood,
    Myſelf and thee I know :

No

No more a child of wrath
   Thy smiling face I see;
And praise thee for the work of faith
   Which thou haft wrought in me.

4 With me thy spirit strove,
   Almighty to retrieve;
Thou faw'ft me in a time of love,
   And faid unto me, live.
By thee made free indeed,
   I felt thy gracious words;
Thy mantle over me was spread,
   And I became the Lord's:

5 Jefus, thy Son, by grace,
   I to the end shall be;
Made perfect through thy comelinefs
   Which I receiv'd from thee.
I drink the living ftream
   To all believers giv'n,
A fellow citizen with them,
   Who dwell in yonder heav'n.

6 With all thy chofen band
   I truft to fee thee there,
And, in thy righteoufnefs, to ftand
   Undaunted at thy bar.

HYMN II. *The Heavens declare the Glory of God.*

1 THE fky's a veil, the outward fcene
Proclaims the majefty within;
Which boundlefs light, tho' hid behind,
Breaks out too great to be confin'd.

2 The heav'n thy glorious imprefs wears,
Thy image glitters in the ftars:
The firmament, thine high abode,
Seems too the fpangled robe of God.

3 Whene'er its beauty I admire,
It's radiant globes direct me high'r,
In filent praife they point to thee,
All light, all eye, all majefty!

4 Glory to him who ftuds the fky,
(Earth's variegated canopy)

Z 4

With

With lamps to guide us on our way,
Faint emblems of eternal day.
5 Yes, Lord, each shining orb declares
Thy name in dazzling characters;
As precious gems they dart their rays,
And seem to form a crown of praise.

HYMN III. *On Ascension Day.*

1 LO! the Lord by whom salvation
　　Is to fallen man restor'd,
Now resumes his blissful station,
　　Shews himself th' Almighty Lord;
Slow ascending,
Bids us, for a while, farewel.
2 Who his heav'nly state suspended,
　　And for man's atonement dy'd,
By unnumber'd hosts attended,
　　Rises to his Father's side;
Born by angels
Back to his eternal throne.
3 Seraphs, chaunt his endless praises,
　　Guard him to his ancient seat;
Open wide, ye heav'nly places,
　　Your returning God admit:
Heav'nly portals
Let the King of Glory in!
4 Christ his kingdom re-inherits,
　　His before the world began;
Myriads of admiring spirits
　　Hover round the son of man;
Wrapt in wonder
View the wounds he bore for us.
5 "Worthy thou of exaltation,"
　　Lost in sweet surprise they sing;
"Mortals, with like acclamation,
　　Hail your great redeeming King:
Let your voices
Emulate th' angelic choir."

6 Yes,

6 Yes, O Chrift, from ev'ry creature,
　　Praife fhall to thy name be giv'n ;
　Worthy thou of more and greater,
　　King of faints and king of heav'n !
　Kindling tranfports
　Swell our hearts and tune our tongues!

7 Though our Lord is taken from us, -
　　Prefent but in fpirit now,
　This his faithful word of promife
　　Made while fojourning below ;
　" Where I enter
　Thither fhall my fervant come:"

8 Him we praife for his afcenfion,
　　Conqueror of fin and death ;
　Gone up to prepare a manfion
　　For his ranfom'd flock beneath :
　They fhall quickly
　Reign with him in glory there.

9 There already is our treafure,
　　There our heart, our hope, our crown ;
　Thence on fublunary pleafure,
　　We with holy fcorn, look down :
　Earth hath nothing,
　Worth a moment's tranfient thought.

10. We fhall foon in blifs adore thee,
　　Gain the realms of endlefs day ;
　Soon be gather'd home to glory,
　　All our tears be wip'd away :
　There, for ever,
　Sing the Lamb's new fong of love.

HYMN IV. *To the Trinity.*

1 GLORIOUS union, God unfought ;
　Three in name and one in thought,
　All thy works thy goodnefs fhow,
　Center of perfection thou !

2 Praife we, with uplifted eyes,
　Him that dwells above the fkies :
　God who reigns on Sion's hill,
　Made redeem'd, and keeps us ftill.

3 Join th' angelic hosts above
Praise the Father's matchless love,
Who for us his Son hath giv'n,
Sent him to regain our heav'n.

4 Glory to the Saviour's grace,
Help of Adam's helpless race;
Who, for our transgressions slain,
Makes us one with God again.

5 Next the Holy Ghost we bless;
He makes known and seals our peace,
Us he cleanses and makes whole,
Quickens ev'ry dying soul.

6 Holy, blessed, glorious Three,
One from all eternity,
Make us vessels of thy grace,
Ever running o'er with praise.

7 Thee we laud with grateful song,
Sever'd from the guilty throng,
Ransom'd by the Son who dy'd,
By the spirit sanctified.

8 All the persons join to raise,
Sinners to a state of grace;
All unite their bliss t' insure,
In the glorious work concur.

9 O that we his love might taste!
Bless us and we shall be blest.
Cleanse us, Lord, from sins abuse,
Fit us for the master's use!

10 In our hearts, thy temples dwell;
With the hope of glory fill:
Be on earth our guest divine,
Then let heav'n make us thine.

HYMN V. *Another.*

1 FATHER, Creator of mankind,
Thee we attempt to sing;
With thy Son and Spirit join'd,
Our everlasting king;

Us

Us thou doſt in Chriſt receive,
    Cloth'd with Chriſt we come to thee :
Him thou did'ſt for ſinners give
    Their ſubſtitute to be.

2 All our ſins, dear Lamb of God,
    Are for thy ſake forgiv'n,
Jeſus, thy reſtoring blood
    Entitles men to heav'n :
Self-exiſtent, Lord of all,
    Uncreate, with God the ſame,
Bought by thee on thee we call,
    Exulting in thy name.

3 Spirit of Jehovah write
    Thy nature on our heart,
Us unto the Lord unite,
    As thou united art ;
Make us meet his face to ſee,
    Jeſus' righteouſneſs apply :
Holy Ghoſt, our leader be,
    And guide us to the ſky.

4 Three in One, before thy feet
    Our inmoſt ſouls we bend,
Glorious myſtery, too great
    For worms to comprehend :
We can ne'er, on this ſide death,
    Bring the Deity to light ;
Reaſon here muſt yield to faith,
    'Till faith is loſt in ſight.

HYMN VI.

1 JESUS, thou try'd foundation ſtoŋe,
  From whoſe prevailing blood alone
    Thy ſaints expeƈt ſalvation,
My robe thou art, I feel thy grace,
And triumph in thy righteouſneſs,
    Made mine by imputation.

2 Exulting in thy ſtrength I go,
My allotted work rejoice to do,

For

For love divine conftrains me :
Supported inwardly by this,
Through ev'ry obftacle I prefs
    While thy great arm fuftains me.

3 By thy free grace 'till now upheld,
My future hopes on thee I build,
    Nor are my hopes ill-grounded :
Thy promifes are on my fide,
And fafe to glory, lo ! I ride,
    By countlefs deaths furrounded.

4 Before I from the body fly,
He who forgave fhall fanctify
    And perfectly renew me ;
Stronger than Satan Jefus is ;
Sin fhall not always wound my peace,
    Nor finally fubdue me.

5 Who wafh'd me from its deadly ftain,
Shall here cut fhort its guilty reign,
    And weaken its dominion ;
From height to height my faith fhall rife,
Until I gain my native fkies,
    On love's feraphic pinion.

6 Unmov'd, till then, on Chrift I ftand,
And Satan from the Saviour's hand,
    In vain attempts to ftir me :
On Jefus I for ftrength depend ;
My omnipotent redeeming friend,
    Prepare my way before me.

HYMN VII.

1 PRAISE the Lord, my joyful heart,
With the elders bear thy part :
Stand with them around the throne,
Singing praifes to the Son.

2 Strive with them in rapture loft,
Who fhall laud the Saviour moft :
Join with angels to proclaim
All the mercies of the Lamb.

3 Praife

3 Praiſe his great humility,
   Long as life remains in thee ;
   By thy pray'rs and praiſes given,
   Make on earth, a little heav'n.

4 Jeſus, I the theme renew,
   Endleſs praiſes are thy due :
   Anthems equal to thy grace,
   Saints and angels cannot raiſe.

5 I my worthleſs mite caſt in,
   Here the ſong of heav'n begin :
   I th' eternal chorus join,
   Ecchoing the love divine.

6 Ever may I worſhip thee,
   . Praiſe my ſole employment be ;
   Sing the virtues of thy blood !
   Every moment thank my God.

HYMN VIII.

1 MY ſoul with bleſſings unconfin'd,
    Thy tender care ſupplies ;
   Thyſelf the fountain head from whence
    Thoſe bleſſings firſt ariſe.

2 Let me thy gracious gifts receive,
    With gratitude and joy,
   And in thy juſt and ceaſeleſs praiſe,
    Each thankful hour employ !

HYMN IX.

Rom. viii. 16. *The Spirit itſelf bears Witneſs with our*
    Spirit, that we are the Children of Grace.

1 EARNEST of future bliſs,
    Thee, Holy Ghoſt, we hail ;
   Fountain of holineſs,
    Whoſe comforts never fail,
   The cleanſing gift on ſaints beſtow'd,
   The witneſs of their peace with God.

2 With our perverſeneſs here,
    How often haſt thou ſtrove,
   And ſpar'd us year by year,
    With never-ceaſing love !

O set from sin our spirits free,
And make us more and more like thee.
3 What wond'rous grace is this,
   For God to dwell with men !
Through Jesus' righteousness,
   His favour we regain.
And feeble worms, by nature lost,
Are temples of the Holy Ghost !
4 Tho' Belial's sons would prove
   That thou no witness art,
Thanks to redeeming love,
   We feel thee in our heart ;
Continue gracious Lord to bear,
Thine inward testimony there !
5 By thee on earth we know,
   Ourselves in Christ renew'd,
Brought by thy grace into
   The family of God :
Of his adopting love the seal,
And faithful teacher of his will.
6 Great Comforter, descend,
   In gentle breathings, down,
Preserve us to the end,
   That no man take our crown :
Our guardian still vouchsafe to be,
Nor suffer us to go from thee.

HYMN X. *Thanksgiving for the divine Thankfulness.*
1 IMMOVEABLE our hope remains,
   Within the vail our anchor lies ;
Jesus, who wash'd us from our stains,
   Shall bear us safely to the skies.
2 Strong in his strength, we boldly say,
   For us Immanuel shed his blood ;
Who then shall tear our shield away,
   Or part us from the love of God ?
3 Can tribulation or distress,
   Or persecution's fiery sword ?
Can Satan rob us of our peace,
   Or prove too mighty for the Lord ?

4 Founded

4 Founded on Chrift, fecure we ftand,
 Sealed with his fpirit's inward feal;
We foon fhall gain the promis'd land,
 Triumphant o'er the pow'rs of hell.

5 The winds may roar, the floods may beat;
 And rain, impetuous, defcend;
Yet will he not his own forget,
 But love and fave them to the end.

6 Jefus acquits, and who condemns?
 Ceafe, Satan, from thy fruitlefs ftrife:
Thy malice cannot reach our names,
 To blot them from the book of life.

7 This is eternal life to know,
 God and the Lamb for finners giv'n;
Nor will the Saviour let us go,
 His ranfom'd citizens of heav'n.

8 Us to redeem his life he paid,
 And will he not his purchafe have?
Who can behold Immanuel bleed,
 And doubt his willingnefs to fave?

9 Surely the Son hath made us free,
 Who earth, and heav'n, and hell commands;
Our caufe of triumph this—that we
 Are graven on the Saviour's hands.

10 To him who wafhed us in his blood,
 And lifts apoftate man to heav'n,
Who reconciles his fheep to God,
 Be everlafting glory giv'n.

HYMN XI. *On the Birth of Chrift.*

1 AMPLEST grace in thee I find,
Friend and Saviour of mankind,
Richeft merit to atone
For our fins before the throne.

2 Born to fave thy Church from hell,
Once thou didft with finners dwell;
Was to earth a prophet giv'n,
Now our advocate in heaven.

3 Well might wond'ring angels cry,
　" Glory be to God on high,
　" Peace on earth, good will to men,
　" Loft mankind is found again."

4 Join my foul, their holy fong,
　Emulate the brighter throng,
　Hail the everlafting word,
　Welcome thy defcending Lord !

5 Grace unequall'd ! Love unknown ! .
　Jefus lays afide his crown,
　Cloaths himfelf with flefh and blood,
　Takes the manhood into God.

6 Harden'd rebels tho' we are,
　Lo, he comes to fojourn here :
　See him lie where oxen feed,
　This his chamber, hay his bed !

7 God (O hear it with furprife!)
　For a manger leaves the fkies,
　By affuming flefh beneath,
　Render'd capable of death.

8 From their maker turn'd afide,
　As in Adam all have dy'd,
　So whoe'er his grace receive,
　Shall in Chrift be made alive.

HYMN XII. *Thankfgiving for general Mercies.*

1. GRACIOUS Creator, thy kind hand
　　In all thy works I fee ;
　Refiftlefs pow'r and mildeft love
　　Are blended, Lord, in thee.

2 When thou art wrath and hid'ft thy face,
　　The whole creation mourns ;
　Thou art the attractive pole to which
　　Thy ranfom'd people turns.

3 O let my heart be wholly thine,
　　Thy property alone !
　No longer let me think it mine,
　　Or call myfelf my own !

4 Without

4 Without referve I quit the claim,
 And give up all to thee,
For thou, my all-fufficient Lord,
 Art more than all to me.

5 Only do thou refine my drofs,
 And cleanfe me with thy blood,
To make th' imperfect facrifice
 Acceptable to God.

6 Nor fhall I fear, if Jefus pleads,
 Unworthy as I am,
Being excluded from the feaft,
 And fupper of the Lamb.

HYMN XIII. *Thankfgiving for the Righteoufnefs of*
       Chrift.

1 FOUNTAIN of never ceafing grace,
 Thy faint's exhauftlefs theme,
Great object of immortal praife,
 Effentially fupreme ;
We blefs thee for the glorious fruits
 Thy incarnation gives ;
The righteoufnefs which grace imputes,
 And faith alone receives.

2 Whom heaven's angelic hoft adores,
 Was flaughter'd for our fin,
The guilt, O Lord, was wholly our's,
 The punifhment was thine :
Our God in flefh, to fet us free,
 Was manifefted here ;
And meekly bare our fins, that we,
 His righteoufnefs might wear.

3 Imputatively guilty then
 Our fubftitute was made,
That we the bleffings might obtain
 For which his blood was fhed :
Himfelf he offer'd on the crofs,
 Our forrows to remove ;
And all he fuffer'd was for us,
 And all he did was love :

4 In him we have a righteoufnefs,
　　By God himfelf approv'd,
　Our rock, our fure foundation this,
　　Which never can be mov'd.
　Our ranfom by his death he paid,
　　For all his people giv'n,
　The law he perfectly obey'd,
　　That they might enter heav'n.
5 As all, when Adam finn'd alone,
　　In his tranfgreffion dy'd,
　So by the righteoufnefs of one,
　　Are finners juftify'd.
　We to thy merit, gracious Lord,
　　With humbleft joy fubmit,
　· Again to Paradife reftor'd,
　　In thee alone complete.
6 Our fouls his watchful love retrieves,
　　Nor lets them go aftray,
　His righteoufnefs to us he gives,
　　And takes our fins away :
　We claim falvation in his right,
　　Adopted and forgiv'n,
　His merit is our robe of light,
　　His death the gate of heav'n.

HYMN XIV. *Thankfgiving for the Sufferings of Chrift.*

1 O THOU who did'ft thy glory leave,
　Apoftate finners to retrieve,
　　From nature's deadly fall ;
　Me thou haft purchas'd with a price,
　· Nor fhall my crimes in judgment rife,
　　For thou haft borne them all.
2 Jefus was punifh'd in my ftead,
　Without the gate my furety bled,
　　To expiate my ftain ;
　On earth the Godhead deign'd to dwell,
　And made of infinite avail,
　　The fuff'rings of the man.

3 And

3 And was he for his rebels giv'n ?
  He was : th' incarnate King of heav'n]
    Did for his foes expire ;
  Amaz'd, O earth, the tidings hear ;
  He bore, that we might never bear,
    His Father's righteous ire.
4 Ye faints, the man of forrows blefs,
  The God for your unrighteoufnefs,
    Deputed to atone :
  Praife him 'till with the heav'nly throng,
  Ye fing the never-ending fong,
    And fee him on his throne.

HYMN XV. *The General Thankfgiving in the*
        Liturgy, paraphrafed.

1 ETERNAL God, the thanks receive,
  Which thine unworthy fervants give ;
  Father of ev'ry mercy thou,
  Almighty and all-gracious too !
2 In humble yet exulting fongs,
  Thy praifes iffue from our tongues,
  For that inceffant, boundlefs love,
  Which we and all thy creatures prove.
3 Fafhion'd by thy creating hand,
  And by thy providence fuftain'd,
  We wifh our gratitude to fhew,
  For all thy temp'ral bleffings due.
4 But O ! for this we chiefly raife
  The incenfe of admiring praife——
  Thy love unfpeakably we own
  Which fent the willing Saviour down.
5 For him, of all thy gifts the beft,
  Th' exceeding gift which crowns the reft,
  Chiefly for him thy name we laud,
  And thank thee for a bleeding God.
6 Nor fhould we fail our Lord to praife,
  For all the affifting means of grace ;
  Th' appointed channels which convey
  Strength to fupport us on our way.

7 To thee let all our thanks be giv'n,
  For our well-grounded hope of heav'n,
  Our glorious truft that we fhall reign,
  And live with him who died for man.

8 And O! fo deep a fenfe imprefs
  Of thy fupreme unbounded grace,
  That anthems in full choir may rife,
  And fhake the earth and rend the fkies!

9 Make us in deed, as well as word,
  Shew forth the praifes of the Lord,
  And thank him ftill for what he gives
  Both with our lips, and in our lives!

10 O that, by fin no more fubdu'd,
  We might devout ourfelves to God,
  And only breathe to tell his praife,
  And in his fervice fpend our days!

11 Hail, Father! Hail, eternal Son!
  Hail, facred Spirit, three in one!
  Bleffing and thanks, and pow'r divine,
  Thrice, holy Lord, be ever thine!

P A R A-

PARAPHRASES

ON SELECT PARTS OF

HOLY WRIT.

Sanctos aufus recludere Fontes.

PARA. I. *Pfalm* CXLVIII.

1 GEN'RAL praife to God be giv'n;
   Praife him in the height of heav'n :
  Him, ye glorious hofts, proclaim,
  Saints and angels, blefs his name !
2 Sun, his lofty praife difplay,
  His who made thee king of day :
  Moon, adore the god of light,
  God, who made thee queen of night,
3 Stars, your tribute too be giv'n,
  Spangles in the robe of heav'n :
  God, your awful fovereign, own,
  Bright forerunner of the morn.
4 Praife thou curtain of the fky,
  (Hiding heav'n from mortal eye)
  Him that fpreads thy wat'ry clouds,
  Celebrate the God of gods.
5 Higheft heav'n, his dwelling place,
  Lift thy voice, refound his praife.
  Hymn " the dweller ev'ry where,"
  Prefent more fupremely there.

6 Sun and moon, and ftars and light,
  Heav'n and fky, and clouds unite :
  Verbal creatures of the Lord,
  Swift exifting at his word.

7 'Stablifh'd firm by his command,
  Lo ! immoveable, we ftand ;
  Him, th' ineffable adore,
  Own his regulating pow'r.

8 Womb and fepulchre of man,
  Join, O earth, the grateful train :
  Praife, 'till, in the laft great fire,
  Thou and all thy works expire.

9 Ocean, with thy num'rous brood,
  Swell to magnify thy God :
  Roll his praife from fhore to fhore,
  Lift his name and found his pow'r.

10 Praife him, fire and hail, and fnow,
  Praife him, all ye winds that blow :
  Cold and heat—let each extreme
  Join to render praife to him.

11 Storms difpenfing wafte and death,
  Dreadful meffengers of wrath ;
  Spread his fear and praife abroad,
  Weapons of an angry God.

12 Mountains, vales, and hills, and trees,
  Tell how good your Maker is ;
  His exalted praife declare,
  Feather'd fongfters of the air.

13 Beafts of prey, where'er ye prowl,
  Join to make the concert full :
  Cattle, low Jehovah's fame ;
  Meaneft infects, do the fame.

14 Kings and people, rich and poor,
  Celebrate creating pow'r ;
  Who are ranfom'd by the Lamb,
  Join to praife the great I AM.

15 Female, male of ev'ry age,
  From the fuckling to the fage,
  All confpire with one accord,
  Chaunt the glories of the Lord.

16 Worthy praife can ne'er be giv'n,
'Till his faints arrive at heav'n,
There, with all the glorious ones,
Sing his praife and caft their crowns.

PARA. II. *Names of Chrift, expreffive of his
Offices, taken from various Parts of Scripture.*

1 LOW at thy feet, O Chrift, we fall,
Enabled to confefs,
And call thee by the Holy Ghoft,
The Lord our righteoufnefs.

2 God over all Immanuel reigns,
With his great Father one;
The brightnefs of his glory thou,
And partner of his throne.

3 Author and finifher of faith,
In all that know thy name;
A lion to thy ftubborn foes,
But to thy friends a lamb.

4 Sceptre of Ifrael, prince of peace,
Immortal king of kings:
The fun of righteoufnefs that fhines
With healing in his wings.

5 The gift of God to fallen man,
The Lord of quick and dead:
A well of life to fainting fouls,
And their fuftaining bread.

6 Foundation of thy people's joy,
Their pardon and their reft;
On earth our facrifice for fin,
In heav'n our great high prieft.

7 The Lord of life, who fuffer'd death
That we might heav'n regain:
The fource of bleffing, who, on earth,
Was made a curfe for man.

8 Was poor that Adam's needy fons
Treafure in thee might find;
Repairer of the dreadful breach,
Reftorer of mankind.

9 Through

9 Through thy defert a fallen race
   To God may gain accefs ;
   With thy fine linen deck our fouls,
   Thy perfect righteoufnefs.

10 With that celeftial robe endued,
   We ev'ry foe defy ;
   On earth it fhall our armour be,
   Our glory in the fky.

PARA. III.   *The Prayer of King Manaffes para-*
                 phrafed.

1 AUTHOR of all in earth and fky,
   From whom the ftars derive their light,
   When thou art wroth the planets die,
   And melt as nothing in thy fight.

2 Meafur'd by thine almighty hand,
   Unfathom'd feas of liquid glafs,
   Obedient, own thy high command,
   And keep the bounds they cannot pafs.

3 Shut up by their reftraining Lord,
   They in their proper channels flow:
   Obey Jehovah's fovereign word,
   " Here, and no farther; fhall ye go."

4 Thy terrors as a blazing flame,
   Devour and weigh the finner down:
   The mighty tremble at thy name,
   And nations quake beneath thy frown.

5 Tremendous as thy judgments are,
   Thy pity too no limit knows ;
   Thine arm is ftretch'd the meek to fpare,
   And terribly confume thy foes.

6 With fhame, great God, I own with me,
   Thy waiting mercy long hath borne,
   Yet would I not come back to thee,
   Proudly refufing to return.

7 When mercy call'd I ftopp'd my ear,
   How did I from the Saviour rove,
   And, bent on death, refufe to hear
   The voice of thy inviting love !

8 Blind

8 Blind were my eyes, and hard my heart,
 And proof againſt thy ſtriving grace :
I would from thee, my ſtrength, depart,
 And ceaſe to walk in wiſdom's ways.

9 But lo ! On thee I fix my hope ;
 Be thou my friend and advocate :
Gracious Redeemer, lift me up,
 And raiſe me to my firſt eſtate.

10 Faith in thy merit is thy gift,
 By which thou doſt backſliders heal :
Impart it, gracious Lord, to lift
 'My abject ſoul from whence I fell.

11 Deſtruction ſhall not ſeize the juſt,
 'Whoſe ſin already is forgiv'n,
Whom thou haſt reſcu'd from the loſt,
 And number'd with the heirs of heav'n.

12 To ſinners, of whom I am chief,
 Thy healing promiſes pertain ;
Who fell from thee through unbelief,
 By faith may be reſtor'd again.

13 Of boundleſs mercy I have need,
 My ſins have took deep hold on me ;
In number they the grains exceed,
 That form the margin of the ſea.

14 Meek on the earth thy ſervant lies,
 And humbly makes his ſorrows known ;
Unworthy to lift up my eyes
 To heav'n, my injur'd Maker's throne.

15 Bow'd with my ſenſe of ſin, I faint,
 Beneath the complicated load ;
Father, attend my deep complaint,
 I am thy creature, thou my God !

16 Tho' I have broke thy righteous law,
 Yet with me let thy ſpirit ſtay ;
Thyſelf from me do not withdraw,
 Nor take my ſpark of hope away.

17 Mercy unlimited is thine,
 God of the penitent thou art ;
The ſaving pow'r of blood divine,
 Shall wipe the anguiſh from my heart.

18 Then

18 Then let not fin my ruin be,
    Give me in thee my reft to find:
Jefus, the fick have need of thee,
    The great phyfician of mankind.

·19 In my falvation, Lord, difplay
    The triumphs of abounding grace:
Tell me my guilt is done away,
    And turn my mourning into praife.

20 Repriev'd fo long from hell's abyfs,
    Thou wilt not hurl me there at laft,
But chear me with the fmile of peace,
    Nor look at my offences paft.

21 Then fhall I add my feeble fong
    To their's who chaunt thy praife on high,
And fpread, with an immortal tongue,
    Thy glory through the echoing fky.

PARA. IV. *The* xx*th Pfalm.*

1 BELOV'D of God, may Jefus hear
The ardent breathings of thy pray'r,
    And cancel thy tranfgreffions;
Be with thee in affliction's day,
Redeem thee from thy fears, and fay
    Amen to thy petitions!

2 Thy ev'ry need he will fupply;
His faints fhall furely find him nigh,
    The God whom they rely on;
He will not turn away his face,
But fave thee from his holy place,
    And fend thee help from Sion.

3 Thy feebleft pray'r fhall reach his throne,
Thy ev'ry pang is noted down,
    And thou fhall be forgiv'n;
He loves thee, troubled as thou art;
And all the pantings of thy heart
    Are treafured up in heav'n.

4 God is our triumph in diftrefs;
His children's privilege it is
    To fmile at tribulation:

Jefus,

Jefus, to thee we lift our voice,
By grace enabled to rejoice,
  In hope of thy falvation.
5 Ready to hear, O Lord, thou art,
Mighty to take thy people's part,
  And help them in affliction :
Creation kneels to thy command,
The faving ftrength of thy right-hand,
  Shall be our fure protection.
6 In chariots fome repofe their truft,
Of horfes others make their boaft,
  But we in God are ftronger :
Who on the arm of flefh rely,
Trembling before our face fhall fly,
  When we fhall more than conquer.
7 Still may the palm to us be giv'n,
Thy faints, O mighty king of heav'n,
  Continue to deliver :
Support us with thy ftrength'ning grace,
'Till we, in yon celeftial place,
  Sit down with thee for ever.

PARA. V. *Pfalm* cxix, *Verfe* 169, *to the End.*

1 CONSIDER, Lord, my juft complaint,
Wifdom divine is what I want ;
From lack of knowledge, Lord, I groan :
O when fhall I my God put on ?
2 O let my fupplication rife,
As fumes of incenfe to the fkies,
Enter Jehovah's high abode,
The prefence chamber of my God.
3 When I am truly taught thy ways,
My lips fhall only fpeak thy praife ;
My tongue fhall fing of thee alone,
And tell the wonders thou haft done.
4 Affift me in thy love to ftand,
And hold me by thy guardian hand :
Help me to choofe the lot of grace,
The way of life, the path of peace.

5 Lord, I have long'd thy will to know,
And, knowing, all thy will to do :
My meat and drink is thee to pleafe,
And know the Saviour as he is.

6 Tho', as a fheep, I went aftray,
And wander'd from thy holy way :
The way that Chrift my mafter trod,
The narrow way that leads to God :

7 Sought out by grace, brought back I am,
Sav'd by the merits of the Lamb ;
And now, O Chrift, myfelf I fee,
In Adam loft, reftor'd to thee.

PARA. VI. *The* cxxift *Pfalm.*

1 MY heart, whene'er I lift my eyes
To heaven's exalted fphere,
Wing'd with impetuous ardour flies,
To meet thee in the air.

2 Jefus by faith I ever fee,
Who for the finner pleads,
And ev'ry moment look to thee,
From whom my help proceeds.

3 The great artificer of heav'n,
My guard and keeper is,
Who, by his fpirit inly giv'n,
Affures me I am his.

4 Where'er I go he guides my fteps,
Nor fuffers me to fall :
Ifrael's defence, who never fleeps,
Surrounds me as a wall.

5 In my Redeemer's watchful fight,
Secure I ever ftand ;
My guard by day, my fcreen by night,
My fhield on either hand.

6 Knit to my condefcending God,
I dwell with the Supreme ;
Nor open force nor fecret fraud,
Shall fever me from him.

7 His light, his peace, his heav'n is mine,
    And mine his mighty pow'r:
My faithful centinel divine,
    Preferves me ev'ry hour.

PARA. VII. *The* cxxxivth *Pfalm.*

1 YE friends and followers of God,
With robes made white in Jefus' blood,
    Approach the throne of grace:
His temple's hallow'd court draw nigh,
By day and night renew the cry,
    And found the trump of praife.

2 With ardour lift your hearts and hands;
In yonder heav'n Immanuel ftands
    To offer up your pray'rs:
From Sion he your fouls fhall blefs;
Builder of heav'n and earth he is,
    And dwells above the ftars.

PARA. VIII. *The* ivth *Chapter of Amos.*

1 YE Kine of Bafhan, who devour
The needy and opprefs the poor,
Who drown in wine your every fenfe,
And drink the fpoil of violence.

2 God by his holinefs hath fworn
(The awful God whofe law ye fcorn)
Your foes, whom more than him ye dread,
Your deftin'd borders fhall invade.

3 The Lord hath ratify'd your doom,
Yourfelves and your's he will confume.
Aliens his inftruments fhall be,
To fcourge your vile idolatry.

4 Your ftately buildings then fhall fall;
His vengeance fhall deftroy them all.
Your palaces fhall be a prey,
And ftalls for oxen in that day.

5 Shall guilty hands and wanton eyes
Be lifted up in facrifice?
Ceafe to tranfgrefs, and then my ear
Shall meet the incenfe of your pray'r.

6 In vain my judgments are abroad,
  Tokens of an offended God;
  Nor wrath nor mercies can prevail,
  Nor love of heav'n, nor fear of hell.

7 I gave you, in your greateſt need,
  Cleannefs of teeth, through want of bread;
  Each face was pale, and weak each knee,
  Yet have ye not return'd to me.

8 Have I not marr'd the rip'ning grain,
  With ſcorching heat and want of rain?
  And fruſtrated your riſing hopes,
  By wither'd trees and blaſted crops?

9 Your water fail'd, your wells were dry;
  Your thirſt ye could not ſatisfy:
  Your fainting cities yet ſinned on,
  And drew my fiercer judgments down.

10 Your figs and olive trees I ſmote,
  Your vineyards I confumed with drought;
  Mildew and palmer-worms bereft
  The earth of what the drought had left.

11 Contagious ſickneſs next I ſent:
  (Infatuate Egypt's puniſhment)
  My fury next in blood I pour'd,
  And gave your children to the ſword.

12 Horſes (the ruin who can tell?)
  Promiſcuous with their riders fell:
  Caus'd by their ſtench, the infectious air
  Increaſ'd the havock of the war.

13 Obdurate, ſtill, ye felt mine ire
  Reveal'd from heav'n in flames of fire;
  The blazing ruin ſwept away
  Men, towns and cities in a day:

14 Hear then the meſſage of the Lord,
  The awful thunder of his word;
  Since all my judgments ſtrive in vain,
  To kindle fear in ſtubborn man.

15 Myſelf in judgment ſhall appear,
  And call thee, Iſrael, to my bar:

As harden'd Pharaoh blind and proud,
Prepare to meet thy hoftile God.

16 Prepare to meet your dreadful foe,
Omnifcient and Almighty too ;
Whofe terrors heav'n and earth proclaim,
The God of glory is his name.

PARA. IX. *Pfalm* cxix. *Verfes* 161, 162, 163,
164, *&c. to the* 169*th.*

1 PRINCES have perfecuted me,
But, Lord, my truft is ftill in thee ;
Me from my hope they fought to move,
But could not ftir me from thy love.

2 I fly for refuge to my Lord,
For comfort to his healing word :
From Saul my fafe retreat he is,
And all the troublers of my peace.

3 Each paffing hour difplays his care ;
He faves me from the latent fnare :
His love with wonder I furvey,
And praife him feven times a day.

4 Jefus, my mind from earth withdraw ;
Great peace have they that love thy law :
No precept there which thou haft giv'n,
Is hard to them who ftrive for heav'n.

5 I too have look'd thy health to fee,
And tafte the peace that comes from thee ;
Each inward luft have ftrove to kill,
And walk in all thy perfect will.

6 My foul hath lov'd thy ways and thee,
Thy word is life and health to me :
Exceedingly thy word I prize,
The fund where heav'nly treafure lies.

7 Thy teftimonies are my food,
The faving oracles of God :
Studious of them on earth I'll be,
And then fly up to reign with thee :

PARA.

PARA. X. *Salvation recovered for Man by Jesus Christ,*
  Isaiah lii. 1, 2, 3, 9, 10, 11, 15.

1 ZION, awake, put on thy strength,
    Resume thy beautiful array;
  The promis'd Saviour comes at length,
    To chase thy guilt and grief away:
  Thee for his purchase God shall own,
  And save thee by his dying Son.

2 Jerusalem, be holy now,
    Satan no more shall dwell in thee;
  Wash'd from thy sin, and white as snow,
    Prepare thy God made man to see;
  Prepare Immanuel to behold,
  And hear his peaceful message told.

3 Shake off the dust, arise with speed,
    Too long hast thou a captive been;
  Redemption's near, lift up thine head,
    And cast away the chains of sin;
  Forth from thy prison come, and shake
  The yoke of bondage from thy neck.

4 Tho' ye have sold yourselves for nought,
    And forfeited your claim to heav'n,
  Accept the Saviour's love unbought;
    Your treason now is all forgiv'n;
  My blood the fallen race restores,
  And saves without desert of your's.

5 Ye desart places, sing for joy;
    Lost man, your hymns of wonder raise;
  Let holy shouts invade the sky,
    And ev'ry altar flame with praise;
  For I, Almighty to redeem,
  Have comforted Jerusalem.

6 My arm's made bare for your defence,
    To save my Church from Satan's pow'r,
  Depart, depart, come out from thence,
    Defile yourselves with sin no more:
  Be pure ye priests, who preach my word,
  And bear the vessels of the Lord.

7 Look

7 Look out and fee Immanuel come,
  Myriads to fprinkle with his blood;
He many nations fhall bring home,
  And fave them from the wrath of God:
And earth's remoteft bounds fhall fee
The great falvation wrought by me.

PARA. XI. *The* viiith *Chapter of Hofea.*

1 SET the loud trumpet to thy mouth,
  Let all the final warning hear;
My everlafting word of truth,
  To high and low alike declare.

2 Swift, as the rav'nous eagle flies,
  And darts, impetuous on her prey,
Shall their victorious enemies,
  Fill Ifrael's land with pale difmay.

3 Then fhall they cry to me in vain;
  Tho' afk'd with tears, no aid I'll grant,
Becaufe they did my words difdain,
  And trample on my covenant.

4 Me for their God they will not have,
  Therefore I give them to the fword:
Your foes commiffion fhall receive,
  T' avenge my quarrel, faith the Lord.

5 Sin is the God whom they adore,
  And hell-born lufts their rulers are:
Th' apoftate land fhall feel my pow'r,
  The fury of deftructive war.

6 Go, to your gods, O Ifrael, go!
  Samaria to thy calf apply!
Thy idols cannot help thee now,
  Nor fave thee when diftrefs is nigh.

7 When wilt thou turn to me thy God?
  When wilt thou feek my injur'd face?
'Till then my wrath fhall drench in blood,
  The harden'd, unbelieving race.

8 Ye fools and blind, confider this,
  Can they be gods which hands have made?
On you and on your images,
  I'll hurl the ruin I have faid.

9 Who fow in fin fhall reap in pain ;
   My word fhall furely come to pafs :
   Un-number'd mifchiefs yet remain,
   For thofe defpifers of my grace.

10 To punifh their apoftacy,
   The corn fhall perifh ere it rife ;
   Or what comes up fhall only be
   A portion for their enemies.

11 For Ifrael waxes worfe and worfe,
   Nor quakes at my tremendous frown,
   Famine and war unite their force,
   To bring a finful people down.

12 Before the heathen Ifrael flies,
   His boafted ftrength is weaknefs found :
   As when a broken veffel lies,
   Slighted and ufelefs on the ground.

13 Ephraim is up to Syria gone,
   In all the confidence of pride :
   Alas, he goes to war alone,
   Jehovah is not on his fide.

14 Ephraim in vain the King of kings,
   With condefcending pity woo'd :
   The fatal love of earthly things,
   Has drawn him from the love of God.

15 The fierce invaders to repel,
   Tho' they have foreign aid obtain'd,
   Yet fhall th' ungrateful nation feel,
   The weight of my avenging hand.

16 Since Ephraim hath difguifed his fin,
   Beneath religion's fpecious forms,
   His very prayer fhall be unclean,
   And haften to bring on the ftorm.

17 In vain I gave my gracious law,
   The treafure of my written word ;
   No beauty there the worldlings faw,
   Nor priz'd the meffage of the Lord.

18 Wherefore their cry I will not hear,
   Nor yet accept their facrifice ;
   Unpardon'd fin pollutes their pray'r,
   Nor lets it penetrate the fkies.

19 In Egypt they again shall weep;
 I'll visit their iniquity:
 Their sins I will in mem'ry keep,
 Because they have forgotten me.
20 In vain they fence their cities round,
  In forts and ramparts put their trust:
 Their lofty spires shall kiss the ground,
 .By light'ning level'd with the dust.

PARA. XII. *The* cxxvth *Psalm.*

1 WHO, Lord, confide in thee,
  And in thy faith endure,
 Shall as Mount Sion be,
  Immoveable and sure:
 As Christ their rock, unshook, unmov'd;
 Of God eternally belov'd.
2 The rising mountains stand
  Around Jerusalem;
 So God's almighty hand,.
  Guards us who trust in him:
 We never will of safety doubt,
 While he shall compass us about.
3 Ye souls who stand in God,
  Whom Jesus' blood hath bought;
 The guilty sinner's rod
  Shall never be your lot:
 Ye shall not fall, upheld by grace,
 Nor put your hands to wickedness.
4 The upright men in heart,
  Jehovah will defend;
 Will not from them depart,
  But love them to the end:
 He will do well, O saints, to you,
 The Lord will never let you go.
5 But such as will forsake,
  The happy path of peace,
 Deceivers, that turn back
  To their own wickedness,

The

The double wrath of God fhall feel,
And fink unpardon'd into hell.
6 While they who hear his call,
    And plead a Saviour's blood,
Shall reign in joy with all
    The ranfom'd ones of God :
Peace upon Ifrael fhall come,
To endlefs glory gather'd home.

PARA. XIII. *Lord's Prayer. Matthew* vi. 9, 10,
11, 12, 13.

1 OUR holy Father, all thy will
We fain would perfectly fulfil;
But each has left thy law undone,
Unworthy to be call'd thy Son.

2 Who art in heav'n, enthron'd on high,
Diffufing glory through the fky ;
Reigning above, on earth rever'd,
By faints belov'd, by finners fear'd.

3 For ever hallow'd be thy name,
The Triune God, the bright I Am;
At which feraphic choirs and all
The hofts of heav'n adoring fall.

4 Thy kingdom come, e'en now we wait
Thy glory to participate :
Rule in our hearts, unrival'd reign,
Nor e'er withdraw thyfelf again.

5 Thy will, thy law, thy precept giv'n,
Be done on earth, as 'tis in heav'n :
Faithful as angels, fain would we
With cover'd faces wait on thee.

6 Great God, on whom the ravens cry,
For fuftenance, our wants fupply :
Give us this day, and evermore,
Our daily bread from hour to hour.

7 Forgive whate'er we do amifs,
Our wilful fins and trefpaffes,
As we forgive (reward us thus)
All them that trefpafs againft us.

8 And

8 And lead us not by bounty's tide,
   Into temptation, luft or pride:
   But what by mercy we obtain,
   Let pow'r omnipotent reftrain.

9 And O! deliver us thine own
   From evil and the evil one,
   Who fain his darts in us would fheath,
   And bind us with the chains of death.

10 Thou, Lord, can'ft vanquifh his defign,
   Thine is the kingdom, only thine;
   The pow'r, th' eternal majefty,
   And glory, appertain to thee!

PARA. XIV. *The* lxiiid *Pfalm.*

1 O GOD, my God thou art,
   My Father too by grace;
   I dare not from my hope depart,
   Or ceafe to feek thy face:
   My thirfty fpirit pants
   Thy plenitude to prove,
   And comprehend with all thy faints,
   The fulnefs of thy love.

2 In this dry, barren land,
   Where water is not found,
   I fain would fly to thy right hand,
   Where living ftreams abound:
   Thee, thee, I long to know,
   Athirft for God I am,
   And come to thee as needy now
   As when at firft I came.

3 Thy glory and thy pow'r
   I long again to fee,
   To have again, as heretofore,
   Sweet fellowfhip with thee;
   Again to feel thy peace,
   Again thy name to praife:
   Better than life thy favour is,
   To all that know thy grace.

4 With

4 With perfevering hope,
   Thy mercy I'll proclaim,
My hands in fteady faith lift up,
   And magnify thy name.
Thy praifes I'll reveal,
   'Till I from earth remove,
My mouth with joyful lips fhall tell
   The wonders of thy love.

5 Surely I reafon have
   On thee, my God, to truft;
My life thou lifteft from the grave,
   My fpirit from the duft:
Thy grace and boundlefs might
   My theme by day fhall be,
My glory in the filent night,
   To meditate on thee.

6 My fuccour thou haft been
   When ev'ry helper failed,
Or I, ere now, had fell by fin,
   And Satan had prevail'd;
My foul, redeem'd from death,
   To thee her off'ring brings,
And hides her helplefs head beneath
   The covert of thy wings.

7 Thou keep'ft my fteady feet,
   In thy appointed road;
By all the pow'rs of hell befet,
   I follow after God:
In Jefus I am fafe,
   My caftle of refort;
His hand is both my fhield and ftaff,
   My fhelter and fupport.

8 The men who feek to tread
   Thy faithful people down,
And perfecute, in them, their Head,
   And crucify their Son,
Thou, Lord, will furely foil
   In thy avenging day,
And give their bodies for a fpoil
   To ev'ry beaft of prey.

9 But

9 But me, and all who love
   Thy worſhip and thy ways,
Thou far from danger wilt remove,
   And hide us in thy place :
Who ſpeak the words of truth,
   Thou, Lord, on them ſhall ſmile,
But thou wilt ſtop the liar's mouth,
   And ſlay the ſons of guile.

PARA. XV. *Pſalm* cxix. *From the* 40th *Verſe to the* 49th.

1 LET thy loving mercy, Lord,
   Come alſo unto me ;
Now according to thy word,
   My preſent Saviour be :
Unbelievers then no more
   Shall againſt my hope blaſpheme ;
Forc'd to own " the mighty pow'r
   Of God hath reſcu'd him."
2 In thy word my truſt I place,
   And humbly urge my claim,
'Till I of thy ſaving grace,
   A living witneſs am :
Give me, Lord, thyſelf to know,
   Then in me thy word fulfil,
To walk in all things here below,
   According to thy will.
3 Seeking now in ſtedfaſt faith,
   I wait a word from thee ;
Bring my feet into the path
   Of perfect liberty ;
Then, when I the path have found,
   Un-aſham'd thy truth I'll ſhew :
Kings ſhall hear the joyful ſound,
   And ſeek ſalvation too.

Bb 4

4 My

4 My delight is in thy word
    Which I have lov'd of old,
  Dearer is thy promife, Lord,
    To me than mines of gold :
Up to thee my hands I lift,
    'Till I of thy grace receive ;
Give the never changing gift,
    Thy full redemption give.

OCCASIONAL

OCCASIONAL PIECES

ON THE

DEATH OF FRIENDS.

John xi. 26. *Whoſoever liveth and believeth in me ſhall never die.*

> —— Quid ſibi Saxa cavata,
> Quid pulchra volunt Monumenta,
> Niſi quòd Res creditor illis
> Non mortua, ſed data Sommo ?   PRUD.

EPITAPH I. On Mrs. E. B.

IF Candour, merit, ſenſe or virtue dies, ⎫
  Reader, beneath thy feet dead virtue lies ; ⎬
Yet ſtill ſhe lives, if worth can eternize. ⎭
Lives far above the reach of death: But where ?
In heav'n, and ev'ry heart that knew her here.
Vain are encomiums ; praiſe is idly ſpent
On them whoſe actions are their monument.
Thrice ſacred tomb, be loyal to thy truſt,
And guard, till Chriſt revives her hallow'd duſt :
Then, as a faithful ſteward, ſafe reſtore
The precious treaſure thou muſt keep no more.

EPITAPH II. On Mr. G. WALTON.

1 THE debt of nature I have paid,
    Which thou muſt ſhortly pay :
  To learn inſtruction from the dead,
    Thou breathing taper, ſtay.
2 Swifter than thought thy years depart,
    My verſe proclaims their haſte :
  A moment nearer death thou art,
    Than when you read the laſt.

3 Soon

3 Soon muft thy earth to earth be giv'n,
Soon muft thou difappear :
Say, reader, is thy heart in heav'n,
And is thy treafure there ?

4 Like thee the proftrate dead I view'd,
While in the flefh detain'd :
How differ we ? thou 'rt on the road,
I've reach'd my journey's end.

EPITAPH III. On the Death of Mrs. F. T.
June 3, 1754.   *Heb.* iv. 9.   *There remaineth therefore*
a Reft for the People of God.

1 THE robes of light our fifter wears,
Which emulate the fun,
Should caufe us to fufpend our tears,
And make our anthems rival their's
Who ftand before the throne.

2 Glory to him whofe love conftrains,
And faves us by his blood :
By virtue of his dying pains,
She finds the reft that ftill remains,
For ev'ry child of God.

3 In fiery trials day by day
Unfhaken did fhe ftand;
To glory fweetly made her way,
Meek and refign'd as paffive clay,
In her great Potter's hand.

4 Her woes their period have found,
They cannot now enflave,
Nor come where endlefs joys abound,
Nor haunt her peaceful foul beyond
The limit of the grave.

5 Victorious fhe affumes the wreath,
For conquerors defign'd,
The end of perfevering faith ;
And leaves her cares, releas'd by death,
Eternally behind.

6 No more, by Satan's rage purfu'd,
 Affliction fhalt thou fee;
Secure of heav'n for thine abode,
Bleft with the prefence of thy God,
 To all eternity.

7 The happy change that life deny'd,
 Affifting death affords;
Behold her at Immanuel's fide,
Unutterably glorify'd,
 Immutably the Lord's!

8 O may we too maintain our ground,
 From faith to faith go on!
At the laft day in Chrift be found,
And form the circles that furround,
 His everlafting throne!

EPITAPH IV. On the death of Mr. ENOCH WILLIAMS, Auguft, 1757.

Gen. v. 24. And Enoch walked with God, he was not, for God took him.

1 HEARKEN! the Saviour's voice at laft
 Invites his fufferer home,
And tells thee all thy toil is paft,
 But thy reward is come.

2 Till meet for blifs on earth detain'd,
 The conqueft thou haft won;
Through much temptation thou haft gain'd
 The prize, and reach'd the crown:

3 While fhouting angels chaunt their joys,
 And tune their notes the higher,
And clap their wings, for O! thy voice,
 Is added to the choir.

4 Of his inheritance above
 They hail a faint poffeft:
Made meet, by his Redeemer's love,
 To be Jehovah's gueft.

5 Swift

5 Swift as an arrow through the air,
  The tow'ring fpirit flies,
   Intrufted to a feraph's care,
    And convoy'd to the fkies:

6 On the expanded wings of love,
  He feeks his high abode,
  To meet the happy fouls above,
    That are brought home to God.

7 Him they falute with lifted cry,
  As foon as enter'd there,
   " But for thy favour'd miniftry,
    Or we had not been here:

8 From pain to glory fummon'd forth,
  Thrice welcome from below,
   Our fellow-fufferer on earth,
    Our fellow angel now!"

9 While humbly he draws near the throne,
  The Saviour's chryftal feat;
   Gives him the praife, and cafts his crown,
    At his redeeming feet.

10 Lifted above the reach of pain,
   We foon fhall change our place;
    And join Immanuel's fhining train,
     And fee his blifsful face:

11 Rejoicing in that glorious hope,
   We bear his crofs below;
    We quickly fhall be taken up,
     Sublimer joys to know.

12 For our arrival into blifs,
   Our friends in glory wait:
    Cut fhort thy work in righteoufnefs,
     And make their joys compleat!

13 The happy foul whom Jefus gives,
   In him to live and die,
    Its bleft tranfition fcarce perceives
     Into eternity.

14 A fight of him that conquer'd death,
   In our laft moments giv'n,
    Shall elevate our languid faith,
     And charm us into heav'n.

15 Chrift

15 Chrift when expiring Stephen view'd,
　　He fcorn'd death's utmoft pow'r,
　　And calmly fell afleep in God,
　　Amidft the ftony fhow'r.

16 Affift us, Lord, to walk and live,
　　In Sion's heavenly road,
　　And then our fouls to thee receive,
　　When call'd to meet our God.

17 A little while and we fhall foar
　　To yonder promis'd land,
　　And meet our brethren gone before,
　　Enthron'd at thy right hand:

18 Thy praife fhall actuate each tongue,
　　Thy love our hearts enflame;
　　And we with them fhall fing the fong
　　Of Mofes and the Lamb.

EPITAPH V. On Mafter Eustace Bateman.

1 HAIL, happy youth, fo early taken home,
　Caught up to Jefus from the ill to come:
　By thy Redeemer fweetly order'd hence,
　Ere vice had marr'd thy lovely innocence.

2 When twice fix winters he had fcarcely feen,
　His heav'n-born foul difdain'd to dwell with men:
　Ardent the crown eternal to receive,
　And ripe for heav'n, he only dy'd to live.

EPITAPH VI. On the Death of the Rev. Mr. R.B.

Numbers xxiii. 10.　*Let me die the Death of the Righ-*
　　teous, and let my laft End be like his.

1 THRICE happy they who fleep in God,
　Securely wafted o'er the flood,
　　To Canaan's peaceful fhore!
　Whofe lives were as a daily death,
　Who walk'd with God, and liv'd by faith,
　　And now fhall die no more!

2 Such, gracious Lord, we wifh to be;
　Such was our paftor, now with thee,

　　　　　　　　　　　　　　　Our

Our candleſtick below :
A burning and a ſhining light,
He liv'd a while to bleſs our ſight;
    But ſhines in glory now.
3 A Prophet hallow'd from the womb,
To ſeek and bring the wand'rers home;
    Anointed, ſet apart :
Enabled by the ſearching word,
To ſet the meſſage of the Lord,
    Home to the ſinner's heart.
4 His ev'ry pow'r devoted was
To further his Redeemer's cauſe;
    Nor did his talents hide :
A beacon ſet upon an hill,
He liv'd to do his Maſter's will,
    He did his will, and dy'd.
5 A faithful meſſenger he ſtood,
The trumpet and the mouth of God,
    To make his counſel known :
His life one conſtant voice hath been,
Inviting ſinners to come in,
    And aſk th' eternal crown.
6 May I like him my hours employ,
Finiſh, like him, my courſe with joy,
    And ſleep to wake in bliſs !
Like him be number'd with the bleſt !
Jeſus regard my one requeſt,
    Make my laſt end like his.

EPITAPH VII. On the Death of Mr. R. V.

Heb. vi. 12. *Be not ſlothful, but Followers of them who,*
    through Faith and Patience, inherit the Promiſes.

1 THE crown of righteouſneſs is giv'n,
    Our friend is landed ſafe in heav'n :
His warfare now accompliſh'd is,
And face to face his Lord he ſees.
2 Forever now redeem'd from pain,
    He did not run nor ſtrive in vain :
With triumph from his clay releaſ'd,
Tranſlated to his place of reſt.

3 Ear hath not heard, nor eye beheld,
What to the faints is there reveal'd;
Blifsful experience only knows,
The glories of the upper houfe.

4 Far, far from all diftrefs remov'd,
They know the God whom here they lov'd:
Temptation, ficknefs, grief and care,
Shall never gain admiffion there.

5 Then let us feek, in ftedfaft faith,
A city that foundations hath:
Our bright, immoveable abode,
Whofe glorious architect is God.

6 There we fhall all our pain forget,
And only fongs of praife repeat;
In knowledge, happinefs and love,
To all eternity improve.

7 There we fhall as the angels fhine,
The martyr's noble army join;
And fee the Lamb (thrice blifsful fight!)
Encompafs'd with his faints in light.

8 When fhall we to our joy be giv'n;
O when exchange this earth for heav'n?
And caft our crowns before the throne,
And worfhip him that fits thereon?

9 When fhall we hear th' inviting word,
And be for ever with the Lord?
A day with Chrift in glory there,
Is better than a thoufand here.

10 Holy and true, call in thine own,
Accomplifh, Lord, their number foon:
Us to thy fecond coming feal,
And with thyfelf for ever fill!

A P P E N D I X.

Confisting of several Pieces, not properly reducible to any of the preceding Heads.

I.

1 LOOK back, my soul, and take a view,
   Of Christ expiring on the tree :
Behold thy Saviour breathe his last,
   To buy eternal life for thee !
Thy Jesus faints—'Tis finish'd, cries,
Reclines his sacred head, and dies.

2 Shadows and types are done away,
   The temple's veil is rent in twain :
Vanish, ye emblematic rites,
   The real victim now is slain ;
Is slain for sinners to atone,
The priest and sacrifice in one.

3 Methinks I see the purpled earth,
   Startle to feel its Maker's blood ;
The sun retires, and from their graves,
   Saints rise to hail their dying Lord :
Each sympathising rock appears
More tender than his murderers.

4 And did the Saviour thus exchange
   His throne of glory for a cross ?
Left he for this th' ethereal court,
   To die a painful death for us ?
For us he bled at ev'ry vein,
And, slain by man, for man was slain.

5 Obdurate

5 Obdurate heart, fhall mountains heave,
 And nature mourn her beft belov'd,
Shall the rocks tremble at his voice,
 And I alone abide unmov'd !
Shall I not weep his death to fee, .
 Who wept in tears of blood for me ?
6 O Prince of martyrs, touch my heart,
 There at thy mighty ftandard reft ;
Burn purifying incenfe there,
 Fit it for fo divine a gueft :
There let thy pow rful crofs refide,
'Till ev'ry luft is crucified.

II. *To a Friend who afked what God is.*

1 IS there a man whofe daring hand,
 Can number ev'ry grain of fand ?
Can count the drops that fill the fea,
Or tell how many ftars there be ?
2 Who, then, fhall ftrive to comprehend
 Infinity that knows no end ?
Who fhall fet bounds to boundlefs pow'r,
Reftrain omnipotence, or low'r
Eternity to one poor hour ?
3 Believe me, friend, thou can'ft no more
 The vaft defigns of God explore,
Than thy fhort arm can touch the fkies,
Or fathom ocean's deep abyfs.
4 Who fhall difclofe his Maker's plan,
 Or dare his fecret will to fcan ?
Shall feeble, guilty, finite man ?
5 None but perfection, fuch as his,
 Can know th' Almighty as he is ;
His glory never can be brought
Adapted to a mortal's thought.
6 Confider what thou art, and fear
 This unfeen witnefs always near.
Dive not into his deep decree :
The object's too elate for thee,
Thou muft not afk, nor wifh to fee.

Caſt each preſumptuous doubt away ;
Remember thou'rt, at beſt, but clay,
Whoſe only province is t' obey.
}

III. ISAIAH xlix. 16. *Behold, I have graven thee on
the Palms of my Hands.*

1 REDEEM'D offender, hail the day
　　That ſees thy ſin forgiv'n :
　Jeſus hath borne thy guilt away
　　And pleads for thee in heav'n.
2 Imprinted on his hands thou art
　　In characters of blood ;
　The ſtream that iſſu'd from his heart
　　Shall waft thee ſafe to God.
3 For me vouchſaf'd th' unſpotted Lamb,
　　His Father's wrath to bear :
　I ſee his feet, and read my name
　　Engraven deeply there.
4 Forth from the Lord his guſhing blood
　　In purple currents ran :
　And ev'ry wound proclaim'd aloud
　　His wond'rous love to man.
5 My faith looks back and ſees him bleed ;
　　A thorny crown he wears,
　To ſet upon the ſinner's head
　　A ſhining crown of ſtars.
6 Saviour, I fain would take the wreath,
　　To thee, my center, move,
　In all the lowlineſs of faith,
　　In all the heights of love.
7 Thy righteouſneſs my robe ſhall be,
　　Thy bitter death my hope :
　For my offence upon the tree
　　My Lord was lifted up.
8 For me the Saviour's blood avails,
　　Almighty to atone :
　The hands he gave to piercing nails
　　Shall lead me to his throne.

IV. PHIL.

IV. Phil. iv. 5. *Be careful for nothing.*

1 CAN my heav'n-born foul fubmit
    To care for things below !
Nay, but never from the feet
    Of Jefus may I go.
Anxious, Lord, for nothing here,
    In ev'ry ftraight I look to thee ;
Humbly caft my ev'ry care,
    On him that cares for me.

2 Godlinefs is greateft gain,
    For that alone I pray ;
Lord, I never would complain,
    Give thou or take away :
Never would I grieve for ought,
    So Chrift is mine and I am his ;
I would ne'er by taking thought,
    Obftruct my inward peace.

3 He fhall dwell in perfect reft
    Whofe mind is ftay'd on thee,
Whom to keep within my breaft,
    My only care fhall be ;
View the lilies of the field,
    They grow, but neither toil nor fpin,
By their Maker's arm upheld,
    Who cloaths the earth with green.

4 See the ravens, day by day,
    Their Maker gives them food,
Lions, roaring for their prey,
    Do feek their meat from God :
Lean thou on his faithful word,
    Nor, by diftruft, provoke his wrath,
Caft thy burden on the Lord,
    O Thou of little faith.

5 Will the Saviour (who thy peace
    At fuch a price hath bought)
From his work of mercy ceafe
    And fell thy life for nought ?

Doubting

Doubting foul, to him look up,
 His ears are open to thy cry;
God fhall recompence thy hope,
 And all thy need fupply.
6 Thou haft promis'd help to thine,
 And I believe the word;
I will never afk a fign,
 Nor dare to tempt the Lord:
'Tis enough for God to fay,
 I'll feed my people with my hand;
Heav'n and earth fhall pafs away,
 But his decree fhall ftand.

V. *Judgement.*

1 BEHOLD, the awful day comes on,
 When Jefus on his righteous throne,
  Shall in the clouds appear:
With folemn pomp fhall bow the fky,
And in the twinkling of an eye,
  Arraign us at his bar.
2 But firft th' archangels trump fhall blow,
 Our fcatter'd duft it's voice fhall know,
  And quicken at the found;
The fea fhall then give up her dead,
And nations, ftarting from their bed,
  Shall cleave the op'ning ground.
3 Who fhall fuftain his righteous ire,
 When Jefus fets the clouds on fire,
  And makes the earth retreat?
· In vain fhall finners then repent,
When each expiring element,
  Shall melt with fervent heat.
4 The dead in Chrift fhall firft awake,
 The faithful few, who for his fake,
  On earth were juftify'd:
Guarded by a feraphic band,
Aloft they mount to his right-hand,
  In whom they liv'd and dy'd.

5 See

5 See next the guilty crowd arife,
　Beholding, with reluctant eyes,
　　The glories of the Lamb,
　White taunting fiends impatient wait,
　To hurl them from the judgment feat,
　　To hell's eternal flame.

6 Hark ! as they mount, by devils borne,
　To meet their judge, on earth their fcorn,
　　Defpairingly they cry,
　" Fall on us rocks with all your load,
　" And fcreen us from the wrath of God,
　　" And hide us from his eye."

7 In vain on rocks and hills ye call,
　The rocks fhall from their bafis fall,
　　And know their place no more :
　The hills fhall melt when God comes down,
　And mountains crumble at his frown,
　　And groan beneath his pow'r.

8 What thought can paint their black defpair,
　Who this tremendous fentence hear,
　　Irrevocably giv'n,
　" Depart ye curfed, into hell,
　" With everlafting burnings dwell,
　　" Remote from me and heav'n ?"

9 But O thou Saviour of mankind,
　Difplay thy pow'r, and to the blind
　　Effectual light afford :
　Snatch them from unbelief,
　And now compel them to come in,
　　And tremble at thy word.

10 Methinks I hear thy mercy plead,
　The voice of him that wakes the dead
　　Doth over finners mourn :
　" Why do ye ftill your God forget,
　" And madly haften to the pit
　　" From whence is no return ?

11 " Ye reafoners, make the wifeft choice ;
　" Liften, in time, to reafon's voice,
　　" Nor dare almighty ire :

　　　　　　" Turn,

" Turn, left my hotteft wrath ye feel,
" And find, too late, the flames of hell
" No metaphoric fire."

VI. *Contempt of the World.*

1 CAN ought below engrofs my thought ?
    Or am I to the world confin'd ?
Nay, let my pure affections foar
    To objects of a nobler kind !

2 I know I'm but a pilgrim here,
    That feeks a better, promis'd land :
Then may I run and never tire,
    Till that celeftial home's obtain'd.

3 Refolv'd to tread the facred way
    That Jefus water'd with his blood,
I bend my fixed and chearful courfe
    Through that rough path my mafter trod.

4 Contemptuous of the world I live,
    A daily death rejoice to die :
And, while I move and walk below,
    My abfent heart mounts up on high.

5 O light of life, ftill guide my fteps,
    Without thy friendly aid I ftray :
Lead me, my God, for I am blind,
    Direct me, and point out my way.

6 Let the vain world applaud or frown,
    Still may I heaven's path purfue :
Still may I ftand unfhook, and keep
    The center of my hopes in view !

7 Tho' Satan, earth and felf oppofe,
    Yet, thro' thy help, I'll perfevere ;
To Canaan's hills my eyes lift up,
    And chufe my lot and portion there.

8 The way that leads to glory lies
    Through ill-report, contempt and lofs :
Affift me to deny myfelf,
    To follow thee and bear thy crofs.

9 Let Satan never come between,
    Nor feparate my God from me ;
But may my foul, in ev'ry ftorm,
    Find a fure refting place in thee.

VII.

1 DYING Redeemer, flaughter'd Lamb,
 Thou pour'dft out thy blood for me ;
O may I, kindled by thy flame,
 As freely give myfelf to thee !
My heart to thee I now refign,
For, Lord, it coft the blood of thine !

2 To fave my falling foul from death,
 Th' immaculate Redeemer dy'd ;
Lord, my offences drove the nails,
 The foldier I, that pierc'd thy fide :
For this my reftlefs eye runs o'er,
Becaufe I can lament no more.

3 How gladly fhould my head have worn,
 The crown of thorns to hinder thine !
Have fuffer'd in my mafter's ftead,
 And made thy dying forrows mine !
Have ftretch'd my arms upon the tree,
And dy'd myfelf to refcue thee.

4 But O ! no other facrifice,
 The Father's juftice could appeafe ;
Ten thoufand worlds had dy'd in vain,
 Thy blood alone could buy our peace :
The God offended muft be flain,
To expiate the offence of man.

5 And fhall I not his crofs take up
 Who dy'd upon a crofs for me ?
Jefus, through good and ill report,
 I, in thy ftrength, will follow thee.
My mafter liv'd defpis'd, abhorr'd,
And I am not above my Lord.

VIII. *Life and Immortality brought to Light by the*
Gofpel.

1 HOW bleft am I ! no fnare I fear,
While Jefus keeps his dwelling here :
His prefence chaces death away,
Enliv'ning with continual day.

2 By

2 By Satan's rage I ftand unfhook,
   My hopes are founded on a rock :
   Chrift is the ftone on which I build,
   My caftle, guardian, helmet, fhield !

IX.   *To the Rev. Mr. E. W. March,* 1757.

1 SOLDIER of the living God,
      Steward of the myftic word,
   Ufe the gifts on thee beftow'd
      To the honour of thy Lord.
   Free thou didft from him receive,
   Man of God as freely give.

2 Clad with zeal as with a cloak,
      Boldly urge thy rapid way ;
   Firmly grounded as a rock,
      Faithful in the trying day :
   Stand in Chrift thy fure abode,
   Safely hid with him in God.

3 In Immanuel's ftrength go forth,
      Loud his dying love proclaim,
   Dare the feeble fons of earth,
      Conquer in his faving name :
   March with Jefus for thy guide,
   Go, for God is on thy fide !

4 Bear the ftandard of the Lord,
      Fight thy captain's battles well ;
   With the fpirit's two-edg'd fword,
      Put to flight the hofts of hell :
   Single thou thy foes fhall chafe,
   Arm'd with all the ftrength of grace.

5 Satan and the world may join,
      Hell and death with thee engage ;
   Strong thou art, in ftrength divine,
      Safe amidft their blackeft rage :
   Jefus fhall thy foul confirm,
   Lift thee up above the ftorm.

6 Vainly fhall the blinded crew
      Strive thy progrefs to withftand ;
   Thee they never fhall fubdue,
      Guarded by the Saviour's hand :

God

God hath faid concerning thee,
    " As thy day thy ſtrength ſhall be."
7 But if Jeſus ſhou'd depart,
    For a ſeaſon ceaſe to ſmile,
Proving what is in thine heart,
    Leave thee to thyſelf a while,
He again thy ſtay will prove,
Bear thee in his arms of love.
8 When thou do'ſt in ſecret pray'r,
    Find a ready, free acceſs,
When thou telleſt all thy care,
    Sweetly at the throne of grace,
Me to Jeſus then commend,
Think upon thy diſtant friend !
9 Dauntleſs thou his word proclaim,
    Tell his meſſage to mankind ;
Bid them, in thy maſter's name,
    Aſk the pearl for thoſe deſign'd :
Tell them, Jeſus will redeem
All that come to God by him.
10 Faithful to thy ſacred truſt,
    Thus from ſtrength to ſtrength go on;
Stay the weak, bring back the loſt,
    Labour 'till thy work is done :
Fight and conquer, end the ſtrife,
Enter on eternal life.

X. THESS. v. 24. *Faithful is he that c.... , who alſo will do it.*

1 FICKLE and changeable man,
    Terreſtrial joys are juſt as vain,
        And periſh in the taſting ;
But Jeſus' truth I cannot fear,
His gifts without repentance are,
        His love is everlaſting.
2 Mercy unchangeable is his,
    Eternal as himſelf it is,
  Nor will his promiſe fail me :
I own the token he has given,
And ſteadily preſs on to heav'n,
    Tho' fiends and men aſſail me.

3 He never will from me remove ;
For me the Saviour pleads above,
   Still making interceffion :
I hear his pray'r, I feel his blood,
Kept by the mighty pow'r of God,
   Through faith unto falvation.

4 His fpirit for that end is giv'n,
To bear unhurt, unftain'd, to heav'n,
   The foul of each believer :
Deputed by the Lamb he is,
To comfort, guard, and ftrengthen his,
   And ftay with them for ever.

5 Through him united to the Son,
Unalienably fealed his own,
   Nor earth, nor hell fhall move me :
From conqu'ring I'to conquer go;
Jefus hath lov'd me hitherto,
   And to the end will love me.

6 Bent to devour the ferpent ftands,
But Chrift from his own mighty hands
   Will never let him force me :
My Maker is my hufband now,
Nor heights above, nor depths below,
   Shall from my Lord divorce me.

7 If, for a feafon, Satan's chain
Be lengthen'd, Jefus will fuftain
   Me in the fore temptation ;
Will fruftrate the accufer's hope,
And bear my ranfom'd fpirit up
   Above the inundation.

8 His name affuredly I prove
Effential faithfulnefs and love ;
   Shall I, by doubting, grieve him ?
My foul he with a price hath bought,
His law within my heart is wrote,
   And I fhall never leave him.

T O

HOLY SPIRIT,

Modernized from the OFFICE for ORDINATION.

HYMN I. *To the Holy Spirit, &c.*

1 COME, Holy Ghoft, our fouls infpire,
   And warm with uncreated fire !
Thou the anointing fpirit art,
Who doft thy feven-fold gift impart :
Thy bleffed unction from above
Is comfort, life, and fire of love.

2 Enable with perpetual light
   The dullnefs of our blinded fight ;
Anoint and chear us, all our days,
With the abundance of thy grace ;
Our foes convert, give peace at home :
Where thou art guide, no ill can come.

3 Teach us to know the Father, Son,
   And thee ; a Trinity in one :
That, thro' the ages all along,
This may be our endlefs fong ;
   Praife to thy eternal love,
   Father, Son, and myftic dove !

HYMN II. *A Contemplation, fuggefted by Rev.* vii.
9 —— 17.

1   I SAW, and lo ! a countlefs throng
   Th' elect of ev'ry nation, name, and tongue,
Affembled round the everlafting throne ;

With

With robes of white endu'd
(The righteoufnefs of God);
And each a palm fuftain'd
In his victorious hand;
When thus the bright melodious choir begun:
" Salvation to thy name,
" Eternal God, and co-eternal Lamb,
" In pow'r, in glory, and in effence, one!"

So fung the faints, th' angelic train,
Second the anthem with a loud Amen.
(Thefe in the outer circle ftood,
The faints were neareft God);
And proftrate fall, with glory overpow'r'd,
And hide their faces with their wings,
And thus addrefs the King of kings:
" All hail, by thy triumphant Church ador'd!
" Bleffing and thanks and honour too
" Are thy fupreme, thy everlafting due,
" Our tri-une, fov'reign, our propitious Lord!"

While I beheld th' amazing fight,
A feraph pointed to the faints in white,
And told me who they were, and whence they came:
" Thefe are they, whofe lot below
Was perfecution, pain, and woe:
Thefe are the chofen purchas'd flock,
Who ne'er their Lord forfook;
Through his imputed merit, free from blame;
Redeem'd from ev'ry fin;
And, as thou feeft, whofe garments were made
clean,
Wafh'd in the blood of yon exalted Lamb.

Sav'd by his righteoufnefs alone,
Spotlefs they ftand before the throne,
And in th' etherial temple chaunt his praife;
Himfelf among them deigns to dwell,
And face to face his light reveal:
Hunger and thirft, as heretofore,
And pain, and heat, they know no more;

Nor

Nor need, as once, the fun's prolific rays,
  Immanuel, here, his people feeds,
  To ftreams of joy perennial leads,
And wipes, for ever wipes, the tears from ev'ry face."

2 Happy the fouls releas'd from fear,
    And fafely landed there !
  Some of the fhining number, once, I knew,
    And travell'd with them here :
  Nay, fome (my elder brethren now)
Sat later out for heav'n ; my junior faints, below ;
Long after me, they heard the call of grace,
  Which wak'd them unto righteoufnefs.
  How have they got beyond !
Converted laft, yet firft with glory crown'd !
  Little, once, I thought that thefe
    Would firft the fummit gain,
And leave me, far behind, flow journeying thro' the
    plain !

Lov'd, while on earth ; nor lefs belov'd, tho' gone ;
  Think not I envy you your crown ;
No ; if I could, I would not, call you down.
    Tho' flower is my pace,
      To you I'll follow on,
  Leaning on Jefus all the way.
  Who, now-and-then, lets fall a ray
      Of comfort from his throne.
    The fhinings of his grace
Soften my paffage thro' the wildernefs,
And vines, nectareous, fpring, where briers grew ;
  The fweet unveilings of his face
Make me, at times, near half as bleft as you.
O might his beauty feaft my ravifh'd eyes,
  His gladd'ning prefence ever ftay,
  And chear me all my journey thro' !
But foon the clouds return ; my triumph dies ;
Damp vapours from the valley rife,
  And hide the hill at Sion from my view.

                                        Spirit

Spirit of light, thrice holy dove,
Brighten my fenfe of int'reft in that love
Which knew no birth, and never fhall expire!
   Electing goodnefs, firm and free,
   My whole falvation hangs on thee,
Eldeft and faireft daughter of eternity.
   Redemption, grace, and glory too,
   Our blifs above, and hopes below,   }
   From her, their parent-fountain, flow;
Ah, tell me, Lord, that thou haft chofen me!
Thou, who haft kindled my intenfe defire,
Fulfil the wifh thy influence did infpire,
   And let me my election know!
Then, when thy fummons bids me come up higher,
Well-pleafed I fhall from life retire,
   And join the burning hofts, beheld at diftance
   now.

HYMN III. *Happinefs found.*

1 HAPPINESS, thou lovely name,
Where's thy feat, O tell me where?
Learning, pleafure, wealth, and fame,
   All cry out, " It is not here:"
Not the wifdom of the wife
Can inform me where it lies,
Not the grandeur of the great
Can the blifs, I feek, create.

2 Object of my firft defire,
   Jefus, crucify'd for me!
All to happinefs afpire,
   Only to be found in thee:
Thee to praife, and thee to know,
Conftitute our blifs below;
Thee to fee, and thee to love,
Conftitute our blifs above.

3 Lord,

3 Lord, it is not life to live,
    If thy prefence thou deny ;
Lord, if thou thy prefence give,
    'Tis no longer death to die :
Source and giver of repofe,
Singly from thy fmile it flows ;
Peace and happinefs are thine ;
Mine they are, if thou art mine.

4 Whilft I feel thy love to me,
    Ev'ry object teems with joy ;
Here O may I walk with thee,
    Then into thy prefence die !
Let me but thyfelf poffefs,
Total fum of happinefs !
Real blifs I then fhall prove ;
 · Heav'n below, and heav'n above.

HYMN IV. *Affliction.*

1 ENCOMPASS'D with clouds of diftrefs,
    Juft ready all hope to refign,
·I pant for the light of thy face,
    And fear it will never be mine :
Difhearten'd with waiting fo long,
    I fink at thy feet with my load ;
All plaintive I pour out my fong,
    And ftretch forth my hands unto God.

2 Shine, Lord, and my terror fhall ceafe,
    ` The blood of atonement apply ;
And lead me to Jefus for peace,
    The rock that is higher than I :
Speak, Saviour, for fweet is thy voice,
    Thy prefence is fair to behold ;
· I thirft for thy fpirit with cries
    And groanings that cannot be told.

3 If fometimes I ftrive, as I mourn,
    My hold of thy promife to keep,
The billows more fiercely return,
    And plunge me again in the deep ;

While

While harrais'd, and caft from thy fight,
The tempter fuggefts, with a roar,
" The Lord hath forfaken thee quite,
Thy God will be gracious no more."

4 Yet, Lord, if thy love hath defign'd
No covenant blefling for me;
Ah, tell me, how is it I find,
Some fweetnefs in waiting for thee?
Almighty to refcue thou art;
Thy grace is my only refource;
If e'er thou art Lord of my heart,
Thy fpirit muft take it by force.

HYMN V. *The Method of Salvation.*

1   THE Father we blefs,
Whofe diftinguifhing grace,
Selected a people to fhew forth thy praife;
Nor is thy love known,
By election alone;
For, O thou haft added the gift of thy Son.

2   The goodnefs in vain,
We attempt to explain,
Which found and accepted a ranfom for men;
Great furety of thine
Thou didft not decline,
To concur with the Father's moft gracious defign.

3   To Jefus our friend,
Our thanks fhall afcend,
Who faves to the utmoft, and loves to the end;
Our ranfom he paid,
In his merit array'd
We attain to the glory for which we were made.

4   Sweet fpirit of grace,
Thy mercy we blefs,
For thy eminent fhare in the council of peace;

Great

Great agent divine,
To reſtore us in thine,
And cauſe us afreſh in thy likeneſs to ſhine.

5   O God, 'tis thy part,
    To convince and convert;
To give a new life, and create a new heart;
    By thy preſence and grace,
    We're upheld in our race;
And are kept in thy love to the end of our days.

6   Father, Spirit, and Son,
    Agree thus in One,
The ſalvation of thoſe he has mark'd for his own;
    Let us too agree,
    To glorify thee,
Thou ineffable One, thou adorable Three.

HYMN VI. *The evil Heart.*

1 ASTONISH'D and diſtreſs'd,
    I turn mine eyes within;
My heart with loads of guilt oppreſt,
    The ſeat of every ſin.

2 What crouds of evil thoughts,
    What vile affections there!
Diſtruſt, preſumption, artful guile,
    Pride, envy, ſlaviſh fear.

3 Almighty King of ſaints,
    Theſe tyrant luſts ſubdue;
Expel the darkneſs of my mind,
    And all my powers renew.

4 This done, my cheerful voice,
    Shall loud hoſannas raiſe;
My ſoul ſhall glow with gratitude,
    My lips proclaim thy praiſe.

HYMN VII. *Thy Kingdom come.*

1 O WHEN ſhall we, ſupremely bleſt,
Enter into our glorious reſt!

Partake the triumphs of the ſky,
And, holy, holy, holy, cry!

2 With all thy heav'nly hoſts, with all
Thy bleſſed ſaints, we then ſhall fall;
And ſing in extacy unknown,
And praiſe thee on thy dazzling throne.

3 Honour, and majeſty, and pow'r,
And thanks and bleſſings evermore;
Who doſt through endleſs ages live,
Thou, Lord, art worthy to receive.

4 For thou haſt bid the creatures be,
And ſtill ſubſiſt to pleaſure thee;
From thee they came, to thee they tend,
Their gracious ſource, their glorious end!

HYMN VIII. *The Propitiation.*

THY anger, for what I have done,
The goſpel forbids me to fear:
My ſins thou haſt charg'd on thy Son;
Thy juſtice to him I refer:
Be mindful of Jeſus and me!
My pardon he ſuffer'd to buy;
And what he procur'd on the tree,
For me he demands in the ſky.

HYMN IX. *Aſſurance of Faith.*

1 A DEBTOR to mercy alone,
Of covenant mercy I ſing;
Nor fear with thy righteouſneſs on,
My perſon and off'rings to bring:
The terrors of law, and of God,
With me can have nothing to do;
My Saviour's obedience and blood,
Hide all my tranſgreſſions from view.

2 The work which his goodneſs began,
The arm of his ſtrength will complete;
His promiſe is Yea, and Amen,
And never was forfeited yet:

Things

Things future, nor things that are now,
 Not all things below nor above,
Can make him his purpose forego,
 Or fever my foul from his love.

3 My name from the palms of his hands,
 Eternity will not erafe :
Impreft on his heart it remains,
 In marks of indelible grace ;
Yes, I to the end fhall endure,
 As fure as the earneft is giv'n ;
More happy but not more fecure,
 The glorified fpirits in heav'n.

HYMN X. *To the Bleffed Spirit.*

1 HOLY Ghoft, difpel our fadnefs,
 Pierce the clouds of finful night,
Come thou fource of fweeteft gladnefs,
 Breathe thy life, and fpread thy light !
Loving Spirit, God of peace,
Great diftributor of grace,
Reft upon this congregation,
Hear, O hear our fupplication.

2 From that height which knows no meafure,
 As a gracious fhow'r defcend ;
Bringing down the richeft treafure,
 Man can wifh, or God can fend ;
O thou glory, fhining down
From the Father and the Son,
Grant us thy illumination !
Reft upon this congregation.

3 Come, thou beft of all donations,
 God can give, or we implore ;
Having thy fweet confolations,
 We need wifh for nothing more :
Come with unction and with pow'r ;
On our fouls thy graces fhow'r ;
Author of the new creation,
Make our hearts thy habitation.

4 Known

4 Known to thee are all receffes
　　Of the earth, and fpreading fkies ;
Every fand the fhore poffeffes,
　　Thy omnifcient mind defcries :
Holy fountain, wafh us clean ;
Both from error, and from fin !
Let us fly what thou refufeft,
And delight in what thou chufeft.

5 Manifeft thy love forever,
　　Fence us in on every fide ;
In diftrefs be our reliever ;
　　Guard, and teach, fupport, and guide :
Let thy kind, effectual grace,
Turn our feet from evil ways ;
Shew thyfelf our new creator,
And conform us to thy nature.

6 Be our friend on each occafion ;
　　God, omnipotent to fave !
When we die, be our falvation ;
　　When we're buried, be our grave :
And, when from the grave we rife,
Take us up above the fkies ;
Seat us with thy faints in glory,
There forever to adore thee.

HYMN XI. *Divine Breathings.*

1 I GROAN from fin to be fet free,
　　From felf to be releas'd ;
O take me, take me unto thee,
　　My everlafting reft !

2 Come, O my Saviour, come away !
　　Into my foul defcend :
No longer from thy creature ftay ;
　　My author, and my end !

3 The blifs thou haft for me prepar'd,
　　No longer be delay'd :
Come my exceeding great reward,
　　For whom I firft was made.

4 Thou

4 Thou all our works in us haft wrought,
    Our good is all divine ;
The praife of ev'ry virtuous thought
    And righteous work is thine.

5 'Tis not of him that wills or runs,
    That labours or defires ;
In anfwer to my Saviour's groans,
  . Thy love my breaft infpires.

6 The meritorious caufe I fee,
    That precious blood divine,
And I, fince Jefus dy'd for me,
    Shall live forever thine.

HYMN XII. *Pfalm* cxlvii. 1.

'TIS pleafant to fing,
The fweet praife of our King,
    As here in the valley we move :
'Twill be pleafanter ftill,
When we ftand on the hill,
    And give thanks to our Saviour above.

HYMN XIII. *Hebrews* x. 19th *verfe.*

We have Boldnefs to enter into the Holieft by the Blood
of Jefus.

1 O PRECIOUS blood, O glorious death,
    By which the finner lives !
When ftung with fin, this blood we view,
    And all our joy revives.

2 We flourifh as the water'd herb,
    Who keep this blood in fight,
The blood that chafes our diftrefs,
    And makes our garments white.

3 The blood that purchas'd our releafe,
    And wafhes out our ftains,
We challenge earth and hell to fhew,
    A fin it cannot cleanfe.

4 Our

4 Our fcarlet crimes are made as wool,
    And we brought nigh to God :
  Thanks to that wrath appeafing death ;
    That heav'n procuring blood.

5 The blood that makes his glorious Church
    From ev'ry blemifh free ;
  And, O the riches of his love!
    He pour'd it out for me.

6 Guilty and worthlefs as I am,
    It all for me was giv'n ;
  And boldnefs, thro' his blood, I have,
    To enter into heav'n.

7 Thither, in my great furety's right,
    I furely fhall be brought !
  He could not agonize in vain,
    Nor fpend his ftrength for nought.

8 He wills that I and all his fheep,
    Should reign with him in blifs ;
  And pow'r he has to execute,
    Whate'er his will decrees.

9 The Father's everlafting love,
    And Jefus' precious blood,
  Shall be our endlefs themes of praife ;
    In yonder bleft abode.

10 In patience let us then poffefs,
    Our fouls, 'till he appear :
   Our head already is in heav'n,
    And we fhall foon be there.

HYMN XIV. *A propitious Gale longed for.*

1 AT anchor laid, remote from home,
  Toiling I cry, fweet fpirit come,
  Celeftial breeze, no longer ftay,
  But fwell my fails, and fpeed my way.

2 Fain would I mount, fain would I glow,
  And loofe my cable from below;
  But I can only fpread my fail ;
  Thou, thou muft breathe th' aufpicious gale.

HYMN

HYMN XV. *All in All.*

1 COMPARED with Chrift, in all befide
  No comelinefs I fee:
The one thing needful, deareft Lord,
  Is to be one with thee.

2 The fenfe of our expiring love,
  Into my foul convey;
Thyfelf beftow; for thee alone,
  My all in all I pray.

3 Lefs than thyfelf will not fuffice,
  My comfort to reftore:
More than thyfelf I cannot crave;
  And thou canft give no more.

4 Love of my God, for him again,
  With love intenfe I'll burn:
Chofen of thee ere time began,
  I'll chufe thee in return.

5 Whate'er confifts not with thy love,
  O teach me to refign;
I'm rich to all th' intents of blifs,
  If thou, O God, art mine.

HYMN XVI. *Weak Believers encouraged.*

1 YOUR harps, ye trembling faints,
  Down from the willows take:
Loud, to the praife of love divine,
  Bid ev'ry ftring awake.

2 Tho' in a foreign land,
  We are not far from home,
And nearer to our houfe above,
  We ev'ry moment come.

3 His grace will to the end,
  Stronger and brighter fhine;
Nor prefent things, nor things to come,
  Shall quench the fpark divine.

4 Faften'd

4 Faften'd within the vail,
    Hope be your anchor ftrong;
    His loving fpirit the fweet gale,
    That wafts you fmooth along.

5 Or, fhould the furges rife,
    And peace delay to come;
    Bleft is the forrow, kind the ftorm,
    That drives us nearer home.

6 The people of his choice,
    He will not caft away;
    Yet do not always here expect,
    On Tabor's Mount to ftay.

7 When we in darknefs walk,
    Nor feel the heav'nly flame;
    Then is the time to truft our God,
    And reft upon his name.

8 Soon fhall our doubts and fears,
    Subfide at his controul;
    His loving kindnefs fhall break through
    The midnight of the foul.

9 No wonder, when God's love,
    Pervades your kindling breaft,
    You wifh for ever to retain,
    The heart tranfporting gueft.

10 Yet learn, in ev'ry ftate,
    To make his will your own;
    And when the joys of fenfe depart,
    To walk by faith alone.

11 By anxious fear deprefs'd,
    When, from the deep ye mourn,
    " Lord, why fo hafty to depart,
    So tedious in return!"

12 Still on his plighted love,
    At all events rely:
    The very hidings of his face,
    Shall train thee up to joy.

13 Wait

13 Wait till the fhadows flee ;
    Wait thy appointed hour :
Wait, till the bridegroom of thy foul,
    Reveals his love with pow'r.

14 The time of love will come,
    When thou fhalt clearly fee,
Not only that he fhed his blood,
    But that it flowed for thee.

15 Tarry his leifure then,
    Altho' he feem to ftay :
A moment's intercourfe with him,
    Thy grief will overpay.

16 Bleft is the man, O God,
    That ftays himfelf on thee !
Who wait for thy falvation, Lord,
    Shall thy falvation fee.

HYMN XVII. *Chrift the Light of his People.*

1 I LIFT my heart and eyes to thee,
    Jefus, thou unextinguifh'd light,
My guardian ftay and leader be,
    My cloud by day, my fire by night.

2 Glory of Ifrael, fhine within ;
    Unfhadow'd, uneclips'd appear :
With beams of grace exhale my fin ;
    Break forth thou bright and morning ftar.

3 The earth a tracklefs lab'rinth is ;
    Be thou my thread and faithful clue !
Thy kingdom and thy righteoufnefs,
    The only objects I purfue.

4 Light of the Gentiles thee I hail ;
    Effential truth, thyfelf impart !
Spirit of light, his face reveal,
    And fet thy fignet on my heart.

5 Thy office 'tis t' enlighten man,
    And point him to the heav'nly prize ;
The hidden things of God t' explain,
    And fhine the darknefs from our eyes.

6 Witnefs

6 Witnefs of Chrift within my heart,
  My int'reft in his love difplay;
My int'reft in that better part,
  Which never can be torn away.

7 In bondage 'till thou fet me free,
  Fain would I know my part in him:
The brightnefs of his rifing fee,
  And bafk in thy meridian beam.

8 Shine then thou uncreated ray!
  If but a moment thou withdraw,
That moment fees me go aftray,
  That moment fees me break thy law.

9 The word and fpirit both confpire,
  To tell thy Church fhe is forgiv'n;
And lift her daily high'r and high'r,
  'Till all her joys are crown'd with heav'n.

10 To that blefs'd realm of bright repofe,
  Thou wilt conduct my weary feet;
Where peace no interruption knows,
  And where my fun fhall never fet.

HYMN XVIII. *Leaning on the Beloved.*

1 COURAGE my foul; Jehovah fpeaks;
  His promife is for thee:
" I never will forfake nor leave
  The foul betroth'd to me."

2 The chearing word, as heav'nly dew,
  My thirfty foul drinks in:
Jefus commands me to rejoice,
  Who bore away my fin.

3 My Saviour's ever watchful eye,
  Is over me for good:
What will he not on me beftow,
  Who hath himfelf beftow'd?

4 Me to enrich, himfelf he made
  Poor, and of no efteem:
The fource, the true foundation, this,
  Of all my love to him.

5 Dear

5 Dear Lord, into thy faithful hands,
  My welfare I commit ;
And to thy righteoufnefs alone,
  For fafety I retreat.

6 Sorrows and agonies and death,
  Thou didft endure for me,
When all the fins of God's elect,
  Were made to meet on thee.

7 Tho' worthy, in myfelf, of hell,
  And everlafting fhame ;
I cannot dread the frown divine,
  Accepted in the Lamb.

8 Still on thy merit, gracious Lord,
  Enable me to lean :
Ever in thee may I be found,
  My hiding-place from fin !

9 Exult my foul; thy fafety ftands
  Unfhaken as his throne :
His people's everlafting life
  Is founded on his own.

HYMN XIX. *Before Hearing.*

1 SOURCE of light and pow'r divine,
  Deign upon thy truth to fhine ;
Lord, behold thy fervant ftands,
Lo, to thee he lifts his hands :
Satisfy his foul's defire,
Touch his lip with holy fire !
Source of light and pow'r divine,
Deign upon thy truth to fhine.

2 Breathe thy fpirit, fo fhall fall
  Unction fweet upon us all ;
  'Till, by odours fcatter'd round,
  Chrift himfelf be trac'd and found ;
  Then fhall ev'ry raptur'd heart,
  Rich in peace and joy depart :
  Source of light and pow'r divine,
  Deign upon thy truth to fhine.

HYMN XX. *A Morning Hymn.*

1 CHRIST whofe glory fills the fkies,
    Chrift the true, the only light,
  Son of righteoufnefs arife,
    Triumph o'er the fhades of night ;
  Day fpring from on high be near,
  Day ftar in my heart appear.

2 Dark and chearlefs is the morn,
    Unaccompanied by thee ;
  Joylefs is the day's return,
    Till thy mercy's beams I fee :
  Till they inward light impart,
  Glad my eyes and warm my heart.

3 Vifit then this foul of mine,
    Pierce the gloom of fin and grief,
  Fill me, radiancy divine ;
    Scatter all my unbelief ;
  More and more thyfelf difplay,
  Shining to the perfect day.

HYMN XXI. *A Chamber Hymn.*

1 WHAT tho' my frail eye-lids refufe,
    Continual watching to keep,
  And punctual as midnight renews,
    Demand the refrefhment of fleep ;

A fov'reign protector I have,
  Unfeen, yet forever at hand,
Unchangeably faithful to fave ;
  Almighty to rule and command.

2 From evil fecure and its dread,
  I reft if my Saviour is nigh,
And fongs his kind prefence indeed
  Shall in the night feafon fupply ;
He fmiles and my comforts abound,
  His grace as the dew fhall defcend,
And walls of falvation furround,
  The foul he delights to defend.

3 Kind author and ground of my hope,
  Thee, thee, for my God I avow,
My glad Ebenezer fet up,
  And own thou haft help'd me till now ;
I mufe on the years that are paft,
  Wherein my defence thou haft prov'd,
Nor wilt thou relinquifh at laft
  A finner fo fignally lov'd.

4 Infpirer and hearer of pray'r,
  Thou feeder and guardian of thine,
My all to thy covenant care
  I fleeping and waking refign,
If thou art my fhield and my fun,
  The night is no darknefs to me,
And faft as my moments roll on,
  They bring me but nearer to thee.

5 Thy minift'ring fpirits defcend,
  To watch while thy faints are afleep,
By day and by night they attend,
  The heirs of falvation to keep ;
Bright feraphs, difpatch'd from the throne,
  Repair to the ftations affign'd,
And angels elect are fent down,
  To guard the elect of mankind.

6 Thy

6 Thy worfhip no interval knows,
　　Their fervour is ftill on the wing;
And while they protect my repofe,
　　They chaunt to the praife of my king.
1 too, at the feafon ordain'd,
　　Their chorus for ever fhall join;
And love and adore, without end,
　　Their faithful Creator, and mine.

HYMN XXII. *A Prayer, living and dying.*

1 ROCK of ages, cleft for me,
Let me hide myfelf in thee;
Let the water and the blood,
From thy riven fide which flow'd,
Be of fin the double cure,
Cleanfe me from its guilt and pow'r.

2 Not the labours of my hands,
Can fulfil thy laws demands:
Could my zeal no refpite know,
Could my tears forever flow;
All for fin could not atone,
Thou muft fave, and thou alone.

3 Nothing in my hand I bring,
Simply to thy crofs I cling;
Naked come to thee for drefs,
Helplefs look to thee for grace:
Foul I to the fountain fly,
Wafh me, Saviour, or I die.

4 While I draw this fleeting breath,
When my eye-ftrings break in death;
When I foar to worlds unknown,
See thee on thy judgment throne;
Rock of ages, cleft for me,
Let me hide myfelf in thee.

HYMN

HYMN XXIII. *To the Trinity.*

1 ETERNAL hallelujahs,
    Be to the Father giv'n,
Who lov'd his own
Ere time begun,
    And mark'd them out for heav'n.

2 Anthems of equal glory,
    Afcribe we to the Saviour;
Who liv'd and dy'd,
That we his bride,
    Might live with him forever.

3 Hail co-eternal Spirit,
    Thy Church's new Creator!
The faints he feals
Their fear difpels,
    And fanctifies their nature.

4 We laud the glorious triad,
    The myftic one in effence;
'Till call'd to join
The hofts that fhine
    In his immediate prefence.

5 Faithful is he that promis'd,
    And ftands engag'd to fave us:
The triune Lord
Has pafs'd his word,
    That he will never leave us.

6 A kingdom he affign'd us,
    Before the world's foundation:
Thou God of grace,
Be thine the praife,
    And our's the confolation.

HYMN

HYMN XXIV. *2 Tim.* i. 9. *" Who hath faved us and called us with an holy calling ; not according to our works, but according to his own purpofe, and grace, which was given us before the world began."*

1 HOW vaft the benefits divine,
　　Which we in Chrift poffefs,
Sav'd from the guilt of fin we are,
　　And call'd to holinefs.

2 But not for works which we have done,
　　Or fhall hereafter do ;
Hath God decreed on finful worms,
　　Salvation to beftow.

3 The glory, Lord, from firft to laft,
　　Is due to thee alone ;
Aught to ourfelves, we dare not take,
　　Or rob thee of thy crown.

4 Our glorious furety undertook
　　To fatisfy for man,
And grace was given us in him,
　　Before the world began.

5 This is thy will, that in thy love
　　We ever fhould abide,
And lo, we earth and hell defy,
　　To make thy counfel void.

6 Not one of all the chofen race,
　　But fhall to heav'n attain ;
Partake on earth the purpos'd grace,
　　And then with Jefus reign.

7 Of Father, Son, and Spirit, we
　　Extol the three-fold care,
Whofe love, whofe merit, and whofe pow'r,
　　Unite to lift us there.

HYMN

HYMN XXV. *He hath borne our Griefs, &c.*

1 SURELY Chrift thy griefs hath borne,
Weeping foul no longer mourn :
View him bleeding on the tree,
Pouring out his life for thee ;
There thy ev'ry fin he bore,
Weeping fouls lament no more.

2 All thy crimes on him were laid,
See upon his blamelefs head ;
Wrath its utmoft vengeance pours,
Due to my offence and yours ;
Wounded in our ftead, he is
Bruis'd for our iniquities.

3 Weary finner keep thine eyes,
On th' atoning facrifice :
There th' incarnate Deity,
Number'd with tranfgreffors fee ;
There his Father's abfence mourns,
Nail'd and bruis'd, and crown'd with thorns.

4 See thy God, his head bow down,
Hear the man of forrows groan !
For thy ranfom, there condemn'd,
Stripp'd, derided, and blafphem'd ;
Bleed the guiltlefs for th' unclean,
Made an off'ring for thy fin.

5 Caft thy guilty foul on him,
Find him mighty to redeem :
At his feet thy burden lay,
Look thy doubts and cares away ;
Now by faith the Son embrace,
Plead his promife, truft his grace.

6 Lord, thy arm muft be reveal'd,
Ere I can by faith be heal'd !
Since I fcarce can look to thee
Caft a gracious eye on me ;
At thy feet, myfelf I lay,
Shine, O fhine, my fears away.

HYMN

HYMN XXVI. *Faith in the Promises.*

1 WHAT in thy love poffefs I not,
    My ftar by night, my fun by day;
My fpring of life when parch'd with drought,
    My wine to chear, my bread to ftay;
My ftrength, my fhield, my fafe abode,
My robe before the throne of God.

2 From all eternity with love
    Unchangeable, thou haft me view'd
Ere knew this beating heart to move,
    Thy tender mercies me purfu'd;
Ever with me may they abide,
And clofe me in on ev'ry fide.

3 In fuff'ring be thy love my peace,
    In weaknefs be thy love my pow'r:
And when the ftorms of life fhall ceafe,
    Jefus in that important hour;
In death as life, be thou my guide,
And fave me, who for me haft dy'd.

HYMN XXVII. *Divine Aid.*

1 THE pow'r of hell, the ftrength of fin,
    My Jefus fhall fubdue:
His healing blood fhall wafh me clean,
    And make my fpirit new.

2 He will perform the work begun,
    Jefus, the finners friend;
Jefus, the lover of his own,
    Will love me to the end.

3 No longer am I now afraid,
    The promife fhall take place,
Perfect his ftrength in weaknefs made:
    Sufficient is his grace.

4 When thou doft in my heart appear,
    And love erects its throne;
I then enjoy falvation here,
    And heav'n on earth begun.

5 Lord,

5 Lord, I believe and reft fecure,
 In confidence divine ;
Thy promife ftands for ever fure,
 And all thou art is mine.

HYMN XXVIII. *Almighty Power.*

1 WHAT tho' I cannot break my chain
 Or e'er throw off my load ;
The things impoffible to men,
 Are poffible to God.

2 Who, who fhall in thy prefence ftand,
 Or match Omnipotence ;
Unfold the grafp of thy right-hand,
 And pluck the finner thence.

3 Faith to be heal'd I fain wou'd have,
 O might it now be giv'n ;
Thou canft, thou canft the finner fave,
 And make me meet for heav'n.

4 Bound down with twice ten thoufand ties,
 Yet let me hear thy call ;
My foul in confidence fhall rife,
 Shall rife and break through all.

5 Thou canft o'ercome this heart of mine,
 Thou wilt victorious prove ;
For everlafting ftrength is thine,
 And everlafting love.

HYMN XXIX. *Mercy experienced.*

1 JESUS, what haft thou beftow'd
 On fuch a worm as me ;
What compaffion haft thou fhew'd,
 To draw me after thee :
Mindful of thy mercies paft,
 Still I truft the fame to prove,
Still my helplefs foul I caft,
 On thy redeeming love.

2 Haft

2 Haft thou not revers'd my doom,
  Thou haft, and I believe;
Yet I ftill a finner come,
  That thou may'ft ftill forgive;
Wretched, miferable, blind,
  Poor, and naked, and unclean,
Still that I may mercy find,
  I bring thee nought but fin.

3 Open, Lord, my inward ear,
  And make my heart rejoice;
. Bid my quiet fpirit hear,
  Thy comfortable voice:
Silent am I now and ftill,
  Dare not in thy prefence move;
To my waiting foul reveal
  The fecrets of thy love.

4 Chrift hath the foundation laid,
  And Chrift will build me up;
I fhall certainly be made,
  Partaker of my hope;
Author of my faith he is,
  He its finifher fhall be,
Sov'reign grace has fealed me his,
  To all eternity.

HYMN XXX. *Fervent Defire.*

1 FATHER, I want a thankful heart,
I want to tafte how good thou art,
To plunge me in thy mercy's fea,
And comprehend thy love to me;
The length and depth, and breadth and height,
Of love divinely infinite.

2 Jefus, my great high prieft above,
My friend before the throne of love;
If now for me prevails thy prayer,
If now I find thee pleading there,
Hear, and my weak petitions join,
Almighty advocate to thine.

3 O fo-

3 O ſovereign love, to thee I cry,
   Give me thyſelf, or elſe I die ;
   Save me from death, from hell ſet free,
   Death, hell, are but the want of thee ;
   My life, my crown, my heav'n thou art,
   O may I find thee in my heart !

HYMN XXXI.   *Written in Illneſs *, Pſalm* civ.
             Ver. 34.

   " *My meditation of him ſhall be ſweet.*"

1 WHEN languor and diſeaſe invade
   This trembling houſe of clay ;
   'Tis ſweet to look beyond our cage,
   And long to fly away.

2 Sweet to look inward and attend
   The whiſpers of his love ;
   Sweet to look upward to the place
   Where Jeſus pleads above.

3 Sweet to look back and ſee my name
   In life's fair book ſet down ;
   Sweet to look forward, and behold
   Eternal joys my own.

4 Sweet to reflect how grace divine
   My ſins on Jeſus laid ;
   Sweet to remember that his blood
   My debt of ſufferings paid.

5 Sweet on his righteouſneſs to ſtand,
   Which ſaves from ſecond death ;
   Sweet to experience day by day,
   His ſpirits quick'ning breath.

---

* The late Counteſs of Huntingdon had the original of this melli-
fluous piece of poetry ſent her by the Author. The right honour-
able lady Ann Erſkine gave herſelf conſiderable trouble to procure
it for the Editor, for which obliging politeneſs and condeſcenſion,
he returns this public acknowledgement.

6 Sweet on his faithfulnefs to reft,
 Whofe love can never end ;
Sweet on his covenant of grace,
 For all things to depend.

7 Sweet in the confidence of faith,
 To truft his firm decrees ;
Sweet to lie paffive in his hand,
 And know no will but his.

8 Sweet to rejoice in lively hope,
 That when my change fhall come ;
Angels will hover round my bed,
 And waft my fpirit home.

9 There fhall my dif-imprifon'd foul
 Behold him and adore ;
Be with his likenefs fatisfy'd,
 And grieve and fin no more.

10 Shall fee him wear that very flefh,
 On which my guilt was lain ;
His love intenfe, his merit frefh,
 As tho' but newly flain.

11 Soon too my flumb'ring duft fhall hear
 The trumpet's quick'ning found ;
And by my Saviour's power rebuilt,
 At his right-hand be found.

12 Thefe eyes fhall fee him in that day,
 The God that dy'd for me ;
And all my rifing bones fhall fay,
 Lord, who is like to thee.

13 If fuch the views which grace unfolds
 Weak as it is below ;
What raptures muft the Church above
 In Jefu's prefence know.

14 If fuch the fweetnefs of the ftream,
 What muft the fountain be ;
Where faints and angels draw their blifs,
 Immediately from thee.

15 O may

15 O may the unction of thefe truths,
    For ever with me ftay;
    'Till from her finful cage difmifs'd
    My fpirit flies away.

HYMN XXXII. *The Dying Believer to his Soul.*

1 DEATHLESS principle, arife;
    Soar, thou native of the fkies.
    Pearl of price, by Jefus bought,
    To his glorious likenefs wrought,
    Go, to fhine before his throne;
    Deck his mediatorial crown:
    Go, his triumphs to adorn;
    Made for God, to God return.

2 Lo, he beckons from on high!
    Fearlefs to his prefence fly:
    Thine the merit of his blood;
    Thine the righteoufnefs of God.

3 Angels, joyful to attend,
    Hov'ring, round thy pillow bend;
    Wait to catch the fignal giv'n,
    And efcort thee quick to heav'n.

4 Is thy earthly houfe diftreft?
    Willing to retain her gueft?
    'Tis not thou, but fhe, muft die:
    Fly, celeftial tenant, fly.
    Burft thy fhackles, drop thy clay.
    Sweetly breathe myfelf away:
    Singing, to thy crown remove;
    Swift of wing, and fir'd with love.

5 Shudder not to pafs the ftream:
    Venture all thy care on him;
    Him, whofe dying love and pow'r
    Still'd its toffing, hufh'd its roar.
    Safe is the expanded wave;
    Gentle, as a Summer's eve:

Not

Not one object of his care
Ever suffer'd shipwreck there.
See the haven full in view !
Love divine shall bear thee through.
Truft to that propitious gale :
Weigh thy anchor, fpread thy fail.

6 Saints, in glory perfect made,
Wait thy paffage through the fhade :
Ardent for thy coming o'er,
See, they throng the blifsful fhore.
Mount, their tranfports to improve :
Join the longing choir above :
Swiftly to their wifh be giv'n :
Kindle higher joy in heav'n.
——Such the profpects that arife,
To the dying Chriftian's eyes !
Such the glorious vifta, Faith
Opens through the fhades of death !

INDEX.

N. B. The Roman Numerals refer to the Volume, and the Figures to the Page.

A.

of

B.

Counter.

G

Gifford,

H.

Idiots,

Knowledge,

G g 4   *Locke.*

M

who

NATIONAL

Political

Q

QUALITIES, senfible, of matter, what they are, vi. 116. From whence they refult, *ibid.* 122, 123. 132. 139. Would be totally reverfed, if our organs of perception were oppofitely conftituted to what they are, 124, 125. 134, 135. 142.

Quarto Bible, publifhed in the reign of Edward the Sixth, ii. 113. Other editions during the reign of Elizabeth, ii. 115—123.

Query, concerning a paffage in the marriage ceremony, iii. 445.

Quefnel Pafquier, fample of the, 101. Propofition for which he was anathematifed by the Pope, i. 92. His exile, imprifonment and death, 94.

Queftions and anfwers, concerning predeftination, formerly bound up with our Englifh Bibles, ii. 123—127. Their authority vindicated, 124.

R

RAMSAY, Chevalier, collects the conjectures of the ancients concerning the rife of moral evil, vi. 102. *note.*

Randal Anthony, deprived for Ranterifm, i. 106. A view of his tenets, *ibid.*

Ranters, a continuation of the Familifts, i. 104. Held that predeftination was not abfolute, but conditional, 105. Violent advocates for free will and perfection, *ibid. note.* Bore a vehement enmity to the Puritans, 108. Their fhamelefs pretences to veneration for the church of England, *ibid.* Maintained univerfal grace and redemption, *ibid.* 109. Dr. Fuller's character of them, *ibid.* (See more, under the article of *Fifth-monarchy-men.*)

Redemption, not unlimited, i. 120. 123. 129. 141. 143. 144. 148. 266. 295—299. 322. ii. 72. 193. What redemption really is, i. 295. Limited, not difcouraging, ii. 72. Conditional, a modifh tenet, iii 29. The confequence of fuch a fyftem, 30. Not left at uncertainty, 399. A finifhed work, vi. 104. The extent of, 128. Some very pertinent reflections thereon, 129, &c.

Refinement, focial, not natural to man, vi. 49, 50. *note.*

Reflection on the beginning of the year, iii. 454. Not a fource of any new ideas, vi. 24.

Reformation, at what time it took its rife, v. 19. At prefent a fad awful departure from the principles, vi. 150. The fruit fuch declenfion produces, *ibid.* 151.

Reformers, Englifh, were profeffed Calvinifts in doctrine, i. 248. Large proof of this, i. 243—348.

Regeneration, the work of efficacious grace, i. 119. 284. 285. 310.

An

Virtue,

him

E R R A T A.

www.ingramcontent.com/pod-product-compliance
Lightning Source LLC
Chambersburg PA
CBHW052331110726
47901CB00005B/1202